The body came into view slowly for Cully. As she approached she saw the high-heeled shoes lying beside the feet, then noticed the fishnet stockings, then the skirt hiked up above the waist. Aware that everyone had stopped talking behind her and that all the cops there were watching to see her reaction, Cully kept her eyes down and focused on the legs, even when the gore above was bright red in her peripheral vision. She took deep breaths to steady herself.

Then she looked.

It didn't make sense at first: a dead woman sitting on the pavement between ranks of garbage cans. A note on white paper covered her forehead. The body was battered and soaked in blood, like a Mexican party piñata filled with liquid instead of candy and now pounded into oozing ruptures. *People don't bleed like that,* she thought; *they drain, they don't explode. . . .*

Then Cully realized that what she was seeing was not a blouse shredded by a beating and soaked in blood. What she was seeing was a woman's bare torso. . . .

WHERE ANGELS WATCH

WHERE ANGELS WATCH

Randall Wallace

BANTAM BOOKS
NEW YORK · TORONTO · LONDON · SYDNEY · AUCKLAND

WHERE ANGELS WATCH
A Bantam Crime Line Book / August 1992

ISBN 0-553-29254-4
Published simultaneously in the United States and Canada

While a seminarian, I came across the work of a theologian who wrote: The genius of Jesus of Nazareth is that he found the holy, not among the monastic, but among the profane. *Since coming to Los Angeles, I have witnessed the city's legendary profanity; I have also seen moments of shimmering sanctity. I wrote this novel hoping to portray both. But this book is not meant to depict the actual lives of anyone in this city, anymore than it is meant to depict my own.*

Still, it is with a personal sense of living in this profane and holy world that I dedicate this novel

To my sons,
Andrew and Cullen
and the angels that watch over them.

WHERE ANGELS WATCH

Prologue

The Sunset Strip. A half-mile curve of boulevard hanging on the edge of the Hollywood Hills. Above it the high-tech homes of a community of homosexual party lovers who refer to the hills as the Swish Alps. Below, the Los Angeles basin, a billion lights wobbling in the smog.

The boulevard is a black river flowing backward from the sea. From its western end it curls through some of the world's most expensive real estate, past the homes of oil shiekhs and movie sultans; on its way east its banks are lined with glass-tower office buildings, then small shops and restaurants, then car dealerships and finally porno-movie houses and a mud-wrestling place or two before it trickles out of Hollywood altogether.

The Strip is the asphalt river's glamorous eddy. Billboards stretch above it, lit by a million candlepower, announcing megawatt movies in murals with three-dimensional bodies, puffs of smoke, ripples of fabric flame.

But tonight there is a rarity: a billboard without a buyer. The producers who had contracted for the rental to hawk their new blockbuster have just filed for bankruptcy, so the billboard company has painted out the last ad and has displayed one that says: THIS SPACE AVAILABLE.

Down by the base of this sign, next to the gray steel

1

pillars that hold those words a hundred feet in the air, stands a woman.

Her spiky high heels tilt her feet forward and push her calf muscles up high and hard, like the dancer she once dreamed of being. Her knit skirt catches every curve of her bottom. Her breasts are the best that money could buy, and her blouse clings around the raised nipples. The cherry red of the stoplight beside her is nothing compared with the color on her lips, and her hair, yellow as brass and just as soft, lights up in the headlights of a silver limousine as it slides slowly through the intersection.

The limo swings to the curb and stops beside her. She glances over, and the smoked glass in the backdoor sinks low. She steps across the sidewalk to the opening as if she is an actress and another starlet has stopped to say hello. She peers into the darkness of the compartment, and sees nothing. Then the privacy panel behind the driver's head hums down, and he turns his face toward her. He wears sunglasses, even now at thirty minutes before midnight, as if the green glow of the dashboard instruments is too much for his eyes, but he takes them off long enough for her to see his face.

In two years on the street she has learned to be wary. But tonight she steps quickly into the car.

I

The sun rose into a clear blue sky; the winds of October blew across the great western deserts of America and drove the smog out to sea.

Fielding grounders on the sunrise shift for the new homicide division of the Los Angeles Police Department were Detectives Martin "Trigger" Frazier and his partner, Joe Morris. Frazier had lost the last two joints of his right index finger in an altercation at the Dorothy Chandler Pavilion on his first and only visit to an opera; during a discussion of another patron's hairstyle and how it blocked Frazier's view, he had referred to the patron as "Jewboy" and the man had bitten off two inches of Frazier's gun hand. Now Frazier, if he wanted to fire his pistol, had to do it with his middle finger, but that was worth the macho nickname. Morris, his partner, was known as "Micro," having been christened that by a waitress at a cop bar out in Devonshire; if you asked him why, he would go deaf on you.

"Grounders" were what L.A. cops called dead bodies that turned up on the streets with the sunrise. Some guys called them doo-drops.

The first body they found that morning was a laugher. The second was a shot of cold piss to the heart.

They had just brought a double order of extra-cream cinnamon-dusted Krispy Krust Magic Eclairs and two bottomless coffees back to their sedan when the radio crackled and the dispatcher gave them an address,

3

an alley just off Sepulveda Boulevard, and the dispatcher added, "Hey Trigger, I think this is a friend of yours!"

Frazier wasn't worried. The only friend he had was Morris, and Morris was sitting right there.

The alley was familiar; it was behind a carpet store, and the Dumpster there was full of remnants of cut pile and shag—a treasure chest for the winos who lived on the streets. They had been known to fight for the carpet scraps like starving dogs over a meatless bone, and cops were called there regularly. Now the manager of the store was standing at his backdoor waiting for them to arrive, and when Frazier and Morris pulled up, he just pointed toward the back side of the Dumpster and shut his door.

In the shadow of the Dumpster they found a dead man. A naked dead man. A fat naked dead man. He lay on his back, his belly like a half-inflated parachute, his thighs white blobs of blubber spread upon the pavement. His eyes were blue, bright and blank as a doll's, staring lifelessly into the morning sky.

Frazier used a thumbnail to excavate a chunk of Krispy Krust from his own gum line and said, "Old Aspen finally wiped out, huh?"

Before Morris could answer, a black-and-white cruiser swung into the alley and stopped diagonally across its width. Out of the cruiser stepped a uniformed sergeant. Ragg (Rough As Goat Guts) Wilson was a transplanted Texan and never left the station on a motor patrol without first squinting into the hot smog and saying, "I tell yer whut, hits gonner be rough as goat guts out there today, boys. And goat guts is pretty rough." Grins and grimaces all traveled Ragg's face along the same ruts, and three decades' worth of flared-up hemorrhoids had left his lips in a permanently pained smile.

Ragg pulled a roll of yellow police barrier tape out of his car and strolled over to the two detectives. "We got us a John Doe?" Ragg asked.

"Nah," Frazier said, "this is Aspen Jack Merkle. He used to try to sell us hot drug tips on the other winos and junkies when we were working vice."

Ragg looked down at the blubbery body. "He don't look like nobody who spent a lotta time in no Aspen to me."

Frazier laughed. "He gave himself the name Aspen cause one night he was watching 'Life-styles of the Rich and Famous' on the tube down at the mission and he saw this thing about celebrity skiers and one of 'em said he liked Aspen because he liked to shoot the powder there. So Jack here, he tells us one night, 'Just call me Aspen, 'cause I like to shoot the powder.' Dumb shit thought the celebrities meant cocaine."

"Maybe they did," Ragg said. He put his hands into his pockets, squinted at the body and said, "Thought cocaine made you skinny."

"Does, if you can afford it. Jack's main addiction was garbage cans behind restaurants," Frazier said. "He liked to eat before he drank his Ripple. Where the fuck is Woger?" Just then the official blue van of Roger the Coroner appeared at the far end of the alley and rolled up to them, its dusty brakes shrieking and making Ragg wince like he had bitten into a lemon. Frazier made a show of frowning at his watch and called, "Woger, you're wate!"

Roger the Coroner stepped out with one of his assistants, smiled at Ragg and the detectives, and glanced down at Aspen Jack Merkle's body. "Viowent, owa natuwal?" Roger said.

"It was a beautiful passing, Woge," Frazier said. "Probably a heart attack, trying to climb into the Dumpster to sleep last night. The other winos took his clothes."

"Yeah," Morris said, "they can make tents out of 'em."

Roger went to work snapping pictures. He used a strobe to blot out shadows, and the body looked even whiter in the flashes. Ragg wrinkled up his nose. "Pyew-wee!" he said. "Is he decomposin' already?"

"That's just how he smelled," Frazier said.

"Gotta weigh three," Ragg said.

"Three hundred pounds?" Morris said. "Three fifty if he weighs a pound."

"Closer to four," Frazier said.

"Bullshit," Ragg said. He said it like Frazier's estimate was hardly worth a response; the words came out like *Boo-shit*.

"Bullshit?" Frazier said.

"Boo-shit!" Ragg said. "Naw way this pusgut weighs over three sem'ty."

"Twenty bucks," Frazier said.

"You're on, bubba," Ragg said. "Hey Woger, when you gonner weigh this fish?"

"How much did you guess?" Roger the Coroner said, flashing from another angle.

"Less'n three sem'ty."

"Thwee seventy? I'm afwaid you wuze, Wagg," Roger said. He put away the camera and pulled a liver thermometer and a hammer from his bag. The thermometer was eighteen inches long, sharpened at one end and flattened at the other like a spike for a vampire's heart. It measured the exact temperature of a corpse's liver, and with that number and some other calculations based on the surrounding temperature and the corpse's body weight, the coroner could make a damn good guess about the time of death.

Roger pressed the point of the thermometer to the soft roll of fat on the dead man's underbelly and slammed the hammer against the flat head of the probe. Even with a stiff whack it barely penetrated the spongy flab. Roger belted the probe again and it poked in about an inch.

" 'When John Henwy was a wittle baby . . .' " Frazier sang.

Roger was getting pissed. The jokes about his

speech impediment didn't bother him, but he took pride in his expertise with corpses and this one was making him sweat. Roger started whacking at the spike, and Ragg, in a deep voice, announced, "We are here today to celebrate the joining of the two railroads. . . ."

The point of Roger's probe suddenly penetrated the layers of gristle and surged deep into the body, straight to the center of the liver. Panting from his exertion, Roger said, "Help me turn him a wittle, to check the wividity."

Morris and Ragg grabbed the corpse's right arm and groaned like Volga boatmen; they hauled Aspen onto his left side, but the moment they let go, the body's huge weight rolled him onto his back again. Roger, out of practice with bodies of this size, realized the problem and moved the left arm into a position above the head, and the cops pulled again. This time the body rolled over onto its side and stayed. The entire back was stained by purple lividity, where the dead blood was settling. Roger took another picture.

"I got an idea!" Ragg said. "Hold it, hold it, I got an idea!" Ragg was excited about his idea; he didn't have many. He ran to his car, opened the trunk, and pulled out a stack of art pads and markers he had bought for his grandson's birthday party next weekend. He'd have to go back to the art-supplies store, but this would be worth it; Ragg had an idea! He folded one of the pads in half, wrote something on one side of its white cardboard backing, and ran back over to the body, saying, "Get a picture, huh, Woge? Get a picture!"

Ragg had fashioned a book. He set up his makeshift book on the pavement beside the naked corpse's right hand. With the left arm extended and the head lolling upon the pillowy biceps, the bloated body did look strangely like a nude sunbather reading on the beach. The huge thermometer sticking out of his gut appeared to mar the effect, until they looked at the title Ragg had printed in bold red letters: HOW TO COOK PORK.

Their laughter, as Roger took the photograph, was interrupted by another call from the radio in Frazier and Morris's sedan. This time there was no humor in the dispatcher's voice; he gave them an address that was directly across the street from where they were and said, "Maybe you oughta get on this, the rook that called this in sounded a little shook-up."

The electronic blare of the radio fuzzed the words around their edges and compressed any concern out of the dispatcher's voice, but just listening to it made the cops wince as the sound became part of the whole mixture of glare off windshields and smoggy air and early pavement heat that promised a bad day. One more complication, one more chore; Frazier and Morris left Ragg and Roger with the first body and strolled across the street through the morning traffic. A guy in a Mercedes, clearly a recent victim of California's jaywalking laws, saw these two men in shoulder holsters with badges clipped to their belts and lowered his window as he passed to yell out, "Hey, that's illegal!" Morris tossed him the bird and went on without hurrying or looking back.

In the alley on the other side of Sepulveda, behind an auto-parts store, they found another black-and-white cruiser. Two young patrolmen manned it. One was fifty yards up the alley, talking with a Mexican kid on a bicycle who apparently had made the discovery. The other patrolman was pacing beside his police unit, and Frazier and Morris swaggered up to him. The rookie was so young his crew cut looked like original equipment from the police academy. His face was ashen, and he was sweating. Frazier and Morris resisted the impulse to smirk; these young guys got surly when you kidded them about freaking out over their first body. "Where is it?" Frazier said.

The young patrolman pointed toward some garbage cans against the back wall of the store. Frazier didn't see anything unusual at first, then noticed two feet in lace stockings stuck out from behind the cans.

The patrolman, having held it together long enough to do his duty, which was to protect the crime scene long enough for the detectives to arrive, now turned away, bent over, and vomited.

Frazier and Morris chuckled at the rookie as they walked toward the trash cans.

But when they rounded the cans and saw what was leaning against the stucco wall, they stopped laughing. The faces of the two veteran detectives went as white as the rookie patrolman's.

Frazier straightened his back to keep from fainting, and sucked a full breath into his lungs. "Jesus Holy Christ," he said.

Morris straighted, too. He looked away, looked back at the corpse, and winced as he looked away again. Both detectives turned toward the sunrise and breathed deeply for a minute. Then Frazier said what Morris was thinking.

"We better call Ridge."

Doubting Thomas Ridge was trying to pray.

He knelt beside the four-poster bed he had made with his own hands and tried to squeeze his spirit out into the Great Beyond, but felt himself sliding back to earth. He wanted to brush his fingertips against the breath of God, but all he felt was the polyester carpet, hot and wrinkly against his knees.

He raised his head and looked out at the smog-filtered sunlight, silver on the needles of the pine tree outside his window. The apartment building was on a street behind a North Hollywood supermarket, but Ridge's three rooms were on the second floor and looked directly out into a massive pine tree, so that, kneeling, he could see sky and evergreen instead of rows of cars and California stucco. He tried to use the sunlight and the tree to clear his mind, to focus on something natural and elemental so to be reminded of the Maker and maybe reach Him that way. But Ridge's own thoughts defeated him.

Why look at nature to touch God? he asked himself. Why not look at pavement, at garbage in the gutter, at blood on the sidewalk where a fourteen-year-old boy has just blown out the brains of an eight-year-old girl—by accident, since he meant to shoot her brother? At the university Ridge had once attended, a professor of religion had told him that most theologians would consider the purest prayer to be: "Thy will be done." Purest, maybe, but not the realest, the sophomore Ridge had thought then and the thirty-eight-year-old detective of homicide thought now. The prayer most real was the one Jesus uttered when hanging on the cross: "My God, my God . . . why hast Thou forsaken me?"

He lowered his face to the quilt his grandmother had made two decades past, when he was still in college. He closed his eyes and breathed in its cedar aroma, as if he could inhale her goodness. He was here now, on his knees, because of her. The last time he had held her in his arms, with the cancer writhing in her stomach, on a night ten years ago that still seemed like yesterday to him, he had promised her he would keep trying. Not with words; he had never actually uttered his promise. Such formalities as speech had never been necessary to seal a pact between him and her. She had simply looked up at him with those eyes as blue as a Tennessee sky in October and had asked him without saying anything, and he had sworn with his own eyes that he wouldn't give up, but would keep trying to make a truce with God.

His handle in homicide, Doubting Thomas, had nothing to do with his feud with the Almighty, at least not as far as the other detectives knew. They called Ridge that because of the way he accepted nothing at face value. Investigators like to find the predictable patterns of a murder motive—hidden debts, volatile relationships—and work from those; but Ridge did the opposite. He rethought the basic assumptions of every life whose most intimate details were laid bare to him by the act of murder. His solutions had an unexpected and unearthly quality about them; his fellow detectives considered him the undisputed champion of their craft. Though they liked him, they found him spooky. And because they could not follow his thought processes, Ridge had often found himself alone—as he was now.

Oh Lord, thy will be done.

My God, why have you forsaken me.

Thy will . . .

Why have you forsaken . . .

The phone on the floor beside the bed rang.

He answered: "Ridge."

"Ridge, Frazier." Frazier hesitated, and in that small silence Ridge caught the stench of brutal murder. Trigger Frazier might be as subtle as a cinder block, but he was a tough cop with a detective's stubborn pride, and he wouldn't be asking for help unless something had shaken him. Being shaken wasn't easy to admit, so Frazier just said what all the murder dicks say when they've found a hot body: "The dead meat is on the street."

2

Ridge crawled out of the city-issue Dodge slowly, one long leg and then another. Cars these days weren't made for men six-foot-three; when he drove, he had to lean the seat back to keep his head clear of the roof, and stepping out of a car was like rising from a supine position. To the men watching him emerge he appeared angular, all elbows and knees, but when he stood to his full height, there was something both graceful and mean about his body, like a rural length of barbed wire.

He walked straight to Frazier, who led him without a word toward the shady side of the alley. Morris and the uniforms took two steps backward and watched as Ridge walked slowly toward the body, like a frontier marshal on Main Street. Doubting Thomas Ridge, a legend. But there was no swagger in Ridge's walk; it was somber, even reverent. Morris, leaning against the gritty back wall of the auto-parts store, shot a glance at Ridge's gray-green eyes as he passed, and saw in them that Doubting Thomas had already started asking himself questions.

Frazier stopped twenty feet from the body and let Ridge advance alone. Doubting Thomas liked what he called a virgin crime scene, and he liked seeing them by himself, without associates or assumptions. A virgin crime scene; was that what this was? No one else seemed to have been here but the boy on the bicycle,

12

the cops, and the flies. Frazier watched, too, wondering, as Morris did, if the great Tom Ridge would be as shaken as they had been.

Ridge rounded the garbage cans, just as they had, and then stopped abruptly. He stood with his arms at his sides, and slowly paled. Hell yes, Frazier thought, the great Tom Ridge is shocked, too.

Ridge stood motionless for a full minute, his eyes wide. He wants not to believe it, Frazier thought, that's why he's looking all around like that and not really looking at her.

But then Ridge's attention went completely to the body. He squatted in front of her, sitting back on top of his tiptoes like a catcher taking fastballs behind the plate, then tipped down to one knee and looked into the girl's face. With everything else to see, Ridge looked into her face.

A victim is a person. That was one of the scriptures from the training manual Ridge had written for the academy, the slim volume the detectives all called *The Book of Thomas*. This was chapter 1:1: *A victim is a person. Not a piece of meat. Not a crime, or a thing, but a person. Remembering that is the key to solving any murder, or to knowing why homicide is a crime at all.* Every other cop in the world would tell you not to take your cases personally; but to Ridge, taking your work personally was the only way to crack the hard ones.

Practicing what he had preached, Ridge stared now into the victim's face. Frazier could not have said what Ridge saw there, since he had not been able to look at her face for long. Ridge squeezed his eyes shut, turned his head away, then forced himself to look again.

And then he did the strangest thing. He nodded, as if the dead girl had asked him something, and he had answered.

Vehicles started arriving, all at once. Roger the Coroner, finished with his sledgehammer job across the street, showed up with the forensics van; two black-and-

white units arrived and taped off both ends of the alley;
and then a bright red jeep squealed in from the boulevard and slid to a stop with its nose under the yellow
tape the uniforms had just stretched out.

Roger's assistant, stepping out of the forensics van,
stopped beside Morris and the two men stared openly,
like men will do whenever they are in a group and a
notoriously attractive woman arrives. The assistant
smirked and said, "Bull Barrel."

"Bull Barrel" was Detective Scarlet Ann McCullers. If asked for a nickname, she would give you
"Cully." That's what they had called her at the academy.
And for a while, when she had come through the patrol
ranks in record time and scored at the top of the detective's promotion list, they had called her Dickless Tracy.
But the name that really stuck was Bull Barrel. She was
a pistol expert, but the nickname had nothing to do with
her shooting. It derived from an incident that had occurred when she was a rookie and was running her fingertips around the body of a black male bodybuilder she
and her partner had stopped on suspicion of having
committed an armed robbery just moments before;
Cully, full of adrenaline, thought she had found a bull-
barrel pistol stuffed down into the guy's pants, and
jumped back from the guy yelling, "He's got a gun! And
it's a bull barrel!"

She was mistaken.

She had thought that Ragg Wilson, her partner that
day, would keep his solemn oath not to tell anybody else
about the incident. He being a training officer and all,
she was sure he wouldn't spread the word of this and
stick her with a nickname she could never live down.

She was mistaken about that, too.

Some guys thought the nickname made the chip on
her shoulder bigger. But the guys who knew her at the
academy said the chip couldn't *get* any bigger.

Now every cop there stopped what he was doing
and watched as she got out of her car. Five-seven. Waist

tight from two hundred sit-ups every morning. Tight butt under blue jeans. A plaid blouse, big enough to hide the breasts that drew comments when she showed them off. Irish-blond hair—the kind with streaks of auburn in it. Blue eyes. And always in a hurry. Maybe it wasn't so much of a hurry as it was that she always seemed mad.

Like now. She shut the door with a pop and stalked toward Ridge. She was wearing cowboy boots; not new ones, like a woman buys to match an outfit, but old tan ones, scratched up like a rancher's. They made her knees bend a little extra, giving her an angry strut as she came at Ridge.

The other detectives kept watching, and they waited, expecting something. They had all heard the rumors.

The word was that something had gone down between Ridge and Cully McCullers. She had just finished working her first homicide case, and Ridge, the specialist who descended like air cavalry into bogged-down investigations and broke them open with an intellectual assault and then flew off again . . . Ridge, who had never been known to work with a partner . . . this same Ridge had paired himself with her, and together they had covered themselves in violence and glory.

And if you believed the rumors, with some extracurricular dancing between the sheets.

Ridge strode out and met her halfway. When Ridge was concentrating, which was most of the time, his face had an electric quality as emotional voltage sparked beneath its surface, contrasting noticeably with his eyes, fixed as on a distant target, with the left slightly more open than the right. That habitual stare gave him an air of anger when his mind was focused, quite different from the flare-eyed, clinched-jaw look he took on when truly mad. Glimpses of this look were both rare and brief; Ridge's fellow cops knew him to have an explosive temper, and when it went off, things tended to happen suddenly. His laugh was just as sudden, and his grin showed all his teeth. And for a man so inward, he left an odd impression of smiling often; that was because he smiled mostly with his eyes and not his lips. But now he turned his face drab, and to the onlookers, trying to catch his words, his voice was only a murmur.

What he mumbled was, "Hi."

"Why didn't you call me?" she said, sharply and low, moving her mouth so little that the other cops weren't sure she had said anything at all.

Ridge's gaze wandered along the alley pavement, cupped down the center so water would drain. "Call you?" he said. "I did call you. A couple of times."

She had not called him back, and she couldn't deny that she had ignored his calls. "Those calls . . . were personal," she said, and looked up at the blank back wall of the building beside her as if stucco were a fascinating architectural feature. "Is that what the message is here, Ridge? You're sending me a message, right? If I don't return your personal calls, then you're going to forget to give me a professional call when I ought to have one? Is that right?"

"How do you know the calls I made to you weren't professional, since you decided to ignore them?"

She glanced at him; now he was staring right at her. She had to look away. "Let's deal with that later, okay?" she said. "Right now this is a homicide and I'm a detective and I don't know about this till I call in and somebody at the station tells me about it. I was the backup to Frazier today, in case he should get multiples, which he did. Okay? Don't keep me from doing my job."

He nodded. She nodded, too, and started to walk past him. He pushed his palm against the hard cap of her shoulder, stopping her with a soft jolt. "Hang on a second," he said. "This . . . is kinda . . ."

"Kinda what?" she snapped.

"Kinda awful."

"What, and you think I can't look at it?"

He pinched his upper lip between his front teeth, raised his eyebrows, and stepped back. His eyes were angry, daring her to look.

She pushed by him.

The body came into view slowly for Cully, as it had for the other detectives, with the garbage cans at first blocking the line of sight of everything but the victim's feet.

As she approached she saw the high-heeled shoes lying beside those feet, then noticed the fishnet stockings, then the skirt hiked up above the waist. Aware that everyone had stopped talking behind her and that all the cops there were watching to see her reaction, Cully kept her eyes down and focused on the legs, even when the gore above was bright in her peripheral vision. She took deep breaths to steady herself.

Then she looked.

It didn't make sense at first: a dead woman sitting on the pavement between ranks of garbage cans. A note on white paper covered her forehead. Something had happened to her torso.

But Cully's mind couldn't assemble it all. The body was battered and soaked in blood, like a Mexican party piñata filled with liquid instead of candy and now pounded into oozing ruptures. Such a terrible amount of blood! People don't bleed like that, she thought eagerly; they drain, they don't explode. . . . Where did it all come from, had her face been torn away under the note? Had all the blood come from her head? Two coagulated pools of it were on her shoulders, one on the left and one on the right.

Then Cully realized that what she was seeing was not a blouse shredded by a beating and soaked in blood. What she was seeing was a woman's bare torso, with the breasts cut away.

As she gawked, and the reality of what she was seeing ran into her brain before her defense mechanism shut it off and forced her to turn away, she realized she still hadn't seen it exactly as it was. The breasts had been cut, but not completely off. They had been slit down the inside edge and pulled open; they hung loose now from flaps of outside skin, the nipples facing opposite directions. The bags on her shoulders had been breast implants, and they had been cut out.

Only when Cully realized this did she read the words on the note, all capitals, printed in red marker. The note, nailed with a single spike to the center of the dead girl's forehead, read:

FALSE AND MISLEADING ADVERTISING

The building behind the mutilated corpse slid suddenly down like the turning of the whole earth, and the sky rolled into view, a cloudless, hazy blue, and then went dim.

3

Cully awoke with a driverless car moving toward her. No, she was moving toward it, encircled by a strong arm around her waist that took most of her weight and floated her forward, her feet stumbling along behind her like a marionette's wooden shoes dragged too quickly by the master of the strings.

She plopped into the open front seat of one of the black-and-white patrol units. She reached out and brushed her fingers across the on-board computer, just to judge her distance from something. But the keys swam before her eyes.

She had to stand up, to get out of that car before everybody looked at her and said Bull Barrel couldn't take it. She tried to suck in a deep lungful of air, but her breath had the scent of vomit and her head spun as if she were on a sailboat in the middle of a greasy and heaving sea.

Ridge walked out into the middle of the alley, his shadow long on the pavement, the sun hot on the back of his neck. Frazier's shadow moved up and stretched out beside his, and Ridge spoke without looking around. "Complete containment," he said. "Absolute restriction of view to the body. And a complete list of everyone who's seen it so far."

Frazier waited; some other thought seemed to be hanging on Ridge's tongue, and his eyes had that stare that made Frazier anticipate another of what he called

"Ridge's transmissions from Mars." But Ridge only stood there, so Frazier turned around and barked orders.

"Nobody else sees anything, besides Roger and that assistant with him right now! *Nobody,* understand?"

The uniformed cop, the one who had thrown up earlier, nodded his pale head. "Absolutely," he mouthed.

Frazier moved over to the back of the coroner's van. Roger and his assistant were trying to figure out what to do for a body bag. Aspen Jack had taken up the couple the van carried, and Roger had been proud of his ingenuity in unzipping two and putting them together like a double sleeping bag. Aspen Jack's remains now sagged the left side of the van down onto its springs, and Roger was at a loss as to how he was going to bag this latest guest into the Last Stop Motel. Frazier motioned him and his assistant closer and said, "Lock your lips on this one, right? This does not get out. So far we've got four detectives, those two uniforms, and you two. Plus whoever found the body." Roger, Frazier knew, was reliable; but he didn't know the assistant, so he spelled it out for him. "Now I'm telling you again so you understand: this don't get into the press. If it does, I know whose butt to pulverize."

The CA blinked and shook his head as if startled by the suggestion that he might blab.

Frazier said, "Yeah, but if some freako newspaper offers you a few hundred for details about this body, you just think of me going through your employment application, the friends you party with, your tax returns. Think of any lapses in judgment I might uncover."

"Not me, man," the assistant said. "I don't see nothin', I don't know nothin'."

"You sound like my third wife," Frazier said, and turned around to look for Ridge. He spotted him standing near the body, where Morris was using tweezers to lift the note from the face of the murdered girl. Morris raised the paper into the sunlight, and for a moment it looked translucent and its red writing appeared black. Morris carefully loaded the paper into a plastic bag. Frazier walked up and said to Ridge, "We'll take it to the lab ourselves."

But Ridge wasn't listening. Staring at nothing, he said, "He used a bag. No. Two bags."

"Two bags?" Frazier said. He looked at Morris to see whether his partner had any idea what Ridge was talking about. Morris shrugged.

"One would be waterproof," Ridge said, "to hold in the blood. But there would be a tougher one outside the first bag, something like a canvas seabag that wouldn't split from the blows, like the plastic would, if it were the outer bag." Ridge looked at Frazier and nodded slyly as if somebody had just tried to trick him. "That's how he did it. A bag around the girl, then a bag around the bag."

Cully McCullers had walked up behind them. Ridge half turned so he could talk to all three of them at once, his voice dreamy, as if he were only saying what the dead girl's ghost was dictating into his ear. "That's how he had to do it, to keep from getting blood all over. He beat her to death through the bag, and the bag contained the blood. See how she looks like she's been soaked in it? But not much leaked out from her chest because she died inside the bag. Her heart wasn't beating when he did his little surgery. . . ."

Ridge's voice trailed off. The other three detectives looked at each other. Ridge looked at the body, and a series of tremors twitched through his face, small winces like echoes of the pain the girl felt when blows were shattering her bones.

Frazier and Morris turned to the garbage cans and started to rummage through them, looking for the bags. Ridge became aware of what they were doing and opened his mouth to speak, but he seemed to lack the energy to correct them.

"No," Cully said to Frazier and Morris, from behind Ridge. "He wouldn't dump them here. He was careful with everything. Careful to use the bags in the first place, and particular about how he laid her out for us to find her. He wouldn't ditch the bags here because he'd know we'd find them, but he wouldn't hold on to them long either, because they could get him gassed. We'll have the uniforms help us check every Dumpster within a block or two. He probably wadded one bag inside another, to look like garbage."

Ridge looked at her, then looked away, a single glance that said: *You always understand.*

Frazier and Morris walked off to talk to the uniforms. Cully watched them leave, then said, "Thanks."

"For what?"

"You caught me. When I fainted."

"You gonna yell at me now for standing too close behind you?"

"No," she said softly.

"Good," Ridge said, and walked away.

She followed him with her eyes as he moved toward the Mexican kid who sat in the squad car. The kid's bicycle was still lying where he had dumped it on the asphalt and run to the pay phone on the corner to tell the 911 operator that they'd better send some cops quick.

Ridge liked wild-cherry Lifesavers; they gave his breath a faint aroma that sometimes reminded Cully of the cherry-blend pipe tobacco her father used to smoke, before he started boozing and went to Camels. Ridge always had a roll of the sweet lozenges in a pocket of his sport coat, and he took the candy out now. He peeled one circle off the top of the pack, then handed the rest to the Mexican kid.

The kid slipped off a Lifesaver for himself and handed the pack back to Ridge. Ridge motioned for him to keep it.

The corners of the kid's mouth lifted. It wasn't

much of a smile, but it was the best he could manage, after having his paper route interrupted by the sight of the woman between the cans.

Ridge nodded, but didn't try to smile. There was something else on his face, a look that Cully understood because she alone knew the story. It was a story about another boy who had discovered a dead body—two, in fact; mother and father—and the look on Ridge's face was not of pain but more like the memory of pain, a memory that would last forever, even after he had cut out the part of himself that had once felt the hurt.

4

The Mulholland Homicide Division—MULHOM, in LAPD-ese—was the brainchild of Deputy Chief Michael Rowe. Mike Rowe, at thirty-six, was younger than the other four men in line to become chief of police someday, and there were those in both political parties who thought that job would be an unnecessary detour on Rowe's way to the governor's mansion, or even the United States Senate. Rowe had Jack Kennedy's hair and Rob Lowe's lips, and the joke around headquarters was that he could be a one-man population explosion with that combination. He had a pretty wife from old money and three children; and though his family spent a lot of time in Europe, his reputation was of contentment and fidelity in marriage as in all things.

Rowe had championed the idea of an independent homicide division even though the concept carried little political heat. This made him appear utterly nonpolitical, which, as his intradepartmental rivals pointed out, might have been the most political thing he could have done. Still, when the Police Commission approved the restructuring plan—at a projected *savings* to the city of three million dollars per year—Rowe did not do the safe thing and install a leader he could blame if things went wrong. He stepped into the new post and ran the division himself.

Nobody doubted his guts.

24

The idea of the division was simple. In the previous structure each division maintained its own homicide team as well as units in burglary, armed robbery, fraud, gangs, vehicular theft, traffic. But homicide was particularly liable to produce a duplication of teams because deaths could occur in the course of any crime, and the traffic team that was experienced in building a case against a motorist accused of driving under the influence might be more capable of proving the circumstances of vehicular homicide than the homicide unit the old rules said would have to be called in whenever there was a fatality. This was the exact example Mike Rowe used in his verbal arguments before the Police Commission.

What Rowe had suggested, sitting there before the council members in his two-hundred-dollar suit that looked like it cost five times that because of his perfect size-38-regular body, was a creative alternative. "The City of the Angels needs a tighter, more efficient approach," he had told them, in his firm baritone. "Specialists drawn from each division, molded into one unit that addresses what we all really mean when we say murder: the intentional, premeditated killing of one human being by another.

"All this new plan proposes is that we make a simple distinction: that not every death is an act of will, but those that are will be investigated by experts. Experts whose only responsibility will be the apprehension of the perpetrators of intentional homicide. And that we should provide those experts with the lab, ballistics, and the necessary information linkups with other law enforcement agencies and even with the FBI.

"I want to point out, ladies and gentlemen of the council, that this restructuring—should you support it—is not meant to draw responsibility and resources away from the present divisions of the city. On the contrary, it increases their autonomy. Their investigators retain cases that clearly are an outgrowth of their specialties.

In plain English this sends each cop a message that his job is important and he is important, and we have the confidence that he can make a case even when it involves the greatest loss of all, that of a human life."

Rowe had looked down at the document on the table before him, a tight, vivid little ten-pager that he had designed himself on his home computer. He held up his copy. "Each of you has one of these before you. You will see that we have already chosen a location to headquarter this special division: an abandoned structure once used by the city's street maintenance. It's on Mulholland, central to both the basin and the valley. You will also see that the creation of this division will save the city several million dollars. Annually."

The council members did not dissect the document, but if they had, they would have found it airtight. Michael Rowe had always done perfect homework.

When they voted it his way, they did so without thinking of the good they might be doing. When they cast their votes—unanimously in favor of Rowe's proposal—it was with the thought: I hope this guy never decides to run for my job. If he does, I'd better look for a new line of work.

Rowe had been careful to avoid the term "elite": at the time it wasn't fashionable with the city council. But when the division captains chose the detectives who would represent their divisions in the new unit, they looked not only for excellence but also for ego and aggressiveness; this unit would be no place for shrinking violets.

The roster of detectives in that first MULHOM team read like a list of gunfighters. In addition to Tom "Doubting Thomas" Ridge and Cully "Bull Barrel" McCullers, and "Trigger" Frazier and Morton "Micro" Morris, there were George "Tooda" Taylor, Larry "Baby Boom-Boom" Malchek, Charles "Rose Nose" Dugan, Carlos "Banana" Santana, John "the Baptist" Dewey.

The old, cavernous metal building surrounded by

an unpaved parking lot among the pine trees high on Mulholland Drive, a trail of sun-parched asphalt snaking along the crest of the Santa Monica Mountains separating the main business districts of Los Angeles from the bedroom communities in the San Fernando Valley, added to the Old West feeling. They called the building the Can. They may as well have called it the Long Branch Saloon.

The building had a cement floor that a roving city maintenance crew swept once a week without ever removing its residual stickiness or the faint smell of tar that always hung in the air. That floor had once supported the weight of steamrollers and dump trucks filled with sand; no Southern California earthquake since 1947 had been able to crack it. Huge bolts set into the concrete had once anchored the building's metal walls, and though rust had eternally fused the doughnut-sized locknuts to those bolts, the metal around them had corroded away, so that gravity alone kept the Can on its pad. The joke among the detectives was that one of Ragg Wilson's chili farts could knock down the building, but nuclear torpedoes couldn't shake the pad, which was probably why some developer with a city councilman in his hip pocket had never acquired the site for luxury condos.

The rectangular pad was half the size of a football field and the Can rested all around its edge; but inside, the structure seemed smaller because of the way the lights dangled at twenty-foot intervals from the peaked ceiling. The fixtures themselves were inverted metal cones, each with a single forty-watt bulb peeking out from below the base. The illumination was far too meager, but the overhead lights were all on the same circuit, and when Baby Boom-Boom Malchek had brought his extension ladder from home and tried to brighten things up a little by substituting hundred-watt bulbs, he had blown out the main breakers. The city had made repairs and promised to rewire the whole system, but nothing had happened yet. Boom-Boom said he didn't mind so much squinting at his paperwork, but those fixtures looked to him like fireflies with hemorrhoids. But whenever Cully sat at her desk, which stood at the far end of the building, and looked down the length of the Can, the double rank of cones dangling weak lights from their bases looked like a fleet of lost spaceships, all running out of fuel.

Wooden detective desks formed a double line down the middle of the floor, in a rough match with the lights. Everything above the fixtures, ten feet over the desktops, was gloom, except at a certain time each afternoon when the sun would drop to just the right angle and send rays through the slats of the vents on the west side of the Can's roof. Then, for about twenty minutes, the light and shadow fell across the floor in four-inch bars, and the detectives at their desks all looked as if they themselves were in jail.

Along the length of the long walls were rolling doors, massive enough to admit the trucks that L.A. Street Maintenance had once stored here. These doors were now welded shut. The presence of the welded lock bars and the chains that had once operated the door mechanisms gave these former bays an air of security, which may have been why the one on the east side of the building housed the unit's evidence section and the one on the west provided space for communications equipment and computer terminals. Evidence was kept behind a wood-and-chicken-wire enclosure that was never locked. Communications was manned by one permanent operator, plus a part-time computer specialist from the city who had no idea how anything worked. To keep his high-tech promise until the city made good on its commitments, Mike Rowe had brought in his own equipment from home.

Cully's desk at the far narrow end was closest to the locker room, a separate wooden annex that had workable lockers and showers stout enough to serve men who had paved roads all day. On opposite corners of the other end, nearest the parking lot, were the only two private cubicles, both made of glass partitions. One belonged to Mike Rowe, and the other to Leonard Bellflower.

On paper Bellflower was second in command. But he was a cop's cop, a twenty-year veteran, a black giant everybody on the unit would listen to and respect, and even Rowe knew that Bellflower was the one the MULHOM detectives looked to for leadership. And Bellflower had a reputation not only among cops but with the public; the evening news shows loved the jut of his jaw and the gravel in his voice, and they had sought quotes from Bellflower so often that from time to time strangers he passed on the street would stop him to ask for an autograph or would flash him the finger from their cars. Bellflower never took any of it personally; he figured his bulldog face had become a kind of barometer for measuring how the citizens were feeling about their police force at any given time.

The chill of that October morning was blunted by space heaters like the ones used on construction sites, and the cops tried not to think about how cold it would get if winter had any teeth this year. Rowe had promised to stump for some kind of air-conditioning, if the unit survived until summer. Bellflower had arrived late that morning to find the other detectives milling around the communications table, discussing what little they knew of the alley situation from the bits of radio traffic they had picked up. To them it was like listening to a jet dogfight; Ridge was using MULHOM code words like "eviction" for "murder," "termite damage" for "mutilation," and "kitchen" for "female" to throw off the reporters who kept police scanners in their cars and their newsrooms. Ridge had a thing about the press.

But he was not prone to overstate. His radio message that they had found "an evicted kitchen with major termite damage" had the morning shift buzzing.

Frazier and Morris returned first, carrying in two blood-soaked bags, one plastic and one canvas, in a third clear, sterile evidence sack. The bright gory trophy made for an excited show-and-tell, the gist of which was that Ridge had done it again. Mike Rowe came out of his cubicle and stared at the blood with a kind of awe, then nodded stiffly and retreated to his office, where he fought a wave of nausea.

Bellflower, on the other hand, glanced drowsily at the blood. He listened long enough to be sure that he wasn't going to find out anything important from Frazier and Morris, then left the gaggle of excited men and drifted into his office, stopping by the coffeemaker and pouring himself a cup, which he set on his desk and stared at while the steam rose slowly into the chill air.

When Ridge and Cully arrived from the murder scene, walking in separately because they had come in separate cars, the other detectives swarmed them with questions. Ridge seemed not to hear. Bellflower looked up from his coffee and barked, "Hey!" They all heard him, right through the venetian blinds of his glass cubicle.

Ridge and Cully moved over to his office and shut the door behind them. "What's this about a woman mutilated in an alley?" he demanded.

"Ugly scene," Ridge said. Ridge never said more than he wanted to. It was aggravating to people who liked to speculate, but it was Ridge's theory that if you articulated possibilities, you set them in your mind and gave other seeds of inspiration no chance to take root.

"Ugly, what's ugly, Ridge? Every murder we see is ugly. Get the spooky look off your face and tell me what the fuck is happening!"

"Somebody carved the implants out of a woman's breasts. They attached a note to her forehead—attached it with a nail through her skull. She was beaten to death first."

Bellflower wasn't sure he had heard right. "He carved out her what?"

"Assuming the killer was a he," Ridge said.

"Assume the killer was a Martian, Ridge! He carved out her tits?"

"He cut out her breast implants. The bags of silicone that made her boobs bigger. He left them on her shoulders—the bags, I mean. Her breasts were still attached by flaps of skin."

Bellflower took a huge breath and blew it out through puffed cheeks, like a man who has swallowed his whiskey too fast.

"The killer *was* a he, of course," Ridge said.

Bellflower's eyebrows scrunched so low he had to peer through them to see Ridge. "What are you holding back on me?" he demanded.

"We just found the body." Ridge looked down and rubbed his right thumb across his fingertips as if to sharpen his sense of touch.

"Hey. Ridge? I'm the boss, right? You tell me what you think."

Ridge tilted back his chin and scratched his neck. "We've got, I'm almost certain, a male killer; mutilation of breasts alone is a statement, not the kind of attack against another woman's femininity that a psychopathic woman might make; in that case you'd expect the mutilation of the vagina, which didn't happen here. He's careful and theatrical. We know the killer is careful because of the way the body was delivered: there had been a plastic sack around her to contain the blood, and I think she was in the sack when she was beaten to death. She was killed inside a house, or a room, or even a car, and was wrapped up like that so the blood wouldn't spurt. We know it was indoors because anyplace the killer felt safe enough outdoors would be someplace remote enough that he wouldn't worry about spilling the blood. The rage was in the beating, not in the cutting. The cutting was a psychological justification for what had gone before; it was done inexpertly but not in a frenzy; the breasts were cut up, but the bags were both intact, and a lot of crazy stabbing would have punctured them for sure. And we know he's theatrical because she was posed in that alley. He made a picture of her instead of just dumping her. Even the nail through the skull is a statement—a kind of crucifixion."

Frazier and Morris had invited themselves into the cubicle and closed the door on the other detectives while Ridge was delivering this report, and they listened without interruption.

"So that's *all* you can tell me?" Bellflower said. "Just that little bit?"

Cully said, "You left out that she's a hooker." Everybody looked at her. "She had a tattoo—an elephant, I think—on her right shoulder."

Frazier and Morris looked at each other; neither of them had noticed the tattoo. Ridge said, "Yes. She did. But just having a tattoo doesn't make her a hooker. Imagine what we'd think if we found the body of Cher."

"Hey," Morris said, "maybe the meat was in the circus and worked with the elephants."

"Or a Republican," Frazier said.

"Maybe she's got more brains right now, lying in one of Roger's body bags, than you guys got," Bellflower said.

"That's cold," Morris said.

"What's cold?" a voice behind them said, and all the cops in the cubicle involuntarily straightened up. The voice belonged to Deputy Chief Rowe. He walked in and glanced around expectantly, almost cheerfully, with this first chance to prove the expertise of his new unit.

"We've got a murder, an ugly one," Bellflower told him. "Maybe a serial."

"One body? Why do you think it might be a serial?" Rowe asked.

"It seems personal—personal to the killer but not

to the victim," Bellflower said. "When you get that kinda situation, when you find a killing that ritual and obsessive, you can figure you're gonna see more than one before it's over."

Rowe looked at Bellflower first, as if asking his permission before making a suggestion. "We'll want to put an information blanket on all this then, won't we?" he asked.

Bellflower nodded.

"So we don't have any copycats? And if anybody confesses, we'll have some unpublished details he'll have to know so we can be sure he's not just after attention?" Rowe had a habit of asking instead of telling, thinking it gave his men a sense of power and importance.

"Exactly, sir," Frazier piped up. "You let something like this get out, any guy in Beverly Hills wants a divorce and doesn't want to split half his assets, he can murder his wife and carve her tits off and say it was the same murderer."

"God," Rowe said, "is that what the mutilation was?"

"Both of 'em," Morris said. "Right off."

Bellflower didn't like the way the detectives were making fun of their deputy chief's inexperience, whether the DC noticed it or not. Bellflower stood by way of dismissal and said, "You guys make your rundowns and put whatever you need to on the wires."

"By the way, sir," Cully said. "There was a note."

"A note? Oh yeah," Bellflower said, frowning. Mutilators often signed their work: initials carved on a body, letters scrawled in blood on floors or walls. Words on paper were less frequent; usually the butchery itself was the message. "Crazy or coherent?" Bellflower asked, with only casual interest.

"Both," Ridge said. "Right now we'd better make sure all our evidence is taken care of and get a description out on the missing-persons com lines. The victim didn't have any ID."

Bellflower nodded and the detectives and deputy chief filed out of his office. When they had left, Bellflower shut the door behind them, drew tight the venetian blinds, and sat down again at his desk. He stared at the wall for a long time and finally remembered his coffee. When he sipped it, it was chilly.

As Deputy Chief Rowe returned to his own cubicle and sat down at his massive desk, an antique reproduction in blond burlwood, he was not troubled by his isolation from the details of his job or the perspective of his own men. A few weeks before, such a lack of involvement would have bothered him enormously, and he would have considered a subtle bit of ridicule such as Morris had just tossed at him to be an unpardonable affront. But something had happened to change the deputy chief and his relationship with the whole world.

Michael Rowe was falling in love.

Love. What an experience. It was new for him. Yes, he had loved his wife once, in a particular way. She had been right for him; she looked great, she spoke elegantly, she thought the right things about schools and clubs and church and belonged to the right ones.

But this new love was different and he was astonished at its power. He couldn't even think of the relationship directly because the thrill of it was so overwhelming. The awareness of the sexual possibilities with his new lover stood in Mike Rowe's mind like a magnetic mountain. So great was the attraction of that mountain that if he let his thoughts go at it directly, they would latch onto it for hours, days—forever?—and he would be able to think of nothing else. He had to let his thoughts race by it at high speed and touch it at a glance, throwing off a shower of mental sparks.

Only a few times in his life had such overwhelming longings possessed him, but he had always seen his desires as dangerous and awful. He had never cheated on his wife, but this was different; to fall in love like this seemed not to be cheating at all. This new relationship made a difference in every moment of his life. He had been troubled before, and now he was at peace. What a profound realization that was! He hadn't even realized he had been troubled. Imagine! No wonder poets spoke of love as an awakening. This was like he had been dead before and had just been called into life for the first time.

Everything was different. No, Mike realized as he thought about it anew in his office, it was that he was different and now he saw the world differently. Before, when he saw young lovers—two brown-skinned teenagers playing tonsil hockey on a park bench, a fifteen-year-old boy and an even younger girl slouched against each other in the shopping mall and walking toward the video-game room like the world was against them—he felt contempt. Now he felt aligned with them, a part of their passion. Now he saw the beauty in their love and saw love as what kept the world going. Without that beauty the world would be torn apart by the filth that Mike Rowe had to deal with every day.

Murders, muggings, robberies, wife beatings, child abuse. All that came across his desk every day, and the people who thought he was cold to all that just didn't know Mike Rowe. He had to be efficient and that meant staying cool, but as he had fallen in love he had realized how good a person he actually was and how much he wanted the world to be a better place.

He had the nagging thought that to pursue this new passion would surely be adultery—and yet that thought shattered to dust against that magnetic mountain in his mind. Yes, he might end up cheating on his wife, but the man who was married to Cecilia Rowe was not the man he really was, and Mike knew those secrets had to last forever.

The secret that would always be there.

There was nobody he could tell all this to—not
even his lover. Rowe was afraid if he talked about it too
much, it would all go away.

But now he had memos to write, requisition forms
to send out, favors to call in, to help MULHOM, his
new child.

The detectives who had been forced to wait outside
while Ridge, Cully, Frazier, and Morris were having a
conference in Bellflower's office were not happy: the
first murder for MULHOM, and they weren't being
filled in on it, what was this crap? They lingered around
the south end of the Can, surly and expectant, and when
Frazier and Morris emerged, they began to pepper the
two with questions. Frazier responded with characteris-
tic diplomacy: "Shut the fuck up. This case is confidential. You dipshits'll have to wait till we're ready to tell
the world."

This comment reminded everybody that no secrets
worth knowing would ever be in Trigger Frazier's possession, and they all felt better right away. Cully and
Ridge, coming out of Bellflower's office behind the
other pair of detectives, found everyone drifting back to
the central desk area. Ridge paused a moment, and
Cully knew that he was looking at her, but she did not
look back. Turning away from him, she followed the others. Ridge waited another moment, then turned sharply
and moved toward the evidence cage.

Out in the desk area John "the Baptist" Dewey
decided to liven things up with a story about Carlos
"Banana" Santana, who had been his partner in the
Rampart Division. "Hey guys," he said, "I ever tell you
about Santana's kid?"

"My *alleged* kid," Santana corrected.

"Yeah, yeah, his alleged kid," Dewey said, in the
gravely preacher's voice that got everybody's attention.
"The Banana was dating this girl. This *alleged* girl. Who
was married to this wrestler—"

"Allegedly married," Santana broke in.

"Yeah, yeah, allegedly married," Dewey agreed. "And the girl gets pregnant. And not allegedly either, bitch got—"

"Bitch got pregnant!" Santana agreed.

"But it ain't Banana's kid, noooooooooooo!" Dewey said. "Her husband, her *alleged* husband, he's this big dude. And the baby's born, and he's got this pecker that looks like a capital J, man. A perfect banana!"

But Cully McCullers wasn't listening to this story. She was thinking of what she had just done to Ridge, of the anger she had met him with out there in the alley before she had looked at the body, and of the tiny snub she had just committed, volunteering more information about a murder investigation than Ridge was ready to talk about. That was a tiny personal infraction, the kind that carried such weight between once and future lovers. Why had she done it? She didn't understand it herself; and in the logic of romance, knowing that she had just been cruel made her angry, not at herself, but at him.

These were not the first raw edges she and Ridge had rubbed against each other; over the last week they had exchanged little but quick frowns and short words. Nor were she and Ridge the only ones who had noticed the tension between them. A beautiful single woman in a world of men draws all sorts of disguised attention, and the gossip that she and Ridge had become lovers at the end of their last case only served to sharpen the eyes of the men around them. And George "Tooda" Taylor did not need much encouraging; since the first moment he had seen Cully McCullers, he had been waiting for his chance. He had noticed Ridge's lingering; he had caught the subtle brush-off. And now he was sure that Cully was available, maybe even on the rebound, and that made Tooda as delicate as a rutting rhinoceros.

So as the Baptist was telling his story about Banana, Tooda slid up next to Cully and gave her a grin like a Turkish knife thrower. Tooda had a swarthy walrus mustache and a powerful build; the coarse black hair that covered his back and shoulders spilled out above the collar and below the armholes of the tight T-shirts he wore. All LAPD cops are body conscious, knowing the importance of an intimidating street presence, but Tooda went beyond most; he was a power lifter, and his shoulders seemed to start halfway up his head, just behind his ears. He was proud of his body, working on it two hours a day, four days a week, and like many bodybuilders he figured that if his body was a fetish for him, it must also be for women. Standing with his pumped-up arms cocked wide, like a man about to lift a barrel, he said, "Hot case, huh?"

"Yeah," Cully said, "I guess they all are."

Tooda nodded as if her comment were profound. "Hear you had a little trouble out there this morning." He was smiling.

"Huh?" she said. Then she realized what he was talking about, and her eyes narrowed. "Oh yeah. A little trouble." She looked away from him again.

"Kinda tough when you're new," Tooda said.

"I'm not new," she said.

"New enough to faint," Tooda said, and grinned.

At first she wasn't sure; was he coming on to her? And this was how he flirted, by putting her down? "You gotta get used to what happens," he said, rubbing her shoulder like a big brother, but probing his fingers into her muscles and looking into her eyes to see if she liked it.

Any other time she might have dealt with this more immediately. But this was one wave in an emotional sea storm that had tossed her since her telephone had squealed her awake that morning, and with each unexpected surge she felt her reactions lagging farther and farther behind. Every other day she knew who she was, what she was facing, and how to deal with it; but today, with Tooda making a public physical contact of the kind that she had always warded off from her male coworkers, she found herself thinking, I deserve this.

It made her hesitate, and that encouraged Tooda.

But then she snapped her eyes around at him, forced a smile, and said, "Thanks, but I really don't need a back rub right now."

"Sure, babe!" Tooda said, grinning his walrus grin and knowing that nobody had ever put a hand on her before. He nodded and took his hand away.

She looked back at the Baptist and tried to focus her mind on his story.

Tooda patted her on the butt, right where the hard muscles of her bottom joined the top of her legs.

Cully spun around, blinking. He winked at her. She slapped him across the broad flat muscle of his cheek. Most women, if they slap, do it like an actress in a soap opera, with much the same loose motion as a waitress in a diner uses a dishcloth to swat at a fly. Cully McCullers, daughter of an Irish street cop and a cop herself, slapped like a tiger punching the neck of an antelope with its paw. Everybody within thirty feet heard the loud sharp sound, and as Tooda recoiled to his right she followed her first slap with another from her left hand, jolting him back the other way.

Flushing red as a traffic light, he shoved both hands against her shoulders and bounced her backward. The next moment was confusion, the surprised detectives grabbing at Cully instead of Tooda because she was reeling back through them. And no one was quite sure afterward whether Tooda was actually moving toward her to follow up his advantage or not, and the point would always be moot, because a blur streaked in from the far side of the Can and Tooda's head popped. It sounded like a watermelon falling off a picnic table onto hard ground. He went limp and sprawled; Ridge had hit him flush in the neck, right below the ear.

Cops are trained to react to a fight by jumping into

the middle of it, and they are quick to take sides. Boom-Boom, Tooda's partner from Central, swung at Ridge and caught him high on the back of the head. The blow glanced, but it was a cheap shot, and suddenly it was all-out war. The detectives hurled themselves into the melee and locked up like a rugby scrum, shoving each other back and forth along the floor.

Cully stood frozen, gaping openmouthed at Ridge, who was ignoring Boom-Boom's blow, if he felt it at all, and stood over Tooda, yelling for him to get up, until the mass of bodies surged over him and Ridge was swept into the middle of the elbowing, the biting, and the gouging.

Then just as suddenly as the cops had begun to fight, they stopped and held their breath; they had heard the distinctive sound of a revolver being cocked, and that kind of noise puts a sudden chill into every kind of action involving cops. Boom-Boom Malchek, gripping Ridge's waist from behind, felt something metallic and cold against his throat, just beside his Adam's apple, and he determined not to move an eyelash.

"Carl," he said slowly to Banana Santana, who was holding Ridge's left arm. "I think she's got her weapon on me, Carl."

Banana Santana said, "She does, Larry. She sure does."

Rowe and Bellflower had come stumbling out of their offices and were now standing there gawking along with everyone else.

"McCullers!" Bellflower barked.

Cully stayed in a crouch, her eyes wide and steady, her hands solid on the trigger and her breath coming in and out hungrily, ready to shoot.

"Malchek! Santana!" Bellflower said sharply. "I think she's waitin' for you to pay attention."

Boom-Boom and Banana let go of Ridge and stood up. Cully backed off and stood with the pistol still raised. Bellflower and Rowe looked back and forth.

Then they looked at Tooda, sprawled on the floor, his eyes just beginning to focus.

"Holster your weapon!" Bellflower snapped at Cully.

She eased the hammer down, slid the pistol back into the belt holster under her jacket, and stared down at Tooda. "Sorry," she said, softly and without remorse.

5

Leonard "Liberty" Bellflower was a veteran of twenty-two years on the police force and forty-eight years on the streets. He had joined the LAPD after a stint in the marine corps. Unlike most peacetime volunteer leathernecks, Bellflower was not a little guy out to validate his manhood (he was six-one and at the time he joined weighed one hundred and eighty-five pounds); he was a fatherless black kid who felt himself at a crossroads between determination and destruction, and he chose the corps because he believed the thing that would make the most difference in his life was self-discipline, and where better to learn it than standing at attention in front of a cracker drill instructor telling you you ain't nothing but a nigger faggot?

Bellflower had come out of the marines four and a half years later, having extended just long enough to go to officers' candidate school and emerge as a second lieutenant. The corps wanted him to stay; they needed black officers. But Bellflower had another idea. Another dream was emerging in America: that young black kids could become not just rebounders and wide receivers, but doctors, scientists, maybe even politicians, and Leonard Bellflower had dreams. He joined the LAPD and set about completing his education, even before the city was willing to help pay for it. He graduated from USC's night school and proceeded to volunteer for every tough road the Los Angeles Police Department could chart.

His last formal evaluation as division chief noted that "Captain Bellflower has a low tolerance for failure."

Bellflower said the same thing himself, but put it differently to his men. At one time or another everyone who worked for him had been told, "I expect results. Don't expect thanks from me; competence is the minimum I require. Just remember this: you disappoint me, and I'll make sure you are disappointed."

But if you were his friend, he would never forget you. Cully McCullers believed that about Bellflower, perhaps more strongly than anyone else could ever believe it. Bellflower had been a friend of her father's; they had ridden patrols together. When her father died, and was buried by his family, and the department sent no honor guard, no flowers, not even a flag, and his old brothers in blue all thought of other places they just had to be that day, Len Bellflower showed up, in his dress uniform, and when even the priest was gone, he stayed beside the grave and held Cully's fingers in his white-gloved hand, and with his other hand, he saluted.

Now Bellflower was yelling. Not just blowing out words in a loud voice, either. His anger was too big to squeeze through that one little hole of his mouth, and in too big a hurry to get out all at once, so it backed up and built up pressure, pinching his voice off until it was faint and high and popping the veins out on his neck. It even garbled his diction; the first words out of his mouth were, "Got-dammick!"

He told Cully she had just pulled the most unprofessional performance he'd ever seen. Yeah, he knew, he knew, some of the detectives were pigs, but that was completely, utterly beside the point. What was the big surprise, didn't she already know cops were pigs?

Only now he wasn't talking to just Cully, he was talking to Ridge, too. And he'd never yelled at Ridge before. Maybe that's why he lowered his voice a little, right after he said, "I'll tell you what's going on. I know what's going on! The whole department knows what's going on!"

"Don't you glare at me, Ridge, don't you dare glare at me. Cause I'm your goddamn superior officer and if you don't like that you can get your ass out of this whole police department, that's what you can do, but you're gonna hear this 'cause it's the truth and you know it is. You two been playin' grab-ass! That's what you just proved to everybody in the whole unit! And I don't give a damn what you do on your own time, but you belong to City of Los Angeles and that means you belong to me and I will not have my cops turning into high-school sweethearts on me, is that all-together clear?"

Ridge had sat through the whole tirade without looking at Cully. He had turned different colors, from the flushed rose of anger to the bleached pale of shame, but Ridge was a man who knew the truth when he heard it, and now he glanced at Cully, then back at Bellflower, and said, "Yeah, Len, I guess I gotta admit it. She can't keep her hands off me. I wish you'd talk to her about that."

Bellflower was caught off guard. He tried to cover by keeping the anger pumped full into his face, but as he became aware of the extent of his anger, and how ridiculous Tooda had looked on the floor, and how little actual harm had been done, he shook his head and smiled.

Cully, who had sat in silence through all of this, seemed to grow even more still as Ridge smiled, too. She stood suddenly. "You guys are a ton of fun," she said, and walked toward the door.

"Detective, you get back here!" Bellflower boomed.

Cully stopped and turned, but refused to take a step back toward him.

"One of you has got to go," Bellflower said. "I can't

have this case go south on me. What if we don't find this guy, whoever butchered that girl? We might not, you know! First case of this unit? The chief starts looking into our investigation and finds out I had two detectives all over each other instead of this investigation? Holy shit, they'll bury all of us."

Cully looked at Ridge. "I'm not going to be the one who leaves this case," she said.

"Okay," Bellflower said. "Ridge can be backup."

She nodded, started to walk away, stopped again. "Wait a minute. If I don't catch this guy right away, you'll bring Ridge back into it. Won't you?"

Bellflower didn't say anything.

"You'll have to," Cully went on. "Downtown, they'll say they want some action, so you better bring in the big gun."

"Unfortunate choice of words," Bellflower said.

Cully stood there boiling as Bellflower threw a half grin at Ridge. "Won't matter," she said. "I'm gonna nail the guy. I'm gonna cut off one particular body part and shove it in his mouth and leave him with a sign around his neck that says, 'Do Not Bend, Fold, or Mutilate.' "

"You do that," Bellflower said.

Cully turned sharply and walked out.

Ridge caught up to her in the parking lot. "You're carrying your father's gun?" he said.

Only it was a question, and she wasn't going to answer. She kept stalking toward her car, walking quickly. But Ridge's long legs easily kept him beside her. "How mad at me are you?" he asked.

She looked at him fiercely.

"I'm sorry," he said.

"You think I can defend myself?" she said.

"Yeah, I think so."

"You think I can decide whether to go off on a guy or just walk away?"

"Yeah. I think so."

"You think I want every cop in the division to see you protecting me, like you're some kind of caveman and I'm your woman?"

That was the one that made Ridge stop, lick the inside of his mouth, and bite his lower lip, the way she had seen him do before when his feelings were hurt and he was mad.

"What's wrong?" she said. Though she knew what it was.

Ridge just turned his back on her and walked away. Cully got into her car, moving deliberately so as not to slam the door or grind the engine when she started it, and drove away.

Back in the Can, Bellflower sat alone in his office, looking through the glass window and wondering what the fuck he was doing in this job. He saw Walter Hobbs, the evidence clerk, coming from fifty feet away. Hobbs had a fast walk that got faster when he was bringing something, and here he came, on a mission from God.

He knocked and opened Bellflower's glass door all in one motion and laid the pictures on the desk and went out again, all without ever breaking stride.

The pictures were prints of the first photographs of the body, a stack of two dozen, taken from all angles. Meant to be a reference for every detail, in a way they showed nothing. It was hard at first to figure out what the hell you were looking at. Bellflower poked at them with his big blunt fingertips, knocking the stack around, spreading them into some shape and wincing when his mind finally assembled the gore into human form. He had to do that, put her back together in his head, to realize what she once had been.

There it was, the elephant tattoo McCullers had mentioned. Bellflower stared at it.

Then he scattered the photographs with slow dread, and found the one of her face.

He drove down to the morgue. He used his blinking light but not his siren, and got there five minutes before his detectives did.

He went in and stood over the body and stared at her until they arrived. When he heard them out in the hallway, talking loudly like detectives always do before they come in to watch Roger carve the turkey, Bellflower left, by the backdoor.

6

Roger the Coroner kept the autopsy room cold. Cully thought it was to help keep things down, things like the smell, and your breakfast. The truth was that Roger didn't worry about the way his workplace affected detectives. Frazier, who carried a thick sweater in the trunk of his Plymouth and always brought it to what he called the Grand Openings, said Woge was just a bloodless ghoul and liked the room to match his own body temperature.

The chill in the room and the goose bumps on her arms reminded Cully that dead bodies were cold. That, to Cully, was the most unlifelike thing about them, that they took on the temperature of the rooms around them, or the floors you found them on. She tried to think of that coldness now.

The body lay faceup on the chrome-guttered table beneath the bright, neutral white lights of Roger's examination room.

Aspen Jack Merkle lay two tables away, looking deflated; his belly had sagged and spread out, so that instead of looking like a whale he now resembled an overfilled cupcake, oozing out in all directions. Frazier and Morris, there to attend his excavation, filed in behind Ridge and Cully, and Frazier said, "Jeez, Jack looks like he lost weight. I wonder what his diet is, I wanna give it to my wife."

And Roger, coming in, his usual smiling self, said,

"As soon as we open his bowel I can wet you know exactwy what he had at bweakfast."

Cully actually chuckled. She wanted to laugh, she wanted to forget that these people on the steel tables were once suckling babies, runny-nosed toddlers, teen-agers with passionate dreams. Why did something in her keep trying to picture them that way? Why torture her-self with morbid thoughts? You look at enough of these, you've got to forget they were once real.

The Jane Doe did not look like a person. Her face was bruised, blue on the left side, the skull caved in above her left ear. Her chest was brownish red, a stark contrast to the bloodless white of the rest of her body under Roger's lights. The two silicone-filled breast-implant bags that had rested on her shoulders when they found her now lay in a silver dish beside the scale on Roger's instrument tray. Cully thought at first that Roger had already taken out her kidneys.

"Shee-sus, wouldya look at that!" Frazier said. "I can tell already that this girl is Jewish!"

"Jewish?" Roger said. "How's that?"

"Cause she's got a Hanukkah bush!" Frazier said, pointing at the cadaver's pubic hair.

Roger nodded thoughtfully, switched on his record-ing equipment, and spoke into the microphone dangling from the ceiling; he gave the date, the time, the sex and apparent age of the victim (he estimated mid-twenties), and then said, "Most distinguishing physical characteris-tic: pubic hair dyed in stwips of fluowescent cowwers: wed, gween, yewwow, and bwue."

Frazier and Morris looked up at Roger, then looked at each other, and suddenly howled in laughter. "What?" Roger said. "What's so funny?"

Frazier and Morris laughed so hard they couldn't tell him. But the words "wed, gween, yewwow, and bwue" were destined to become the punch line in one of Frazier's favorite stories about Roger. They laughed so hard they were gagging, and then they looked at the severe face of Thomas Ridge.

Cully knew that Ridge did not lack a sense of humor, and it was not their ridicule of Roger's speech impediment that made him scowl; she knew already that Ridge figured Roger had to take care of himself when it came to guys like Frazier, and Roger got along just fine with his own sense of humor. What troubled Ridge was how they were going to keep this piece of information out of the papers. The pubic hair was a good clue. It was distinctive, it might lead them to the victim's identity. So how could he keep this secret, if Frazier and Morris couldn't wait to go around the station saying "wed, gween, yewwow, and bwue"?

Frazier and Morris wiped the tears from their eyes and retreated to the bright glow around the body of Aspen Jack Merkle. Roger went back to the business of excavating Jane Doe. He recited a general survey of the body: skull concavity in on upper left hemisphere, repeated trauma to the face, especially the left side. No signs of strangulation—trachea normal, breathing passages blocked only by blood from internal hemorrhage, possibly the result of battering to the abdomen as well.

He moved down: breasts cut cleanly, implant bags present, assume cuts were for purpose of removing the bags.

Ridge stopped Roger there. "Have you weighed them yet?" he asked.

"The bweasts?" Roger said.

"The bags."

"Oh. Yes," Roger said; but he meant no, he hadn't, and he tossed one of the bags onto the scale right then and came up with a reading of exactly one hundred ten grams.

"Thank you," Ridge said, and Roger went on.

He confirmed the trauma to the rib area, moved down to the groin, and reported "the aforementioned pwensence of dye in the pubic wegion."

Frazier and Morris heard Roger say this, and that set them off again.

And Cully, God help her, began to snicker, too. She couldn't help it. She put her hand up to her face and tried not to laugh and it just spilled out of her. She straightened her face, trying to look grave, and thought, Cuwwy, wook gwave! And that did it for her; she began to laugh so hard she had to leave the room and wait for Ridge in the hallway.

She waited in the hall for half an hour before Ridge came out. In that time Roger had carved away the top of the woman's skull and examined the brain. He had stared up and in and through every opening in her body, both natural and unnatural. He had clipped the ribs like snipping off the top of a wire basket and had taken her organs out one by one and weighed and examined them, then twisted the whole mess up inside a plastic bag and returned the whole shebang into her chest, closing it back up with a nice loop stitch. He had tape-recorded all his spoken observations and had taken flash pictures of everything significant in the procedure.

The implant bags he had kept as evidence.

Ridge had stayed to watch; somebody had to. Now, when he walked out into the corridor, Cully said immediately, "I'm sorry, I don't know what happened to me, I just—"

"I know what happened," he said. He even forced a smile.

"I mean, I just started thinking, 'The pwesence of dye in the pubic wegion. Wed, gween, yewwow, and bwue . . .' "

"I know," Ridge said.

"What's happening to me, Ridge?" she said. "I'm turning into as big a pig as Frazier." She gazed down at the floor, big black-and-white squares of linoleum.

"No you're not. You're just turning into a cop. And you know, maybe Frazier's not so much of a pig." When her eyes snapped up to his face he added quickly, "Well, okay, Frazier is a pig, but sometimes we have to be pigs, don't we?"

"What did the rest of the autopsy tell us?" Cully said, still feeling like the giggles weren't far away.

Before Ridge could answer, Frazier and Morris came out to join them; Roger had decided to pause for coffee and a peach Danish before he scooped out Aspen Jack. "I hear her vagina was a Flying Dutchman," Frazier said.

"A Flying Dutchman?" Cully said.

"Yeah!" Frazier said. "No semen!"

Cully snickered again. Ridge's eyes flicked at her, then turned on Frazier.

"That's right," Ridge said. "No semen."

"The bitch was a hooker," Frazier said. "Had to be. That bush? Come on!"

Cully, stung by Ridge's glance and smarting from her own laughter, said, "A stripper, I think." When they all looked at her, she said, "Did you see her legs? Long muscular development."

"Most working girls stand around a lot," Frazier said doubtfully.

"Standing and walking give you knottier muscles. Hers were long and ropy, like a dancer's. Almost nothing gives you that kind of development except dancing and maybe gymnastics, and with those store-bought boobs and the tie-dyed pubic hair, I'd say she didn't spend her time on a balance beam." Impressed with herself, Cully smiled and glanced back at Ridge. "Anything else?" she asked.

"Another tattoo, besides the elephant on her shoulder," Ridge said. "Right side of her butt. This one shows an elephant, with an erection, trying to mount a mouse. And the cartoon has a caption. Just two words: 'Love Hurts.'"

* * *

Back at the Can Bellflower asked them what they'd found, and they gave him the reports. He stared at the windowless walls, and interrupted Cully in midsentence.

"Here's what you do," he said. "Make up twenty copies of her picture and pass 'em around to whoever's not working on anything special. In fact, pull 'em off whatever else they're doing. We want the identity of this victim. Go ask the hookers on Sunset. Love Hurts? That sounds like Sunset Boulevard to me. Go ask 'em. Ask their pimps. Do it right now. Show 'em the picture and find out her identity. Follow that where it leads."

"But Captain—" Cully began.

"Hurry up," Bellflower said, and turned back to the wall.

7

The pole gleamed. It wasn't brass, no, it was gold, pure, rich, and sensual; that's what Porsche told herself as she made love to it, stretching her fingertips slowly upward on its polished surface, toward her blackness beyond the spotlight.

She bent at the waist and arched her spine, clawing her fingernails down the polished metal surface as her breasts swung out, one on either side of the pole. They were enormous and glistened with jewels of sweat, beaded on the surface of the baby oil she slicked on them before every performance. She had been nicely built even without the implants, but high, bulging knockers were the rage among strippers these days, and since she'd had hers turbocharged into 44-Ds, her weekly take—on and off the stage—had tripled.

She shook her shoulders back and forth and her breasts batted against the pole—not too much, but just enough to show the men sitting perfectly still beneath the pounding music, with the red lights from the spot gels reflecting in their eyes, that her boobs were soft and squeezable. She pulled her pelvis up to the pole and humped it slowly, one, two, three. . . . Then cupped her right hand beneath her left nipple and pouted, comforting the breast as if it were a crying baby.

She tossed her head so that the luxuriant hair of her blond wig swung around her face, then wrapped one knee around the pole and slid to a seated position as the lights went out and a blare of horns and drums told the hypnotized men that the dance was over.

The lights stayed out until she was backstage and wrapped up in her terrycloth robe. Out on the stage Freddy was hollering, "Hey guys, knowwhat, knowwhat? Ya believe in karma? In karma? Knowwhat? I'm gonna live right so if I get reincarnated I can come back as that pole! Huh? Huh?" Freddy never got a laugh but so what, nobody came to this place to see a comedian.

She spritzed on some counterfeit Giorgio and slipped into a silk kimono, garters and stockings, and high heels. In the dressing room a couple of the girls were doing some crystal meth in a glass pipe, and another offered Porsche a hit off a joint, the same one Porsche had left in the ashtray before going out to do her act. Porsche wanted to sit down and kick back for a minute, but she knew she wouldn't get up again if she did. She had an hour before her next tour of the stage, enough for a couple of trips around the world if she had been as good as she thought out there. The manager scheduled them that way so they could do a few clients in between shows. It was the least he could do, since he paid the girls next to nothing.

The guys who wanted some action would usually drift over by the door from the backstage area into the main bar. Some would only wait and stare at the sign that said DO NOT ENTER and try to work up the guts to make an approach when the girls came out. A couple of those types were standing there as she pushed open the big metal door. She pretended not to see them and made her way to the bar, ordering rum and Coke and sitting with a vacant stool on either side of her. The whole idea was to be easy, but it added to their excitement and her bargaining advantage if they came to her.

"Hey," a voice said behind her, and she turned around, smiling. He wore sunglasses, a blue suit and blue shirt and blue tie, and his hair was so oiled and black it looked almost blue itself. He hadn't been beside the backstage door; he must have been sitting farther down the bar. "How much?" he said.

"Excuse me?" she said.

"Come on. How much?"

"How much for what?" she said.

"Party." He drew the word out as if pissed off for having to say it. "Two hundred," he said.

Cops weren't allowed to mention money; if they did, it was entrapment. Two hundred was a lot of money, and the guy with the blue hair didn't look that turned on, but she said carefully, "For everything? Everything is two fifty."

"We'll have to ask the guy," he said.

"This party isn't for you?" Porsche said.

"For my boss," he said. "He's out in the limo."

Porsche didn't like secondhand deals; she had been around enough to know how bad they could go. But they were talking good money, so at least she could go out onto the sidewalk, where it was safe, and check it out. She stood and took his arm, laughing and talking as she walked out with him so they'd look like old friends and she wouldn't put off the other customers who might still be in the mood if she made it back with enough time to entertain another new friend before she danced again.

They stepped out onto the sidewalk, where the cars streamed back and forth in the colored glare of Sunset Boulevard. A silver limousine was parked at the curb, its motor running and music playing so loudly inside that she could hear it even on the curb. Bluehair unlocked the backdoor, opened it, and stepped back. Porsche leaned down to speak to the man inside, and found no one there. When she straightened quickly and turned on Bluehair, he had removed the sunglasses, and was staring at her.

Blinking, she looked at his face.

He smiled. "Wanna talk about the two fifty?" he said.

"Two's enough," she whispered to him, as if they had a little secret, and she slid into the back of the limo.

He walked around and got behind the wheel, and the limo pulled away from the curb, the lights of the boulevard sliding down its polished curves.

Cully stopped at the grocery store on the way home. She bought herself some trout and fixed it for herself, with some Minute Rice and a salad. She poured herself a glass of white wine and sat at her kitchen table. The air conditioner hummed. The water valves in the apartment next door went on and off as the dishwasher worked, and Cully wanted to throw her wineglass against the wall, just to make some different sound.

She heard the first rumble and thought it was an earthquake. She gripped the table and started to duck under it, in the panic that Californians learn, then heard the noise again and realized it had come not from the earth but from the sky.

Her apartment was on the second floor. She walked to the sliding glass doors off the living room, pushed back the curtains, shoved open the door, and stepped out onto the balcony. The lightning was far off, drifting across the San Fernando Valley. The whole valley was hushed, as if the sky had cleared its throat to ask for attention, and two million citizens in the bedroom of Los Angeles crouched down in their homes and waited for the rain. On the horizon out toward the Pacific the sky glowed a surly red. Thunder rolled across the flat floor of the valley. The freeways were a string of lit diamonds one way, rubies the other, rushing away before the rain.

It came at once, with hardly a sprinkle to start. The sky split and rain fell in torrents as if the clouds had held up a huge lake of fresh water until its weight tore through and gushed toward the parched ground. Cully stood in the shelter of her balcony's stucco awning and watched the storm batter the streets. A rain like that would wash Los Angeles, clean away the oily dust of six dry months, and clean the air, too. But it couldn't make the people clean.

Cully saw his old Corvette pull into the parking lot, the wipers slapping uselessly against the downpour. He got out and tried to cover his head, but gave up and sprinted toward her door. He did not see her on the balcony, he just knew that she would be home that night, looking for shelter against both storms: the one that rained on the outside world, and the one that raged inside her.

She stepped back into the apartment, slid the door shut, and waited for his knock. She heard him outside, brushing the water off his sleeves, probably smoothing his hair, and then he rapped twice. She opened the door. "Hi," he said.

"Hi." She stepped back and said, "Come on in."

"I can't," he said. But then he did anyway, starting and stopping, starting and stopping, till he stood three feet inside her door. This was like Ridge, she thought; he would have planned this, he would have rehearsed what he wanted to say, and it was in his mind that he would say it all at the door and wouldn't ever be inside. He fumbled a moment, his eyes blank, his mind a book where he had lost his place.

"Want some coffee?" she said.

"Uh, no. Yeah! Uh . . . no. I really can't stay, I just wanted to come by and talk with you. Just for a minute."

She tottered between heading into the kitchen to make the coffee and sitting down in the living room to listen to the speech that he had obviously prepared. Outside, in the liquid air, the thunder rumbled, closer now.

"Cully," he said, "I don't know what to say to you. Nothing, I guess, is the right thing to say. Better just not to say anything, it's not something you talk about."

Cully knew what this "it" was, that they couldn't even refer to in a discussion of not talking about it.

"But it's sort of happening that we have to talk about it, don't we?" He didn't give her time to answer. "And that's why I came tonight, to say what I need to say."

With that preamble finished, he stopped and took a breath, then plunged on. "I don't want to hurt you, Cully. And I don't want to lie to you. I guess those are my main things, don't hurt and don't lie. I can't say I don't want to love you. And I can't say I do want to love you, either, because that's not a question of want. Not for me, anyway.

"I don't know a lot about being in love. I guess I don't know a lot about loving. I can love somebody who's gone—like my brother, or my grandmother. I loved them when they were alive and I love them now. That's easy to say. Now that they're gone, loving them doesn't carry any responsibilities.

"But loving somebody alive is different. If you love somebody, you don't want to hurt them. And . . . and you act like that's what's happening with us. That I'm hurting you."

She wanted to shake her head and say that wasn't so, but he was trying so hard to be honest that she couldn't get herself to lie.

"The night we spent together was . . . different from anything that ever happened to me," he said. "And I wouldn't change it. Even now. I don't want to lose you because of it. If we don't love each other, and I was mistaken about what happened then, then it's okay with me to just live with that illusion. I don't want to give up that moment in my memory. It made me hope for something and believe in something. And if we do love each other, then I'm willing to try to never let it out again, if letting it out hurts you. I just . . ."

She wanted to say something, anything. She couldn't.

"Is it hurting you?" he asked. A drop of the rain embedded in his hair broke loose and slid down his forehead, like a tear that had been left behind and was now wandering, lost.

"Tommy," she said, "all I can tell you is this. I'm not ready. I'm not ready for this."

He nodded, as if he understood. Did he understand? She didn't. Why couldn't she cross the five feet between them and throw her arms around him and bury her face in his wet chest and let him carry her into the bedroom and make love beneath the thunder and the rain?

But she could not. He nodded sharply, said, "I'll see you tomorrow," and was gone.

8

But it was not tomorrow.

Cully's phone rang at 4:30 that morning and Ridge's voice said, "Detective McCullers."

"Ridge?" she rasped, her voice harsh in the deep sleep that had swept over her, after she had put it off for so long.

"We've got another dead girl," Ridge said.

The body rested half sitting, half reclining, like a child fallen asleep and slumped down in a church pew. Only this girl's back was against the plywood doors that shuttered the racks of a newspaper stand off Ventura Boulevard. The plywood had once been painted a deep blue, but the sun had baked off some of the paint and bleached the rest turquoise; now the gray thirsty wood beneath had drunk in some of the gore, giving the body a blurred purple outline like a satanic corona. The short overhang of the newsstand roof had held the rain off the torso, but the sidewalk had been a river; the congealed blood above the waist faded gradually with the rinsing all the way down to the feet, waterlogged and white, so that to Ridge she looked like a genie, called from hell to materialize from a wisp of smoke.

Ridge had the body screened off by the time Cully got there. Roger had to come all the way from his home in Pacific Palisades, so the Coroner wasn't there yet when the detectives arrived. Cully walked straight up to

Ridge and didn't even say hello; they were two professionals, on the job. "Who found her?" she said.

"Driver of the truck that was delivering the bundles
of the morning paper. He spotted her there and thought
at first it was somebody sleeping under a red blanket.
But street people usually don't have notes nailed to
their heads, and when he saw the square of white paper,
he took a second glance."

"He called nine-one-one?"

"Yeah, from that phone booth across the street."

Cully looked. The booth was at the edge of a service station, but the station was closed all night. "So the
call went right into Mulholland Division?"

Ridge didn't look at her. "They routed it straight to
me. I guess they just hadn't heard yet that this was your
case."

"It won't be my case much longer, if this is a serial." She tried to keep the anger out of her voice, but it
was there. She knew her selfishness about this case was
ugly and forced herself to think about the immediate
problem. "So now we've got a whole newspaper knowing about this," she said. "No way this driver doesn't tell
some reporter he wants to impress."

"Maybe not," Ridge said. "He'll tell, for sure, but
maybe we can make a deal there. That is, if you want me
to. I'm not trying to butt into your—"

She turned from behind and walked toward the
cordon of black-and-white patrol cars, angled together
to shield the body from view. Ridge followed her, knowing it wasn't him she was mad at. As they closed in on
the body she said, "You're sure it's the same guy."

"No doubt about it. Same beating, same mutilation,
same note."

Cully looked at the body, made herself look long
and hard. The rain had stopped and the air was fresh
and cool, but Cully looked until she felt clammy and
about to smother. Finally she turned away and took a
few deep breaths.

Ridge stood there and waited for her.

She tried to get her brain working again. "Okay," she said. "Okay. Okay. We need to canvass the neighborhood and see if anybody saw anything."

He hesitated and then said, "I've got the uniforms out doing that already. I didn't mean to step on your toes; but they were here, and I thought we ought to get started as quickly as possible. . . ."

"Great, Ridge, do whatever you want," she said, and walked away from him again. This time he didn't follow. And then wondered, how long was she going to keep saying it, and not doing it?

Deputy Chief Rowe arrived freshly shaven and smelling of expensive cologne. He had run six miles before breakfast and had still had time for an hour in his home weight room, so he looked bright-eyed and ready for anything as he showed up promptly at nine. When Bellflower walked into his office and told him about the second murder, the deputy chief only half listened to the details, seeming more interested in the mechanics of mobilizing the resources of his new unit, should this case prove to be as great a problem as Bellflower seemed to think it was. The news clearly surprised him, but he dealt with it as he would have some unpleasant fiscal problem, like the threat of a budget cut. Before Bellflower was finished, Rowe had picked up his phone and told his secretary sitting at the desk outside his door, "Get Ridge and McCullers in here immediately."

Bellflower already had them waiting. Cully could see Bellflower and Rowe through the cubicle glass, and she saw Rowe's animation. It was the energy of an ambitious bureaucrat being handed an opportunity, and she knew what was coming. The stenographer, a gray-haired Lotto addict named Marybelle, put down the receiver and nodded to the detectives, and they moved into the office, Cully leading the way. "So what have we got?" Rowe said brightly. To Ridge.

Ridge hesitated, then said, "Uh, I'm only backup on this case, sir."

"But you were the first detective there, Ridge," Bellflower said sharply, and tried to soften the blow to Cully a little by explaining to Rowe: "The dispatchers hadn't yet gotten the word that I'd assigned Detective McCullers to work the case."

"Mmmph," Rowe said, and Cully saw that Rowe approved of the smooth way his captain had just eased the one woman in MULHOM out of the lead in the case by pretending to put her in it. "So what did you find?" Rowe rephrased, but still looked to Ridge for his answer.

"The same thing," Ridge said. "Breasts mutilated, surgical implants taken out. Note nailed to the girl's forehead."

"And we don't know a thing yet," Rowe said.

Ridge cleared his throat. Bellflower looked at him. Ridge cleared his throat again and looked at Cully. When she still didn't speak up, he said, "Well, we can say a few things."

"What's that?" Bellflower wondered.

Ridge said, "We haven't gotten a preliminary report from the coroner yet, but we did the autopsy on the first body yesterday, and she had not been exposed to intercourse in the twenty-four hours preceding her death."

Both Rowe and Bellflower stayed perfectly still, a tactic they had learned to employ in supervisory meetings where appearing smart was less important than not looking stupid. Rowe then nodded thoughtfully, to camouflage the fact that he had no idea why the fact Ridge reported would be significant. But Bellflower finally blurted, "So what?"

Ridge hesitated. "I believe this time the girl will show evidence of intercourse."

"So that would mean . . . what, two different killers?" Rowe said.

"Uh, no," Ridge said, not completely able to mask his impatience with an intellect that was slower than his. "What that suggests is that yesterday's body was his first victim."

"Well, isn't that . . . isn't it obvious it was his first victim?" Rowe said.

"No, sir, not necessarily. We've been going through the records to find which violent murderers may have been released lately, or may have escaped; or which patients with violent sexual histories have been released from mental hospitals recently. We had also started looking into other homicides with disfigurement or excessive violence, because in cases like this we always have to confront the possibility that what seems like a new killer is really an experienced one who is only producing a mutation in his old pattern. Now we think all that is unnecessary."

"Excuse me, Tom, you're the expert. . . . But how do we know that?" Rowe seemed almost amused.

"I think the first killing was a surprise—not just to the victim but to the killer himself. He had never done this before—not beat a woman to death. I think this because of the difference in the state of rage; the beating was done furiously, wildly; the amputation of the breasts was done more carefully, almost as a justification of what had happened before. But let's start with the things we can be pretty sure about. Getting the victim into the bag was premeditated; the double sacks were on hand. So he may have planned to beat her up. Or maybe he only wanted to get her into the sack, maybe he wanted to smother her. We can't say yet what made him hit her the first time, if he intended it all along or if it was a spur-of-the-moment thing, but it seems to be unplanned. The first time."

Now Bellflower jumped in. "You're saying you know all this from the fact that the girl's snatch was a Flying Dutchman?"

"That along with the observation that this victim

was raped—or at least had intercourse," Ridge said. "When Roger's boys shifted her body to lift it onto their cart, she dripped something. It appeared to be seminal fluid."

"I don't get it," Bellflower said.

"He picks up the first girl, he gets her into the bags, and for some reason he hits her. Let's put that reason aside for a minute. He hits her. And then he hits her again. And again. Now, if he had planned this first murder, it would be just like the second; but it isn't. There was intercourse in one and not in the other. That suggests another possibility. He picked the first girl up for sex. Humiliating, violent sex, but sex, not murder. And suddenly he's beating her. He gets carried away, and he kills her. He's surprised by what he's done, so surprised he loses his intention of sex and now turns to justification, carving up the body and leaving a note that blames the victim for the murder. He dumps the body. And he wakes up the next morning and he still hasn't had his sexual gratification. So he goes after another one, and this time he gets the sex first."

Mike Rowe nodded as if he understood. Maybe he did. Ridge went on, "Of course if we'd been less careful about letting out the specific details of the killings, we might be dealing with a copycat, but the wording of the note is the same, and we've kept that secret, so we can be sure this is one killer, not two." Rowe nodded; Ridge continued. "If neither body had been sexually assaulted, we would be dealing with a different kind of killer— someone impotent, who had fantasized about this thing for a long time. If both bodies had, we draw the same conclusion. But the difference in the two means something very specific about this man."

Rowe tuned back in. "And . . . and you know all this from that one discrepancy?"

"I'm guessing," Ridge said. "Maybe I mistook a drip of body secretion for seminal fluid because that's what I thought it would be. Of course if the coroner comes back and says her vagina was clean, then I'm wrong."

Bellflower picked up the telephone and punched in a number. "Roger?" he said. "Bellflower! You got victim number two on the table? Yeah. I just wanna know, is her snatch a Flying Dutchman or a battleship?" Bellflower paused and listened. "Okay, thanks, Roger." He hung up and looked at Ridge, with a kind of spooky awe.

"Battleship?" Rowe asked, frowning.

"Lots of semen," Bellflower said.

It took Rowe a moment to get it; then he lowered his face, closed his eyes, and rubbed his fingertips on his forehead, as if to press into his brain a reminder that he was dealing with underlings who had their own jargon. Then he looked at Ridge and said, "You mentioned the reason he might have hit her, the first time. Do you have that figured out?"

Ridge stayed quiet, his eyes very still. "I'm not ready to speculate on that," he said.

"Well, Detective—" Rowe began.

"Ridge left something out," Cully interrupted.

They looked at her like she had farted.

"The body was dumped in a shelter, out of the rain," Cully said. "This guy wants the bodies found. He's putting on a little show."

Rowe and Bellflower missed the point. They nodded like bored parents with a child who has asked too many times for attention; it was obvious that Cully was just trying to kick her way back into the forefront of the case. Cully saw she had strained their patience; they even looked a little embarrassed for her.

"She's right," Ridge said flatly, and then they all looked at him.

And Cully thought, Damn if my only friend here isn't Ridge.

"So what do you suggest we do now?" Rowe said, again to Ridge.

"That depends on how Detective McCullers wants to proceed," Ridge said. And then they all looked at Cully.

She said, "We'll get the reports from the uniforms who canvassed the neighborhood to see if anybody saw anything."

"The first thing we've gotta know is the ID of the victims," Bellflower insisted.

"Right," Rowe said decisively, and then thought for a moment about what his decisive order should be. "Double the number of detectives you've got working that picture detail in Hollywood."

The room fell silent. Dead eucalyptus leaves scuttled like rats across the roof of the Can. Rowe glanced around, but everybody was looking down, until Bellflower cleared his throat and said, "Uh, sir, I think the standard manpower will be sufficient here."

"But this is one of those lurid cases the press likes so well," Rowe countered.

"Yes, sir, that's right, and I agree we should work it hard. But your street people, sir, your hookers and pimps, they're real tuned in to the level of police presence. Doubling our manpower's just gonna scare off the very people we need to be talking to."

Rowe hesitated, but only for a moment. He knew how to make his eyes go blank, but his lips betrayed him, not by speaking but by pursing and clamping down, as if refusing to suck on something bitter, something like being told by a subordinate that he didn't know as much as the people he was leading. Rowe smiled suddenly and said, "But Commander! You're forgetting the kind of people we're talking about here. Street cops, green detectives, sure, I would agree with you that they would be counterproductive out there. But this is MULHOM!"

Rowe nodded and raised his eyebrows in punctuation. Bellflower nodded, too. But there was a deep pain in Bellflower's eyes.

* * *

When they walked out of Rowe's cubicle, Marybelle said, "Detective Ridge, there is a Mr. Gulker from the *Times*, who has called you twice."

Ridge nodded. "Yes. Thank you," he said to Marybelle, and then looked at Cully.

"It's your case, you take it," Cully said.

"It's your case, you take it," Ridge said.

Cully accepted the message slip from Marybelle, walked along the long row of desks to her place at the end, and sat down. She stared at the blank blotter and tried to make her stomach stop doing angry flip-flops over the way they'd handed Ridge leadership in the investigation. Then she dialed the number.

Gulker was out. Cully left a message that she had to reach him, urgently, and two minutes later her phone rang. "Detective McCullers, Charlie Gulker," he said, in that treble voice of his that always sounded like he was about to laugh; in person he looked like he hadn't eaten in days, and his thin face was pinched into a frown behind steel-rim glasses.

"Hi, Mr. Gulker, remember me?"

"How could I forget?" Cully had met Gulker a few weeks before, when Ridge had made a deal with him to keep Ridge's name out of a story in exchange for the inside details of the case, once it was broken, and Gulker had kept his word, which made Cully feel he had a heart, even though other cops told her that was always a dangerous assumption when it came to journalists.

"I have a deal to offer you," Cully said, "something similar to our last one. But you're going to have to act quickly. One of the drivers of your morning delivery trucks found a body this morning, in what we think is a serial murder. He's sure to go to some reporter with—"

"He's already come to me," Gulker said.

"Oh," Cully said. "Okay. So you know. Just what do you know?"

"Everything," Gulker said.

"Okay . . . then you know what the note said."

There was a pause at the other end of the line. "Sure," Gulker said.

"All right. Then I guess you can just print it, and then we can tell everybody else in town that the *Times* did irreparable damage to our chances of catching the killer, and also made copycat murders more likely, by publishing details we needed desperately to keep secret."

"Whoa, Detective, slow down," Gulker said, and chuckled. "I just had to make sure I was dealing with somebody smart here. If you're going to make a trade, I have to believe you're going to have something worthwhile on the other end. If I go in and tell my editors I want to sit on a murder story as juicy as this one, I better deliver some hot stuff later on."

"Well you're just gonna have to gamble, and trust me, Mr. Gulker, cause I can't tell you what I don't know yet. All I can promise is that you'll get what I have, before anybody else does."

"Call me Charlie, okay?"

"So it's a deal? You'll just say a murdered woman was found, something like that, but you won't give details?"

Gulker hesitated again. "Am I supposed to keep Ridge out of this story?"

Cully sat with the receiver propped beneath her head, and her mind wandered to Ridge's dark family history. When Ridge was a boy, his mother and father were found shot to death in their bed, out in the rural southern community where Ridge had grown up, and the circumstances were such that no one ever knew whether it was a double murder or a murder/suicide. Then Ridge's younger brother had become a minister and he, too, had suffered a tragic death. These deaths, Cully suspected, with the unanswerable questions they left dangling in his life, were the reasons Ridge was the detective he was. Cully knew for sure that Ridge kept a low profile with the media because he knew how they would love to explore and exploit the murky waters of his family, and that, to Ridge, would be like building a public latrine above their graves. Gulker knew and respected that fact, and this made Cully trust him.

"Ridge isn't on this case," she said.

"If it's a serial, and you don't catch the killer right away, then he will be," Gulker said.

"If he is, then you can make a deal with him. Right now it's my case. But," Cully added after a moment, "I know he'd want his name kept out."

"What's your relationship to Ridge?" Gulker asked.

"We were partners."

"Were?" he said.

"Are. Sometimes. He . . . trained me," she said, and realized how hesitant she was sounding. "Exactly what are you trying to find out?"

"What is there for me to find out? There's a rumor you two are involved."

"Look, Gulker—"

"I'm just doing my job, Detective. And I'm telling you something. I've promised Ridge not to publish his name, not to make him a celebrity. He's been a great source for me, but he's also a great story. And if I hear his history from some other source, then it's fair game— and it's fair game because some other reporter will break that story first, and then it won't matter how loyal and respectful to Ridge and his family I was, somebody else will have the scoop that I had in my back pocket for so long. So I'm just telling you to shoot straight with me."

"I shoot straight," Cully said.

"I know," Charlie Gulker said, with that curious chuckle in his voice, and he hung up.

The second autopsy was easier only because she was alone. Roger was there, of course, with his saws and his microphone, but he was so much a part of the morgue that to Cully he wasn't alive. And the body on the table seemed somehow more remote from life than the first victim had been. That was odd because this one was not as badly beaten. That is, she had not been hit so many times as the first girl, and the collapse of the left half of her skull was more orderly looking, like a single blow meant to kill, not surrounded by a swarm of bruises that looked like practice strokes.

Maybe it was the implant bags. They were so large they looked like shoulder pads, laid as they were now beside the victim's head.

This second girl lacked the tattoos and dyed pubic hair of the first victim; the second Jane Doe's only distinguishing feature was an inch-long birthmark roughly in the shape of Florida, just below where her left breast had been. The blotch had been covered with makeup, but when Roger cleaned it off, it stood out clearly. Roger took the photographs he needed, then loaded in another roll for Cully and shot twelve frames of the face. Cully took that roll with her, back to the old tin building on Mulholland.

There at the Can she dropped the exposed negative off at the makeshift darkroom Rowe had established next to the evidence cage. While she was waiting for the prints she moved across to the communications bay and ran her checks through missing persons. It was a dull task, taking the size and weight of the victim and the age and hair color, and trying to connect that description with anybody who had been reported missing. The computer could select the subset for her, and even call up pictures for the ones who seemed possible. Cully had to stare at some photographs and wonder how the years would have affected the faces she saw. How would these girls, whose high-school yearbook pictures she was looking at, have changed in becoming hookers or strippers? The effort produced no result other than to make Cully think about time, and how many people in the course of it became more corrupt, and how few became nobler.

The photo technician tapped her on the shoulder and told her the prints she wanted were ready. Cully retrieved them, along with the other run of prints she had ordered of the autopsy face shot of the first victim. She took the two stacks of eight-by-tens to the folding table by the communications bay and placed them neatly side by side, then fetched two index cards from her desk and used a marker, not unlike the one the killer had used to make his sign, to write on them *Jane Doe I* and *Jane Doe II*. Frazier, walking by at that moment to pick up pictures for himself and Morris, noticed what she was writing and said, "Hey, Roman numerals. We're gonna number 'em like Super Bowls, huh?" and left her alone again.

On the table above the two mounds of pictures she placed the small white index cards. To Cully they looked like gravestones.

From the top of each pile she took several of the prints, then drove across to Hollywood and walked up and down the hooker streets and showed the picture. Nobody, as Ragg Wilson would say, knew nothin'.

She stayed two hours past the end of her shift. Homicide detectives have flexible hours, and they all expect to work overtime. Cully had no justification for overtime today; if the hookers had changed shifts, she might have continued with some hope of talking to different ones, but it was a weekday evening and the street was quiet. Still, she walked up and down, the photograph in her pocket, and after a while she stopped showing it and just kept walking. Kids in leather jackets and with haircuts like the bright comb of a Roman legionnaire's helmet waited in line outside the rock clubs for a dose of heavy-metal music. Others filtered in and out of record stores. Valets ran to the doors of German luxury cars and opened them for the patrons of the open-air restaurants along the strip.

Cully walked. She stopped at a corner phone booth and put in a call to the station to say that she was going off shift. Bellflower told her to go home. She said she would, but her beeper would stay ready.

She walked for two more hours.

She circled back to her car, parked in a red zone outside a boarded-up restaurant on Vine Street, and drove over Coldwater Canyon, back into the valley. At Ventura Boulevard she stopped at the Hughes supermarket and bought herself one of the fresh pink salmon steaks they had on special. She bought skin cream and a box of Oreos. She paid in the cash-only express line and headed down toward the exit door that was farthest away from her car but closest to the entrance of the small pharmacy that rented floorspace inside the market.

When she decided to take that way out of the store, she thought she had already made up her mind to head into the pharmacy. But just as she reached the pharmacy the supermarket's automatic exit door sprang open for a box boy shoving in a train of grocery carts, and Cully suddenly stepped through, out into the thin light of the parking lot. She stood there breathing slowly as the sodium vapor lamps threw hazy domes against the red-black sky and glanced harsh glints off the chrome carts as they rattled past. The box boy heaved the last of the carts by her and the door stayed open, with Cully caught in the safety beam.

She turned, went into the pharmacy, and bought herself a home pregnancy test.

When she got to her apartment, she had no appetite, so she shoved the fish into the freezer and ate a bowl of canned soup. She had left the paper bag from the pharmacy on the kitchen counter, and when she took the bowl back to the sink and rinsed it and tucked it into the dishwasher, she picked up the bag and brought it back to the kitchen table.

She opened the test and read the instructions. They

were simple enough. She didn't open the little box with the test tubes, but nudged it around the table with her fingertips in a distracted game of cat and mouse. She unfolded the accompanying literature and read that, too. It made her angry. It was dry and clinical. It ought to say: *You're wondering if you're pregnant. And you're scared to death.*

But the printed words were about assuming no liability for inaccurate results, and about probabilities of false positives. Legal talk, mathematical talk. Words to make it seem less personal and human.

Then it hit Cully why that woman on the slab today seemed less real to her than the first one had. It did have to do with those implant bags. So big. Like she had wanted to make herself so different. Cully, full-chested herself, had plenty of small-breasted friends who had told her of feeling unarmed in the war for attention that all women wage at one time or another, and though breast augmentation seemed a little unnatural to Cully, she had never seen anything about it as fundamentally different from braces on crooked teeth or blond highlights bleached into dull hair. But today in that autopsy room something had happened to Cully. She had triggered a protective mechanism to let herself view that second body, and it was a mechanism that said, *This woman was a slut and deserved to die.*

Sitting there alone at her kitchen table, Cully thought: If I were Ridge, I would pray for forgiveness for my cruel spirit. I would ask God to help me stay human.

She was not Ridge.

But she might have his baby inside her.

And if she did, what was she going to do about it?

Looking at the box, she thought again of the literature. And she thought of Roger's pictures of the battered woman on the slab.

Hell, no wonder nobody said they knew her. Was a pimp going to look at that crushed face and say, "Yeah, sure, that was one of my girls! Oh yeah, sure, I guess you could say I knock 'em around sometimes to keep 'em in line, but fuck no, I don't know nothin' about this here!"

How stupid could the detectives be? They weren't ever going to find out the victims' identities this way.

Cully grabbed her personal phone book out of her purse. She flipped through it and found the name of a friend from college, an old friend she was always reminding herself she had to look up, but hadn't seen in two years.

A woman answered Cully's call on the third ring. "Gail?" Cully said. "It's Cully! Cully McCullers!"

"Cully!" her friend said. "How are you!"

"Good! How are you?"

"I'm great, just great! It's so good to hear from you! I've kept meaning to call you and get together!"

"Yeah, me too. How's Robert?"

There was a pause; Cully wondered if she'd gotten the name wrong. Then Gail said, "We split up. The divorce was final two months ago."

"Oh . . ." Cully winced, and silently reproached herself for blundering, and for being so out of touch with an old friend that such a blunder was possible. "I'm so sorry to hear that."

"Don't be. He's met a woman who thinks he's God, and he agrees with her." The phrase was too pat and Gail knew it, even though Cully forced a laugh. Gail said, "I've met a great new guy. And I've changed careers."

"Really?" Cully said. "That sounds great!"

"Yeah, doing layouts for an ad agency. My new boyfriend owns it, actually." Gail gave a dirty laugh, and Cully remembered all over again why they had been friends in the first place. "And I heard you're a *detective*!" She said the word with a little squeal, like somebody just starting the first plunge on a roller coaster.

It made Cully grin. "Yeah, do you believe that?"

"Yeah, I do, actually," Gail said. "Like father, like daughter."

Cully's father had never made detective, but Cully let the comment go.

"Listen, Gail," she said, "I'm sorry to say this, since we haven't talked in so long, but I'm calling because I need a favor."

"Sure! What?"

"It's police work."

"Yeah?" Gail said. Cully could hear the excitement in her voice.

"You are still drawing, aren't you?"

"Well . . . yeah, sure, I still draw!" She wanted to be qualified to do this favor. It sounded a lot more exciting than doing layouts.

"I can't tell you exactly what this is about, but it might be emotionally hard. What I need is your help in a homicide case."

"Yeah?" Gail said.

Cully gave her instructions, and she could feel Gail's excitement growing in the uh-huhs she muttered as Cully told the story. Then Cully told Gail they would have to meet at the morgue.

Gail paused, then said she was willing. Cully hung up, then called downtown to be sure one of Roger's assistants would still be on duty, then called Gail back.

Cully left the test kit unopened on her kitchen table and drove down to the chamber of guttered tables and body lockers.

9

When the lights come on in Los Angeles, it is as if something huge, something as distinct and separate as the globe of Earth itself spinning through black space, has come alive.

During the day the city lies naked beneath a relentless sun, and moments after each fresh dawn, anything that is delicate begins to shrivel: cut flowers and car finishes, painted wood and unpainted tourists exposing virgin flesh to the sun god; all wither under its patience. Even the air dies and settles across the dry husk of a city like a brown shroud.

On the worst days, when it has destroyed the most, the sun celebrates as it leaves, reveling in bands of red, pink, and purple across half the breathless sky. The darkening Earth rolls over in defeat.

And then the lights come on.

No city in the universe glows like Los Angeles. A thousand square miles of lights blanket the valleys, accent the mountains, stream through the canyons; the freeways crisscross the whole mass like pulsing arteries, pumping illumination to keep the body brimming with light. From the air the city is like a fissure where a round dead rock has cracked open to reveal its living core. In other towns the lights have a certain architectural character, from the lonely beacon of a rural porch lamp to the stately, arrogant towers of Manhattan; but in Los Angeles it is the people who give the lights their quality.

It is as if those people have come thousands of miles—from Kentucky, Central America, Hong Kong—just to turn on a light in L.A.

Michael Rowe drove through the city, on one of its arteries of streaming light, and he thought of survival in L.A. terms. *Now is all there is. Only the moment survives.*

He drove to a restaurant off the Harbor Freeway, not far from Chinatown. A French chef, reputedly backed by an Italian movie producer with alleged connections to tainted money, had opened the place only six weeks ago. There was no sign above the front door to announce the restaurant's presence, and Rowe understood that the number for reservations was unlisted, but when he found the address, and confirmed it against the note his secretary had given him, he was surprised to see the line to get in stretched halfway down the block. Antihype, Rowe thought. I'll never understand that business. He meant the enterprises of Hollywood, and what its insiders called the Business.

Rowe parked down the street and walked slowly past the line of people, who did not at all seem to mind their wait. The young women, half of whom had blond hair, blond by any means necessary, wore skintight dresses, mostly in black or white. The young men wore shiny suits almost exclusively in shades of gray, with no ties. They talked and laughed and felt safe on these streets, though Rowe could have told them assault statistics for that neighborhood that might have given them something to think about. Then again, they had the look of people afraid of nothing except missing out; even while conversing with one another, they cocked back their heads to peer at the dimly lit doorway at the front of their line, and they interrupted themselves to stare carefully at everyone who walked past, as they looked at Rowe now.

There are many places in Los Angeles, as in other cities, where a police badge will gain admittance; Rowe knew instinctively that this was not one of them. But when a tuxedoed maître d' stepped into his path, the deputy chief had the golden key. "I'm here to meet Mr. Lannon," he said quietly.

The maître d' closed his eyes, nodded his head with a gentle smile, and led Mike Rowe past the two men who stood on either side of the doorway, whose tuxedos seemed much too tight around the shoulders.

Inside, the place was stark white plaster with high ceilings; booths stained a dark oak and spreading ficus trees in the corners gave the room its only color, for the tile floor was white, too. Rowe had worried that he would be underdressed, but now he fretted that the opposite was true; his blue suit stood out, and his necktie was the only one in the place. Even the waiters wore band-collar shirts beneath their tuxedos. The maître d' led Rowe to a corner booth, the throne room, the place of honor—the table of Josh Lannon.

Lannon had started out in Hollywood as an actor, but he had a talent and drive that wouldn't let him be just a mannequin in someone else's movie. In the last decade the films he had written, produced, directed, and starred in had grossed over one billion dollars.

At thirty-eight years old Lannon was a man's man: he liked to hunt (with a camera, not a rifle), climb mountains, race sailboats, lift weights. He was always good for an appearance at charity golf tournaments, where he would even play a few holes and laugh at how awkward he felt, though he was actually more graceful than many of the actors who were out of work often enough to practice the game. It was at one such tournament that he and the deputy chief had met. Lannon had a voracious appetite for cop stories, and Rowe was at ease with celebrities. Their friendship seemed natural, and good for both of them. Lannon loved the flavor that cops' tales lent to the screenplays he wrote; and Rowe's career with the LAPD did not suffer at all by his cultivating a relationship with the power and influence of Hollywood, especially when that relationship resulted in

on-screen statements of gratitude to the Los Angeles
Police Department for its technical advice and coopera-
tion, along with a more tangible demonstration of that
gratitude in the form of a new three-million-dollar ath-
letic facility for the academy, in a no-strings-attached
donation from Josh Lannon.

The rumor was that Lannon had also been the
source of the money being used to renovate the Can
into a state-of-the-art homicide facility, but that donation was anonymous, and Mike Rowe would never con-
firm the rumor. Rowe was a discreet man.

As Rowe walked up, Lannon was talking with a
blonde whose hair piled like clouds around her face and
made it look smaller, when it already had the look of a
Scandinavian porcelain doll. Lannon glanced up and
smiled, stood and shook Rowe's hand, even while finishing the anecdote he was telling the girl. She threw her
head back and laughed beautifully while Lannon said,
"Mike! You found it!"

Rowe nodded. "Yeah, I'm glad you gave me the
address, these guys don't believe in signs."

"Sometimes the best hype is no hype, huh? Oh, this
is Sonata Grimwade."

"Miss Grimwade," Rowe said politely, and offered
his hand. The girl laid her fingers in Rowe's palm, studying his face with sudden intensity.

"Sonata, this is my buddy Michael Rowe," Lannon
said. "Mike is deputy chief in the LAPD, you believe it?
He's giving me some tech help on my new screenplay."

The girl's eyes went suddenly blank, and the smile
left her perfect lips before she could look away. Lannon
sat down and slid over, beckoning Rowe to take the
place he had been occupying himself. Eyes all over the
room shot a quick glance at Rowe, and just as quickly
looked away. Rowe was obviously a civilian, someone
not in the Business, and therefore not worth second
thoughts. It was not just his suit that betrayed him, but
the fact that Lannon, whose manners were well-known,

had made room for him that way. Lannon held doors and brought coffee for cleaning ladies in studio office buildings, but he wouldn't give up his seat to anyone else in the Business.

"Great to see you," Josh Lannon said.

Rowe nodded, pressing his lips together in a suppressed smile. The glances from around the room had made him nervous.

" 'Scuse me," Sonata said to Lannon. "I need to visit the sandbox."

Lannon smiled and nodded her away. Rowe watched her back, her tiny butt outlined by a minuscule pink skirt, her slender legs lengthy and tanned. "Pretty girl," Rowe said.

"Yeah." Lannon sighed. "But her hair weighs more than her brain."

Rowe chuckled. "You ought to write that down," he said.

Lannon shrugged, lifted one corner of his famous mouth as if his cleverness were nothing. "I already have. Last weekend in Malibu. In fact I just keep Sonata around 'cause she sets me up for the line." Lannon had already said the same thing to four other people, but he repeated the joke naturally, as if for the first time.

The girl reminded Rowe of his wife, or rather of all the things his wife wasn't. He was about to say so, but he stopped himself; before Rowe had fallen in love, he could have made such a comment, but now he felt it would be disloyal, and he didn't want to hurt his wife, even the image of her he carried in his own mind.

"What's the matter?" Lannon said.

Surprise showed on Rowe's face; he was amazed at how sensitive Josh Lannon could be to every nuance of the people around him. "Oh," Rowe said, "I've got a lot on my mind. It's . . . been a strange day."

"Strange how?" Lannon said, genuinely curious. He was working on a screenplay about cops, and he craved the details of a cop's day and emotions like a junkie craved his drug.

Without meaning to, Rowe found himself talking about his day. "I had my second-in-command come into my office, and tell me . . . something kind of weird."

"Weird how?"

Rowe paused. "Off the record, okay? I mean you won't use this anywhere. I'll just tell you because you're a friend and . . . heck, maybe you can help me figure it out."

"Sure!" Lannon said. "Hey, you hungry?"

"Yeah, maybe . . . I'll order in a minute."

"Okay, go on, go on, you were saying. . . ."

"He comes into my office, there at the Can, and he shuts the door behind him and says, 'I need a minute with you, sir,' and I say, 'Sure, what's up?' And he sits down and he has the strangest look on his face. He . . . You know about these two murders we've just had, the two alleged prostitutes?"

"I read about them in the paper, yeah." Notices had appeared about the discoveries of the bodies; police cordons and coroner's wagons always drew attention. But other than the statement that the two victims were women apparently in their twenties and the vague acknowledgment of the suspicion that the two cases might be related, MULHOM had revealed nothing of substance, and the reporters had not uncovered anything. "I wanted to ask you about that," Lannon said eagerly. "It seemed really interesting. You guys were real stingy with details, though. The papers didn't say anything about them being hookers."

"We don't know that for sure," Rowe said carefully. "At least we didn't, not before this commander walks into my office. See . . ." Deputy Chief Rowe dragged a palm across his eyes, so blue and gentle they looked like those of a cartoon lamb. "He knew them. At least one of them, he said, and maybe the other."

For a moment Lannon didn't say anything. His

eyes, like rich chocolate puddles, darted back and forth behind the horn-rims he had begun to wear lately. The glasses were the buggy round kind from the 1930s and might have looked quite ugly on a face less handsome; some of the tonier news magazines that carried Lannon's off-screen photograph in reviews of his latest movie had been uncharitable enough to suggest that the glasses were just part of an attempt to make Lannon look more intellectual. But Michael Rowe, looking at him now, did not think Lannon's glasses were props. From the first moment he had met Josh Lannon he had been surprised by the penetrating power of his brain, and his eyes looked very thoughtful now. He nodded slowly and simply said, "Hmm."

"What are you thinking?" Rowe said, his brow bumpy with concern.

"I don't know, Mike. Maybe I'm just in my writer mode here, and my imagination is a little too pumped up."

A waiter had swung by with an extra place setting for Rowe and a frosty water glass, and Rowe had been self-consciously spinning that glass with his fingers on the glass tabletop; now his eyes locked on Lannon's. "Then maybe I should take up screenwriting, too," Rowe said, "because I think I've been wondering the same thing."

"Two girls get killed, and the same guy knows them both? But hey, let's not get carried away."

"Exactly," Rowe said. "Though he told me he wasn't sure he knew the second one. And of course he did come in and volunteer the information—"

"Well, what'd he say, what'd he say?"

"I'm gonna tell you!" Rowe said, finding himself smiling. But then his smile faded as he recalled his conversation with Bellflower. "He said he knew the first girl who was killed. He recognized her from a tattoo. And get this. He said he was with her on the night she was killed."

"Sheesh! He had sex with her?"

"That's what he was telling me, yeah."

"Does that mean . . . does that mean some traces of him might be on the body? I mean his hair, his skin under her fingernails, his . . . body fluids? I mean is he telling you this because that new genetic testing stuff could connect him to the girls? And make him look like the killer?"

"No," Rowe said. "At least I didn't think so. He even used a condom; he made a point of telling me so. And there was no semen found in the first body, though there was a sample taken from the second, and we're having that tested. Of course with a hooker, who might have been with any number of men in a day, with or without condoms, with or without them breaking . . . I'm not sure what the genetic testing would prove. All it seemed to me was that he was admitting to something he was ashamed of. I mean, a black police commander going out and sleeping with white hookers? It's not the image anybody wants to project, and *I* was sure disappointed in him. But I didn't have the feeling he was protecting himself, not from suspicion of murder, anyway. It was just that he knew the first victim, and maybe even the second, and he couldn't say so without telling everybody just how he knew them. And he wanted to help the investigation, but he didn't know how to just up and say what he knew. I felt sorry for him. At first."

"At first."

Rowe nodded, feeling those intense chocolate eyes still on him. "But since then I've started to wonder. I've heard he's had some pretty big emotional problems. His wife dead, other relationships falling apart, that sort of thing. And now he tells me he knows this dead hooker."

"You're not saying 'alleged hooker' anymore," Lannon observed.

"No. I'm not. He knows this dead hooker very well. And maybe, he says, *maybe* the second one. It's like going out and finding these hookers is a compulsion with him. And these murders look like compulsive, obsessive killings."

"They do," Lannon agreed, nodding.

Rowe and Lannon exchanged looks for a moment, and then the deputy chief shook his head. "I'm making too much of it. Way too much. I'm sure that's exactly what he was afraid of, in coming in to tell me. He's a cop, and not an administrator like me; he's a former street cop. He knows how suspicion gets started. He trusted me. And listen—that's exactly why everything I've said about this is completely confidential."

"Everything you say to me is completely confidential," Josh Lannon said. He looked away from Rowe's lamb's eyes and said, "Listen, I have to ask you a favor, and I'm real sorry about it."

"Anything."

"It's my mother. She's . . . I don't know how to put it. She started calling me, and . . . we were out of touch for a long time. Never communicated. Since I've been successful, we've talked a grand total of twice, both of them fights over the telephone. Now I get a call from her, saying she's bringing out a new line of perfume, called TAMI, but no, she's not exploiting *my* name, she's exploiting *hers*. To top it all off she's scheduled a 'premiere' of the 'fragrance line' at some toilet shopping mall out in the valley and announced to everybody that I would be there, without clearing it with me, of course." Lannon paused, and shook his head slowly.

Mike Rowe ached for Lannon's dilemma. He had first heard of Lannon's mother when he saw Josh on a network talk show and the actor was reflecting on the ways stardom had changed his life; he had told the audience that the best thing about success was that it had served as a catalyst for the healing of the relationship between himself and his mother, who, Lannon told them with appealing candor, had gone through some difficult times that had been difficult for him, as a boy, to understand, but that he was struggling to understand now. The lofty, almost maudlin warmth of this approach, coupled with Lannon's far more interesting escapades with beautiful young women, had kept a discussion of his family life out of the tabloids; his mother had refused interviews, even from the publications that offerred juicy fees, and maintaining the privacy of that aspect of his life had seemed easy. But Rowe could tell how much Lannon loathed to see a publicity campaign launched by his mother. "You're trapped," Rowe said gently.

"I've put off thinking about this," Lannon said. "Everything else in my life, I address what's wrong, but this I can hardly face. Now it's tomorrow, and I've got to show up."

Rowe nodded, feeling Lannon's pain.

"I'm sorry to ask you this, Mike, but could I use a few of your guys to get in and out? Some cops smart enough not to be a big presence, you know what I mean? I'm walking a line like a razor, trying to be there for my mother but not there, you know?"

"Of course, Josh. Absolutely."

"I just need a few guys. I've already spoken with a couple of friends who work for you—I took that liberty —but I didn't want to say anything was cleared till I could talk with you."

"You've got any help we can give you," Rowe said, and wondered who it was that Lannon knew in his command.

"Thanks. I can't tell you how much I appreciate it. Here comes Sonata. Look at the way she's posing." The girl had stopped to talk with a tableful of men whom Rowe took to be agents or studio executives or others in the Business.

"She doesn't seem like your type, Josh."

Lannon laughed. "What's my type?"

"Why are you with her?"

"Sometimes you can find out more about women by being with a shallow, vacuous slut than with a complicated lady," Lannon said. "And it's part of my job to know about women. Hey, I tell you what. I'm taking her by the house later. Not the main house, I mean the little one. Why don't you come by and join us?"

"You're kidding," Rowe said, his face showing his displeasure.

"Of course I'm kidding," Lannon said, punching him on the shoulder. Then Josh Lannon looked into Rowe's eyes, nodded soberly, and grinned as Sonata appeared again at his table.

After Deputy Chief Michael Rowe had left his table and gone home, Josh Lannon ate his usual meal: twice-washed romaine lettuce with no dressing, broccoli seasoned with pepper only, six ounces of Dakota lean rib-eye steak—from cattle specially nourished to produce beef with less cholesterol than either chicken or fish—and finished with one sip of Cristal champagne. The waiter left the whole bottle, of course, and Sonata drank three flutesful. Lannon observed that and thought, Sonata drank three flutesful. He smiled to himself; he might make that a title: *The Three-Flute Sonata.* Or else he might turn the inspiration into a song; Lannon sometimes wrote the musical title tracks of his films.

When the meal was done, Lannon nodded almost imperceptibly to the maître d', who relayed gestures that resulted in Sonata's car, a leased, white, slope-nosed Porsche, being brought to the rear of the restaurant, and Lannon and the girl stood and made their way quickly through the kitchen, Lannon calling out boisterous and good-natured greetings to the chef. The great man and his companion were into the car and away before most of the restaurant's diners, much less the gawkers on the sidewalk, realized it. Lannon left two twenty-dollar bills on the table, purely as gratuity, for there was never any suggestion that he would pay for his meal. He had more money by far than anyone who had ever entered the place, including its wealthy financial backer, but Lannon's presence was a royal endorsement, priceless for the restaurant's future, and to have accepted payment for his meals, even if Lannon had insisted, would have been a violation of the actor's star status, Hollywood's unforgivable sin.

Sonata drove through the wide downtown streets, sparsely traveled at this hour, then whipped the car into the streaming river of freeway lights. The Porsche sat low and hummed in and out of lanes as the girl gunned her way through the traffic, and Lannon sat back and enjoyed her driving. Sonata, he knew, had owned a succession of boyfriends, first surfer types and then the richer boys with fast cars, and she was superb behind the wheel of a sports car.

She drove to Van Nuys. She took the right exit, but Lannon had to help her find a couple of the turns to the house, since she had only been there once before.

Van Nuys, bordering upscale Sherman Oaks and the even haughtier Encino, has a tarnished image among the bedroom communities of the San Fernando Valley. With a General Motors factory at its northern end and car dealerships on its southern flank, and its main thoroughfares dotted with businesses whose signs offer PAYROLL CHECK CASHING with the inevitable added inducement YO HABLO ESPAÑOL, its days seem hotter, its smog more toxic. Its blocks of residential communities are crammed between commercial developments, but there are some small, cozy neighborhoods, and it was to one of these that Sonata drove.

The house was at the end of a cul-de-sac and had a long driveway flanked by a high fence on one side and a tangle of vines on the other. She pulled down this driveway and under the carport, angled in such a way behind the house that the car was shielded from the street. Lannon led her in through the kitchen.

No one lived here. Josh Lannon called it his playpen. Lannon's possession of this house was a secret even from its owner; the rental was handled on a cash basis, extra cash compensating for no questions being asked.

Lannon opened the freezer compartment of the refrigerator and found a single overlarge ice cube in the bottom of the ice-maker tray. Frozen within that cube was a single joint of marijuana. Lannon shattered the ice cube in the sink and took out the joint, protected from moisture by a plastic wrapping. They lit the joint over one of the gas burners of the stove and took several lungfuls each, then ground up the remainder in the garbage disposal and washed it away. After that they went quietly into the bedroom.

Lannon flipped on the stereo and chose a videocassette, then powered up the big-screen television. He turned around and Sonata was at his shoulder, waiting. He kissed her, a hard movie kiss like the first plunge of new lovers, then broke away laughing. "Tell you what," he said. "I've got an idea. Let's see just how good you really are." He was talking about acting and not about sex; acting was what Sonata was always wanting to talk about, whatever the subject seemed to be. "Remember that scene in *Being There,* when Shirley MacLaine has sex with herself and Peter Sellers watches?"

"Hey," Sonata said. "Yeaaah."

Lannon grinned. He switched on the tape, and onto the big screen of the projection television came images filmed at a sex show in Tijuana: a woman performing with a burro. Lannon looked at the screen and laughed, then his laugh faded and he watched, his eyes cold. Sonata was bored with the tape; she had seen it the last time she was here. She stepped out of her clothes as if she were getting ready for a shower.

Lannon turned and pressed one of the wall panels. Touch latches behind the panel kicked it out, revealing the hidden closet. In that closet were handcuffs, masks, leather girdles, and other sexual implements made of rubber and steel. In a snickering parody of Peter Lorre he said, "Can I interest you in a little variety, my dear?"

Sonata giggled. Lannon ducked down into the closet, and when he rose up, he had strapped a huge, pink, hard rubber artificial appendage around his head so that it stuck out like a massive nose. "Let's play Pinocchio," he squeaked in a munchkin voice, and chased the naked and laughing girl around the room until he cornered her and threw her onto the bed. They nuzzled for a moment, and then he pushed her onto the floor.

"Just a second," he said. Recessed into the wall beside the bed was a panel of remote electrical switches, and he used them to kill the sound on the videotape and turn on the CD player; *Scheherazade* seeped softly from the hidden stereo speakers, and Lannon altered the lighting so that it took on a purple hue. Then he lay back on the bed and let the girl watch him take off his clothes. "Okay," he said. "Action."

Later they showered, Sonata asking for comments on her performance. But Lannon was subdued. They dressed and she drove him to his main house in Bel Air.

Sonata was a little disappointed that Lannon hadn't been more effusive in his praise of her acting, and as an instructional experience she rated it only as mediocre. But she still believed she was going to get a major role in his next movie.

And for weeks afterward she would think of this as the best sex she had ever had.

Mike Rowe lived in Hancock Park. But mostly Mike Rowe lived inside his own brain.

Hancock Park lies in the flats of the L.A. basin, with the sex shops and drug alleys of Hollywood forming its northern boundary and the main financial and cultural districts of Los Angeles surrounding the rest of it. Part of the neighborhood's impact results from its suddenness; traveling south on Highland Avenue, past the barnlike buildings where moving companies rent storage space and import shops sell cheap furniture, a driver headed toward the museum of art might turn early to avoid some of the congestion of Wilshire Boulevard, and wham, find homes that sprang from old money. The houses here were built in a day when size and style mandated a certain quality. In nouveau riche sections of Encino or Beverly Hills it is easy to find massive houses where warped ceilings are camouflaged with acoustical spray and stately columns are plywood, delaminating in the sun, and colored windows are single panes of clear glass painted with translucent stain.

But in Hancock Park the mahogany staircases are solid, not veneer; the English Tudor roofs are covered in real slate; the mantels are hand-carved. Because the neighborhood is surrounded as it is, the homes cost half of what they would ten minutes farther west on Wilshire, and living in Hancock suggests both class and frugality, exactly the right image for a young deputy chief of police who could find himself standing for public office in the not-too-distant future.

Mike Rowe felt at home in Hancock Park. It was like his mind: stately, classical, and removed from the squalid clamor that surrounded it.

When he parked in the circular drive of his two-story brick Colonial home, he pulled up behind his wife's Jaguar and thought of how perfect it was for his wife to use for taking her friends to luncheons, and he was happy that he had bought it for her. When he entered the house quietly and reset the burglar alarms, he did it with the warm feeling of providing for his family's security. When he climbed the stairs and stepped into his daughter's room and kissed her hair and pulled the blanket up to her chin, he felt like the world's most loving father, and when he undressed quietly and slipped into bed beside his wife, who slept deeply because of the medications she took for her headaches, he felt like a good and loyal husband.

Lying on his back beneath the satin sheets and the

down comforter, Rowe stared up at the carved beams in the ceiling, then closed his eyes and thought of his lover. He stroked his fingertips across his chest and surrendered to fantasies long forbidden.

Next to him his wife snored softly, and he did not hear her, for she did not live inside the fortress in his mind.

Leonard Bellflower lived in an apartment complex where nobody knew he was a cop. Six years before, he had rented a place for about three months when his wife had thrown him out of the house, and during those months the apartment manager was banging on his door constantly to have him come and quell a family fistfight or chase belligerent drunks away from the swimming pool or look at a burglarized apartment, as if he could track down the thief before the stolen goods were sold. So this time Bellflower showed check stubs and provided credit references and told the apartment manager only that he worked for the city.

Bellflower felt bad about that, though. A cop is a cop, and being a cop was supposed to stand for something. And yeah, sure, he didn't get knocks on his door at night this time, but he didn't stand for anything, either. The apartment manager somehow had the impression that Bellflower worked for the Rapid Transit District, and that made Bellflower feel worse; a few years back when he worked out with weights three times a week, you could tell he was something intimidating—a bodyguard or a cop. Now he looked like a bus driver.

Bellflower's new apartment was in Tarzana, out in the hot part of the valley. His home had been in Woodland Hills, the next community up the Ventura Freeway, and Bellflower wanted to stay close to where his children were. Tarzana was lily-white; Len Bellflower was the only black in an apartment complex of nearly a hundred units. But Woodland Hills was WASP territory, too, and that was all right, because Bellflower figured being around people who didn't know you and were inclined to think the worst of you only helped you remember to be a good example.

Bellflower's apartment came furnished. It was on the third floor and was two doors down from the elevator. It looked out toward the freeway, and the noise was bad if you listened to it. But beyond the freeway there were mountains, twenty miles away on the far side of Northridge, and every day Bellflower would look toward those mountains and tell himself that even if the smog hid the mountains, the mountains were still there.

Tonight when he arrived home from the Can, he fixed himself a TV dinner, same as he did every night. He alternated between mandarin chicken and Salisbury steak and mushrooms, both with seven hundred calories each, only the meal topped fourteen hundred for Bellflower because he always fixed himself two servings. He would drink one glass of wine with the meal; wine was a pleasure he had denied himself through the twenty-two years of his marriage because of his wife's problems with alcohol. Now the apartment's new refrigerator held two green bottles of Chablis and three cans of diet soda. Without them, the nineteen cubic feet of the inside of the Frigidaire would have looked like a field of snow in the sun.

Bellflower popped his two dinners in the microwave, poured his wine, sipped it in the kitchen while the oven nuked his food, then took a fork from the drawer, pulled a couple of paper towels off the dispenser, fished his dinners from the oven using the towels as potholders, and sat down at the round table in his dining area to eat. The dining area was lit by one of those apartment-complex chandeliers meant to be artistic; this one looked like a tangle of clear Christmas lights that had been crapped on by a metal sea gull; rusty drips of iron flakes obscured the pointy little bulbs. Bellflower had to turn the dimmer switch all the way up to see what he was eating, but somehow the ambience was neither appetizing nor romantic.

When he finished, he took the fork and his wineglass back to the sink and rinsed them out. He left the foil trays his dinner had come in on the table. He reached into the cabinet above the stove and stretched out his full length, so that the muscles pulled along his rib cage, and touched a small folder with his fingertips. He fetched it down.

He opened the folder and looked at the photographs inside. They were in muddy color, taken with amateur equipment in too little light. Two hookers who wanted to get into the big time of centerfold posing had taken sample pictures of each other. They called them their demos and had showed them to any regular customers they thought might know something about how a girl got ahead in the world.

One of the girls in the pictures was the first girl the detectives had found murdered.

One of the men she had given her pictures to was Len Bellflower.

Bellflower ripped the photographs into strips. He twisted the torn strips into tight bands and put them inside the foil trays of his TV dinners, then crumpled the trays and packed them into one of the boxes they had come in.

Then Bellflower took the rest of his kitchen garbage from the can under the sink, shoved the boxes into it, and carried it all down to the Dumpster in the back of the building.

On his way back to the elevator Bellflower passed the apartment manager, who said, "When you guys gonna get those routes worked out? My maids have been late three days in a row and it's all because of the buses."

"We're working on it," Bellflower said, and walked slowly on.

* * *

Cully and Gail met in the morgue parking lot. Gail was still rail thin and, ever the artist, wore a long shawl over a floor-length skirt. The only real changes Cully noticed were rare streaks of gray in the straight red hair and a few new wrinkles at the corners of her eyes. After she and Gail hugged, and pulled back laughing to look at each other, they made the small talk that told so much. Cully said her work was a challenge, and didn't have to explain what she meant, since they were talking outside the city morgue. Gail said she'd had some rough years before the divorce, but she was happy now. She declared that the only thing really different about her was that she now wanted to be called by her middle name, which was Bryn.

"Okay, Gail," Cully said, and they both laughed again. Then Cully took a long breath, wet her lips, and said, "What we're about to do is not going to be pleasant for you. Some people have a curiosity about morgues and autopsies. It's a natural curiosity and you may have it, too, but I can promise you that afterward you'll have moments when you hate me for bringing you here. So I want you to understand why I'm doing it. Someone has started murdering women, beating them to death and then mutilating them. We took photographs of the first victim and showed them around, but those pictures look like nothing that was ever alive. So I want to try something different with this second victim. I want you to draw me a picture, not of the way she is now, but the way people who knew her would like to remember her. That's why I'm putting you through this."

Gail tried to smile. Cully squeezed her hand. They went into the building, where Roger's assistant rolled out the slab and pulled back the sheet of Jane Doe II.

Gail didn't move at first. Cully thought she was much tougher than she had expected. Gail stood there and looked at the gray face, all battered on the left side, and the head with the top of the skull sawed off and then sewed back on like an egg mended with thread, and the artist in her seemed to find the sight fascinating.

But suddenly she pressed a palm to her mouth as her stomach bounced. Blood drained from her face, and she looked at Cully with bright, watery eyes. Cully led her into the hallway.

After a visit to the parking lot for a few breaths of cold air and a cup of black coffee from the employees' lounge, Gail said, "My God. You do this for a living."

"No," Cully said, "for a living I catch the people that do this."

Gail took another minute, and then said, "Let's go."

They went back into the slab room. The assistant had left Jane Doe II out, but had re-covered the dead girl's face with the sheet. Cully and Gail approached again, and Gail forced herself to the very edge of the slab. She lifted her sketch pad, flipped back the cover, and took a deep breath. She nodded once, sharply, like a rodeo cowboy on a bull when he wants to tell the wranglers to open the chute, and Roger's assistant pulled back the sheet.

10

Cully sat in the blue light and cigarette smoke, looking at the bare stage, a platform of hardwood flooring three feet above the real floor. The platform was surrounded by a low bar with stools like those in a soda fountain. The drinks here were weak mixtures of hard liquor at four dollars a pop, but nobody came for the booze.

Cully was alone at a two-person table against a side wall. She had Gail's sketch of Jane Doe II in her purse, and later she would show it to the owner. He'd know she was a cop the moment she flashed the drawing, but right now he didn't know, and she wanted to see this place operate the way it really was, without the warning glances the manager would give to the girls and the bartender when he knew the heat was around.

The ceiling was painted a flat black, and a mirror ball hung above the stage, in front of a single brass pole glinting in the spotlight from the sound booth in back. The sound system poured out a Top-40 tune, surprisingly melodic and romantic for this kind of place, Cully thought; she had expected something throbbing and crudely sensual.

The smoke stung her eyes, and when the waitress came and asked if she wanted a drink, Cully was tempted to say yes. "Got anything in a bottle?" she asked, and when the waitress said they had Corona, Cully said she'd take that.

She thought about her father. How many of these places had he been in? How many of these shows did he see?

Big Jim McCullers had been a good cop. A tall, muscular Irishman with one of those smug smiles, full of life and passion and ego. He had heart, and nobody knew it better than Cully. Something had eaten him up, and for the last ten years his little girl had tried to figure out what. Cully blamed his job. Maybe she was wrong, maybe the job didn't cost Big Jim his life, but it sure as hell cost him his marriage. In the endless days of his patrols, after he had seen children abused, shot down, buggered, battered, he would come home and scream at his wife for being so stupid as to let Cully and her brother play in the front yard, and boy, could Big Jim scream. After the divorce, and a couple of episodes of depression, the department had shifted him from patrol to vice, and Big Jim got to sit in bars all night long, looking for illegal sales of alcohol to minors. A guy sitting at a bar all night has got to drink something, right?

But Cully didn't blame the department for the cirrhosis that killed him. People have to be responsible—to themselves. That's what she had told Ridge, during their first assignment together, on that first night she was sure they had fallen in love, when she had spilled the whole story about her father: what happens to you is up to you, she had said. She had told him something else, too, something she had learned from watching her father's decline, and it had to do with her whole attitude about being a cop. What she had learned from her father, she had told Ridge, was that when somebody commits a crime, somebody suffers; but it's almost never the perpetrator who suffers the most. And she had decided that, by God Almighty, the perpetrators should have their fair share of suffering.

It was an awful thing to admit. Saying things like that could get you thrown out of the department as a head case. Some cops thought it, but none said it out loud. But she could tell Ridge because Ridge knew it already—you couldn't keep secrets like that from Ridge. He would look at you and ask a couple of general questions and *wham,* he would know your core. Ridge would understand why she was here right now, he could figure it out and find her if he wanted to. He was that good. Even mad, she felt close to him.

She pulled Gail's drawing from her purse and looked at it. In the blue light it looked even more alive, more like a stripper. Gail had done a real job. Only one side of the face to go on, but she hadn't simply sketched in a mirror image; she had somehow caught a sense of the spontaneous, the fleeting quality real faces have. She had even colored in the eyes and put a tarty red bloom on the showgirl lips. This sketch looked nothing like the death shot of the battered corpse that the other detectives were carrying around.

The club owners all along Sunset Boulevard had already seen that photo and denied knowing the girl; Cully knew that from the coverage lists they had filled out—one of Rowe's obsessions with being methodical. She could go back to them again, but they didn't want to know the girl, and when a man can prepare to lie from the moment he knows you're a cop, it's impossible to know if he's telling you the truth.

But nobody had talked to the other strippers. That was Cully's angle. And though she knew the need to prove yourself is a weakness, it was a great motivator for her, and she wanted to see the looks in the faces of Rowe and Bellflower when they saw she had out-performed everybody, even the great Tom Ridge. Asking Gail to help, instead of one of the police artists, was an inspiration. All of the men in MULHOM, Ridge included, would have said a sketch was unnecessary, that Roger's death photos were good enough. And they probably were, if all you compared them with were the charcoals the department's artists would have sketched. But Cully felt a tug of sympathy for the dead women.

They were helpless now to protest that they looked so much better in life. This picture would invite, rather than discourage identification. Sitting in the bar Cully thought, with pleasure, There are times when being a woman is almost like cheating.

She looked up as the lights on the stage dimmed. A spotlight drilled a white tunnel through the smoky air and the music began to pound. A big male voice came through the sound system: "From Phoenix, Arizona . . . Belle Starling!" A girl in a cowboy hat, vest (with no shirt), red-white-and-blue bikini bottoms, and white boots came strutting out onto the stage, her hands on her hips, doing a walk that was supposed to look like a cowgirl shuffle in a main-street parade. Cully winced. This girl is not graceful, she thought.

And then another thought hit her. The sound booth. The strippers who worked these places might be as peripatetic as Gypsies, but the guy who worked the sound would be a permanent employee and ought to remember any girl who had worked there.

Cully slid out of her seat and moved back to the sound-booth door. The window in it was smoked glass, but she could make out a slim male figure bent over a control panel lit by a high-intensity study lamp like high-school kids are given when they go away to college. Cully tapped at the door. She could see his silhouette as he moved to the window and peered out. She didn't know if he could see her face in the shadows, but she smiled anyway. He opened the door.

"May I come in?" she said.

"Sure," he said. He was younger than she had thought from his profile—maybe early twenties. He had auburn hair that glowed orange in the colored light washing back from the stage. He still had freckles, and his expression was dazed—not from drugs or booze, Cully sensed, but from looking at naked women for five hours every night. "Can I help you?" he said. His voice was deep, like an announcer's on a TV game show.

Maybe he was another Hollywood hopeful working to make ends meet; nobody should aspire to being a booth man at a strip show.

"You the deejay?" she asked in a voice with just a hint of Ridge's Southern accent. Play this naive, Cully, she thought, even stupid if you can pull it off.

"The sound-and-light tech," he said. "Uh, Mr. Carpazian doesn't allow any customers in the booth. . . ."

"I'm sorry, I don't want to get you into trouble," Cully said.

The kid looked toward the entrance. The boss was busy checking the take at the ticket window where they sold the tourists "temporary memberships," and from the distance he couldn't see into the booth anyway. "No problem," he said.

"I'm looking for somebody," Cully said. "I thought you might know her. She's the sister of my best friend, back in Atlanta." Keep it simple, Cully, she told herself.

From her purse she pulled Gail's drawing, fishing it out slowly so as not to wrinkle it, as if she didn't have ten extra color xeroxes in her car.

He glanced only once at the page. "That's Porsche."

"Portia?"

"Like the car," the kid said. "Guess it was a stage name."

"My friend's sister was named Juanita."

The kid smiled, dipped an ear, and pumped his eyebrows just once. He wasn't going to try explaining why Juanitas move to LA and turn into Porsches.

"I wanted to find her. My friend wants her to come home."

"You a private detective?" the kid asked.

"I wish. Maybe someday, I kinda like this. Actually, I sell real estate in Brentwood. I really do want to find Juanita, though, her sister's real worried about her. Do you know where she's working now? Or where she lives?"

The kid looked toward the cowgirl dancing on the stage, but his eyes didn't move with her writhing.

Feeling his hesitation, Cully said, "Juanita always was a wild one. We're not gonna be surprised if she's getting paid now for what she used to do for free."

The kid looked back at Cully. "She has a pimp named Clarence," he said. "Drives a Clenet and works the corners around Sunset and La Brea. Don't tell him I sent you."

"Thanks," Cully said.

The kid looked away again and turned up the music, though it was too loud already.

Cully drove down Sunset, her senses alert, her thoughts rushing but clear, like a hound who has just caught the scent of its prey.

Above the boulevard the billboards glowed, and they were all that Hollywood was and ever had been. The sensational, the stupendous, the vivid, the monumental: all the movies coming out that month with huge promotional budgets. The billboards were created for that space alone, that mile-long section of Sunset Boulevard, and the billboards were alive. They erupted, they moved; a fifty-foot pistol a hundred feet above the street belched puffs of steam at five-second intervals; a billboard umbrella opened and closed above the two cinema lovers who stood drenched in shimmering plastic-foil rain. None of the advertisements was even the same shape as the others: parts stuck out above and beyond the dimensions of the normal billboard rectangle, as if the news on them was so big, so important, that nothing conventional could contain it.

Why do they do this? Cully wondered. These things have to cost tens of thousands of dollars, maybe hundreds of thousands. And why? Who sees these, except the people who drive into Hollywood from Beverly Hills

—the stars, the producers of these same movies? Don't they know what they want to go see? Will any of them, will *one* of them, go to see a movie because of its billboard? Or was it something else, some other process that didn't make sense to us mortals, crawling here on earth: that these signs were a kind of acid test for them, a part of the Deal. *You want me to star in a movie, you want me to produce it? Then prove you love me; before I make the picture, swear to me and my lawyer on this contract that you'll put my name in lights big enough to see from the moon.*

Something about all that ego must be succeeding, or why did this whole Hollywood process keep sucking in ego and puking out money?

False and misleading advertising . . .

That's one thing you could say for false and misleading advertising; it worked. And here was something else that worked: girls strutting up and down the streets, leather skirts clinging to rolling bottoms, black nylons stretched tight, breasts inflated with silicon and punching out elastic blouses as thin as paint.

People still did this? With the AIDS scare? They came down here and bought sex? Or, Cully wondered, was sex really what they bought, and if it was, why buy it here? Was it better here, or was the idea of it better here, beneath the glare of the lights with a girl who had come out to see the lights and be a part of the glamour, maybe even end up on one of these billboards instead of under one.

False and misleading advertising . . .

Rage. It was rage. You didn't do what he had done to another human being without being full of rage. But at whom? At what? Not at this, Cully thought. Hollywood is just a figment. It's a lie, but it's an impersonal lie. Rages are personal, at somebody.

At yourself?

That was when Cully's thoughts turned personal. What was she going to do if that little test on her kitchen table back home said she was pregnant? She had known Thomas Ridge intensely for a matter of weeks, but weeks weren't the measure; during that time they had risked their lives together, and had saved lives. Surely that was enough to say they were close. To say they were close? Cully! What are you asking yourself? Are you feeling like a slut because you're pregnant?

Yes. She was pregnant and knew it. She could feel it. And in her heart she knew it.

Did she love Ridge? If she'd asked herself that question the night she slept with him, the only answers would have been yes and yes and yes.

The next morning . . . Well, she hadn't had time to think about it the next morning. She had killed a man the next morning.

And after that . . .

Ridge was unlike anybody she had ever met. But did she love him? How could she know? How could she find out, when she already had his baby inside her?

Okay, Cully, keep it together. Watch the road, make the turn, park in the shadows, and look at the girls standing on the corner and smiling at the cars driving past. They look right into the drivers' eyes. What do they look for, some signal, some recognition? Just interest, they can recognize interest.

She watched a driver pull to the curb and a too thin blond girl, no more than sixteen, walk over to lean down and talk to him. Making a bargain. Setting a price. Wanna party? That's how they opened the negotiation, at least that's what the detectives had told Cully when she was training in vice. Back when she was a rookie in the Van Nuys Division, the guys in the sexual crimes unit had talked about using Cully for a phony hooker and had asked her to come to work the next day dressed for the part. But Bellflower got wind of it and shut down that assignment. He had started in the vice unit, had made all his bones there and risen to supervisor before he made lieutenant and they moved him on, and he knew all the tricks. Bellflower said if the guys wanted to see Cully McCullers in something besides the business suits she usually wore, they'd just have to find some other way to get her there; but nobody, he said, would buy this woman as a Hollywood street-corner whore. Beverly Hills, maybe, but not Hollywood.

It was easy to like Bellflower.

The girl Cully was watching now did some talking. She was not going to get into the car. She nodded toward the motel across the street, and the guy handed her a bill, probably a ten. That's how it worked; the girl would rent the room at the two-hour rate. She wouldn't get into the car. Travel parties were a special deal that had to be cleared with her pimp first. *For local flights, we use the runway across the street, with Clarence, our friendly air-traffic controller, nearby to be sure all the landings were safe and the fares all collected.*

Cully pulled her car down the block, turned around in a side street, then parked at the curb on the motel side of the boulevard. The john was already in the parking lot, waiting for the girl to come out of the motel office. Cully watched the girl walk out and hand a key to her customer. The hooker was even skinnier than she had looked from across the street; probably a crack freak. But her customer didn't care. She must have told him to go on in and get ready; he took the key and went into the room first. The hooker watched him enter and close the door, and then she walked over and knocked at a door three up from the one her customer had gone into.

That's where Clarence would be. The hooker would tell him what room she was working in, and he would be watching when she came out, waiting for a signal that everything had gone okay and the guy had paid; otherwise Clarence would have the pleasure of knocking the john around a little.

Cully waited as the door opened a few inches and the girl said something through the space, then moved down to her customer. When the hooker had entered the john's room and shut the door behind her, Cully got out of her car and walked to the door the girl had just left. She bumped the door with her knuckles. "Clarence."

The locks rattled and the door opened two inches. Clarence had one of his size-thirteen Guccis planted firmly behind it. He was bound to have cash with him and would be ready for trouble; Cully had no doubt he was holding a pistol. Through the gap in the doorway she saw that he was tall, six-six at least, and had a round, close-cropped head. The whites of his eyes were a dingy yellow, and the small irises darted at everything around her before they locked onto Cully. "Yeah," he demanded.

"McCullers," she said, flipping open the inside of her lapel to show her badge. She did it with her left hand, leaving the right one free. "I'm the law."

He hesitated, then drew the door back slowly, hissing "Shit . . ." under his breath. His right hand did something behind his back and then came into view to match his left, hanging at his side. "What you want?" he said.

Cully, again with her left hand, pulled out the drawing Gail had made for her and handed it across to Clarence. The pimp looked, and kept his eyes down too long as he tried to calculate what was going on here and just what he would say.

"Who's that?" Cully said.

Clarence handed the drawing back. "Girl."

"One of *your* girls," Cully said.

"What you talkin' bout? I'm from outta town, jus' waitin' for my date to show up."

"She was murdered, Clarence."

Cully couldn't tell if Clarence was surprised. You can't always tell, not with an experienced liar like Clarence. Once he started calculating, he was harder to read. But if Cully had guessed, she would have said

Clarence had not known. The girl hadn't shown up after
a date to give Clarence his money, but that probably
had happened before.

"I don't know nothin' about nothin'."

"What's her name?"

"Get outta here. You got a warrant? Get outta
here."

"One of your girls is dead, Clarence. Beaten to
death. Cut up. Maybe you didn't do that. Maybe you
did."

It was in Clarence's nature to bully women, and
when he didn't know what to do, intimidation was his
first weapon. "You here alone?" He half smiled, showing a diamond in a front tooth, and his eyes fixed on her
in a way that said he'd have no problem with knocking
her teeth out and driving away. It was a chilling stare, a
threat well practiced and frequently carried out.

"Let me tell you something, Clarence," Cully said.
"Somebody did something ugly to this girl. Real ugly.
And I'm a cop. You know what that means, Clarence? It
means I'll kill you, you big dumb son of a bitch. I'll
shoot you down right now and never lose a night's sleep.
I'll say you went for that gun in your belt behind your
back. You're a suspect in this murder, and when I tried
to question you, you went for it. And now you're dead."
Cully's eyes didn't move. They were blank, staring
through him. Clarence didn't know where her pistol
was, or how the hell she could pull it before he pulled
his, but as he tried to stare her down he seemed to get
the idea that she looked too damn certain of what she
was saying.

"What you mean, a suspeck? I din do shit to that
girl, 'cept take care of her."

"Well, you didn't take too good care of her, did
you, Clarence? Want to see what she looks like now?"
Cully returned the drawing to her left coat pocket, and
with the same hand pulled out the coroner's shot of the

girl, with her face battered in and the nail hole through the bridge of her nose.

Clarence winced.

"Who did it?" Cully said.

Clarence tried to turn his face away from the picture, but his eyes kept cutting back to it.

"Talk to me, Clarence. You might be an accessory to murder here."

"No ma'am, no way, huh-unh, no way."

"She worked for you, you set up her tricks. She wouldn't go work a private party unless you okayed it." Cully watched him; his round forehead was shiny with sweat. "Figuring it out, aren't you, Clarence? If you saw this guy, he might decide to pop you. Just to shut off the trail. Better talk to me; maybe I can get to him first."

"I don't know the guy. He had a limo, that's all I know. And up-front money. Bound to, the way Porsche went off with him."

Porsche. Cully had wanted to hear him say the name, without volunteering it herself. The detective's rule was to hold back anything you knew so that if you heard it someplace else, you could figure you might be getting the truth. "How do you know she went off with him, did you talk to the guy?"

"No. No way. I was across the street, lookin' out for her, when this limo stops and she just up and gets in, like she ain't supposed to do. Ask me, bitch got what she deserves."

"You saw this limo pull up, and Porsche get in. But you didn't see the driver?"

"Headlights was on. Lotsa light off the windshield."

"You recognize anything about the limo?"

"Like what?"

"Like what color. Like a license number."

"It was plain. Silver," Clarence said, shrugging. Cully remembered the pimp owned a Clenet, a custom car packed with chrome and modeled after parade cars like the Dusenberg. No wonder he couldn't remember.

"But you didn't notice anything about the car?"

"See lotsa limos."

"Did the car come from down the street? Or was it waiting at the curb, before she came out?"

Clarence looked at Cully, a new wariness in his eyes.

"Was he out cruising the boulevard for girls, Clarence? Or was he looking for Porsche specifically? I want to know if he knew her."

Clarence calculated whether either answer could hurt him and seemed to decide that neither could. "Limo was waitin' a few spaces back and pulled up to her when she came out on the sidewalk."

"Then he must have been inside the club, watching her dance, and decided she was the one he wanted."

"For a bitch cop you pretty smart."

"So this limo pulls up, and Porsche hops right in. Without talking to you first, or having the driver or the passenger talk to you."

"Right."

"That how it's supposed to happen? You're not supposed to clear the deal? Negotiate the price? Make sure she's gonna be okay?"

"Sure I am! Sometime the bitch know the man." Clarence shrugged. "Price already set, she know she okay."

"And she just got right in it."

"That's what I said!" Clarence was getting testy. "She gave me a nod, like she sayin' it's okay."

"What'd she mean?"

"Fuck do I know! She mean it okay, you unnerstand Engliss?"

Cully was quiet for a moment. "Oh. One more thing. You know Porsche's real name?"

"Maggie somethin'."

"Where'd she live?"

"With me, for 'bout three months."

"Let's go, Clarence."

"Where? I tol' you I don't know nuthin'!"

"To your place. I want to see her things. And maybe get a home address so I can notify her family."

"I don't got nothin' o' hers. She din come back, I threw her shit out."

Clarence thrust the picture back at Cully, then wiped his fingers on his suit, as if the photo were something he'd been forced to fish out of a toilet. Cully took the picture in her left hand, turned to leave, then turned back. "You know, Clarence," she said, "you use these girls, you buy new cars and new suits off what they do, and all you're supposed do is protect them. But you look more at a car than you do at a driver. Guess you're not worth a shit at protection, are you?"

Clarence made a move toward her—to grab her or shove the door shut, she wasn't sure which. But she crouched, straightened her right arm, and felt the forearm brace that her father made and wore when he was undercover spring the revolver into her hand. She had the pistol aimed at the pimp's groin before he could close the few feet between them. He froze.

"I jus' had to see where you were packin' it," Clarence said, and shifted back a couple of feet. He grinned, flashing the tooth.

Cully kicked him between the legs, and leveled the pistol again as he doubled over. "That's where I pack it," she said, and walked back out to her car.

When Cully left the motel, it was 1:15 in the morning. She drove home.

Back at her apartment she showered and went to bed. She didn't go back into the kitchen, didn't turn on the lights there, left the test kit lying on the table in the darkness.

It lay the same way in her dreams: cold, silent, clinical, with a heartless message inside that she was unwilling to listen to.

11

The clock read 6:15 when she opened her eyes. It had arrived there in jerks; she had seen it every hour since she turned out the lights.

The sun had just begun to drain the darkness from the sky, but had not yet hit the print fabric of her window curtains with the stream of light that woke her like chimes of color after she had slept well. This morning she lay there in the warmth of the covers, with a cold stomach, thinking of the test kit with the glass tubes and the chemicals.

She rose, slipped on her robe, and padded into the kitchen. Methodically she prepared the test, collecting her first urine of the morning and pouring a sample into the tube that held the test chemicals. A mirror lay at right angles to the tube in its holder so she could see its bottom when the reactions were complete. No dark ring at the bottom, no pregnancy. A dark ring—and a baby was growing inside her.

She couldn't think of that. She couldn't read the test either; she'd wait till that evening.

She forced her way through her morning exercises and drove to work. Ridge's car wasn't in the parking lot.

Cully went to her desk and sat down to write her report, explaining how she had found out the victim's name and where she had worked. She mentioned Clarence, in the jargon of police documents, as a "business associate suspected of pandering"; she might eventually have to verify his alibi, but other than that nobody else had to talk to Clarence. She wrestled for the better part of an hour with the report, cramming in the details and knowing the only important ones were: who owned the silver limo, and was he the killer?

"Hi," Ridge said.

She looked up to see him standing in her doorway.

"Hi," she said.

"May I come in?"

May I come in. "Sure," she said. When he had taken a seat in the wooden chair beside her desk, she added, "Kinda formal, aren't we?"

"Well, you've had a little starch in your britches lately, don't you think?"

"Wouldn't you? I mean if you were me?" He sat with his elbows on his knees, listening, as he always did, to what wasn't being said.

He looked at her, and maybe he nodded; the movement of his head was so slight it was hard to tell. Then his eyes shifted to the bare metal wall, seeping rust onto the concrete floor. "I . . . uh . . . came up with something I thought you might use. On your case," he said.

"Oh? Really. What was it?"

"I found out the name of the second victim."

He tried to say this casually, but after he did, the room got so quiet they both could hear the fan humming in the space heater on the other side of the Can. "How?" Cully said.

"I . . . uh . . . went through the phone book and called doctors who specialize in breast implants. There weren't that many. I mean there were quite a few, but I was able to narrow it down by asking if they used silicone or saline bags. I checked Roger's second autopsy report; the ones in Jane Doe Number Two were silicone. Then I just asked each guy if he'd done a patient with a Florida-shaped birthmark under her left breast. Not the sort of thing a guy would forget. And bingo, the fifth guy I talked to . . . had her name."

She drummed her fingers on the half-written report lying on her blotter. "Her name?" Cully said. "Is . . . that all you found out."

"Oh yeah, sure." He tried to sound like it was just a little thing he'd done and she'd missed, like it was something insignificant to find out the exact identity of the murder victim. "Oh yeah. Except about where she worked as a stripper."

"As a stripper."

"Yeah, you know, you said at the autopsy you thought the girl was some kinda exotic dancer."

"Right, that's what I said," she said sharply. "But how the hell do you know about where she worked, Ridge?" She heard her voice rise. "She told that to the tit doctor?"

Ridge cleared his throat. "Uh, no. I found out about where she worked from Clarence."

"From Clarence."

"Yeah, you know, her pimp. See, the doctor had her address, of course, he had to have that, and she didn't mind giving it to him because he was her doctor, it was all legitimate, the operation and all. She paid in cash, of course, and the doctor guessed she wasn't exactly a nun, but he's a doctor, he had the Hippocratic oath to live up to, new boobs without discrimination."

Ridge's rambling made her angrier; he was trying to sneak up on his point. "Clarence," she prompted.

"Clarence, yeah, right. So this morning I went to her home address, which was Clarence's place, and I roused him out of bed and talked to him. He told me about some lady cop who had shaken him down last night. Kicked him in the dick, he said. Not the balls, the *dick*, he said." Ridge smiled. "Good ol' Clarence, huh?"

The winner and still fuckin' champion. That's what the other cops said about Ridge, and the longer she knew him the more she understood why. All her running around. Kicking a citizen. And he'd found out everything he needed to know by using his head and the telephone.

Cully sat there taking deep breaths and blowing them out through her nose. She wasn't sure if her face was red, but it was hot.

"What's the matter?" Ridge said.

"What do you think is the matter?" Cully answered sharply.

Ridge looked down at his crossed legs and brushed some imaginary lint off his angular knee. "I don't understand why you're angry," he said.

"You don't think maybe *I* want to run *my* investigation? And I especially hate looking like a fool."

"Like a fool? Nobody else even came close to figuring out what you did. And besides that, who's competing?"

"Ridge? I'm gonna shoot you."

He shrugged, one of those "who can understand a woman?" shrugs.

"All right," she said. "All right. So we both talked to Clarence. And we ought to know *something.*"

"What do we know?"

"Me? I don't know anything. But I'll tell you what's bothering me. The girl."

"The girl?" Ridge seemed intrigued.

"That's right, the girl. If she hadn't had a pimp, it would be one thing. She'd go with anybody and take her chances. But she has a pimp to make sure she's protected and to make sure she's paid. This victim, Porsche, she had a pimp, but she went anyway. Why? Because she recognized the guy. He rolled down the window, she saw his face, and she went with him."

"Yeah. She did."

"So," Cully said emphatically, "it's somebody that hooker knew." She cocked an eyebrow and lifted a corner of her mouth in a smirk.

"Cully!" He shook his head and blinked, dazzled. "That's terrific!"

"Yeah. It is, isn't it. So maybe you outthought me on Clarence, Ridge. But I beat you to that conclusion."

Ridge slipped some sheets of paper from the inside pocket of his sport coat. They were doubled over, folded lengthways, and had the serrated edges of computer printouts. "I got a list from the DMV off all the limousines registered in the Los Angeles area. Thousands of them. Black's the most common color, then white, then silver—but still we're talking about thousands of them. And most are owned under corporate names. For instance, you remember a few weeks ago when Rowe brought the chief up here in that silver limo that he borrowed from his buddy Josh Lannon? Well, I checked the list and Lannon's name isn't on it, that limo's probably registered to one of the few hundred tax-shelter production companies down there. And even if we know the actual owners, there are tens of thousands of potential drivers, so the list won't do us much good. But, uh . . . I believe I did scribble some thoughts on the back."

Cully turned the list over. On the blank side of the back sheet, Ridge had written: *Somebody the hooker knew.* Cully looked up at him, and he was smiling, but only with his eyes.

12

"Let's go for a drive," he said. He stood. "Come on! Let's go." He was cheerful. The bastard.

Cully stood and followed him out of the metal building toward the parking lot. The construction workers had arrived and were putting the finishing touches on the cinder-block addition to the back of the Can, a large rectangular annex that was to be the Mulholland Homicide Division's own shooting range. Cement trucks and Bobcat mini-bulldozers had churned up the ground, and they had to walk over deep ruts, Cully wobbling in her western boots and Ridge graceful in his coffee-colored English wingtips.

They reached the cars and the dirt was hardpacked, covered with layers of thin dusty leaves from the eucalyptus trees high above their heads. Ridge stopped at his car, put his back to the driver's door, and said, "Let's talk a minute."

"Come on, Ridge," she said, looking around for anybody else driving up. It was a cool morning, with a clean blue sky beyond the bony-white knuckles of the eucalyptus branches and the trees smelled fresh and fertile, and she didn't want Rowe or Bellflower or the other detectives to come up and see them standing there talking like two people who were . . . well, involved with each other.

"We're detectives working the same case. We can talk, can't we?"

"What do you want to talk about, Ridge?"

"About you."

"About me. Come on, Tom!"

"We need to talk about you, I think. For just a minute."

"We don't need to talk about me, we need to talk about a murder case! Two murder cases!" *Okay, Cully, settle down; and lower your voice.* "We've got two women down on Roger's slabs, and both of them from the same killer. This guy, whoever's doing it, is in a hurry. He's not sitting around talking about himself! He's out there right now getting ready to carve up his next one." She was almost shouting again. "So what are we doing standing here?"

Ridge's face was steady, but his eyes drifted as if searching for a target somewhere in the mists of his mind. "That's probably exactly what he *is* doing."

"That . . . what is? I don't follow you. Getting ready to kill his next victim?"

"Yeah. Sure. But I meant talking about himself. Murderers are self-absorbed. Killing somebody else is kinda the ultimate way of saying that what I want is more important than what you want, isn't it?" Ridge glanced away, toward the purple mountains on the opposite rim of the San Fernando Valley. He pondered his own hypothesis for a moment; or at least that's what he seemed to be doing, she couldn't be sure. Then he looked back at her. "Just figure he is intelligent enough to have committed at least two murders without being caught yet, and he's aware enough that we're after him, so that he'll be thinking about how and why he does things, and how and why *we* do things. So a little bit of personal thought on your part isn't out of line here."

"Boy, are you hard to argue with!"

"So why are you trying to argue?"

She threw up her hands. "Okay, Ridge! I give up! What do you want to talk about?"

He studied her face a moment. "Your boots," he said.

"My boots?"

"Yeah." He nodded. "Your macho boots. And your macho new four-wheel-drive whateveritis. And your spare guns, hidden all over your body."

"Lots of cops—" she began, but he cut her off.

"Lots of cops are full of crap. You aren't. But you're scared. That's what the guns are about. Don't even start to argue with me, I've seen it before. I've felt it myself. I've even done it myself, started to carry an extra gun, brass knuckles, speedloaders, a spring gun, a switchblade—because after you've been in a shoot-out, you start reliving it in your thoughts and your dreams, and you realize how easily you could have died, how a little piece of a second could have changed things forever. . . . And then one gun doesn't seem like enough, and two doesn't either. And then you want to carry a bazooka. And drive a tank. And you want a big tattoo on your face that says 'Don't Fuck With Me!' " He paused. "And you want to kick every dirtbag you talk to, right in the balls."

"All right, okay, okay!" Cully said. But she wouldn't look at him. She looked at the tree bark flaking off in thin strips. At the valley. At the leaves she was nudging with the hard toe of her boot.

In a quieter but not gentler voice Ridge said, "You're right about the responsibility. That we've got to catch him. That *you*'ve got to catch him—because a cop that doesn't take this as a personal contest between himself and the killer will never make it in homicide. But if you're gonna be the one who catches this guy, then you've got to take care of the part of you that does the catching. Not the part that buys the jeep and hides the guns. But the part that thinks and feels." He bumped himself up into a standing position, away from the door. "Get in the car."

She did.

* * *

Cully didn't ask where they were going; Ridge liked to talk and think in moving cars, though he usually liked to be the passenger because of the way his mind wandered over everything but the road. Cully preferred to take the wheel; she liked to show him that she could drive and think at the same time. But today she just buckled in beside him and sat quietly as he steered the swaying sedan down the switchbacks of Coldwater Canyon and into the San Fernando Valley.

After a few minutes she said, " 'False and misleading advertising.' What do you think that means?"

"I've got a theory about that, too," Ridge said. "I think I've figured that out."

"I bet you have," Cully said.

"The murderer is somebody who feels nobody loves him," Ridge said. He looked at Cully for a moment and then swung his eyes back to the street.

They rode on a little and she said, "What do you mean? How do you figure, about feeling unloved?"

"He blames the victims for what happened to them."

"Shifting responsibility for the killing from the murderer to the victim."

"Exactly."

"Then the dead girls are a message," Cully said. "It's not the note that's the message, it's the whole package. This guy is outraged, and maybe . . . afraid of something, too. Fear and anger jumbled up."

Ridge nodded. "Yeah," he said softly. "The greater the viciousness of his emotion, the stronger his justification of the crime."

"Which he may not see as a crime at all."

"Maybe not. Almost surely not. And all this is connected to attraction, because these girls have gorgeous bodies, beautiful faces. They're the cream of the crop among strippers. They're not just targets of opportunity, they're selected. He's drawn to them, overwhelmingly, compulsively—but then something makes him feel threatened and full of rage."

"Yeah," she said, stumped. They reached the flats of the San Fernando Valley at the bottom of the mountain. "Ridge? One of our textbooks in the detective training course said that with serial killers there is usually a progression. It starts with a compulsion. Like go pick up hookers. Then compulsion becomes obsession. Like killing hookers. And then . . . obsession becomes . . ." She didn't want to say it, it seemed so ugly.

"A sport."

She nodded.

"We chose a pretty job, didn't we, darlin'?" Ridge said.

"Yeah," she said quietly.

Cully saw him drift off into his own thoughts. He had turned onto Moorpark and was rolling through the residential area of Studio City. "Where are we going?" she asked.

"There's something here I wanted to show you."

He made another turn, and stopped on a street lined with king palms, then swung into the driveway of a house with broken windows and peeling paint. The grass, which had been meager in its best days, was now brown bristle in brick-baked earth. The rest of the place was as pocked and pitted as the practice house at the SWAT training facility.

There was a for-sale sign chiseled into the dead lawn.

"This your dream house, Ridge?" she said, and turned to him with a sarcastic smile. Instantly she knew she had said the wrong thing; disappointment crinkled the corners of his mouth. But then her voice changed. "You're buying this? I mean . . . really . . . you can afford real estate?" "Real estate" was said with awe in Southern California, since owning it was an impossible dream for most cops.

"I haven't bought it. But I'd like to. It's a probate,

you've got to put in an offer and if the trustees accept it they go to court and other people can bid if they want to, but they have to bump your bid by ten percent."

"It's . . . in kinda rough shape," Cully said, and as she said it a battered and half-furless cat jumped lazily from one of the broken windows.

"It's two hundred twenty thousand dollars."

"Two hundred . . ."

"That's what they're asking. Maybe they'd take less. But with a probate they work off an appraisal, so they couldn't take very much less."

"Yeah, but two hundred thousand!"

"Here's what I figure. Just listen a minute. It needs a new kitchen. Heck, it needs a new everything. But a new kitchen, that's twenty, maybe twenty-five grand. The bathrooms could be redone, too, but they're solid, they could be cleaned up way better than you'd imagine. The floors need refinishing, the walls need paint, all the doors need stripping, the whole place needs going over. But if it was in good shape, it'd be worth three."

"Three? Three hundred thousand dollars?"

"One just like it down the street sold for more than that last April."

"More than three hundred thousand?" She was stunned. She had not looked seriously at houses in a couple of years, but she had thought of owning a house herself someday; this bit of news made her feel just how far out of reach that goal was. She did some math in her head. "Twenty percent down on a loan, Ridge. And they figure I think one percent of the loan per month in house payment. That's forty grand up front and maybe sixteen hundred a month in payment. You can afford that on a cop's salary?"

"Not on one," he said.

He kept looking at the house. She looked at him and then fixed her eyes on the house again so she wouldn't have to answer, and could pretend that she hadn't understood.

* * *

For two days she had been on the radio, even on two of the early-morning talk shows, telling everybody about the introduction of her new fragrance line out at a mall in the valley and how he was going to be there.

Mom.

As Lannon drove there alone in his Range Rover he wondered how she had gotten somebody to finance all this. She was one of those people who have a great sense for money yet never have any of their own. Lannon guessed she had simply offered her name and promotional services to the fragrance manufacturer, along with the concept. The people who made the perfume hadn't been in the fragrance business previously; mainly they made motor oil. Lannon had checked.

He had not spoken to his mother in over five years. Lannon, in a quest for privacy from the hundreds of people who wanted him to read scripts or appear somewhere or give money, changed his home number a half-dozen times a year and had never notified her. Then, about two months ago, she telephoned his agent's office and left a number of her own. When Josh called back, to what proved to be a motel in Arizona, she apologized for troubling him, then asked for a part in his new movie. She said she wanted to play the role of his mother. When he told her there was no part like that in the picture, she said, "I understand that, son. But you're the screenwriter, so write one."

It had not been an easy conversation for Josh. She ended up asking for money and he had agreed to send her some. He sent a check by overnight mail for ten thousand dollars. Three days later the check came back in a plain envelope, with only her name where the sender's address should be. There was no letter, no note of any kind; she had simply sent the check back.

A few weeks later she began appearing in advertisements in national newspapers, announcing the introduction of her new fragrance. In a Los Angeles news conference she told everybody on the face of the planet that her son, Josh, was going to be at the "official introduction of the fragrance" out at the valley mall, and the news people started checking with his agent to see if that was true. His agents replied that they had no comment; that sent the reporters back to Mom, who said, "See? He's going to come!"

Now what could he do? He had talked about his past, but never about his mother. Now here she was.

The shopping center wasn't even a good one. And even as Josh Lannon drove along the hot boulevard, past taco stands and muffler-repair shops, he coldly admired his mother's genius. The scheme would never have worked in Beverly Hills, but to attach the Lannon name to a perfume for the waitresses who smelled like sweat and bacon grease? The lines of cars Lannon found around the mall that morning told him just how shrewd his mother still was.

But her son had instincts, too. He was going to go in early. Before they would expect him, he could beat the crowd and the television cameras. He could avoid being in any film footage, holding up some glittery bottle of the stinking perfume, but no one could report that he had abandoned his mother.

But as he parked the Rover on the outer perimeter of the parking lot and walked across the lot, wearing a tracksuit and sunglasses and a Dodgers hat, and slouching along like any other guy out in the valley, Lannon had a great idea, like those that had marked his career as a writer, actor, and director. Why not laugh at all this? he thought. Why not tell everybody it was a cheap publicity stunt by brazenly using it to hype his next movie?

Without being recognized, he passed through the doors into the Mall itself, but then found the stores inside weren't open yet. He went to the big sliding glass partition that blocked the entrance to the department store where his mother's big event was to be held. Inside he could see the displays for TAMI, a "fragrance of exquisite flare," and an autograph table. He stood unrecognized among the other early arrivals of the mass of mindless admirers who would appear that day, and he looked through the glass in blank amazement. Sure, she had used him, and that made a knot in his guts; but he could pull himself back from that knot, had learned to do that a long time ago, and could admire the pieces she had pulled together even as he resisted being one of them.

Then he saw her. Tami Lannon. Mom. She looked old, pale and powdered, but better than she had when he last saw her. She wore a sequined headband and a shimmery outfit that looked like a pair of pajamas, tightly belted at the waist to show off those big bouncy knockers she still had, and the waist that was still pretty small for a woman bumping sixty. Her hair was freshly dyed, a luxurious hay yellow, and though her face was a little puffy now, she had great bone structure, and when Lannon studied her objectively, he saw their family similarities and resolved again to discipline himself never to drink, never to eat fat and sweets, and so to look young forever.

And she had those lips, full and opaque, like red wax. As he stood there she glimpsed someone standing at the door and glanced away before she registered that it was him. When she looked back, her lips formed a puckered circle of surprise, as if she had not been sure he would come. Josh wasn't sure; maybe the surprise was real. He could read other people, but he could not read his mother.

She waved to the man in the white short-sleeved shirt and kelly-green tie who was scurrying around setting up the display, and nodding like an excited puppy, the man rushed over and opened the door. He introduced himself as the store manager and Josh shook his hand. The manager kept talking, but Josh didn't look at him anymore, he just looked at Mom.

She ignored the manager, too, cutting right through whatever he was babbling about to say to her son, "You'll sit right over here, with me."

"Okay," Josh said. "But no pictures."

"You won't have your picture taken with your mother?"

"I'm not here to endorse the product." Josh felt the store manager watching him, hanging on every word, and added to his mother, "I'm here to endorse you."

"That is so wonderful," the manager said breathlessly, and Tami Lannon smiled. Josh noticed she had had her teeth capped since she had seen him last.

The doors opened, the crowd arrived. "He's here!" Lannon heard someone saying in the crowd. "Really!" When word went around that Josh Lannon was actually there, the doors were plugged with people. A photographer was in the department store snapping pictures, and Josh's mother planted a huge kiss on her son's face. She kept her lips pressed to Josh's cheekbone while the photographer's autowinder whirred through a whole roll of film, then looked toward the crowd and said loudly, "I want to thank Mr. Vernon Mietzel, my partner, and I want to thank my son, Joshua Lannon, for coming today." A stocky bald man, apparently Mr. Vernon Mietzel, moved up on Josh's flank and stood there with a smile as wide as a jack-o'-lantern's as Tami Lannon grabbed Josh and pressed her lips against him again, holding him by the jaw with her long fingers so Mietzel's photographer could snap pictures, and all Josh could say was, "If Vernon's gonna kiss me, I gotta go."

The crowd loved that. Two video teams were just arriving, one from local news and one from a syndicated tabloid show, and they were elbowing their way to the front, angry that the proceedings had already begun. But the people in the leisure suits and Levi's and the print dresses made way without anger; the impatience of the camera crews gave the whole event a feeling of importance and urgency. Mietzel was asking for more pictures when Bellflower showed up, his two blue-uniformed officers blowing whistles to clear the crowd. Lannon called in a stage voice, "What? Cops? You mean a publicity stunt for my next picture? Gee, Mom, what did you teach me?"

At first nobody knew how to take it, then everybody laughed, and his mother kissed him a third time. Lannon smiled at the cameras. "This is my friend Leonard Bellflower. He was my main source for my new picture, *Blue's Blues*. Thanks, Len. I have a tight schedule on my next picture, but thank you all for coming today."

With that, Lannon headed through the inside of the store, where none of the crowd had thought to be. Bellflower and his boys covered his retreat, just like they planned. Lannon was able to stroll through the whole empty department store without being hailed by any admirers or detained for a single autograph, and while half the fans deserted the perfume display and ran to the front entrance to look for a motorcade, Lannon reached his Rover on the back side of the parking lot and drove to the lot of an auto-parts store two blocks away, where he rendezvoused with Bellflower and his boys for another thank-you.

Lannon gave each of the two uniforms who had helped him a couple of second-row seats for a Lakers game and asked Bellflower if there was anything he could do for him.

"Nah," Bellflower said, "glad to help out." Then he added, "But you know, I have been meaning to ask you if I could borrow your limo again."

"Sure, Len, anytime, you know that."

13

At exactly eleven A.M., Mike Rowe arrived at the Can. His car was brand new, its first day in the parking lot. Rowe wasn't sure if eucalyptus trees dropped any kind of sap that could pit the high-gloss finish, but just to be sure he parked in the sun away from the trees and the construction. When they had the lot paved, he would have his own space marked out.

He opened the trunk and took out two cases, each containing a Beretta nine-millimeter automatic pistol, then stood with the cases under his arm and checked his watch. At exactly 9:05 a blue Range Rover turned off Mulholland and plowed across the dirt, tossing the flat leaves in a spray behind the all-weather tires.

Lannon, at the wheel, wore a Dodgers cap, a denim coat, jeans, work boots, and big sunglasses. He could have passed as one of the construction workers. He sported a mustache that was a slightly lighter shade of brown than his hair and looked naturally bleached out by the sun. It was an excellent fake.

Lannon hopped out of the jeep, slapped Rowe on the shoulder, jumped back away from the Mazda as if it might scorch him, and said, "Hey, new wheels! Man, that's hot looking!" He leaned down to look inside the deputy chief's Mazda. "You'll have to take me for a ride, sometime."

Lannon was so easy for Rowe to like, truly like; he did things like make a fuss over a new Japanese car, even though he had a line of Ferraris and Lamborghinis and racing Porsches in the automobile stable of his estate over the hill in Bel Air. Rowe knew Lannon would never have time for the joyride, but it was nice to hear him say he'd like one.

"How did everything go at the shopping center?" Rowe asked as they were crossing the expanse of dirt.

"It went," Lannon said, then added quickly, with a smile, "Bellflower was just right, thanks for sending him."

They walked together around the side of the building and through the side door, where Rowe was sure no one would be because Bellflower was preparing a morning conference of detectives. They turned through the metal building into the cool concrete corridor that connected to the cinder-block cavern of the firing range.

They found the range lit and ready; empty, but with the targets hanging in two bays, waiting for the push of the buttons that would activate the overhead pulleys to run them out to the desired distance. Lannon tucked his sunglasses into the pocket of his flannel shirt and looked around, his deep chocolate eyes shining. Rowe watched him, and delighted in his approval.

They cranked out the targets and fired eight rounds each before they said a word to each other. They rolled the targets back, checked them—Rowe had let a couple stray into the white so that Lannon's score wouldn't look so bad—and started reloading, when Lannon slipped his earmuffs down around his neck and said, "So, Mike . . ." He waited till Rowe had his muffs off before saying, "What's going on?"

"Usual stuff. You know."

"Come on!" Lannon said. "I don't want any of the stuff you don't want the press to have, I don't want to be responsible for that kind of information. But tell me about it, I couldn't stop thinking about it. We got Jack the Ripper out there, or what?"

Rowe checked his safety a second time and laid the

pistol on the elbow table. "That's what the press would call it, if they got ahold of it. Every time a woman gets cut up, the press calls it the return of Jack the Ripper."

"That's what's happening? The women are really getting cut up?" Lannon frowned. "Come on, Mike, give me some details."

Rowe hesitated, but only for a moment. "It's mutilation. The guy cuts out their breast implants."

"Their *what*?"

"Yeah," Rowe said.

"Got any leads? Pervert, con, escapee . . . Mental case, maybe, though I hope not, they're not very interesting—" Lannon caught himself. "Jesus, I'm sorry, Mike, that was awful to say. Somebody's out there killing people and I'm hoping for an interesting villain. See there? It's like I've been telling you, you do this movie shit for too long and you lose perspective on real life."

"I think that happens to all of us who deal with this kind of thing—from one side or another," Rowe said, basking in his intimacy with this man who fascinated so many millions of people. A dim awareness flickered across his brain, an awareness of how easy it was to spill sensitive information in friendly situations, and that Ridge was wise to hold his thoughts so closely to himself. "We've got a couple of really good detectives taking the point on this one. And it's our first big case in MULHOM. We'll get this guy. I just hope we do it before too many other women get cut up."

Lannon nodded, and gave Rowe an open grin of pure white teeth that said, *Buddy, I admire you, too.*

Ridge drove back to the Can. All the way up the hill Cully sat beside him, not saying a word, but she felt he was the one being silent. It was not until they reached Mulholland and were steering left and right along the crest road that he tried being all business again and said, "Did you have your artist friend draw a picture of the first victim, too?"

"I didn't want to put her through it twice," Cully said. "I figured I'd start with victim two because we'd already spent more time showing Roger's photographs of victim one."

"Well, the artist was a great idea," Ridge said. "You think you could get her to do a drawing of victim one if you told her that what she did on victim two had already struck pay dirt for us?"

Cully felt a stab of guilt, remembering how Gail had struggled to do the drawing, and Cully had not yet called her to let her know the plan had worked. Success would mean a great deal to her; artists don't get many chances to feel courageous and effective. "I'm sure she'd do it again for us," she said.

They reached the Can, and as Cully went to her desk to call Gail Ridge stopped by the computer tables to check whether any of the missing-persons bulletins had turned up anything. Zero there.

On his way back to his desk Ridge ran into a knot of detectives hooked by an old friend, Odom "Two Moons" DeFuller. The stories that Odom had earned his nickname by twice baring his backside were entirely slanderous; he was originally dubbed "Two Moons" because of a fondness for Moon Pies early in his career, when he would eat two of them for lunch. What Odom liked to called himself was DeFuller DeBetter.

When Ridge ran into him, DeFuller was telling a story about Trigger Frazier, who had been his partner years ago in the Rampart Division and was still counted as a friend. Frazier was a racist and DeFuller was a blue-black Afro-American straight out of South Carolina, but the two of them had gotten along great because Odom DeFuller had his own take on police work, which was that you beat back the shit and pissed on 'em if you could, and that kind of attitude warmed Frazier's heart. It was Odom DeFuller who, the day Marvin Gaye was shot by his own father after physically abusing the old man in a drug-induced fit, took one of Gaye's album covers down to the shooting range, drew a bull's-eye around the singer's nose, and grouped three rounds right through the picture, then hung it up on the station house wall with a sign that said: MARVIN GAYE'S GREATEST HITS.

Odom was something of a hero for Micro, Trigger, Boom-Boom, and the Baptist. As Ridge walked up, Odom cut himself off in mid-punch-line—he was that much of a gentleman—and shook Ridge's hand. "Hey, country boy, how you doin'!"

"Good, Odom!" Ridge said. "You?"

"Can't complain. Hey, I heard about you takin' down that dealer in Mexico City. *Boom boom.* Nice job."

"That was mostly McCullers," Ridge said. "You know her?"

"Naw. Heard about her, though," DeFuller said, and left it at that. Then he asked, "What you up to?"

"Butcher case."

"What all you know about him?" DeFuller said, winking at the others, knowing how much Ridge would have deduced and how little he would say.

When Ridge didn't answer, Morris chimed in. "Likes strippers. Has a fixation for big tits."

"Likes strippers and has a fixation for big tits? Hell, I know! The butcher's a cop!"

Everybody laughed.

Cully reached Gail at work and told her how it had gone with the first drawing. Her friend was surprised and excited. When Cully asked if it would be possible for Gail to come down and do it again for another victim, Gail said she could leave right away.

"I wouldn't want to get you in trouble with your boss," Cully told her.

"Are you kidding?" Gail said. "My talents needed in urgent police business? Helping to track down a killer? This kind of thing could *make* our agency!"

Ridge and Cully headed down to the morgue. She drove this time. Ridge sat looking toward the traffic, with no matching movement in his eyes. Cully was familiar with that stare; it was as if the motion of an automobile made him throw his mind into neutral and let it drift.

At times like these, Ridge was not aware of concentrating; it was like relaxing. His brain flowed in a sea of memory and projection, instinct and intuition, operating as if independent of his body. There were those in the LAPD who thought of Ridge as the Zen detective, a "Zen Baptist," as Ragg Wilson once put it, and they would nod in smug satisfaction whenever they saw him this way. But Ridge employed no mystical techniques and subscribed to no Oriental philosophy. To Ridge, his own kind of meditation was a completely private and selfish act; he liked to do his own thinking in his own way, and he was willing to live with the consequences of the sometimes strange results.

His thought process involved moods, feelings, nonverbal fragments that he could never have explained afterward. Today, riding with Cully, he was thinking of what DeFuller had said.

It was not that Ridge had any reason to suspect a cop in the killings, and in fact he instinctively discounted that remote possibility; policemen have plenty of opportunities to participate in violent situations, and anybody with a tendency to turn brutal would have shown that side in a drug arrest or a traffic citation or even in training encounters at the academy. But DeFuller had gotten him thinking on a different slant. Who would hate a hooker enough to do that to one of them?

The urge to kill was personal, but the target was impersonal; one victim, and maybe something particular about her, made her a target, but two victims, with only general similarities, said they were types to the killer, not individuals. They were part of a group. And was there some other group who would have such violent contempt for prostitutes that they could do this?

Cops did not hate hookers. They were too much like neighbors on the same street. Hookers caught violence but seldom dished it out themselves, and they lived by a transaction that men willingly made. Cops hate wife beaters and child molesters far more than they hate the businesswomen who often had been the victims of both. Hookers make good informants, too. They had even been known to fall in love with cops, and cops with them.

So who would absolutely hate hookers? Not clergymen; they tried to see every whore as Mary Magdalene. How well Ridge knew this. Years ago, a lifetime now it seemed, he had attended a seminary, grappling with the fundamentalism he had soaked in during his youth. He had only recently experienced any resolution of his feelings about professional Christians, as he called them, and he knew he held clergymen to impossible standards and tended to suspect them of everything; but he could not see how any killer with a secret rage like this one could hide himself within their ranks for any length of time without his dark urges exposing themselves in many other and less lethal ways.

Artists? No, they were fascinated by prostitutes and used them as models. They painted beautiful pictures of them. Ridge remembered something about Vincent van Gogh, himself a failed seminarian: hadn't van Gogh tried to give his ear to a hooker?

Who, then? Who hated them?

Ridge became aware that this was not the right question. It was almost the right question, but not quite.

"You're mad at me, aren't you?" Cully said.

Ridge turned and his eyes focused on her. She wasn't sure he had heard her, so she said it again. "You're mad. At me."

"No, I'm not," he said.

He seemed surprised at the suggestion.

Or maybe, Cully thought, he's just given up on me.

Gail made the second drawing, intent this time, confident. When she looked at the body on the slab, she saw the living face she was sketching, not the death mask.

Cully watched but did not think about the case. She was wondering if there was any other reason why her nipples could be feeling tender.

Ridge, oblivious to Cully's quandary and sensitive to the way she seemed unaware of him, stood by and looked at Gail sketching the corpse and thought of van Gogh with one ear. He understood the mad Dutchman. Cutting off an ear was nothing to the pain of loving and not having that love returned.

They headed into Hollywood with Gail's drawing of the first victim. It was early afternoon and the hookers were scarce.

Hollywood is not awash in hookers, though television, movies, and novels could leave that impression. Even at ten P.M. on peak tourist weekends, they don't clog the sidewalks like pine logs in an Oregon river. The drop-in kind of sexual trade, trawling the streets for a random pickup, is a hard business, and most girls soon graduate into the safer and more lucrative world of referrals, stripper/pimping, and organized whorehouses, or they die from the drugs and demons that drove them to the streets in the first place.

Sometimes they are as easy to find as a Middle Easterner behind the counter of a convenience store, other times they're scarce; and at this time of day Cully and Ridge found the pickings slim. They drove the corner of Sunset and Highland, passing back and forth, and in an hour they found only two girls smiling and waving at men in passing cars. They questioned both; that is, Cully did, while Ridge sat in the car and scrubbed his fingertips over a furrowed forehead. Neither of the girls recognized the woman in the sketch, and when Cully came back to the car the second time, she was frustrated.

"Nothing. I think we ought to find their pimps and try them."

"The kick-Clarence-in-the-balls route, huh?" Ridge said, still distracted.

"Yeah, maybe," Cully said, twisting the ignition key too hard and grinding the starter. "You got a headache, or what?" She drove back down Highland; they would have to clear the corner for a few minutes before the girls came back, like starlings shooed from a seeded lawn. Ridge still sat there distracted, and it angered Cully that he had lost interest in what they were doing. "You hate the work part of being a detective, don't you, Ridge?" she said as she drove. "Just bores you to tears, doesn't it?"

He sighed and shrugged. She was right; grunt work like stakeouts and pounding the pavement hoping to find a random acquaintance of an unknown victim sapped his energy and depressed him. There ought to be some better way, he thought, some idea that could get them somewhere. He stared out at the sidewalks sliding past his window and tried to imagine Jane Doe I resurrected from her slab and out walking the streets again. His eyelids drifted almost shut and behind them he could picture her, standing on a corner somewhere, letting her looks attract a glance and then smiling to show she was available . . . or prancing down the street with that hooker strut, her buttocks tense and that tattoo, *Love Hurts,* rolling underneath the thin fabric of her skirt.

Ridge's head snapped around toward Cully. "That tattoo," he said, suddenly exuberant. She frowned at him. "She didn't get that back in Idaho or wherever she came from! That's something you have done when you've already become a hooker. That's something she did here."

"So—" She got it, but didn't have time to say it before Ridge explained.

"There're only a couple of tattoo shops around here. I mean the trendy Hollywood ones, where she would have gone."

"Why didn't you think of that before, Ridge?" Cully said, trying to sound bitchy but hearing the affection sneak into her tone. "You're slipping."

He just smiled.

The nearest tattoo shop was on the Sunset Strip, with a big painted sign of a red tattoo heart above a wooden hut directly beneath the huge billboards.

They walked out of the sunlight into a small square parlor with big windows facing the sidewalk. The walls were vertical wooden planks painted canary yellow and hung with hundreds of tiny framed designs in red, green, and blue. Behind the counter was a bearded man in a tight T-shirt. Tattoos spiraled on him like ink ivy rooted somewhere beneath his shirt and growing wherever there was bare skin: down his arms to the last knuckles of his fingers, up his neck to his hair and beard line. Until her second glance Cully didn't realize that the man was bald; the bare pate of his head was tattooed with roses.

He studied them, and Cully realized what a strange couple they must appear, Ridge in his tailored suit and her in her leather jacket, jeans, and boots. The bald man smiled—to her relief, his teeth weren't tattooed—and said, "Whatever turns you on!"

The same motto was lettered in a sign above his head.

Ridge scanned the walls, as if he hadn't heard. The tattooist was used to tourist gawkers, but these two were studying the designs like first-timers, so he helped them out. "Flowers and figures, the delicate and the delectable . . . Tiny and teasing, romantic and pleasing . . ." He would've added, "Nearly painless, and absolutely sterile," but he had found it best not to mention the actual needle process until first-timers had already settled on a design.

"What about mottoes?" Ridge asked, still studying the options on the walls.

The man waddled around the counter, and Cully saw that the waddle was from a limp. One of his legs was artificial and the shoe on it was glossy and unwrinkled, while its mate on the real foot was scuffed and battered. The false leg added to the tattooist's old-salt image, and he used it theatrically, planting the peg leg in the center of the room and pivoting around it almost running with the real foot as he hawked his talent and laughing at himself even as he did it. "Look! All around! Samples and examples, but what you want you get from Pierre La Pointe! You want something classical, something far out and funky, something absolutely, really and truly unique? Pierre is there!"

He bowed, showing them the garden on the top of his head.

Cully was speechless. Ridge seemed to be, too. La Pointe, or whatever his real name was, decided to make his point another way. He pointed out the window of his shop, toward the Italian restaurant across the street, where the sidewalk tables were filling up with Beverly Hills richbitches ordering forty-dollar lunches. "See the waitress over there, the one with the long brown legs? That's 'Ecstasy Enlightens.' " He patted his left hip. "Up there on the hill, guy that owns the house with Cinzano awnings out by the pool, you can see there? He's 'Danger.' " The tattooist touched his own right shoulder.

Ridge lifted a frame off the wall. It contained the elephant-mounting-a-mouse design they'd found on the left buttock of the first corpse. "How about this one?"

The tattooist took the frame, glanced at it, and said, " 'Love Hurts.' "

"Love Hurts," Ridge said. "How many times have you done that one?"

The guy only stared back, unsure where this was going.

Cully unrolled the portrait in her purse and showed him. "Love Hurts," she said. He looked at the drawing; Gail had made the girl look pretty, alive; there was no hint in the picture of what the subject looked like now. "You recognize this girl?"

The tattooist smiled. "I'm sorry, folks, I'm like a doctor, lawyer somethin'. Client confidentiality, know what I mean?"

Cully showed him her shield. "Know what I mean?"

"Love Hurts," the guy said immediately. "Sure, Love Hurts. Great-looking girl."

"Know her name or where she lives?"

"Hey, man, I don't have people fill out applications. But if you want to find Love Hurts, just hang around. She works the Strip."

"She's a hooker," Cully said, being careful to keep all this in the present tense so as not to spook the guy.

But calculation flickered in the tattooist's eyes. "I haven't seen her for a few days. She usually stands right out there, most nights. Is there anything wrong?"

"When did you last see her?" Cully said.

"Couple of nights ago. Tuesday, I guess. Yeah, Tuesday, 'cause I was trying to sell a girl on 'No Holds Barred' and I pointed out to her Love Hurts."

"Did you see who she was with? Love Hurts?" Cully asked.

"Nah. She had a customer, though. Last time I saw her she was getting into a silver limo."

Doing a computer search was one of the most mind-numbing tasks a detective had to do. It ranked right up there with camping for two days in a van outside the apartment of suspect's ex-girlfriend on the off chance that he might show up there.

The heart of MULHOM's computer system was the eight-year-old PC that Mike Rowe had brought from home. He had upgraded his home system and donated the old stuff to the department. The scrounging nature of that appealed to the cops' basic spirit; MULHOM had less modern equipment than any police division in town, but using the ragtag stuff was a kind of arrogance that said, *Hey, we're better, we can use our brains.*

The old computer was slow, but it was simple, too, and the fastest processor in the world is no help if you don't know how to use it. Rowe knew how to use this one, and he had taught his detectives how in one morning. A computer search typically began with a data base —a collection of information from some other law enforcement agency's computer files. The detectives would call up the other agency and then use the telephone modem to have the data loaded into the MULHOM machine. Then they told their machine to search for something, like a certain zip code in a list of addresses, or a certain make of car registered in a certain year. Then Rowe's old machine would chug along and highlight any matches. The detective working the computer would then electronically cut out the listing and paste it into their working file.

It was slow, but it got the job done. Rowe had brought in an old printer, too, a daisy-wheel behemoth that was much slower than the new laser machines, so the detectives tended to work with information straight on the machine and only print out when they needed to make a formal display; but when they did, the product looked official and impressive.

Ridge took the first stint in the chair—two hours of drudgery that left his shirt wet and sticking to his back. He took the list of limos that he had drawn from the Department of Motor Vehicles and scanned it, pulling out every limo registered as silver or gray. Then Cully took over, and Ridge walked to the snack room and had a dinner of diet soda and peanut bars.

Late that afternoon Mike Rowe stepped into Bellflower's office and said, "Commander, I understand the lieutenant governor is in the building. You might want to dress this area up a little."

Bellflower looked around his office. What was wrong with his office? There was paper on the desk, sure, but how was that so bad; shouldn't an administrator have some paper? His pictures were of his family; his kid from nursery school right through college. His wastepaper basket was full. Was that it? Did a full trash can say that a man was not a fit administrator? Still, he should get it emptied. He was just picking up the phone to call building maintenance when Ragland walked in.

"Commander," Ragland said, "I was just wondering where we were on this butcher thing."

Bellflower put down the telephone. Mike Rowe stood there, too, watching Bellflower look stupid and awkward.

"Have you got any leads?" Ragland said. The lieutenant governor waited, but not long enough to give Bellflower a chance to answer. "How about forensics, do you know what they've said?" Another wait, this one a little longer, as Bellflower wondered which question he should answer first. "No?" Ragland said. "No. So how about this one, Commander: Can you assure me with certainty that these murders are the result of one killer, and not of two or more? That they aren't copycats? That anybody who wants to get rid of a hooker isn't taking this opportunity now to do her in?"

Bellflower had had enough. He picked up the telephone and had Ridge and McCullers paged.

Ridge popped in first, then Cully showed up from her cubicle.

"Tell Lieutenant Governor Ragland how all this is going," Bellflower instructed them.

"Starting where?" Cully said, looking at Ragland. Apparently there weren't going to be any further introductions.

"Start with forensics," Rowe said.

"Okay," Cully said. "The nails were hammered in the same way with both the girls. After death, or near the time. What seems to happen is that he beats them unconscious, with some hard object like a baseball bat, then stands over them and nails the note into their heads. There is no tissue of any kind on the girls, no tissue from her killer, I mean. No skin under the fingernails. No semen."

"He doesn't even rape them?" Ragland said, with surprising curiosity.

"Possibly there is intercourse," Cully said. "We have collected a sperm sample, though we can't be sure that was from the killer. The vagina of one of the victims yielded traces of the kind of lubricants used on condoms."

"Wonderful!" Ragland said. "We've established that the killer practices safe sex." He smiled as if he thought this funny, or ironic; no one else in the room smiled. "So is that all we have? Oh, wait; you said he uses a foreign object to knock them unconscious. How do you know that?"

"Because of the lack of tissue," Cully said.

"Oh, yeah, sure, that's right. Well. That's all we have, huh?"

"The girls are dismembered with a blade whose size is consistent with a standard kitchen carving knife," Ridge said. "All that's in the coroner's report."

"So basically all you're giving me is what I could read myself," Ragland said.

He looked at Ridge and Ridge said nothing. No one else spoke.

"Well, gentlemen, we're starting to hear about this

case, and I hope you won't leave me dangling here."
Then, as he was leaving, he shook hands around the
room. Friendly and firm, reminding Ridge of the way
the death-row jailors are when they lead a prisoner on
that last walk toward his execution.

14

Love always and eternal. Love smelling like honeysuckle, tasting like fresh bread, love lasting and unique. Love aching.

Love meant none of that to Thomas Ridge. He didn't even like the word; the thought of it reminded him of greeting cards with drawings of pudgy little humanoids dreaming hearts and saccharine sayings. Who bought those things?

Not people who looked at mutilated bodies in the middle of the night.

Love to Ridge was something else.

It was a bed in a pitch-dark room during a Tennessee winter, so cold that sliding beneath the sheets was like stretching out naked on a frozen pond; but the sheets were clean and smelled of January sunshine, and the twenty pounds of quilts piled above his skinny boy's body exhaled the scent of cedar whenever he heaved them up to turn over. The trick was not to curl into a ball but to stretch out straight as a board; if you didn't, the cold would stab you fresh when you finally did uncurl. In the blackness of the night, where sticks kept the windows propped shut and the closest light was in the Big Dipper, Ridge lay in a bedroom that had held his mother when she was a girl, and his grandparents when they were first wed, and the weight of his grandmother's handiwork pressed down upon him in the darkness like the weight of a hundred ancestral hearts, and he grew warm. No matter how cold or black the night, there was a clean, solitary place within it that said someone remembered him and held him a place.

That was love.

Scarlet McCullers? Just her name made him smile. And the thought of her body made his breath shallow, and he could remember her taste and her aroma. Of course he wanted her; who wouldn't? But he wasn't prepared to call that love.

Love was something you proved when you were angry, when you were tired. When you wanted to betray and tried to convince yourself that you owed no loyalty. Love was where you stood.

Ridge's mother and father had been found shot to death in a bed, in a house just down the road from his grandmother's.

His grandmother had raised him and his brother in a house with a coal fire and water that tasted like the breech of a rusted gun.

But he had known love there, and that was the only kind of love Ridge ever wanted, or would ever need.

The lights played on the hood of his car, sliding up toward the windshield as he drove along the boulevard.

The rock-and-roll clubs, the restaurants, the shops with thousand-dollar dresses in the windows, and the storefronts where Italian sports cars pressed red phallic noses to the glass like metal puppies with half-million-dollar price tags.

And the women in shiny skirts, watching the traffic.

He looked for one he knew.

He needed to know her; he didn't want her pimp around.

One pass down the Sunset Strip, and he saw three different girls, but they weren't right somehow. He didn't want to turn around right away and make another pass; he knew how the local vice squad worked, and he didn't want to be obvious in his trolling. He'd give it a few minutes and try again. He decided to drive all the way to Highland to go around back west along Hollywood Boulevard.

But as he turned up Highland he saw a girl in the shadows; a brunette, early twenties—old by the standards of the street, old enough to listen. He swung the car to the curb, and she moved to his window. She didn't smile, didn't know him. "Party?" she said.

He nodded. She reached her hand into the car, and he reached over and they brushed fingers. The girl knew the law; undercover cops were not allowed to make any physical contact with a hooker they were about to bust; otherwise the case would be thrown out as entrapment.

"You'll have to meet me—" she began.

But he cut her off. "I don't want to go to your place," he said. "I want to go to a hotel." There was one right across the street. He looked at it, thought a minute, and said, "That one there. I'll go over to the bar. You meet me for a drink. If you feel safe, you stay. If you don't, you go."

She nodded. He went.

He drank his first vodka quickly and had called for another when she walked in. The bartender gave her a glance, but when she sat down next to a paying customer and gave him a peck on the cheek, he let her stay.

"Glad you came," he said.

"Glad to be here," she said. "You're a nice guy."

"How do you know?" he said.

"I can always tell," she said.

He drank half of his second vodka and turned the glass between his thick fingers. "Did you hear about the girl that got murdered? The dancer? She thought she could tell."

For a moment the hooker said nothing; but then she smiled again. "Some people have bad karma."

"Drink?" the bartender said, appearing in front of her.

She looked at the bartender, then at the man beside her. "I'll just have some of his," she said.

He checked into a room without any problem and came back into the bar and took her upstairs. She waited for him, to see what he wanted to do first. Room service? Another drink? Or get right to it?

He took off his coat, sat down on the bed, and put his face in his hands.

She had seen this before; guilt, nerves, it was all easy to break down. She walked across the powder-blue carpet and reached over his lowered head to rub her palms up and down his back. Her body pressed against the back of his head.

He rose up and grabbed her wrists. His hands were strong, so big they enveloped her bones like stalks of celery, and she felt just as brittle within his grasp. "What is it, baby?" she said, suddenly scared, wondering if she had misread him. "What do you want?"

"I want to talk," he said. "That's all. Just talk." He let go of her wrists.

"Sure." She backed up and sat down on the arm of the chair nearest the door. "Anything you say."

Couldn't she ask what about? Couldn't she help him get this out? "I just . . . I just . . ." He took a deep breath and started again. "The only people I can talk to are whores," he said.

Oh great, she thought, a yakker. Oh well, they always paid. Hookers had a joke about them: guys either came in your mouth, or came in your ear. Either way they paid the freight.

He saw the bored look come into her eyes. He saw that she was not offended by the word "whore." Why should she be? How stupid, how naive he was to expect anything else. He felt disgust for himself, but that was freedom, the freedom to be disgusted. "I'm a shitty lover," he said. "I'm a shitty man."

"No," she said.

How could she know? But it didn't make any difference. That was the thing about whores, it didn't make any difference.

He began to cry.

Her boredom grew, he saw that through his tears. But she didn't need to understand, he just needed to say it. "Sometimes, it wells up in you," he said. "You want to fight back, you want to make them pay. Nobody else makes them pay. You want to make them pay."

She walked over and kissed him gently. The gentleness was magic. He came alive.

When it was over, he fell asleep.

She slipped out of bed silently, skilled through practice. He was snoring; he had fallen dead asleep right after, like he hadn't slept for a couple of days. Silently she found his pants. His wallet wasn't in them, but then she found it in a pocket of his sport coat. Two hundred thirty dollars there. She took it all. But as she was sliding the wallet back into the coat, her fingers touched something else—another wallet? She pulled it out; it was a badge. Leonard Bellflower, Los Angeles Police.

She put the badge back and returned all but fifty dollars to the wallet. But before she put the wallet back, she searched through it and found a business card. She didn't mind giving a cop a fifty-percent discount, but it wouldn't hurt to keep his card; in her line of work, you never knew when you might need a favor.

15

While Ridge sat dozing in his bare apartment, his restless brain spiraling thoughts of love, Cully lay in the raw blackness of sleep, in dreams that did not reach her consciousness but twitched her reflexes and gnawed like rats in the corridors her thoughts traveled during her waking hours.

And in North Hollywood a girl was walking toward the silver limousine that had settled to a stop just behind her car, parked in the lot of an all-night coffee shop that served notoriously tasty pancakes. She was hungry from a night of mud wrestling, during which she had made fifty dollars in salary and one hundred seventy-three dollars in tips, picked up from the tourists, mostly Japanese, who crowded the midweek shows. When she saw the limo stopping, her first thought was that it contained someone she knew: someone to whom she previously had rented an evening of her time, or maybe one of the Toyotas—the name she gave all the Japanese down at the mud-wrestling club—who came to Los Angeles with thousands of dollars to throw away and a fierce desire for blond Americans.

She had been followed before—and to this very coffee shop. She had never felt any danger from cars trailing her or men stopping to flirt. A body like hers was its own insurance policy. Naked, or in the bikinis she wore in the mud-wrestling club, she was so firm and curved that men were enthralled—and that was even

149

before she'd had her breasts surgically inflated; since then, she was awesome. Her bleached hair, cut long and straight on top and cropped close around the ears, fell in wild profusion and bounced when she was dancing. She had found those bounces effective in generating tips, and even when she was in street clothes, she tended to toss her head, as she did now, leaning down to the right rear passenger window as it buzzed down.

The lights came on briefly in the rear passenger compartment. No one was there.

She looked up toward the driver; he was watching her in the rearview mirror, and when he saw the curiosity on her face, he turned and smiled. "Hi," he said.

"Hi!" she said.

"Want to go for a ride?" he said.

"A ride? Yeah! Sure!" He punched the automatic button to unlock the doors, and she bounced into the backseat, still smiling.

He drove through to the far side of the parking lot, then swung out onto Laurel Canyon Boulevard and up toward Mulholland. "Don't worry about your car," he said.

"Oh, pfoooph, that little piece a' junk?" She had never before been embarrassed about what she drove. "I—"

Whatever she was about to say, it wasn't important; she forgot it as soon as he flashed another smile at her in the rearview mirror and said, "I saw you dance. You're terrific."

"You liked it? Gee, that's so great." She felt like a schoolgirl.

"You tired after that work? I mean, you were working hard. Lotsa guys wanted to give you money." At the mud-wrestling club, which wasn't a club at all, but a place where ten dollars would buy anyone admission, patrons held up bills to draw over the girl and her spotter, a man wearing a referee shirt and a whistle, whose job was to collect the money and make sure the patron did not touch the girl while she undulated her body an inch from his nose and breathed hotly in his ear. The spotter got ten percent, and that night he had kept her busy. At the club she was proud of her status as one of the top earners of tips, but here, in the backseat of this limo, she wondered if that made her seem cheap. She popped up into the middle jumpseat, and as the car headed up the hill toward the crest, she rested her forearms along the padded top of the open partition and smiled at him. "I'm so glad you got to see me," she said. "But you must not a' liked me, you didn't offer me any money! I'd'a remembered."

"I just said you were terrific." His lip curled again into a smile.

She tried wildly to think of something to say, but then he asked, "Want to see the lights from Mulholland?"

"Sure! That sounds great. After I've been dancing for so long I like to kick back, ya know? I mean I can dance *forever,* but I mean I like to take a break, ya know?"

"Yeah," he said. "I know."

At the crest of the mountain they swung west, following the snaky road past the gated drives of the estates, peeking in and out of views of the valley carpeted by lights. He reached over and gently squeezed the fingers of her right hand, dangling beside him. She grinned and squeezed back.

They passed a couple of turnouts, but at one there was already a van parked, and for some reason he didn't choose the other. "Hold it, hold it, *I* know a place that's really private," he said, and he swung into a parking lot beneath eucalyptus trees, their trunks blank stalks in the moonless night.

"What is this place?" she asked.

"It's a kinda office for the police department," he said, swinging the limo around the back of the ugly metal building. "Nobody'll bother us here."

16

Josh Lannon had learned to overcome fear and anger. He knew he had acquired that ability, and the knowledge gave him strength.

Whenever he faced something that could make him afraid, he reminded himself of his past successes in overcoming fear.

Things that frightened most people did not frighten him. Fighting didn't scare him. He had had many fights growing up, and he was not afraid of fighting. The fear of fighting was the fear of humiliation, and he had learned not to feel humiliated by physical combat, win or lose. But it had been many years since he had been in a real fistfight. Now people knew who he was. In the old days they thought he was too pretty to be much of a fighter, and that gave him the first punch, and with that advantage most bar fights were a foregone conclusion.

Acting used to give him a jolt of fear. Walk out in front of the cameras for the first day of shooting, and you find fear. His first times he feared they wouldn't like him—*they* being the director, the other actors, the studio, the public. Later he feared the critics. Then he feared the audience again as he tried to change his image. In time he had experienced the disapproval of all of them, and had found that disapproval varied according to success. What a backward thought. Success should be the finding of approval, but Josh Lannon had discovered —as his mother had seemed to know about her perfume

—that people approved whatever they perceived was a success.

But acting had become an automatic process for him, devoid of risk or fear. Now what Josh Lannon feared was the writing of a screenplay. When he sat down in his garret, his stomach trembled.

His garret was a room in the tower of his Tudor house. The octagonal room—he had designed it personally—was paneled in three-hundred-year-old wood from an inn near Stratford-upon-Avon, and though Lannon knew Shakespeare had been dead for over a hundred years when the inn was built, the actor could sit in this dark oak womb and bask in the light from the leaded windows, and feel the ghost of the Bard.

But Josh Lannon knew that reverie alone would not get a script written. To do that he had to get words onto the page, and each time he switched on his word processor, he knew that what he would write would expose his talent and his intellect, his instinct and his wit, to the judgment of others, and that was enough to make Josh Lannon shudder.

His garret helped him with that fear. The word processor itself, and the telephone hidden behind the doors of the Dutch mahogany cupboard beside the pine tavern table that served as his desk, were the sole modern intrusions. The room was illuminated only by candles and sunlight; the fixtures and furnishings were antique, right down to the frames of the medieval sketches. The screen of his word processor glowed in soft orange letters, and at first it looked forbidding; but Lannon knew how to push himself, and as he began to pile lines of those letters onto that screen, he could fall into a trance in which his imagination would flow and all the realities he had known would be left behind, and his spirit would spread its wings on the rising currents of his fantasy, and glide into flight.

He could write for hours, once he had escaped that way. But this day he knew he would not get that much done. He needed to sit awhile alone in his room, to clear the smell of his mother from his mind.

He sat in the stillness, stared at the orange screen, and breathed.

A tap sounded at his door. A tap—that was all it was, and Lannon knew who this had to be. "Who is tapping, gently tapping, tapping at my chamber door?" he said.

But instead of seeing the humor and answering "Nevermore," his visitor just said, "It's me. Josh."

Okay, Lannon thought, so the cop isn't an artist. But he's polite, and he had the sense to tap, not just knock his knuckles against the door and barge in. Mike Rowe possessed a polished gentility like no one else Lannon had ever known. "So come on in," Lannon said.

Rowe walked in reverently, and Lannon looked at him from the remoteness of his reverie and tried to think of an image that captured Rowe's gentleness. He saw Rowe in feminine terms; it struck him that Rowe had come in like a retired schoolteacher entering a foreign museum that she has spent all her savings to visit. The gentle cop looked at the musty leather chair pads, the ancient brass sconces mounded with the drippings of countless candles; he looked at Lannon, smiled, and said, "Wow."

"Have a seat," Lannon said. Rowe looked doubtfully at the chair in front of the desk table. "Yes, there."

Rowe sat, and seemed not to know what to do with his hands. First he crossed his arms across his chest, then uncrossed them and folded his hands in his lap. Then he interlaced his fingers, and his thumbs did a dance of their own, taking turns pressing into the center of the opposite palm. "I'm out of my league here," Rowe said.

"Out of your league? Why?"

"I don't know anything about writing. Of course I'm not writing; you are. I just don't think I know anything that will help you."

Lannon laughed. "You want to know why I think you'll be a great resource for me? Because I've talked with lots of street cops. I know their macho bluster and their bad habits. But nobody's ever portrayed the true police *leader,* the one who has to fight with budgets and policy and management and gets the job done on that level. That's what you can tell me."

Rowe shook his head, but smiled. "Then you're going to have to ask me questions. Because I don't have any idea where to start."

Lannon was about to open with a question on Rowe's training, just one of those tell-us-how-you-got-here questions to get him rolling.

Then the door banged open and in walked Lannon's mother.

"Joshy," she said, shaking her head sadly. "Joshy."

Lannon's butler was behind her, blinking furiously, not knowing what to do. "She came in the gate, right after I buzzed through Mr. Rowe, sir. I couldn't stop her—"

"That's all right, Contardo," Lannon said quietly.

"Should I telephone the police, sir?" the butler said.

"Go to hell, you little beaner!" Tami Lannon said quietly.

Lannon glanced at Rowe, whose eyes were as tall as candle flames. "No," Lannon said, smiling. "We won't need to call the police."

The butler retreated back down the stairs, never taking his eyes off Lannon's mother.

"You think you can pull that stuff with me?" Tami said.

"Mother, meet Mike."

Tami never took her eyes off her son. "You come to my event and you make a joke out of it by trying to turn it into your event?" She put her hands on her hips, and though Mike Rowe may not have caught it, her son Josh saw that she was posing, displaying her figure, striking the posture of anger before . . . yes, there it was, the trembling lip of hurt, the tears welling in the eyes—though not spilling down. "All I ask for is a little help. That's all I ask. And I have to stand outside your house and wait for somebody else to come, somebody you'll *let in*, before I can get in myself."

Lannon frowned as he tried to figure out the purpose of this visit, and then his face cleared. "I see. It's something else, isn't it? You want me to come to some other appearance. Right? Isn't that right?"

She dropped the tremble and the tears. She almost smiled. " 'The Today Show,' " she said. "They'll set up the satellite feed, you don't even have to go to New York."

"When?" Lannon said.

"Day after tomorrow. I've already told them you'd be there."

"Then tell them I won't be there."

"Joshy . . . baby . . ."

"I'm having my publicist call every editor and program director in this country to tell them I have nothing to do with your product, and nothing to do with you."

"Bastard."

"Whore."

"You can't say that to me."

"I just did. And if you don't leave right now, I'll call Contardo. And he'll have you arrested."

Her face looked very pale beneath the dyed black hair and the powder and the cherry lips. She walked down the stairs, and they could hear the door slam as she left. Echoing back up through the stairwell, they heard the latches as the butler locked her out. Lannon knew Contardo would watch to be sure she went out the gate.

Lannon looked at Rowe. "Well, Mike, you've met my mother."

"Josh, I . . ."

"You don't know what to say. Of course you don't."

Lannon stood, moved around, and sat down again on the front edge of his desk table, just above Rowe. "What you saw, with my mother, was ugly to you. But it was beautiful to me. Because I've never been able to talk to her like that, without blowing up, without losing all my composure. That was one of the most beautiful moments of my life." He paused. "And you helped me achieve it."

Rowe was looking at him, not sure he could let himself believe what was happening.

But Lannon was sure. He could read people. Especially when it came to the things that ruled them, the things that bubbled below the surface and wanted to take control. He leaned down and kissed Rowe on the cheek.

Rowe sat blinking. His heart clattered in his chest, blood sang in his ears and warmed his face. He heard a pounding . . . but it was at the door, not inside his head.

"Mr. Lannon!" a voice came from outside the door.

"Go away, Contardo," Lannon said, his voice steady, his eyes locked on Rowe's. "If my mother is giving you trouble, then call the police."

"But it is the police who are calling, sir," Contardo said. "They say Mr. Rowe left them this number. I told them you were busy, but they said to tell Mr. Rowe that they've found another body."

17

Cully was awake. She lay there in the warmth of her bed, thinking about the glass tube with the chemicals and her urine in it, sitting on the tile shelf next to the toilet in the bathroom.

The phone buzzed once. She knew before she answered it that they had found another body.

This one had been dumped in the parking lot of the Hollywood Bowl. Workers arriving to put up tents for the circus scheduled to go on that weekend found the body, and John the Baptist and Cowboy Cooley had done the honors.

Cully climbed out of bed and dressed without going to the bathroom. She wasn't putting it off. No, she just felt like getting dressed first.

She brushed her teeth. She brushed her hair. Finally she put her brushes down and turned to the tile shelf.

The small mirror was tilted so you could see the tube from the bottom. A brownish-red ring was distinctly reflected there. Clear as a wedding ring. Circle of fire.

All the detectives showed up for this one. The morning "homicide huddle," as Rowe called it, was held in the center of the Can, where the arched roof was the highest and the inverted gymnasium lights glowed like cold distant suns. They sat around a conference table that was actually three card tables shoved together, and their metal folding chairs were stiff and chill.

For this meeting Rowe had brought in a pudgy guy with hair that bristled straight out from the roll of fat on the back of his neck. Rowe introduced him as "Dr. Blein, the department's chief consultant in criminal psychology." Blein didn't look at the huddle of detectives, but rather leaned forward over his potbelly and studied the bowl of his pipe as if it were being introduced instead of him. "I've asked him to study the files of this case to see if he can help us out," Rowe told everyone.

Cully glanced at Ridge. What files of this case? He shook his head, not knowing which files Rowe was referring to, since they had created none. Since Bellflower was downtown going over budget details at the city's accounting offices, Cully assumed Rowe had gone into Bellflower's office and taken the reports out of his desk. Bellflower wouldn't care; he left his office door, his desk, his car, his locker in the dressing room, all unlocked. Bellflower was not particular about his privacy.

Rowe asked if there were any new leads on the case or any "new directions developing" since yesterday afternoon.

Cully told them about the lead with the silver limo. "We've got lots of checking still to do," Cully said.

"Silver," Blein said, listening thoughtfully to the sound of the word from his ample lips. All the detectives watched him as he squinted at nothing and nodded several times. But the pause produced no insight, at least none that he was ready to share.

"Yes, doc?" Frazier said. "Does silver have anything to do with hating tits?" Blein swiveled his head slowly and blinked at Frazier, who grinned and said, " 'Cause I've got a silver car, and I was just thinking it's definitely the wrong color for me."

A bunch of the guys laughed too loudly.

"Gentlemen!" Rowe said sharply.

"Sorry, Deputy Chief," Frazier said, still grinning.

"I just never liked shrinks. I never liked nobody who thinks he's smarter than I am."

Morris leaned closer to Frazier. "That's why you don't like nobody. That's why guys like to bite you."

Everybody laughed except Rowe—and Blein, who frowned quizzically and said to Frazier, "People bite you?"

Frazier glared back at him and snarled, "Sure! Didn't you ever hear the term 'eat me'?"

"That'll be all of that, Detective," Rowe snapped. He turned to Cully and Ridge. "Why don't you share with Dr. Blein your theories on this case. What motivates our killer? How does it happen?"

In a calm, flat voice Cully started to lay it all out, how they figured the killer would first scout the girl when she was on stage in the strip joint. He gets the girl into his car, a limo. She goes without consulting her pimp first, so something about him makes her feel safe. She knows him from somewhere, she trusts him because he's got enough money to have an expensive car, we're not sure. Maybe they flirt a little, have a drink, smooch a little. Then he asks her to get into the bag. That's the trickiest part, that's what he'd have to sell her, without alarming her. But once she's in, he hits her. He beats her to death. Then he does the mutilation and dumps her. Maybe the killing happens at his place, so there's no exposure except in carrying the body out again.

Blein nodded as if amused.

"What?" Cully said, with a sharpness that surprised her. She found herself irritated at the way Blein's upper lip slid out above his lower in an amused little pucker; and she was irritated even more at the thought that maybe she was just like Frazier.

"I just find all this conjecture amusing," the psychologist said.

"If you can figure this out better and faster than we can, it would be a big help to all of us." Cully's eyes were focused on Blein. "Might be a big help to the next victim, too."

"I know all of you are doing the best you can." Blein managed to make it sound as if their best effort was pretty feeble.

"So what do you figure?" Cully pressed.

"The killer is full of hostility."

"Do tell," Cully said.

"He had trouble with his mother, and the attack on the breasts is a symbolic act of hostility against femininity and nurturing," Blein went on.

"You go down to the morgue and look the dead girls in the face and tell them what happened was only symbolic," Cully said.

"I see," Blein said, looking at Cully and nodding sagely. "You identify with the victims."

Cully's jaw hinged down like a bulldog's, ready to bite, but it was a laugh that burst from her throat. "Of course I identify with the victims! Somebody's out there beating them to death and carving their breasts off!"

"Detective McCullers . . ." Rowe said quietly.

"Look," Cully said to Blein, "I don't mean to be hostile. I just need you to give us something we can *use*. Like why he seems to choose women with breast implants. Why he cuts them out. Why he leaves the note. Tell us that."

"Those are tough questions," Blein said.

"No shit," Cully said.

To his credit Blein did not retreat. He gained points with all the detectives by dropping some of his haughtiness and telling them plainly what he knew and didn't know. "The main problem for me concerns his sexual rage," the psychologist said. "Mostly because I'm not sure the rage is sexual. At least not entirely. It's linked to sex, there's no question about that, but it's different, too." He paused, and found all the detectives were listening. "Sexual rages have an element of repression, and the eruption of violence is like a dam bursting. In the killer's psyche the violence is identified as self-defense. But this individual, so far, has got me baffled. The level of violence is consistent with the sexual repression sometimes associated with homosexuality, but homosexual killings rarely involve mutilation of a woman. Yet all the evidence gathered so far suggests the killer is a man. Maybe we're looking for a bisexual, or someone who is omnisexual; by that I mean someone for whom sex is not a directly biological drive but is rather an image, something connected to power and control. I tell you frankly I'm not sure.

"The murders themselves are intensely violent, but the mutilation and preparation of the body afterward is calm, tightly controlled. Whoever this is has the ability to unleash wild emotions and then take charge of them immediately afterward. And then, with the note, he justifies what he has done."

"He left a note?" Mike Rowe asked, frowning with surprise, his mind so far from the business around him that he had forgotten, or perhaps had never really heard when he was told about it.

"Well, yes," Dr. Blein said helpfully. " 'False and Misleading Advertising.' I think it pertains to—"

"Excuse me?" Rowe said, cocking his head toward the psychologist.

" 'False and Misleading Advertising,' " Blein repeated, speaking distinctly and then waiting to be sure the deputy chief had heard him. "It's a strange message, certainly, especially as it seems to pertain to the surgical enlargement of the women's breasts. But maybe the killer doesn't mean it about the breasts. The note nailed to their foreheads is like a sign from the Middle Ages when someone was hung or burned at the stake: murderer, thief, traitor, and so on." Blein stopped. "You tell me what it means."

"It's a detail we need to keep secret," Cully said, looking around the room to be sure everyone caught the reminder. "When this case really hits the press and the nuts start lining up to confess, we need to be sure that only the real killer knows what he wrote on the notes. Right?"

"Right," Deputy Chief Rowe said quietly.

Blein paused and then said, "I'm sorry. I wish I could be more helpful, and I promise I'll keep trying. But right now I feel I ought to tell you this: the killer exhibits classic symptoms of a condition I call Transitional Compulsive Rage—TCR. This killer has murdered three women in the last four days. Other serial killers don't murder with such frequency. This one will kill repeatedly, as he has already done—perhaps even a woman a day for a while. And then his rage could subside for a period; a few months, or even a few years, before it reappears. It may even have occurred in the past, though I am inclined to believe Detective Ridge's assessment as indicated in these notes that the first woman you found was in fact his first victim. In any case, I can tell you this: if you do not catch him in this cycle, you may not catch him at all."

The meeting broke up slowly. The detectives had natural appetites for the hunt, and this case was like waving juicy meat in front of hungry dogs. They lingered around their chairs in half-conscious hope that Rowe would come to his senses and assign some additional experienced backup for this rookie female who had drawn the assignment; but as the deputy chief walked away without a word, they gave up and drifted back to their desks and the routine cases that occupied them: Tooda and Boom-Boom to clean up the incident of an undocumented Mexican who died outside a barroom with the jagged end of a broken bottle ground into his guts, and Banana and the Baptist off to write a close to the tale of a recent arrival from Oklahoma who decided his new California girlfriend ought to know how to load and use a shotgun for personal protection, and in one of their practice runs got his head removed by the double blast of a twelve-gauge.

Dr. Blein sat in his chair, sucking on his lips and staring at the concrete floor, permanently stained by the decades of shelter the Can had given to paving equipment and materials. He sighed, as if to exhale the last scent of tar in the air, then stood and started toward the door. He had almost reached it when he heard Ridge say, "Excuse me, doctor."

Blein turned to look up at the tall detective who had followed him. Blein was shorter than people imagined him to be when he was sitting and had now to cock his head back at an awkward angle, for Ridge was close and had spoken in a low voice. "Yes?" Blein said.

Ridge stayed close, but stooped his head so Blein didn't have to look up so much. "I just wanted to ask you about something. I wasn't completely sure about what you were saying."

"Nor was I," Blein said, smiling. He had worked with Ridge before and knew him to be a man who valued an expert's opinion, as long as he could make sense of it. As long as the expert's opinion made sense.

"You know how we work, doctor. We look for categories. It never solves a case for us, but it helps organize our machinery. I need to ask you about the issue of homosexuality. I feel like we talked around it a little, and I need a more specific opinion. Are we looking for somebody gay here? Somebody who may have a record of crimes as a gay—or against gays?"

Blein's eyes, watery behind his glasses, held Ridge for a moment. Then the psychiatrist, accustomed to confronting emotionally charged issues head-on, said, "You know I'm gay, don't you, Detective." It was not a question.

Ridge said, "It's not an issue with me, one way or the other."

"Yes, but you know," Blein replied. "The others here don't know. In past cases, when they've brought me in to analyze a homosexual killing and the rest of the people here start in with the fag jokes meant to advertise the kosher quality of their own sexual orientation, I've noticed you watching me, to see what my reaction was."

Ridge smiled. "I just noticed you, noticing whether anyone else thought the jokes weren't funny."

"You're saying you don't care if I'm a fag."

"I'm saying I find your work excellent, doctor. And helpful, even if I don't always agree with it. And as for your sexual orientation, as far as I'm concerned it's just so much the better if your personal experience helps you rule something out, or rule it in."

Now Blein smiled. "Maybe you ought to be a politician," he said.

"When you have a southern accent," Ridge said, "you learn to deal with people's prejudices, and their assumptions about your own." Ridge grinned.

Blein found the smile infectious, and matched it; but then the doctor's smile faded. "You want a gut feeling. One not as cautious as my professional opinion? Okay, I'll give you one. You're not looking for a gay killer here. These murders have nothing to do with homosexuality, not in a true sense—and that's not gay rhetoric, that's straight from my gut. The killer may have some gay orientation, but if he does, it's just one more thing that he's suppressed, and *suppression,* that's the key to this. This person feels that who he is cannot come out. That he lives a lie. And he blames other people for that. It's his victims who are false and misleading, who make him live the lie. He's attracted to them, too; he wants them, and your detective colleagues were right to challenge me on my Freudian connection of the exaggerated breasts to the mother. I'm not sure what the core attraction is, if it's the implants themselves or big breasts in general, but it's surely a fascination with the overblown, the extreme."

Blein took a breath, sighed again, started to speak,

then frowned. He looked straight at Ridge. "You want to know who to look for, Detective? Look for somebody who's repressed. Somebody deep in the closet, in *every* sense. Somebody who hides the truth, even from himself."

"You think the guy who's doing this may not even know he's doing it?"

"I can't say for sure. But there's a lie at the heart of this, and the murder comes from the lie. He wants to confess. In some ways he wants to be caught. But that lie he tells himself—that he doesn't really do it, or that he's not wrong to do it—will always win out."

"He's gonna keep killing till we stop him," Ridge said.

"I don't know, Detective," Blein said. "Such judgments aren't mine to make." And with one final look at Ridge, he walked out into the sunlight.

Mike Rowe headed straight into his office, muttering an order to his secretary to hold all his calls. Cully saw Ridge follow Blein, and as the other detectives moved away she took the opportunity to walk back to her desk, where she telephoned her gynecologist.

She told the receptionist that she needed an appointment right away. The receptionist said that Cully's regular doctor was at the hospital doing an emergency cesarean, and after that he had a full day of surgeries scheduled, and then he was leaving for an international symposium in Europe; but they had a new associate who could see her, would that be all right?

Cully had put off the pregnancy test for so long; buying it, taking it, reading it. But now that she knew its results she felt desperate to see a doctor. She told the receptionist that if her regular gynecologist was unavailable, then someone else would have to do.

The receptionist said that Dr. Finnerman was available right now. How quickly could she get over there?

Cully hung up and saw Ridge still talking with

Blein. She scribbled a note that said she had an appointment to get her teeth cleaned and would be back shortly; she left the note on Ridge's desk.

She drove down through Coldwater Canyon into Beverly Hills, thinking not of her pregnancy but of what Ridge had said about her cowboy boots and the jeep she had bought. Her other car, the BMW—it just wasn't right for her, that was all. Sure, she had loved it once and it had been the first new car she had ever owned, but it wasn't her, it was yuppie, and besides that it had gotten shot up. Sporty cars tend not to hold their value when you put bullet holes in them. She was just trying to be practical, that's all, to be a cop. Wasn't that what she was? What was it with Ridge, why did he have to say all that? Come on! When Ridge thought about it, he was bound to realize how mean-spirited it was. She could have said the same kind of thing to him—that he wore those finely tailored sport coats and pressed shirts and gentlemanly ties because he was trying to escape the redneck that lurked inside him. How about that?

She realized she was driving too fast, jerking too sharply around the canyon curves and plunging the jeep side to side as the open wind raked her face. She backed off the accelerator, but still she held her phantom conversation with Ridge.

He only liked her one way; maybe that was it. He wanted her to fit into his image of her, which was his image of himself. Refined and controlled, in those business suits she used to wear to hide her figure. If that's what it was, it was pretty lousy, laying it all on her, telling her that the jeans and boots and flannel shirts just weren't *her*.

She reached the medical building on Wilshire and swung into the underground parking lot, then took the stairs to the lobby level. She punched impatiently at the elevator button, stepped back, glanced at her watch, and punched again. The lit numbers above the elevator doors showed that a car was on its way down, but then it stopped on the floor above. Cully turned away, starting to pace, and saw herself reflected fully in the mirrored end wall of the lobby. She studied herself, from her tousled hair, to the shapeless shirt hanging too far off her shoulders, to the jeans and the boots, which made the jeans bunch around the knee and look even baggier than they already were.

Why did Ridge have to be right about everything?

And as Cully stepped into the elevator and rode it up to the twelfth floor, she thought, And what would Ridge say about this?

The doctor's group had redecorated their waiting area in a warm pink, with Laura Ashley wallpaper and overstuffed chairs and sofas. When Cully arrived, three other women were there, and all three were taut with pregnancy. Cully gave the receptionist her name and sat down in one of the armchairs, feeling like an intruder within its warm and womblike embrace.

Scattered about the coffee tables were various issues of four different parents' magazines, along with one battered copy of *National Geographic*. Cully chose the *Geographic*.

She flipped through and saw an article on the Shakers. It was a topic as far from pregnancy as she could find, and that was the one she started to read.

She found she had made an ironic choice. The article focused on the impending extinction of the Shakers, the group of "Shaking Quakers" who experienced ecstasies of the spirit that caused their bodies to tremble. They were dying out; less than two dozen were left. They lived liked the Amish but had taken separation from the world a step further and practiced celibacy. It didn't seem surprising that they would die out if they didn't reproduce, but they had never depended on procreation; in the past their numbers had been maintained, had even grown, because people came to them and found with them something they were willing to give up everything else for.

Cully read that people like television stars and New York art collectors were starting to buy up whatever they could find that had been made by Shaker craftsmen now that they were on the verge of extinction. The Shakers considered work a kind of prayer, an act of worship. So no matter how small the task, from sweeping a floor to making a spool to hold thread, they did it beautifully.

They reminded Cully of Thomas Ridge.

Okay, she thought, the Shakers are ultimately ridiculous. A person has to have priorities. The world is full of the important and the insignificant, and anyone who doesn't discriminate a little is going to be mindless, and aimless.

So Cully reasoned. But something about this article haunted her.

She thought of her father, a cop who had died in the line of duty—not from a gunman's bullet but from bottled-up desperation. She thought of Ridge's brother Bobby, who had been a minister and died at the task—not a missionary eaten by cannibals, but a local pastor eaten by his own frustrations and despairs. Cully was an appreciator of simple beauty, and she could understand stars and New York sophisticates wanting to own the Shaker handiwork—because who of us wouldn't like to do his own work better, and doesn't need inspiring? And also because art is a kind of pointing out of the beauty we have missed, and anybody who can find beauty in the smallest task is someone who can touch every one of us.

So no wonder they could once flourish, even though they were celibate. And what did that say about the world now that they were dying out?

It was the kind of world that the other women in this room were bringing children into.

Cully couldn't think of that. She forced herself to focus on the article again.

But her mind wouldn't stay on the pages. In the picture of a lone slender man sitting in a stark house of worship, she saw Ridge. She knew Ridge sometimes thought of his own work as a kind of prayer. He couldn't pray on his knees; Cully had never seen him try it, but instinctively she knew it wouldn't work for him any more than it would work for her. His mind analyzed too much, the way he analyzed the motives and incentives of anyone who had come into contact with a victim in one of his murder cases. But these Shakers presented another idea: work was prayer. You did it with love and passion.

Cully thumbed through the pages, studying the photographs. She came across a portrait of the Shakers' founder, a woman who had lost four children. The woman had gone through a period of tremendous despair and emerged from it preaching that bliss and salvation lay in putting away worldly things.

Well, no wonder, Cully thought. Four children? What unimaginable pain. The worst thing Cully could imagine was to lose—

She slapped the magazine shut and tossed it onto the table. The woman across from her, so pregnant she couldn't cross her legs, glanced up from her magazine for a moment, then lost herself again in some story about child care and bliss.

Every victim I ever see was once the baby of somebody, Cully thought. But you can never dwell on that, Cully; not if you don't want to end up like your father.

Maybe that's what this is, maybe I shouldn't be thinking at all.

She knew homicide detectives aren't supposed to think, any more than surgeons are. A doctor has to look at the person under his knife as a system of viable tissue that he is trying to make more viable. If he thinks of the flesh below the blade as part of a human whole, with unique and desperate emotions, his hand will tremble and he cannot do his job.

But she had come to believe Ridge's heresy among professional police officers: to be the best detective possible, one must understand the full humanity of everyone involved in a crime—the victim, the killer, and the person doing the investigating. That is, yourself.

The trouble was, doing this could make the job agony. Cully knew cops could grieve for victims. On a bad day they could even grieve for killers. But once a cop began to grieve for himself, like her father had when he began to drink himself to death, his life was finished.

And she knew what Ridge would say about the Shakers, and their belief in work as prayer. He'd say that sometimes your work has been lousy and you fight to improve it. Sometimes you've done your best, but it seems insignificant. But the ultimate outcome of your work is not up to you. And since you never know how important your work is, you can only do it as beautifully as you can, and offer it up to God, mysterious and unseen, as the best you can do. If that was faith, then Doubting Thomas Ridge had it.

Sitting there in that office, with the pink chairs and rugs and the wallpaper so new it still smelled of paste, she knew she loved him. She was not the brooding, spiritual person he was; at least she tried not to be. She wanted to avoid all those internal arguments, and that was why she wanted to be a cop. Out there on the streets, things were simple. I feel this, I do it. I see this pimp, I despise him, I will kick him in the groin and kill him if I have to, but I won't have to because he knows I'll do it, so he won't make me.

But Ridge made her feel that she was the same kind of person he was. How? Why?

Because she loved him. She loved Ridge and she had slept with him and it was not just a separate physical event. He made love like—well, like a Shaker would make love, if sexual intercourse were on their approved list of things you gave your whole self to and lost yourself in and experienced a joy of the spirit so great that the body shook in ecstasy.

Now there's a thought to boggle your brain. . . .

"Ms. McCullers," the receptionist said, "Dr. Finnerman will see you now."

Dr. Finnerman, it turned out, was a woman, a slender brunette scarcely older than Cully. She was a sharp mix of pretty and plain, with short bobbed hair and bright brown eyes behind horn-rim glasses, and Cully liked her immediately. When the doctor asked how she was doing, Cully said, "I'm pregnant," and she saw no judgment in the keen eyes.

"You've done an in-home test," Dr. Finnerman said. "Let's do one that's a little more accurate, just to be sure, and then we can talk in my office."

The nurse ran a quick test and it confirmed what Cully knew. She showed her into Dr. Finnerman's office, a corner room with potted ficus trees screening the sunny windows. Dr. Finnerman was studying Cully's file. When Cully took a seat on the sofa, Dr. Finnerman left the file on her desk and came and sat in the armchair beside her.

"Is this your first pregnancy?"

Cully shook her head. "In college . . ."

"You had an abortion."

Cully nodded.

"Scarlet, that's such a terrific name. Do your friends call you Scarlet?"

"Uh, no. They call me Cully."

"Cully. I like that, too. Well, Cully, I assume from the look on your face that congratulations are not in order."

"No. I guess not," Cully said.

"Have you already decided how you want to handle this pregnancy?"

"Yes. I want an abortion."

Dr. Finnerman nodded. "I've just looked through your file, and everything there shows you're completely healthy. There's no medical reason why a termination of this pregnancy should have any impact on your options for the future."

Cully nodded, and chewed on her lip, and kept her eyes on her hands and her hands in her lap.

"Cully, I try not to volunteer any advice unless I'm asked for it. But if I might make an observation . . . you don't look entirely at ease about this."

Cully felt tears rolling down her face. They surprised her, even though she felt them there; she had thought she would be able to hold them back. She sniffed hard, laughed, and rubbed at them with the back of her hand. Dr. Finnerman pushed a box of tissues closer to her on the side table, and Cully snatched out a couple.

"You aren't married," Dr. Finnerman said.

Cully laughed for some reason she didn't understand and said, "No."

"Do you want a baby?"

"I'm not married."

"That isn't what I asked you."

Cully paused. "I haven't thought about it. I just mean . . . I can't have one. Not right now."

Dr. Finnerman nodded, and took a moment before she said, "Then I want to tell you something. It's a way of looking at things. It's strictly my own and may not apply to you at all, but I'd like to tell you."

Cully looked up from her wad of Kleenex and nodded. The doctor had her undivided attention.

"Every twenty-eight days," she said, "your body produces an egg. That egg has the potential for life in it, when one sperm out of the several million that are present during sexual intercourse unites with it. Life is a miracle. And there is no more beautiful miracle in all of life than the birth of a baby. Now what is in you right now is not yet a baby. It's a fertilized egg. It may become a baby and it may not; nature itself aborts one pregnancy in four, and nobody knows why. All I can tell you is that every egg in you has the potential to become a child."

The doctor seemed to Cully to want to go on; but she stopped there, and Cully knew it was because if she went any further, she would be advising Cully which choice to make and she wasn't going to do that. Cully took a deep breath. She said, "I don't think this one should become a baby."

"All right," the doctor said. "I'll tell Dr. Knowles and have him schedule a procedure as soon as he returns."

"If it's all the same to you, I'd be more comfortable having you do it," Cully said.

"All right," Dr. Finnerman said. "The soonest I can do it is next week. I know that seems a long way away, but it won't hurt you to have a few days to be sure of your decision."

They stood and shook hands. "Thank you," Cully said.

The doctor smiled and escorted Cully to the door. Before she walked out, Cully turned and said, "Do you have children?"

"No," Dr. Finnerman said. And after a short pause she added, "I can't."

On her way down in the elevator Cully felt a silence at her center, like she had just cried on the shoulder of a friend.

And then she wondered, Would Dr. Finnerman have said anything different if I had told her I'm in love with the man who caused me to be here today?

18

Cully wondered how she was going to keep it off her face, at least until she told him. She wanted to say it first: "I'm pregnant, Tom, and that's why I've been acting the way I have." She at least wanted that much chance, to say it her own way, before he looked at her and read her for himself.

It might be easier if she was sure she wanted to tell him at all.

It would be easier not to tell him. Just take care of it herself. Did he have a right to know? That question felt wrong to Cully; it wasn't a question of his right over her body; if she felt a man had rights over her body just because she had made love with him, then she would never have sex with any man—at least that's what she told herself. The thing was, with Ridge she hadn't had sex, she had made love, and that was what nagged her. She knew he was wondering what was wrong with her. She knew the way she was acting—snapping at him, not looking at him, not responding when he wanted to talk about the future—was gnawing at his insides. But how was she going to tell him?

She couldn't tell him, because she knew what he would want. He would want that fetus to become a baby. Their baby. And she wasn't ready for that.

Cully parked out under the eucalyptus trees and walked toward the Can, watching her boots kick slowly through the flat brittle leaves blanketing the dirt of the lot. She felt as frail as one of those leaves, parched by the sun. Press these leaves and they dissolve into dust; press her, and she felt she would dissolve into tears.

Suddenly she stopped. Parked in front of the Can was a silver limousine. She was five feet from it, had almost walked right into it. Its back windows were blacked out; the sight of it chilled her. It looked deadly, dark, and cold as a hearse. The one window she could see through, on the driver's-side door, showed there was no one at the wheel; but as she moved around the rear of the limo she saw a man in a tuxedo leaning in at the open rear window of the door on the Can side of the car, talking and laughing with someone in the rear compartment. She assumed this man in the tuxedo was the driver, but it was not until he had looked up and grinned at her for several seconds that she recognized him. "Louie!" she said in surprise.

"Hellooo, Meez Detective MeeCullers," Louie said, a smile like piano keys lighting up the brown Mexican planes of his face. Louie had pale scars here and there, from his days in Mexican prison and his time as a bounty hunter for bail jumpers; but the sheen of his clean-shaven chin and the luxuriant shine of his jet-black, slicked-back hair said just how much he was enjoying his new nonviolent career working for the limo company. He was a friend of Ridge's; he had helped Ridge and Cully with surveillance on their last case, and she hadn't seen him since.

"It's great to see you!" she said, and uncharacteristically for her, she hugged him.

"Ooo, my God, will you marry me?" Louie said, turning his cheek to accept her peck there and squeezing her shoulder gently in that blend of flirtation and decorum that Hispanic men, both rich and poor, use so well.

Ridge stepped out of the back of the limo. "Hi," he said.

"Hi," Cully said.

"I thought we ought to do our reconstruction."

"Yeah," Cully said. "Good idea."

Ridge pulled his nine-millimeter pistol from the holster tucked beneath his left armpit and handed it to Louie. Louie flashed the ivories again, said, "You two don' do notheen I wouldn' do," and headed toward the new concrete shooting range Rowe had built for the detectives on the back side of the Can.

Cully, left alone with Ridge, was silent, and Ridge waited, wanting to ask her where she'd been and giving her a chance to tell him; but she turned and ducked into the limo. Ridge followed, and closed the door behind him. Louie had left the limo switch on full auxiliary power; Ridge pushed up a button on the door and the window closed with a hum and the soft whoosh of a tight seal.

Cully had slid without thinking into the main rear seat of the limo, so Ridge had slipped into the smaller seat facing her. He said, "So . . . you want to get started?"

She frowned at him for a moment and then her mind clicked into gear. "Oh. Yeah. I guess I should get out, huh?"

"Whatever you want to do," he said. "But I figured maybe this time you'd be the girl and I'd get to be the man." She gave him a look and climbed back out of the car as he moved over into the place she had just occupied, the place where the killer was likely to ride, if in fact he was using a limousine to pick up his victims.

The reenactment of a crime—Ridge liked to use the word "reconstruction," pronouncing it with an extra southern emphasis on each of its syllables—is an essential element of a homicide investigation, especially one in which the methodology of a murderer was unclear. Cully had practiced from the files of actual cases while she was preparing for her detective's examinations, but she had never gone through the actual process, and she found herself jittery at doing it with Ridge. She knew she could face the details of the killings themselves, the pictures in the MULHOM folders she had seen lying on the rear seat. But doing this with Ridge was another matter. Whatever they did together, he tended to sense more than she was ready to tell him; and what was going to come out between them now, in a session of intimate role-playing?

She shut the door and stood back from the car a few steps. He lowered the window and looked out at her face. Their eyes locked.

"I . . . don't know," she said.

"Don't know what?" he said.

"How far away from the car she'd be. Is she standing out on the sidewalk on display, waiting for a customer to spot her and pull over, or has she already made some kind of contact with him, so she's expecting him when he pulls up?" Cully thought a moment. "My guess is there was some kind of preselection. Clarence seemed to think there was, in Maggie/Porsche's case. And neither one of the girls seemed to be the drug-addict variety of street hooker. These girls had the money to finance boob jobs, and their gigs as strippers gave them a chance to stimulate business. I think this last piece of business came to them before they were just standing on the street."

In the shadows inside the car Ridge nodded. "Makes sense," he said. "Both our victims were pretty, unusually pretty for hookers. Their looks are somehow part of the selection process. If I'm the killer, I can't really tell how you look out on a street at night."

The role-playing was a surprising process; taking up the physical positions of the people involved in a crime, and using as many props as were available, gave a detective unexpected new angles, and Cully, glancing toward the vacant front seat of the limo, said suddenly, "Ridge. We haven't talked about the driver. What about an accomplice? If he uses a limo, his driver's got to know *something*. Maybe everything! Or maybe not everything.

But he's involved, right? Maybe the driver assists in the initial contact with the girl!"

She smiled at Ridge, smug with her insight. Ridge nodded, frowning. He looked impressed.

"Of course," Cully said quickly, seizing the initiative, "maybe he doesn't use a driver. That would be clever. An accomplice would open up a whole area of potential exposure for him, and this guy feels too smart and careful for that. And . . . there weren't two men involved in the intercourse; I saw the lab results on the sample Roger took from victim two, and the genetic tests showed the presence of only one man's fresh sperm." Cully stopped and thought a minute. "You know," she went on, "maybe this guy *is* a limo driver. We should have thought of that; we'll have to check it out."

Ridge nodded again, gravely. Then he turned, pulled a computer printout from the folder beside him on the seat, and said, "Uh, yeah. I took the liberty of requesting a list of all the registered chauffeurs in Southern California. I thought we could cross-check it against our records on sexual crimes."

He put the list back into the folder and Cully nodded tightly. Ridge always acted so casual about having thought of something first, and that matter-of-factness pissed her off almost as much as it did that she had not beaten him to the punch. "Then let's just say she gets into the car," Cully said sharply, and snapped open the limo door and slammed it behind her.

Ridge closed the window again. Cully, sitting now in the seat opposite him, said, "It's hot in here," and turned and shoved her torso through the large opening between the driver's and passengers' compartments. She twisted on the limo's ignition and the air-conditioning came on automatically.

As she settled back into her seat Ridge said quietly, "I guess the privacy partition would be closed."

"Yeah. I guess it would," Cully said. "You want to go ahead and close it?"

"Sure." Ridge reached to the panel of controls set into the limo's ceiling, above where the main passengers sat. As the partition hummed up they found themselves awkwardly alone in a cool, shaded cocoon. "I . . . guess you'd be over next to me. If you were my date for the evening," Ridge said.

"Right," she said, and ducked over to the rear seat, positioning herself against the opposite window.

"Why are you mad at me?" Ridge said.

"You mean . . . me the hooker? Or me Cully?" she said, knowing which he meant.

"You Cully. If it's because I requested a computer list—"

"It's because I should have thought of it, Ridge. It's because I've got too much on my mind. It's because you always think of things first and you're a smug asshole."

Ridge nodded in exaggerated smugness and said, "Yeah. You're right."

"You see you're an asshole."

"I see I always think of things first."

She laughed in spite of herself. He was always able to do that, exaggerate whatever he had done to make her mad, making her laugh at herself. She had never been able to do that, not with a man. But Ridge always seemed to delight in her pride, to love her competitiveness. The ego games he played with her were his way of flirting. She shoved him on the shoulder. "Prick," she said.

"I don't think the hooker would call him that," Ridge said.

"No," Cully agreed. Her gaze fell on the folder on the tufted upholstery between them. Two photographs had slid partially out when Ridge had replaced the computer list, and Cully glimpsed half of one victim's face, the way they had found her, beaten to death and with the note nailed to her forehead. That one glance was enough to sober Cully up. Her lips pressed into a pale line. "Back to business," she said.

Ridge nodded and opened the folder. He carefully laid out two rows of photographs on the burgundy carpet at their feet—one set of the first victim and one set of the second. The photo lab had numbered the pictures in blue felt-tip marker, each number preceded by an *A* or a *B,* and without the letter code it would have been difficult to tell one girl from the other. Ridge took a breath, studied the arrangement of photos, and said, "You notice how similar they are, in their mutilation and the final position of their bodies?"

Cully nodded. "So we've got an attention to detail and a compulsion toward order, which younger serial killers don't usually display."

"You've been studying your criminology books again."

She nodded.

"That's good. So the experts that study this kind of thing say our guy's maybe thirty-five years old. And if we—"

"Thirty-seven or eight."

Ridge stopped and looked at her.

"Not thirty-five," she said. "Thirty-seven or thirty-eight, that's what the FBI book said."

"Oh," Ridge said, miffed. To Ridge, experts were fine as long as they agreed with him and didn't get in his way. "So if we—"

"I read it last night," Cully said, watching his eyes so she could see them jump. "That's why I'm so sure."

"Thank you," Ridge said. "That's very helpful. So now. We ask ourselves if the killer brought anything to the crime."

"The bags," Cully said.

"The bags," Ridge agreed. "The bags and the nail. And something like a hammer to drive the nail through her skull."

"You think that means he planned everything? From the very first?"

Ridge thought and shook his head. "I still think the first one was completely unexpected for him. He may have hit the first one just once, and knocked her out and thought he may have killed her, then put her into the bags and really went to work on her as all the anger and fear that Dr. Blein talked about took control of him. If my theory of the first one being a surprise is accurate, then he may have killed her at home, where he would have all the things he used: the bags, the knife, the hammer and the nails, the stuff to make the sign."

"Then for the second," Cully said, "he knew what he would need, and took it all with him, if he didn't want to take the risk of doing the second murder at home." She looked around her. "He could even do it here, in the limo, if he trusted his chauffeur enough. If he *had* a chauffeur. I wonder if he might even have been able to do the killing without the chauffeur knowing." She looked at the overhead console. There were separate controls for the front and back compartments. "If he had music playing," she said.

Ridge switched on the radio. It was set on a popular rock station, and he left it there, dialing down the volume so they could have the element of authenticity but could still converse comfortably. "Good," he said. "That's good. Oh, by the way, I had another conversation with Dr. Blein. He said something interesting: 'There's a lie at the heart of these murders.' The killer may not always be aware of what he's doing. He may blot it out, or his mind may be sick enough that he can just forget what he's done or about to do, put it out of his mind, like you would a headache. But that doesn't mean he can't premeditate."

"No," Cully said. "He'll react from his gut, like an animal. He'll be a lot more dangerous."

"That's what I think, too," Ridge said softly, his words lost in the music.

"Did you bring some bags?" Cully asked.

Ridge pulled two bags from the cabinet in the console of the limo, next to the liquor cabinet. "The lab has come back with their report on the bags, too. The canvas one is naval issue, and they're not that easy to come by, the army-navy stores don't have them, but a lot of sailors do, and they can be special-ordered by anybody from the manufacturer. We're having the manufacturer FAX us a copy of their shipping lists. The plastic bag is from a major trash-bag maker and can be bought in any supermarket."

"I guess we better figure out how you get me in them," Cully said.

Ridge hesitated. "Why don't I play the victim this time?" he said. "It might be interesting."

"Don't be ridiculous. I'm not afraid to get in the bags. I just want to know what you say—what *he* says—to get me in them."

"Okay," Ridge said. "Okay." He took a breath, and she noticed that it was a little shaky. Their eyes met, and in each other's gaze they saw the effort to put aside who they were and take up the roles of killer and victim. It was a moment both intensely intimate and scary. "I think they . . . we . . . make small talk," Ridge said. "No matter how much or little we know each other. You just got in the car and we break the ice."

Cully crossed her legs, settled into her seat cocked toward him at an angle, and pulled her shoulders back so that her breasts would push out seductively, in the posture she imagined a hooker might take. When there were so many blanks to fill in, the role-player has to make some guesses, and it always helped that all good homicide detectives had big egos and the biggest egos made for the biggest hams, and the biggest hams were the best role-players. "So talk, baby," she said seductively.

"Well," Ridge said, a bit more self-conscious than

she was, and having more trouble getting into his part, "I guess we could talk about why I chose you."

"Yeah?" she said. "And why was that?"

"I like big knockers. And you got 'em." He said this like he was getting into the role; but then he hesitated and looked embarrassed.

"What is it?" she said, more like herself.

"I think he would reach over and feel them."

"So feel them, Tom. You've felt them before."

"Yeah," he said. She settled into her pose again and he reached over and brushed her right breast, then slid his hand across the flannel of her shirt and stroked his hand across her left one. She saw what she thought was a flicker in Ridge's eyes. Did he notice something? Did her breasts feel fuller to him than they had before? They felt fuller to her. Oh my God, she found herself thinking again, what if he guesses my secret before I can tell him?

But Ridge sat back slowly in his seat and blushed a little. "Are you gettin' turned on, honey?" she said in a low raspy hooker voice.

He didn't answer. He sat there in thought.

"What now?" she asked, Cully again.

"I'm wondering when he notices the implants. Is it when he feels her breasts? Or did he pick up on them visually, when—if and when—he saw her dancing before?"

"That's something I've been meaning to ask you," Cully said. "Can he tell? Just by looking?"

"Not with her clothes on. I mean I don't see how he could differentiate between naturally and surgically well endowed, if the girl was dressed. But undressed is a different story. They might be a little too perfect. They might not bounce the same. And a natural breast would be a little softer and hang a little differently, especially if it was as large naturally as the store-bought ones are."

"I didn't know you were so expert on the subject."

Ridge sniffed and averted his eyes. "Well, men, you

know, notice such things." He sniffed again. "I understand breast jobs are so common now that it's almost
impossible to find a stripper or mud wrestler in Hollywood who *hasn't* had one. It's the girls without them
who look different. You've got to understand how few
women have the . . . you know . . . *outstanding* figures like you have naturally. Okay, let's go on." He
changed his voice to get back into his role. "So, baby—"

"Wait a second. What about feeling, do they feel
different with the implants? I mean I've known some
women who've had them done, but I never actually felt
them."

"I don't think he could feel an implant through her
clothes. Not unless he squeezed really hard. If he
touched her bare breast, he might notice the difference,
if he had much experience."

"What would the difference be?" she wondered
aloud.

"Well, gee, I—I mean I guess the breast would feel
very full and . . . nice and firm, I don't know."

"What do you mean, you don't know? You talk like
you've felt them. Breasts with implants."

"Well . . . Yeah, you know. At Tucker's bachelor
party, last year. They hired a couple of girls to go
around topless, in this banquet room where all the guys
were standing around drinking beer. And both these
girls had, I mean, these amazing figures. And they were
pretty open, I mean, you know, and I figured they had to
have implants and I wondered how breasts like that felt,
and I, you know—I felt 'em!"

"These girls were, what, hookers? At a cop party?"
She was frowning.

"Come on. Of course they were hookers."

"And they were there like . . . looking for business?"

He was getting tired of being defensive. "They were
there for humor. For entertainment. But yeah. Sure.

They were there to do business, if any came their way. Now, could we get back to—"

"Did *you* sleep with them?"

"What!"

"Did you sleep with them?"

"Of course not!" Ridge said, so irritated that she believed him instantly.

Her tone changed. "Well, I mean, it would be perfectly understandable if you had. You were single and lonely. It would have been natural."

Ridge slapped both hands to his face. "I don't believe this! No. It would not have been natural. Look, I'm no saint, okay? But I've never gone looking for a hooker. And never let one find me. No matter how single or lonely I am. Not that I don't understand why some men do—but I always thought it would just make me feel more single, and more lonely. Okay? Are we clear on that?"

"I don't know why you're so angry," she said angelically. After a pause she added, "There's not a jealous bone in my body." She smiled, and Ridge found himself grinning at her.

"Okay," he said. "Now. He wants her in the bag. I want you in the bag. What do I say?"

Her mind focused again; she got back to their somber business. "I think . . ." she said. "I think you just . . . tell me to do it. I'm a hooker. I get paid to do all sorts of weird things."

"Get into this bag," he said.

She picked up the plastic bag, unfolded it, and wiggled her way into it. It was more difficult than she expected; she had to reach deep into the bottom of the bag to spread it out with her hands, then take off her boots so the heels wouldn't catch on the plastic and tear it. The bag was full of static and clung to her clothes. But finally she wriggled into it, sitting out on the carpet between the two limo seats, and brought the plastic up to her chin. "Now what?" she said.

"Get into this second bag," he said, opening the canvas sack and helping her tilt herself over so that she could slide her feet over the second bag and he could bring the sides of it up around her. He pulled both bags closed over her head for a moment. "Now how do you feel?" he said.

"Uncomfortable," came her muffled voice. There was a pause. "And really scared." She pulled the bags down and popped her head out, taking a greedy breath. She knew it would have been several minutes before she ran out of air, but still she had felt as if she was smothering.

"Come on," he said, trying to help her out of the bags.

"No. Wait," she said, and stayed there a moment, feeling what it was like inside those bags, letting her eyes slide around to the pictures of the dead girls, the look of the inside of the limo, and finally to Ridge's face. "It isn't pleasant in here," she said. "In fact it's really confining, and sticky, and claustrophobic, and un-pleasant. And I'm thinking that no hooker would be anxious to do this."

"Then why does she do it?" Ridge asked.

She paused again and stared at Ridge, without seeming to see him. "Because . . . because he asks me to. And I'll do it. Not for the money. Money wouldn't make me do this. Not if I'm a hooker. If I'm a hooker, I pass on the customer who wants me to do this."

"What if I force you? What if I threaten you? With a weapon? With this knife I have?"

Cully shook her head. "That won't do it," she said decisively. "I'm a *hooker*. I've seen a lot of ugly, danger-ous shit. You pull a knife on me in this car, and I fight. I jerk open the door, I scream. I know enough to put up my fight before I get into a bag. Before I get tied up and confined."

They sat there frowning.

"Unless . . ." she said.

"Unless what?"

"Unless I want to. Unless I really, truly want to do this. To do anything you ask me."

"Why would you feel that way?"

"I'm not sure. But let's try something for a minute." She slipped quickly out of both bags, leaving one inside the other for convenience sake, and took up her place again, beside him on the rear seat. "Okay. Tell me to get in the bag."

"Get in the bag," Ridge said.

"Sure, baby," she said. "Anything you say." Without hesitating, she climbed back into the bags and pulled them up above her ears, gripping the top inside edges of the bags to close herself off. "Now how do you feel?" she said through the double layers of plastic and canvas. She waited a moment and, hearing nothing, let the bags drop down past her neck again. She found Ridge looking at her strangely. "What is it?"

"I don't know," Ridge said. "It's weird. You'd think it would be exactly what a man would want, to have a beautiful woman say, 'I'll do anything you ask me, anything you say. All you have to do is ask.' The weird thing is, it doesn't sound good. It doesn't sound . . . it doesn't sound . . . *intimate*. It seems the opposite of that. Like a complete act. And to see the woman carry it out, and instantly do something that's so . . . so humiliating, and even dangerous . . . it's kind of disgusting. And . . . and . . ." He shook his head.

"And what?" she said.

"It kind of makes me mad," Ridge said.

Louie had fired a dozen clips on the new MULHOM range, and had then cleaned and oiled Ridge's pistol at the bench behind the shooting line. He was just putting the rags and gun oil back into the racks when they appeared in the doorway and he stepped out into the sunshine with them. "How'd you like the new range, Louie?" Ridge asked.

"It's great," Louie said. "I don't get to shoot much anymore, and I suck. Hey, listen, a guy came in while I was here, big black guy. I tol' him I was with you."

"Bellflower," Ridge said.

"I tol' him I was the leemo driver, and you and Deetective MeeCullers was doin' the reconstruction."

Something seemed to be bothering Louie, so Ridge asked, "He didn't hassle you, did he?"

"No, no," Louie said. "I jus' kinda worried like I was takin' his spot or somethin'. You know how guys are about the shooteen range, everybody likes his own bay, like everybody picks his favorite pew in church, or his favorite stool at a bar."

Ridge nodded and grinned. Cully could see why Ridge liked Louie so much. An educated, ethereal southerner and an earthy Mexican-American ex-con, and they thought alike. "So were you in his spot?" Ridge asked.

"I don' think so. There was lots of casings on the floor on the far left, and on the right, where he shot. I jus' took the middle."

"Then you were okay."

"I jus' don' like cops thinkin' I'm outta place here," Louie said.

"You're with us, Louie," Cully said, and gave him a squeeze on the arm. They walked back toward Louie's limo.

"Hey, you guys know what? Somebody else has had a stretch up here."

As people do when someone says something that at first makes no sense, both Ridge and Cully nodded. But then she said, "Huh?"

"A stretch," Louie said. "A limo. Somebody works up here drives one."

"No," Ridge said, puzzled. "I don't think so. Why—"

"These tracks. Right here." Louie kicked at the dirt beneath his polished shoes. Tire tracks, made on a night when rain had liquefied the dirt around the Can, were molded and baked into the path that skirted the shooting range and led around behind the Can. "Those are limo tires," Louie said.

"You sure?" Ridge said.

"You know me, Meester Ridge," Louie said, with his piano-key grin. "Louie is limos, limos are my life! That's a tread design they use only for limo tires. They just started making it. Costs twice as much as regular tires and ain' a damn bit better, but some dumb shits buy 'em cause some dumb shits'll buy anything." Louie laughed and they walked on to his limo.

"Thanks, Louie," Ridge said, and shook Louie's hand. Cully reached up again and pecked him on the cheek.

Louie handed Ridge his pistol back and said, "Sweet piece, Mr. Ridge." And then he winked, as if he wasn't talking about the nine-millimeter automatic at all.

19

They walked into the Can together, both preoccupied. Thoughts were clogged like gridlock traffic in the center of Cully's brain. Making conversation to get herself back on track, she said idly, "Who would drive a limousine up here?"

"I don't know," Ridge mumbled. "Louie gets excited and starts wanting to play detective." Ridge seemed unsettled, and Cully understood why; she felt the same way herself. Reenacting a murder, with the man she loved, left her with a cold and perverse feeling, as if she had licked a gravestone. As if to wash the same taste from his own mouth, Ridge stopped at the cooler, where a five-gallon bottle of mountain spring water perched inverted over a valve and belched bubbles up through its fat body as he filled a cup for her first, then one for himself. He bumped his paper cone against hers, lifting up a silent toast, and they drank simultaneously, in communion with the living and the holy.

They moved to Cully's desk and sat down, she in her chair, Ridge on the edge of the desktop, distant and withdrawn. Maybe he was just lost in thought, but he seemed to her to be waiting for her to tell him something, and Cully thought again about her trip to the doctor, and she wondered how she was going to tell Ridge what she had found out there.

"Something's bothering you," he said. "What is it?"

"Huh? Oh. I guess . . . it's all the guessing we

have to do. I mean the crime seems so crazy, but we know it makes sense to the killer. Some awful sick passion drives him, and we're trying to track him logically, with lists and computers and arrest records, rational things like that. I mean, here, we've got a list of chauffeurs, to check against the list of known sex offenders. The offenders list against the list of limo owners . . ."

Ridge seemed to have thought of all this before, many years before. He knew that killers lived in their own reality, and that detectives had to pierce that reality to catch them. That was not what sapped his strength. It was that he had been trying to talk with her, and now he was giving up.

She started to tell him, just blurt it out. Instead she found herself saying, "Doesn't this make you sick? Doesn't being around killers just make you want to vomit?"

Ridge nodded. All the life was gone from his eyes. It made her feel guilty. She ought to tell him; she had to tell him. She half hoped that he knew already, and yet she knew that he did not.

Working all that day on their various lists, they came up with nothing. "This won't get us anywhere," Ridge said at last.

"Let's not give up," she said.

He looked up and his eyes held on her, and she could feel that everything out of her mouth was significant to him, as if he were searching for something solid to plug up a hole in his heart. She looked away first.

"We're going at this the wrong way," he said. "This killer's not going to be on any of these lists. I didn't understand that at first, but I do now. He's never been caught before, for anything."

"How do you know?"

"His . . . I don't know, his *contempt* for the victims. And for us. It's like he thinks he's untouchable. He can defy us with the sign, he can arrange the body, he's not afraid. He believes he's above us all in ruthlessness and cunning."

Cully nodded. "So you think instead of getting closer, we're getting farther away."

He said nothing. She went back to her lists.

After two more hours of working through Cully's silence, Ridge wanted to ask her what was wrong, just come right out and ask her if he was repulsive to her. But that's a question that no man can bring himself to ask.

Mike Rowe stayed in his office for four hours, then drove home, his fingers tight around the steering wheel, its leather covering turning slick in his hands. His chest was hot inside his shirt; his armpits had turned into a tropical bog. He struggled to drive, to keep his mind on the road.

He reached his house, pressed the remote control above the visor, and his garage door opened automatically. The engine's sound amplified as he pulled inside; his senses were oversensitive to every detail. He got out of his car, punched the closer on the wall, and watched the door swing shut, closing with a hollow bang.

He stood for a moment inside the garage, feeling safe. Then he left by the side door and began the walk up the fifty feet of serpentine flagstone to his house. He had almost reached the backdoor when, from behind the false bucket-and-windlass well that Cecilia had imported from England and planted with flowers, out stepped Josh Lannon.

Rowe stopped all at once. After a dumb moment his mouth was able to whisper, "Josh!"

Lannon smiled easily. "Sorry I startled you." He was talking quietly, with all the easy innocence of a boy who has climbed up a trellis to have a midnight roof conversation with a school buddy. "I was just thinking about this murder investigation you're into, and it's really got me going. I mean it's fascinating, isn't it!"

"Yes," Rowe agreed.

"I mean, I can't get my mind off this, and—I'm sorry if this seems insensitive to you, Mike, for me to be thinking of this professionally. I mean, *you're* thinking professionally, of course, but your profession is to save lives and I'm just creating entertainment. I had a screenplay thought. But after you left I was stewing about some of the stuff you've told, or I've overheard from your guys—I mean, mutilations! Notes nailed to their heads! And that phrase. 'False and misleading advertising!' And I wondered: is it possible that whoever is doing this is not aware of it? I mean, could anybody who does something so extreme as to kill another human being have a side of his mind where the murdering part lives, and have that side be separate from the peaceful part?"

"You mean . . . could there be a killer . . . who doesn't know he's a killer?"

"Fascinating, isn't it?"

A light went on in the thin bathroom window above their heads on the second floor. Lannon slapped Rowe softly on the shoulder. "Sorry," he said softly, "when my imagination gets going, it's hard for me to turn it off. I just had to come by and ask you. I'll probably be thinking about it all night."

Rowe was thinking about it already. "If it were possible . . . for a killer to hide his identity, even from himself, then . . . anybody could be the killer."

Lannon grinned and bugged his eyes like a mock Halloween mask. "Great screenplay, huh? I'll see you tomorrow. Sweet dreams."

Lannon walked quietly into the shadows. Rowe stood at his backdoor until he heard Lannon's Range Rover pull away.

He moved quietly upstairs to his bedroom suite, showered, and then lay down on the bed. Warm and dry. Safe. This physical feeling overwhelmed all others; the panic was illusion, this peace was real. In this comfort his conscious mind leaked away, and Mike Rowe, efficient manager of task forces and the political processes that establish them, receded from the world, and a single nightmare took his place. In this dream he was younger than the daytime Mike Rowe was, and more muscled than the Mike Rowe of the waking world had ever been; thickly muscled, like a gorilla. He was pressing his hands, palms forward, along the ground, turning up earth like a farmer might till the soil. Only the earth was not dirt but bodies, naked female bodies. They did not bleed, they were not hurt; their bodies were shiny and taut, and he strained them through his powerful fingers and yet he could not feel them. All he could feel was something sticky on his hands. It had no color, but it smelled terrible.

All night long, in his dream, the young dream animal deep in Mike Rowe's brain kept pausing in his plowing and sniffing at the stench upon his hands.

20

In the morning Mike Rowe telephoned Josh Lannon and asked him to meet for breakfast. Lannon's voice sounded groggy, but he claimed to be wide-awake and "ready to ride this day toward the sunset." He had been working on an idea for a cowboy picture and was trying to come up with some authentic-sounding yet fresh western expressions. Breakfast sounded like a great idea. He wanted to do some shooting up at the Can. They could meet at that place that served the great pancakes, in Studio City.

Rowe was already there, in a back booth beside the windows, when Lannon arrived. Lannon was wearing jeans, tennis shoes, a scuffed leather jacket, and a Dodgers cap pulled down low, almost to where the new glasses framed his dark eyes. He spotted Rowe and walked steadily back to him, his eyes straight ahead and cast down as if to keep anyone from looking at him directly. But anyone who did would recognize him right away; he had worn exactly the same clothes when he played an undercover cop in his last picture.

He sat down opposite Rowe and flashed his fabulous smile. "Mornin', pardner," he said, and chuckled at himself. In the clear light of the new day from the window to Lannon's right, Rowe could see the wrinkles around his eyes, and the color in the famous face looked shallow, almost yellow.

"You look tired," Rowe said.

"You oughta see yourself," Lannon said. "I've been working on a script and have to get up early to write. What's your excuse?"

"I just haven't been sleeping well."

"You got a lot on your mind."

Rowe couldn't argue with that. The waitress, a sixty-year-old Hall of Famer in the waitress leagues, came and tossed a couple of coffee cups on the table. In her other hand she gripped the handles of two pots. Rowe decided on regular, Lannon took decaf. Rowe said he didn't have a lot of time so she should take their order now; he wanted scrambled eggs and sausage. Lannon ordered four grapefruit halves, water, and a small stack of pancakes—no butter, no syrup. The waitress left without needing to write anything down.

"She didn't recognize you," Rowe said with a smile.

"Either that or she doesn't give a shit," Lannon said. Then his eyes grew more attentive, holding on Rowe's pale, strained face. "This murder thing is eating you up, isn't it?"

"Yeah," Rowe said. "Yeah, it is."

"Well, you hang in there, pal. You got a rough job."

Rowe frowned down at his coffee and tried to think of what he wanted to say next. But again Lannon beat him to the punch.

"This has been a tough couple of weeks for me," Lannon said. "I had a meeting with the new head of the studio. You know how old this guy is? Twenty-seven. They say he's a genius. Of course the last two guys in that job were geniuses, after my films came in and made the stockholders a billion in profits. But now it's a new genius."

Their food came, four plates and saucers balanced on two soft liver-spotted arms. Lannon looked down at one of his grapefruit halves and took a spoonful of it. For a moment he seemed to have lost interest in his story, but then he went on. "This new genius, he didn't ask for the meeting. I didn't know that till later. My lawyer set up the meeting, so I went. And when I got there, this kid's door was open, and he's talking with one of his other executives, another guy in diapers. And the new head kid, he's saying he wants the word out that the studio's not making any more cartoons. *Banger* is over."

Banger was Josh Lannon's most famous role. He'd done several movies as that character, though in his last several films he had tried to live down the violent macho image that had been his legacy of those films. "And then," Lannon said, "the kid invites me in. We meet. He's nice, we're smiling. Then he says, 'You wanted to see me?' And I said, 'I thought you wanted to see me.' Then he says, 'Your lawyer thought we ought to meet, since your deal with us is expiring.' I tell him yeah, sure, I'm sure we can come to terms. And then this little . . . this little . . ." Lannon gritted his teeth. "This little gentleman looks at me and says, 'He didn't tell you, then. We don't want to renew your deal.' "

"Josh, that's crazy," Rowe began.

"My last picture lost money for them."

"It made millions, I thought."

"It took in fifty million at the box office. It cost more than that to make and advertise. Get it?" Lannon said, digging into his grapefruit again. "They think it's over for me."

Rowe didn't know what to say. That seemed preposterous to him, but then the whole business of celebrity and glamour and receipts calculated in multiples of one hundred million seemed preposterous. He wanted to help, to understand, to lend some kind of support. He tried to read Lannon's face; and what he saw was not pain. Lannon was angling his face toward the booth across from theirs. A younger waitress, a woman in her early thirties, was waiting on the couple there, and when Rowe looked, he saw that her glance had stuck on Lannon's face; she seemed to be asking herself if it really could be he. And when Rowe looked back at Lannon, he saw that Josh was keeping his face turned toward her just enough so that she could be sure.

In that moment Mike Rowe saw Josh Lannon in all his helpless vanity.

What he felt for Lannon at that moment was not disgust, nor was it pity. It was not jealousy either. It was grief. Josh Lannon had fought so hard to fill up a great reservoir of fame, and he had just begun to feel the first few drops of a leak that would inevitably become a flood, draining it all away. Lannon was smart enough to know that.

Rowe felt privileged to share the great man's pain, and he grieved for him. He knew that, without fame and adoration, the Josh Lannon he knew—full of confidence, warmth, charm, and good humor—would die.

21

After the too obvious attention of the waitress, Rowe said they ought to head up to the shooting range; he laughed as he suggested it, saying he thought it might be the only quiet place they could find. And yet he was sincere; he thought the soundproofed concrete room where they fired their pistols would be a far better place to finish their conversation than the coffee shop where it had begun. Lannon said he could come up to the Can and fire a few clips before he had to get back to work on his screenplay.

So they drove up the mountain, Rowe cutting through the morning traffic in his new sports car and Lannon slipping his Range Rover across Ventura Boulevard to gas up at the service station opposite the coffee shop before following up Laurel Canyon.

Rowe never liked waiting for anybody, and he especially disliked the idea of Josh Lannon arriving to find him standing around and killing time until he should arrive. Rowe wanted Lannon to see him as decisive and independent; he sensed that the moment Lannon felt him to be a clinger, someone whose life had no center of its own but revolved around a relationship with a celebrity, then that relationship would change forever.

Knowing that made Rowe more determined to confront Lannon with the question that still lay between them like a cold snake slid between two lovers in a warm bed.

Rowe unpacked his pistol and slapped in a fresh clip. He clipped a new bull's-eye onto the overhead wires and ran the target back to twenty-five feet. Still no Lannon. Rowe began squeezing off rounds.

His first three shots were out of the black, and when the fourth one didn't catch the target at all, just made a soft pop inside his ear mufflers and vanished like he had never fired it, Rowe knew how rattled he was. He hadn't missed a target that badly in years.

He advised himself to slow down and relax. He tried to step out of himself and look at his own body as if he were standing fifteen feet away, where the target was, and could see himself standing there in the ear mufflers and the protective glasses. He saw himself raise the pistol and point it at the target—at himself—and he thought, That's it, that's how I see everything; I'm a sensitive person in a violent world, and all this violence is getting to me.

He squeezed off several more shots, and the whole group found the black, the last one cutting the center of the target.

There you go, he thought. Just pay attention, and everything will come easy to you, just like it always has.

Rowe pulled the trigger again, but his gun would not fire; it was empty. Had he shot that many times already? He set the pistol on the stand in front of him and quickly stripped it down, practicing for speed. The nine-millimeter automatic came apart into four pieces; he could disassemble it in less than five seconds and have it back together in less than ten. He liked to do this. He knew the time was coming when the other MULHOM detectives, not just Bellflower, would start using the range, and when the detectives were there watching him shoot, he would take his pistol apart right there in front of them. Then they wouldn't consider him just another administrator and not a *real* cop.

He felt a hand on his shoulder and spun around to see Lannon. Lannon grinned at his jumpiness and said,

"Whoa! It's me!" Rowe didn't hear the words behind the mufflers, he just saw them mouthed.

Lannon took the second pistol case Rowe had brought him, as he always did, and unpacked another nine-millimeter. He loaded and fired off twelve rounds. But then he didn't check his target. He punched the button and brought the target back, but he barely glanced at it. Lannon was distracted, too, and seeing this made it easier for Mike Rowe. He took off his ear mufflers and blurted, "Who is it, Josh?"

Lannon frowned at him, then slid his own mufflers off his ears to hang like a collar around his neck and said, "What?"

"Who is it?"

"Who is what?"

"The leak inside MULHOM."

Lannon looked at him steadily, the chocolate eyes focused and unblinking; then he turned away from Rowe into his shooting bay, pulled the empty clip from the butt of his pistol, then shoved a fresh one in.

"Come on," Rowe pressed. "Somebody, one of my detectives, is telling you things that nobody outside of MULHOM is supposed to know. I want to know who it is."

Lannon's eyes flicked toward him once, in a glance both charming and sheepish. "I don't know anything, Mike. All I know is what you've told me."

"No," Rowe said. He could feel he had seized the initiative; he felt vigorous and natural and good about himself. "That phrase, 'false and misleading advertising.' That was secret. So I started thinking it might have been me, I must have told you, without realizing. I've been going crazy, wondering if I was saying things I wasn't aware of. It's been driving me nuts, trying to remember when I first heard the phrase, and when I first could have said it. And then I realized what it had to be. Somebody else in MULHOM is leaking information to you."

"Leak," Lannon said, his face twitching unpleasantly at the word. "You make it sound like I'm a reporter or something."

"No, come on, Josh, I understand your curiosity. And I'm not mad at you about it. And look, I know I'm putting you in an uncomfortable situation here, because you wouldn't want to betray someone else's trust any more than you'd betray mine. But this is important, this is my unit! I've given direct orders about leaking—to anybody! And okay, don't call it leaking! But somebody told you something essential about our investigation. I understand it was a juicy fact, one of those great little pieces of cop atmosphere you love to collect, but still it was off limits to anyone outside the unit. And I want to know which one of my detectives it was."

"I don't know many of your detectives, Mike. Though I do want to, by the way."

"You're changing the subject. I want a name."

Lannon took a deep slow breath and let it out. "Don't get mad at him, okay?"

"I can't promise that."

"Then I won't tell you."

"Josh—"

"It was innocent, Mike! And you can't blame a guy, I mean, think about it. I'm a star! I know that doesn't mean shit to you, but it knocks some people over, and they say stuff to me that they wouldn't even think of saying to anybody else. And it's because they trust me. Think about it, come on. I'm not gonna get somebody else in trouble."

"But—"

"But nothing. You've gotta promise me you won't come down on him about this. I want you to promise you won't even say anything to him about it."

"I can't promise that!"

"Yes, you can. And you'll understand why, when I tell you who it is. You won't even be mad anymore."

"Who is it?"

"Len Bellflower." Lannon waited the slightest moment, watching him. "See? Hey. One of the characters I worked on in my last cop story was black—and what do I know about being a black cop? I thought Bellflower could tell me some good stuff, so I introduced myself and talked with him a little. Then when I needed some help with that promo thing my mother was doing, Len was one of the guys I asked to help me. When I called him about it, we talked a little about what he's been doing lately, and he was telling me about MULHOM and the new case you guys had, and he let the phrase slip. He probably figured you'd already told me. So come on, get over it, okay?"

Mike Rowe felt so silly. Silly, and relieved.

"Listen," Lannon said, "I've been wanting to meet some more of your detectives, but I can see that's a problem for you."

"No. It's not a problem. I mean . . . no, really, it's not a problem at all."

"Well, you know, you've just seemed to want to keep them to yourself."

"Josh . . . I haven't. Honestly. I've protected your privacy, and . . . and theirs . . . and the department's. But I certainly haven't wanted to keep them from you. Who would you like to meet?"

"I don't know," Lannon said. "It's not like I've got a list or something." He paused. "I'll tell you who I would like to see, though. The detectives who are in the lead for you, working the dead dancer case."

"Sure, that's no problem. I'll introduce you." Rowe had been holding his pistol through this whole conversation; he had forgotten it was in his hand. Now he tossed it onto the padded elbow stand of the shooting enclosure, made sure the gun was empty, and began to wrap it in its felt storage cloth; he could clean the pistol later.

Lannon began to put his gun away, too. "I don't really want to meet them. I don't want to intrude on their privacy either, like you say. And I appreciate your willingness to help me with my research, Mike, but I really do think it would look like I was taking advantage of our friendship if I started asking too many questions about an ongoing murder investigation. Maybe if I could just, like, see them. Observe what they were doing —from a distance, I mean. See how they are when they're under pressure, see how they go about it. That's all."

Mike Rowe had just felt his first flash of jealousy, and it was not a sexual or romantic threat that tweaked him, but something professional. He had not wanted another cop—any other cop—to be important to Josh Lannon. But now he was so relieved that his stomach fluttered.

They walked through the cinder-block corridor that connected the shooting range with the Can's shower and dressing area, and stored the pistols in Rowe's locker. "I really don't need to meet 'em face-to-face, okay? I just wanna see how they stand, what their faces are like. I want to pick up their body language. I need to see them, the way real guys are when they're in a real homicide case."

"McCullers isn't a real guy," Rowe said with a smile.

"Huh?" Lannon said.

"I mean, she isn't a guy at all. McCullers is a woman."

"Really. Hmm." The corners of Lannon's mouth went down, as if that fact ought to interest him but didn't. "Come on. Show me," he said.

With the mischievous air of a schoolboy showing a friend a forbidden adult secret, Rowe motioned Lannon over to the shadowy mouth of the locker room and pointed out to the desks a few yards away. McCullers was there, bending over her desk, and Ridge was beside her, peering at a second long roll of computer printout.

"Mmm," Lannon said, noncommittal. "She's a looker, isn't she?"

Rowe had long ago put Scarlet McCullers's physical appearance aside in his appraisal of her as a detective. He thought of her objectively: superb academy grades, superior test scores, highly motivated, and with a personal liability in the form of her father's record with the department, a liability that may have stimulated her tendency toward rebellion. This was the official line on McCullers, and Rowe bought it. Rowe more than bought it; he *wrote* it. Now he looked at the taut young woman again and said, "Yes, she is attractive, isn't she?"

"Who's the guy with her?"

"Ridge. Thomas Ridge. They call him Doubting Thomas."

"Doubting Thomas, that's great!" Lannon whispered. "Why do they call him that?"

"They all have nicknames; who knows where they come from," said Rowe, who had no nickname at all.

Lannon had pulled a pad from his pocket and was jotting notes. Rowe looked over at the pad and saw the words: *Intense. No wasted motion. No smoking no fidgets. Determined Relentless Pursuit.* Lannon lowered the pad and said, "What are they working on, do you know?"

"Of course I know, Josh," Rowe said. "They've found some witnesses who have mentioned a limousine, in silver, or gray. They have a theory that maybe whoever is killing the girls is somebody recognizable, because the girls get into the car without their pimps' permission. So they're going over the lists of limo owners, looking for names they recognize."

"Whew. Sounds like a lot of grind. I thought detectives were supposed to be brilliant."

"Mostly the work is an agonizing bore."

Abruptly Lannon looked at his watch. "I gotta go. Thanks. They look serious and dedicated. Real clean. I like that. The girl, she's beautiful, huh? I know actresses don't look that good. And listen, Mike, I hope you catch the guy. Charge him with plagiarism, huh? Who's he think he is, choosing my phrase to nail to the head of his victims?"

Lannon was gone and Rowe was back in his office before it struck him that Lannon had said "my phrase." Not a phrase Bellflower had leaked to Lannon, but *Lannon's* phrase. And then he realized that he had told Lannon about messages being left with the dead girls' bodies, but he had never said anything about the notes being nailed to anybody's head.

Had Bellflower leaked that information, too?

All morning Detectives Thomas Ridge and Scarlet McCullers worked; all morning Deputy Chief of Police Michael Rowe stayed in his office. Through lunch they worked; through lunch he stayed. No one noticed the slight separating of the closed slats of the venetian blinds that shielded the glass walls of his cubicle from the rest of the Can, or the wild, worried eye that from time to time peered out through that space. No one heard the pacing, the sudden turns back and forth across the concrete floor within that cubicle; no one saw the tortured man there.

But he noticed Ridge and McCullers, noticed everything about what they were doing, noticed them with a passionate devotion, as if they could deliver him from his torment. They would find an answer, and that answer would deliver him. Whatever that answer was; once they had it he would *know*. And during those endless, almost unendurable hours all he came to want was clarity, to be sure beyond all doubt whether the man he loved was destroying him and others around him, whether he had stepped through gates that promised heaven and found himself in hell.

At midafternoon there was a flurry of action around the desks of Ridge and McCullers that nearly brought Deputy Chief Rowe from his cubicle; but the activity of the other detectives who brought them messages and the phone calls they quickly began to make did not escalate into the fury that the deputy chief knew preceded an arrest, so he remained behind his screened glass walls. But soon after that first flurry came a second: more detectives hurrying up, more phone calls, this time with shouts and smiles, and this time Rowe emerged from his cubicle.

"What's up?" he said tightly, approaching the knot of detectives gathered around Ridge's desk.

Cully McCullers, in the center of that knot, stood up from the corner of the desk where she was seated and hung up the phone. "We found her car," she said. When Rowe frowned at her, his face strained and pale, he looked bewildered and angry, and she realized he was not up to speed with the rest of them. "The girl's," she said, explaining. "Victim number three. A couple of hours ago Malchek and Santana showed her picture to the manager—"

"Her drawing," Santana corrected.

"Yeah, her drawing," Cully said.

"McCullers had this brainstorm!" Santana fairly shouted to their boss. "Had a friend, this artist, do a great sketch. It was nothin' like the shit we'd get from our old guys, these pictures made the girl look real, man, alive, you know what I'm sayin'? And we found her, man, with that picture we found her!"

Cully, thrilled to have won the praise of the others, quickly added to Rowe, "It was volunteer work from a friend of mine, sir. She won't charge us. She came from work to do this third girl this morning—"

"Go on, please!" Rowe pleaded.

"Yes, sir. Sorry. Using the drawing we had made, we discovered the third victim's identity, and where she worked—a mud-wrestling place down in Hollywood. The manager knew the exact time she left work—he has them punch in and out on a time clock. And she owned this little red Nissan Sentra; that's what she was driving. So we put out an all-points on the car, and a few minutes ago John the Baptist found it—in the police impound lot. It had been towed away from the lot outside the coffee shop at Laurel and Ventura."

Maybe Tom Ridge noticed the deputy chief go a little more pale at that moment, for Ridge was the only one quiet enough and distant enough from the group emotion to have noticed Rowe's distress from the moment he joined them. But if Ridge did notice, he kept silent.

"A private contractor sweeps that lot three days a week with a small pavement washer. He did it this morning. And he remembers the car being there at exactly three-nineteen. We know she left work at two-forty-seven, and it takes ten minutes to drive from the mud-wrestling place to the coffee shop. That means she got there no sooner than two-fifty-seven. So now we've got a window, twenty-one minutes. We know that during those twenty-one minutes, right around three in the morning, the killer picked her up. There were only a handful of people at the coffee shop then, and they, or the waitresses on that shift, might remember something. Malchek and Santana are going back there tonight, or in the morning I should say, to check it out."

"That's all?" Rowe said.

Cully saw the disappointment in his face and realized that what the detectives took as a victory, a point of definite progress, a real sniff at the heels of their prey, was for their supervisor only a set of inconclusive details. "We are checking the car," she said.

"Let me know if you find anything," Rowe snapped, and turned back to his cubicle.

But once inside he began to sweat, and his torment began again. The coffee shop, at Laurel and Ventura. The exact place where Lannon had suggested they meet for breakfast that very morning.

At seven that evening Len Bellflower returned to the Can after another long day at City Hall. He was sorting through the piles of memos and reports on his desk when he looked up to see Deputy Chief Rowe.

Rowe looked around the rusty walls as if he had casually dropped by to see how Bellflower had decorated. He pursed his lips and nodded approvingly. "I like the way you're fixing it up in here," he said.

Bellflower, whose only contribution to the appearance of his office had been to screw to the metal wall a photograph of his son in the robes of his college graduation, thought Rowe was joking. "Yeah, I call my design style 'Early Deterioration.'"

"Say," Rowe said, "why didn't you tell me we have a mutual friend? I didn't know you two knew each other."

"Who?"

"You and Josh Lannon."

"Oh. Yeah."

"I understand you give him background for his cop movies," Rowe said. He wanted to sound casual, as if the only reason he was bringing this up was that he had discovered they had something in common.

"I did on one," Bellflower said.

"You're being modest. He tells me you're a great technical adviser. I approve of that, by the way, I think it's good for the department when our guys help the mass media be more accurate and positive about us."

Bellflower wrinkled his brow, as if uncomfortable with praise he felt he did not deserve. He puffed out his cheeks in puzzlement and sighed. "Maybe I was better than I thought," he said. "But if I was, you'd think he woulda used me again." When the deputy chief kept frowning at him, Bellflower added, "I mean when I bump into him we talk about the Lakers or the Dodgers or something, but he hasn't asked me a cop question for maybe two years."

22

She had studied tap dancing since she was four years old and ballet since she was seven. She knew every song in *The Wizard of Oz* and every line of dialogue, and Judy Garland and Mickey Rooney had replaced Shirley Temple on the throne of her dreams, and then Fred Astaire and whichever beautiful woman he was partnering with had taken their place. Her imagination of what a dancer should be had hardened there, at that pinnacle of the popular art.

She was thirty-seven, and there were women fifteen years younger who would have killed to have the body she had right now. The wrinkles she saw in the mirror, framed by the square row of clear glass bulbs, were a slow sad erosion of her hopes, but she had been worked on by the best makeup men in Hollywood. She had learned from them how to cover up anything; in a spotlight her face looked like it belonged to somebody twelve years younger. And her body . . . well, in some ways it was better than ever. She did ten aerobics classes a week. She worked out with weights. She dieted like a boxer training for a championship fight. The only thing she couldn't keep from sagging was her breasts, but that was okay, the doctor in Westwood, with two small baggies of silicone, had brought them back up to their teenage angle and hadn't even left a scar.

Her name was Suzie Kirkwood, but she had had three other last names, from the three biggest mistakes she had ever made with men. The first raced motorcycles. The second was an actor—at least that's what he told people at the restaurant where he waited tables for most of his adult life. The last was a karate teacher at the place she had taken classes, and he was the only one who had ever beaten her up. But he was gone now, too, out of her life, out, out, out for good.

But there was this problem with money. She had to pay the rent, and song-and-dance was dead in Hollywood. There had been a time, back in the seventies, when a dancer could earn a living in Hollywood. "The Carol Burnett Show." "The Andy Williams Show." "Sonny and Cher." They all used dancers. They all paid residuals when the shows went into syndication. But that was years ago. The car she bought with her last replay check from the Burnett show was ten years old now.

And Suzie Kirkwood had always earned a living. She had the body, she still had the face, and hot damn, could she move. So she went down to La Cienega, a boulevard that hits Sunset right at the base of the Hollywood Hills. As it runs down toward the L.A. basin it becomes fashionable, a place for art galleries and fine restaurants, and right between the sleaze of Hollywood and the haunts of *Architectural Digest* are a couple of blocks of entertainment for discriminating businessmen. Japanese businessmen, mostly—who like all-American-looking girls with great bodies, girls like Suzie Kirkwood.

Suzie always arrived an hour early, just as she had when she had done the Academy Awards show. She would start naked in the dressing room; it was girls only and none of the others would get there for half an hour. She would have already done her hair and face at home, and here she would make up her body, always standing so there wouldn't be any chair marks on her butt. She was a pro.

She would pull on three g-strings, each slightly

larger than the last, then the garter belt, then her hose. Then the bra and the negligee. She tied blue ribbons in her hair. Her one prop was the shepherd's staff.

Then she would limber up and go out on stage as Little Bo Peep.

He was sitting four rows back, in the twilight between the hot glare of the stage and the cold darkness of the seats. The Kit Kat was an old theater, with the back few rows of seats now ripped out for a bar, but patrons bought their own drinks and took them to their seats and sat there like a proper audience. What they did with themselves sitting there in the dark was their own business. But he wasn't drinking, wasn't diddling; he was watching, and Suzie Kirkwood had always loved an audience.

It was her habit, among her other professional traits, to pick out somebody in the audience and perform for him. It made it personal. She would pick him out early; her soundtrack started with a cloud of violins playing chords without rhythm, and she would wander out onto the boards like a girl searching for a lost sheep, a demure, innocent beginning far more intriguing than the bump-and-grind openings the other girls did, but hey, most stripteasers didn't understand that the tease was the most sensual part. It was during this violin section, when she was shading her eyes against an imaginary sun and scanning the far hills of the auditorium for her lost loved one, that she saw him there in the third row. He wore sunglasses and a hat, but she could tell he was into her act already; he was smiling, his lip curled up like he was about to laugh and blow a kiss at the same time. There was something familiar about that smile. And when she looked back at him, after giving up on ever finding her sheep, she thought there was something distinctive about his mustache.

The percussion surged into her soundtrack, the crunch of an electronic drum machine pulsing, pulsing, and Little Bo Beep grew hot from the sun. She was alone here in the meadow, why not take off this frilly dress and cool her body in the stream? Suzie slipped out of the dress slowly, revealing one shoulder and then the other, slowly, turning to face the curtain and showing the audience the pure expanse of her trim back. She stripped down to the petticoat, her breasts mounded high above it, her legs long and sensual below it, and still her posture was demure.

She glanced at him, her first erotic glance of the act, as if Little Bo Peep had just had the first sexual thought of her life, and she saw the smile break out on his face; he appreciated the artistry of it. And right then he reached up and raked the sunglasses down to the tip of his nose, so she could get a better look at his eyes.

Suzie Kirkwood danced. Her timing was never better, her moves never more graceful—and passionate. She knew when to surprise with a sudden movement, and knew how to unbutton and wait, and wait . . . and then reveal casually the breasts she knew were stunning.

She knew, too, not to look at him anymore. That was the way you played to men you wanted. She'd had enough of attractive men, even famous men, captivated by her, mesmerized by her dancing at the Oscars and Emmies and Grammies, back when all three used dancers. Some of them had even hit on her, at the celebrations that followed the broadcast, and after torrid one-nighters a couple of them had called her back for more. But those affairs had never lasted long; actors were expected to go with actresses and dating a dancer was a little like slumming. But she had known they were attracted. And she knew that the trick was to pretend not to notice, but to play to them, to aim everything in their direction. When she knelt on the stage like a Muslim in prayer, pointing her muscled rear in the air and dangling her breasts beneath her, he was her Mecca; when she rolled over and arched her back so that only her hair, butt, and toes touched the stage and her nipples pointed up and her breasts glistened in the lights, her body was the compass needle and he was magnetic north.

When she played with the staff, she was more demure than usual; she didn't want to look like a slut in front of this man.

Back in the dressing room she looked around at the other girls layering on their costumes before they strutted out to peel them off; Suzie scanned their faces, thinking they must have seen him, too; but the others never looked at the customers, even when they were dancing themselves, much less when somebody else was.

Suzie took what she called a West Virginia shower, wetting paper towels in the sink of the tiny dressing room lavatory and wiping her body with them. She put on fresh perfume and dressed in the clothes she had worn to work: jeans, boots, and a tuck-in blouse. She hung up her Little Bo Peep wardrobe so it would be ready for tomorrow, and glowed inside with self-respect for the way she had worked, kept going, kept believing in the Hollywood dream, kept being out there, till it paid off.

Still nothing happened. No knock at the door, no call on the pay phone. That was the way it had always happened before, if somebody was interested in her. Of course she never pursued those calls, those notes from customers, even the ones with money in the notes. Especially the ones with money in the notes; she would hand a note like that right back to the waitress who had brought it, tell her to give it back, and not give a damn whether she actually ever did. Suzie Kirkwood was not a whore.

She had a moment of doubt, standing there in the dressing room, ready to go home and waiting for an invitation she was suddenly not so sure was ever going to come. And then the door swung open and one of the waitresses poked her head inside. "Bo Beep," she said.

"Yeah!" Suzie said.

The waitress handed her not one note, but four. *What a performance!* Suzie thought. *Four notes! Not just one but four. I killed tonight!* Three of the notes had bills wrapped inside; she gave a total of eighty dollars back to the waitress. The fourth note was printed on a slip of vellum notepaper, very fine. It said: *Side door. Five minutes.*

Suzie walked out to the side door and stood there in the light of the building across the street, and thought about moving up in the world.

"Bo Peep?" a deep friendly voice said.

She turned, her eyes wide with anticipation. He pointed to the limousine, at the head of the alley. Suzie Kirkwood nodded. She did not smile, but inside she was excited, even happy.

In the shadows behind the Can he parked the car and switched off the engine, but he kept the trim lights, soft yellow bulbs around the edges of the door bottoms and below the recesses of the drink cabinets, glowing with the gentle mood of candles. He turned around and looked at her, face-to-face, and then he laughed without making a sound. Then the smile faded from his lips, and he kissed her. Her eyes fluttered shut long before his lips reached hers, and she put everything she had into that kiss.

When they pulled apart, he laughed again and said, "Well, I guess I'm gonna have to come back there or you're gonna have to come up here."

She waited for him to tell her which one he wanted her to do. Neither choice seemed obvious to her; it would be whatever he wanted.

Laughing like a schoolboy, he dived back through the privacy partition and fell onto the carpeted floor, pulling her onto him. They kissed again, locking up in a teenage embrace, all positioned and self-conscious. She moaned, she gasped; she tilted her head back until her neck was a long taut pillar and she made her breath shudder as he kissed her there. She was thrilled; and yet she was not having fun. He wasn't responding, and she felt it was her fault. He had been with so many beautiful women; were they so gorgeous, so sophisticated, so glamorous, that a little stripper from North Hollywood had no chance of turning him on?

She tried harder, gasping for air, squealing "yes, yes, yes," spreading her fingers wide as if electric shocks were going through her body as she pressed her palms to the muscles of his shoulders and slid her hands down all the way to his buttocks. She acted, the way she had seen it done in the last movie she watched where a couple had sex, where neither of those actors were in love, nor could they act.

He saw through her. She felt it.

But she could ignore those feelings. Look at where she was, look who she was with! He would tell her what he wanted.

She had been with men before who could not perform. Then it was their fault; now it was hers. But he didn't blame her; a split second before it became embarrassing for her, he slid to a seated position on the carpet of the passenger compartment and said, "I'd love to see you dance."

She smiled and began to pull off her top; it hid most of her figure. That was it; wait'll he got a real look at her body. "We need some music, don't we?" he said, and without waiting for a reply he switched on the stereo and punched in a tape of driving dance music, the same kind they played at the club.

She kept thinking she should be comfortable now, stripping to the familiar music. But the space inside the limo was cramped, and she felt awkward having to lean over to wiggle out of her jersey instead of pulling it straight up over her head and keeping her back arched so that her breasts stood out. She had to sit back on her heels to show him, and when he looked at her, it was with the face of an appraiser, with an expression that said, *I've seen worse; and I've seen better.*

She was beginning to panic. *What if I'm here—with him!—and nothing happens?* She unzipped her jeans and tried to stay in time with the music, but her movements were all out of rhythm. Here she was, damn sure she was a better *dancer* than most of those other women, and now she couldn't even do *that* right!

"Come here," he said. Only it was *c'meer,* and now *he* was starting to sound like a bad movie. She waddled over to him on her knees and he leaned forward, like one of the customers at the club might. Only she didn't keep the proper legal distance this time, pulling his face in between her breasts and gently wagging them against his cheeks. She covered them with her own hands and pressed them up higher, but she was reluctant for him to touch them; she didn't want him to know they were surgically enhanced. Down at the club, where almost every girl had had a boob job, she had come to believe they looked natural even when she was naked.

He brushed her hands away and grabbed them both, hard. She moaned, another movie moan of pleasure. She reached down between his legs. "Don't do that," he snapped, and she pulled her hand away—but not before realizing that he still wasn't having a good time.

"Sure, baby," she whispered. "Whatever you want to do."

"Whatever I want to do," he repeated, and his big hand clamped the base of her jaw and slowly lifted her until her head was pressing the roof of the limo. She had been with several men who liked their sex rough, especially those who couldn't seem to have it any other way. Rather than being alarmed, she was encouraged; at last he was getting into it.

"Yeah, baby. Yeah," she said.

"You like this?" he asked. And then he slapped her, so hard she fell back against the jump seat. The roughness of the blow surprised her; she looked up through her tears and saw that he was watching her, almost curiously, just to see how she would take it. She answered by slipping her jeans down past her knees, and touching herself and moaning, staring into his eyes as she did it.

He frowned. He seemed distracted. Had she not been so worried about her own performance, she might have seen that what was in his face was the same panic she had been feeling, the fear that said, *I can't do this, I can't perform, I am unattractive, unsensual, unsexual, null and void.*

"I want you to do something for me," he said.

"Anything, baby. Anything."

He opened one of the rosewood compartments tucked into the console beside the liquor display. He pulled out two packages and unrolled them. They were bags, one plastic, one canvas. "Get into these," he said. "I've got an idea. It'll be fun."

"Yeah, baby. I like it wild. I like it new." The lines sounded so wooden to her—and yet he seemed to believe them, just like the guys at the club, the ones who handed the spotter a twenty-dollar bill when everybody else was offering fives, seemed to believe her when she moaned in their ears and whispered "Ooo baby, this is sweet." "Do you want me to take my clothes off?" she asked him.

"What do you want to do?"

"Whatever you want," she said.

His voice came in a bellow. "Then take your goddamn clothes off!"

The roar did frighten her, spiking her eyes with fear and making her breasts shudder. But when she saw him smile slowly, and his mouth droop open, and his eyes fixate on her breasts, she knew he was getting excited from the sense of domination. Now she tried to show more fear; she turned her wriggling inside the bags into a minstrel-show burlesque. "Oh please," she squealed, "don't hurt me."

He pulled the top of the plastic bag up over her head, and twisted it shut. He lifted her over and pulled the canvas bag up, too.

"Are you gonna come in here with me?" she said.

But outside the bag, he was gasping for air. The thought of her in there, waiting, willing him to do anything, filled him with contempt. Contempt and anger. He was angry enough to . . . angry enough to . . .

He knew what he was angry enough to do; and the thought of it filled him with energy and sexual excitement.

"Baby?" her voice leaked through the bags. "Baby . . . ?"

The first blow caved in the inside of her left temple. She felt nothing after that.

Mike Rowe was in a nightmare of his soul. Out on the streets, blurred by night fog, he drove around. Around, that's where he meant to go, but the car pointed toward Josh Lannon's house and Rowe knew what he had to do. He would talk to Josh, confront him, force him to give himself up.

As he got closer to Lannon's house it all seemed easy and clear. He wondered at himself, that he could have been so upset, when it was all so clear. All he had to do was tell him. *Josh, you're going to turn yourself in. You're going to confess, you're going to seek help, you're going to plead insanity, for God's sake!* There was no need to bring Rowe's name into it. Absolutely no need at all. But if it came out . . . well, if it came out, then Mike Rowe would live with it. It would be the first decent, courageous thing he had done in his whole life.

He almost smiled.

He reached the bottom of the long curving street, walled by banks of bougainvillea, that led up to Lannon's estate, and was just about to turn up when the silver limousine slid past him in the fog.

Rowe raised his hand to wave, but as the limo slid on around the curve, its taillights rosy against the bracts of bougainvillea, a possibility struck him. It seemed so remote at first that he tried to brush it off as fantasy, but the timing was so striking that it seemed arranged by fate: what if Josh Lannon were on his way out, right this very moment, to pick up another girl?

Clarity. He could find out once and for all. If he caught Josh in the act, then Josh couldn't deny anything! Rowe whipped his car around and drove after the limo.

He stayed well back. The limo was easy to follow, even in the fog, even when they reached the boulevards. As Rowe tailed the silver stretch his spirits bubbled. If Josh was not involved in these murders, if it was all a terrible mistake, a kind of bad joke, then maybe Rowe was about to find that out for sure. If he caught Josh Lannon in the act of abducting a girl, preparing for her murder—what was it Ridge and McCullers said he did first? Ask the girl to crawl into a canvas bag?—then he would have caught the murderer, and any other testimony about them having a relationship would seem completely unbelievable, like vindictive ranting from an insane actor.

He wondered where Josh would pick up the girl. What nightclub would he pick? Were there private places along this route that Mike Rowe had never heard about? The limo took several turns, moving deeper into a residential area.

Rowe thought of another possibility—that this trip would prove inconclusive. Maybe Lannon was going out to visit a friend. Maybe it was another man. Just a friend. Or maybe a lover. And if it was a lover, then that would just make confronting Lannon just that much easier.

The limo rolled down a long avenue without street

lamps. On one side were houses, set well back; on the other side was a vacant field. The limo switched off its lights. Halfway down the block it pulled over to the curb and stopped.

Rowe stopped, too, his lights shut off, and watched as Lannon got out of the limo, opened the trunk, lifted out some heavy object, and carried it into the darkness. Lannon kept the motor running; the exhaust made a gray breath in the foggy night. He was away from the car for less than two minutes and then got back in and drove off.

Mike Rowe's hands shook so badly he could barely start his engine. He pulled up to where the limo had been and walked out into the shadows.

Out in the field he came upon the body, a note nailed into her head.

Rowe ran back across the field, his mind howling, his knees buckling. He fell twice, tearing out the knees in both of his trouser legs, not feeling the rocks and briars that cut his skin. He reached his car and tore at the handle, the sweat on his hands slippy as grease. But finally he jerked the door open and threw himself inside. Josh Lannon sat calmly in the passenger seat.

Rowe screamed, just once, then gawked, his jaw open and trembling, his teeth too far apart to chatter. But Lannon sat motionless and looked back at him, his eyes very still. In a soft and unsteady voice he said, "Listen to me, Mike. You have to control yourself and listen to me. You're the only hope I've got. You're the only hope either of us has."

He sounded afraid. His breath shuddered in his chest. He put a hand to his heart, as if to keep it from pounding through the breastplate of muscles he was so famous for. "Thank God . . . thank God it was you," he went on. "When I first saw the headlights of somebody following me, I thought it was him."

"Who?" Rowe said, surprised to find he still had a voice.

"Bellflower!" Lannon said, and scanned the street with darting eyes. "Do you have your pistol?"

"What?"

"Listen to me, Mike! We can both die here! Do you have your pistol?"

Rowe had to struggle to remember. "Yeah. Yeah!"

"Good! Keep it handy! My God, my God, we've got to think! I feel . . . I feel like that guy in *Shogun*, who decides to kill himself and then he's so weak he can't stand up afterward! I thought you were him, checking up on me to see if I would really do it, and I decided to park and sneak back and have it out with him, even if he killed me! I didn't expect to be alive right now—"

"Josh, make sense, what—"

"Bellflower, Mike! He's the one killing the dancers! Don't look at me that way, Mike, I'm so scared!" Lannon gripped the dash with his thick fingers, each one leaving a trail of sweat that glimmered in the glancing moonlight. "But it makes sense when you think about it, doesn't it? I started suspecting him—but who am I to suspect anybody, I'm not a detective!—but I started suspecting him when he would talk to me about women in the movie business, new actresses and all that, and ask me if I could get him dates, and it wasn't like other guys would ask me, it was like he had this really strange, sick look in his eye. Then you told me about the way he confessed to you about knowing one of the victims. Still I didn't think much about it, I mean so what? But *then* I heard about the killer using a silver limo, and I have a silver limo, Mike! *And I've been loaning it to Len Bellflower!*"

Mike Rowe's ears began to ring. Outside the car the darkness seemed to crawl with demons.

"So when he asked me if he could use my limo for a date, tonight . . . Well, I said yes, Mike, what else could I say? I've loaned it to him before; I mean, I keep the damn thing so I can loan it to friends. Hell, I don't drive it! He picked it up like he always does, but this time, this time I followed him, Mike!"

Just like I followed you, Rowe thought.

"He went to a club, picked up a girl, and drove her up to the Can! The Can, do you believe that! I thought, well, sheez, it must be okay if he's taking her up there, I mean who would kill somebody there? I thought I was all wrong about him, my imagination just getting carried away. I drove home—but when I get there, he's there! He beat me there! And he grabs me, and opens the trunk of my limo, and shows me this girl that he murdered! He says he saw me watching him, and now I'm gonna take the body and dump it or he's gonna shoot me right there and say he caught me doing it."

An island of doubt troubled the river of emotions in Mike Rowe's brain. "Then why didn't he just do that?" Rowe said quietly.

"I don't know, Mike," Lannon said, his voice sad with defeat. "I'm sure he'll get around to doing that, since I know his secret. But right now it seems like a game to him. I don't know, you tell me! What is it with a man who can do such a thing to a woman? You're the cop, you've studied these things, what's in the minds of the people who commit the thousands of murders there are every year? Is it power, the thrill, what? But I tell you this—I think he planned this all along. I think he knew that if he ever got caught, he had me to fall back on. He used my limo—" Lannon's voice broke, and he grabbed at his eyes and sobbed.

In that moment the flow of emotion in Mike Rowe's brain surged over any doubt and carried him away. "Don't worry," he said with real strength. "I'm a cop, too. And I'll take care of this."

"How, Mike? How? He's got this planned out, I'm telling you! How long has he had to think about it? Even telling you, days ago, that he knew one of the victims was just a real smart way of covering himself.

He's been a cop for years, he knows everything there is to know about hiding evidence."

Rowe looked away from Lannon's gray, frightened face. Lannon was right. Rowe swallowed back the bile creeping up from his stomach.

"Unless . . ." Lannon said. "Unless we can think of a way to nail him for this ourselves . . ."

Five minutes later Mike Rowe walked back to the body and shot it.

23

"McCullers!" came rolling down the hallway, and Bellflower turned into the doorway. He stopped and looked from Ridge to Cully and back again. "We've got another one," he said.

She lay in a field, beside a road to nowhere.

It was an open space at the south end of Balboa Park, on what had once been an access road to the Sepulveda Dam, a flood-control system built by the Army Corps of Engineers. Back when the engineers built the dam, the Ventura Freeway had not yet been planned; now the freeway cut across the road and made it a rising dead end. At one end the resulting open space was owned by the city of Los Angeles and contained a complex of baseball diamonds for Little League players, but at the other end was nothing, a sunbaked desert of gnarled wild walnut trees and sagebrush, unmaintained, unwatered, ignored.

It was here that someone had dumped the body of Suzie Kirkwood.

Ridge and Cully walked across the powder-dry, sandy earth as the sun went down in a haze of smog and pinkened the dirty air. In the bloody light the place looked like Golgotha.

The woman who found the body was an actress—or once had been. She was in her fifties now, and like other women who had once made their living with their faces she kept hers covered now. Sunglasses big as twin coffee cups blocked the upper half of her face, and the lower half seemed all lipstick. Mascara ran down from behind the sunglasses, and she shook in convulsive weeping. The terror had hit her, the adrenaline after the shock. There was no doubt her grief was real.

"She's dead! She's dead!" the woman was sobbing.

Nobody doubted that. The woman lay on the rock foundations of the raised road like a lizard sunning itself in the first rays of morning. Her legs were spread wide, like she had been arranged there. She was naked, but that wasn't apparent at first. On first glance she seemed to be wearing clothes; but what looked like a leotard was gore and blood. Her breasts had been carved away and two bloody balls of breast implant lay like earrings on either side of her head. Her face was covered with the note, nailed to the bridge of her nose, with the same familiar message.

They stared at the body, then walked back down to the bottom of the earth ramp, where the neighbors had gathered to watch. The actress kept her back to them, and to Ridge and Cully this was a good sign.

Ridge took the lead; he was most effective with women in trouble. "I understand you're the one who found the body," he said in a gentle voice.

"It wasn't me, it was my dog," she wailed. "Oh Suzie. Poor Suzie!" The woman's voice rose to the cracking point, and she cried in a soprano whistle.

"I'm so sorry you had to see it," Ridge said, and it was clear he meant it. "I hate to put you through this, but it might be easier to talk about it. If you'll think about it now, and not put it out of your mind, you won't have the nightmares."

That sobered her up. The nightmares. What a horrible nightmare it would be. But Ridge talked exactly like he understood just what she was feeling, and would feel.

"Can you tell us exactly how you—or your dog—

found her, and what you did? We need to be sure we've preserved the murder scene and not contaminated it in any way."

"I was out walking her. We always go on our walks at this time, it seems . . . safe. And she started to bark, and tore away from me, she pulled the leash right out of my hands. And she ran up here. We were on the street, I never walk her up here because she gets those prickers in the pads of her feet. But she ran up here barking, and I chased after her, calling to her, but it was like she had caught . . . the scent."

"Yes," Ridge said, nodding, understanding, encouraging.

"There she was. Suzie! And she was just . . . licking! At . . . at . . ."

"Dogs don't mean anything by that," Ridge said. "It's instinct, you can't blame them."

"Do you think she'll be a killer now? Now that she's tasted . . ."

"Your dog?"

"Once an animal has tasted blood, they say . . ."

"Whatever she tasted," Ridge said, "is nothing that will make Suzie more dangerous to you or your neighbors."

But the actress looked at Ridge crookedly, like something was out of joint. "Suzie?" she said.

"Suzie. Yeah," Ridge said. "Your dog."

"Suzie's not my dog," the actress said. "Suzie's the . . . body."

"Wait a minute!" Cully said. "You *know* her?"

"Yes!" the woman insisted. "That's what I've been saying!"

"You know the dead woman!"

"I know her! I know her! How many times do I have to say that to you people?"

"How do you know her?"

"We worked together on the Academy Awards show once. It was the big production number with the different costumes from the movies up for the wardrobe design Oscar, and they asked some of the original cast members to model. You remember I played the part of the Victorian nurse in *Pale Yellow,* the year it won Best Supporting. Suzie was one of the dancers, we used to take class together."

Cully recovered first. "Let me get this straight. You knew this woman?"

"That's what I'm telling you!" The actress held up her hands and stared at Ridge in frustration.

"You walked up here and found a body. And recognized it."

"My dog—Climax—ran from me. She stopped and was licking Suzie's face, licking at the blood there. I couldn't . . . I didn't know what to do. I saw it was a body! But my dog was there like, like eating it! And I couldn't just let her stay there and do it while I ran back to my house and called the police. So I came up here to pull her away. I grabbed the leash and pulled, but Climax just didn't want to come. I saw the note on the face, I knew what it was, I was terrified, but I had to get my dog. I tried not to look. But she licked again and the note came up and I saw it was Suzie."

Cully and Ridge looked at each other. It never comes down clean. Life is not neat. Death is even messier.

The camera crews were all over the place. As Ridge and Cully walked to their car they were followed by reporters dragging microphone lines and shouting, "Officer, could we get a statement? Could we get a statement, please?"

Cully had to hustle to keep up with him and found herself suddenly the object of attention when Ridge snapped at the reporters, "I'm just here as an observer! Talk to somebody in charge!" He barged his way into the car, slammed the door, and started the engine. All the reporters surged at her and she waved them off, hopping in with Ridge. The cameramen had to dive out of the way as he gunned the car away from the curb.

"Great," he was saying, "that's just great. We forget to ring the field with barriers and now everybody knows!" He paused, then slammed the wheel. "Dammit!"

"Everybody ought to know," Cully said.

"Yeah, but we should have told them, if they were gonna know! Now they'll be asking if this is the only one mutilated exactly this way. 'It's not? Then how many have there been? That many? And you didn't tell us before?' " He slammed the wheel again. "It's my fault, I shoulda thought of this."

"I'm lead on the case, I should have thought of it," Cully said. "I guess I'm not thinking very straight right now," she added quietly.

He caught the softness in her tone. He hadn't heard softness like that from her in a long time. He turned to look at her. "Are you okay?" he said.

"Ridge . . ."

"Yeah?"

"I'm pregnant."

She felt as if something amazing and ridiculous—like a bouquet of purple balloons—had suddenly appeared where her nose used to be and Ridge noticed but didn't want to mention it. He stared at her, glanced back at the traffic, stared at her again—but this time at a distance, as if unsure if her whole head was going to split open and start sprouting flowers. Finally he said, "You sure?"

She nodded.

He swung the car off the boulevard and onto a side street, where he stopped under a gnarled California oak. He shut off the engine and twisted around in the seat to face her. He reached into her lap, where her hands held each other, and drew her left one halfway to him and held it there. "I know you're a detective," he said. "You're your own person, somebody to be reckoned with. All of that. I know I'm not supposed to be protective. I know I'm not supposed to show affection. But is it all right for me to tell you I love you?"

She nodded. He drew her over, gripped the back of her head, and hugged her. But she pulled back and he let her go.

"I think we ought to talk about what I'm going to do," she said.

He looked away from her. "I see," he said.

"You see what?"

"You're not saying you want my help in deciding. You just want to make sure I'm okay with your decision."

"That's not fair, Ridge!"

"You haven't made up your mind?"

But she had. She took two deep breaths to speak, before she could actually get it out: "I . . . I'll have it done with my doctor, just as soon as I can get in."

He nodded. It wasn't like he was agreeing with anything.

"This early it won't be any problem at all," she said. "I'll only miss about a half day's work."

He studied the steering wheel. He felt its smoothness. "You're sure it's mine?" he said.

She exploded. "Fuck you! Goddammit, Ridge! Fuck you!"

"No, fuck *you*. You tell me about this . . . How long have you known?"

"What?"

"Don't stall! How long have you known?"

"A couple of days. And . . . it took me a few days to get around to taking the test, to be sure. I've sorta had some other things on my mind, Ridge!"

"Pregnancy isn't some minor little thing, is it? Something that's not a priority?" He wasn't shouting, his voice wasn't that loud. But his face was red, and he was sweating.

No, Cully thought, it's a big thing that gets shoved aside because it's too big to think about.

Ridge said, "So you tell me this a couple of days after you've finally gotten around to confirming what you already knew. And then you tell me, just to tell me. Like you feel obligated to some bullshit feminist kind of idea that says a man's just some kind of disposable breeding device, and it's in some handbook somewhere that he should be informed but God knows why if all he's supposed to do is nothing. Just stand there. Just . . ." He stopped talking long enough to look at her.

She was crying. She hated herself for crying and tried to stop, but the tears kept rolling out of her eyes, even when she turned and tried to get interested in the oak tree.

"I'm sorry," he said softly.

"I'm sorry, too. I was just trying to take care of it." She sniffed, and stiffened. "I'm sorry, I know crying is awful, and makes you feel awful. I'm not trying to do that, I'm just trying to take care of it myself."

"You're trying to take care of it *alone*. And you're not alone. No matter what you decide to do. If the decision is yours, okay. I'm not disputing that, it has so much more to do with you than with me, the decision *is* yours. But I love you. That's all I want you to know. And to admit. Just admit that you know that I love you."

"I admit it," she said at last.

"Good," he said. "Then everything's going to be okay."

Back at the station they had a big parlay with all the officers involved: Ridge and Cully, Frazier, Morris, Odom DeFuller, Baby Boom-Boom Malchek, Tooda Taylor, Len Bellflower, and Mike Rowe.

"Time to go public," Mike Rowe said.

"But that's gonna give us all sorts of crackpot shit

to track down," Tooda said. "We'll get a hundred confessions, and a dozen copycat murders."

"We ain't got a lotta fuckin' choice," Cowboy Condell said.

"That's right," Bellflower said, "the tale has already been told. The newspeople are calling already, and they're asking how much we've held back."

Cully's phone rang. When she answered, the voice at the other end said, "McCuwwers?"

"Wo—Roger?" Cully said.

"We have an intwesting situation with this new body," Roger said.

"Interesting how, Roger?"

"It has two buwwets in it."

Cully put the phone down and told them what Roger had said.

"This is a break," Tooda said. "We can tell the press this is a new murderer—that we haven't had anything like this before."

"I think we have to tell them the truth now," Mike Rowe said, and everybody else agreed—which made Tooda nod his head, too.

"But why the fuck has he gone to shooting them?" Frazier said.

"Exactly," Ridge said.

"Who knows why?" the deputy chief said. "But we haven't been able to break this case on our own. Maybe if we let the public know how dangerous a killer we're looking for, we'll get some usable leads."

Ridge looked at Rowe then, and Rowe looked away. But before he did, Ridge saw a sadness in the deputy chief's eyes, a sadness that would haunt him.

24

The next three hours they spent running down the person that Suzie Kirkwood once had been. They found her phone number listed without an address but got the address from the telephone company, and roused a judge out of bed for a warrant to search her apartment.

What they found was a two-bedroom place off Beechwood Drive, a street that was the first residential stop of many aspiring actors, singers, and dancers on their way to meet their Hollywood destiny. Three-story apartment buildings lined a broad street running straight toward the Hollywood sign, and Suzie had lived on the middle floor of one of these. When Ridge and Cully entered her apartment, let in by a building manager who had not yet gone to bed when they rapped on his door at two in the morning, they smelled her perfume and a litter box. A black short-haired cat with a long Siamese face drifted in from the kitchen, mewed, and brushed against Cully's legs. Cully found a half sack of cat chow in the kitchen broom closet and filled the cat's bare dishes with food and water. She watched the cat hunker down over the food, then rejoined Ridge in the living room.

The place still had the residue of life: a coffee cup left beside the sofa, a rental video—*Gone With the Wind* —still in its box on the glass-top coffee table, waiting for a devoted viewer whose eyes would now stare eternally at the inside of a cheap county coffin, unless Ridge and Cully found evidence of next of kin.

They searched through her shelves and drawers and found matchbooks from the Kit Kat Klub.

They had brought cardboard evidence boxes, and one was all they needed to carry the handful of personal documents they would take back to the station. But as they were leaving, Cully stopped at the door, unfolded a second box, went back into the kitchen and returned with the cat. She avoided Ridge's eyes as they walked to the car, and when she dropped the box off at her own apartment, he said nothing until she came back to the car minus the cat. Then Ridge looked at her and said, "You know, if you had a dog, and you died inside your apartment, your dog would guard your body until he died, too. Your cat, however, would eat you."

"I don't want to discuss it," Cully said, and started the engine.

It was almost three when they reached the Kit Kat. The manager was gone, but the bartender was still there cleaning up, and a couple of the dancers were drinking at the dark bar. They said that Suzie had left early, after the first show, and nobody had seen her since. The manager was angry about that, they said, but he'd get over it.

The bartender had the manager's name, but swore he had no address or number where he could be reached. Ridge and Cully knew the manager wasn't going to know anything, but they decided to put him through the wringer the next day, just to make up for not being there when they wanted to talk with him.

When they were back out at their car, and the night was cool and damp against their faces and against the stinging surfaces of their hot eyes, Ridge said, "Let's get something to eat." Cully was too tired to answer, but not too tired to eat, so they drove to an all-night deli on Ventura Boulevard in Studio City.

It was a showbiz kind of place, done in black and

red. Posters of Broadway musicals crowded the walls. Cully and Ridge sat down opposite twin bowls of matzo ball soup and drank decaf coffee as if they expected to sleep anytime soon. But the jangle that would keep them up until dawn was not from caffeine. Like the endless loop of a show tune that grooves its way into memory and haunts with unwilling repetition, they heard an echo beating against their will. It was death, and it was the silent noise of something that creeps from another world and settles into this one, and seems commonplace but doesn't belong, like the fragments of an ancestor's bones inside a baby rattle.

"What are you thinking?" Ridge asked as Cully's spoon scraped across the porcelain bottom of the soup bowl. She did not bother to raise this last half mouthful to her lips.

She shook her head. "I don't know. What are you thinking about?"

He wished he could think of something good to say. Something that would blot out the noise and the smell, the look of the death in Cully's eyes, and the trembles from the life in her belly. And then he smiled. It was a real smile, the kind that was easy when he looked at her.

She was surprised; and she surprised herself by smiling back. They looked at each other for a long time. "Don't do this to me," she said.

"Do what?"

"When you look at me that way . . ." She didn't finish, and she wasn't looking at him anymore. She was glancing around at the tired waiter who wanted to be an actor, at the tired uniformed cops, sitting in the booth on the opposite side of the room, who wanted to be on day shift.

"I'm sorry," Ridge said. But he leaned forward and said it like he wasn't sorry about anything. "But let me tell you something. I'm sorry our jobs make it awkward when I look at you, and I'm sorry for the situation you're in. The predicament. But I want you to know something. I'm not sorry it happened. I . . ." He squeezed his eyes shut and bounced the side of his fist on the table as if the wood was his brain and he was trying to chisel the words out of it. "I don't mean I'm glad you're pregnant, not if you decide you don't want . . . No . . . I guess I do mean I'm glad you're pregnant. If you have the baby, or you don't . . . I want you to know that I love you. And the idea that you and I could get together, and produce something . . ."

He had trouble talking. Liquid was rimming his eyes and clogging his throat, as if the tears had come up from his lungs.

She stared back at him, her face pointed slightly to one side, her eyes wide and round as the soup spoon in her hand.

"That idea, just the idea of it, is so beautiful, it's like it came from God," Doubting Thomas Ridge said, and then sat there marveling, as if he could not believe that those words had come from his own mouth.

What is inside me is an idea from God, Cully thought. Ridge was the only man she had ever known— hell, he was the only human of either sex—who could say something like that.

She reached across the table, covered his fingers lightly with her own, and said, "Tom. Take me home."

His place was closest; they drove there without discussing it. He parked in the front of the building, beside the pine tree, and they climbed to the second-floor landing. She stood quietly as he opened the door, then she took his hand and let him lead her inside. When he shut the door and she still stood there, saying nothing, he looked at her as if he still didn't understand, but then he finally did when she turned to him there in the middle of his nearly empty living room and kissed him full on the lips.

It was a long kiss, and when they broke apart, she said, "I need a shower."

"Me too," he said.

And then they both laughed.

She began to unbutton her blouse. He loosened his tie. But then he gave up on his own buttons and decided he would rather help her with hers. "Now wait a minute," she said, giggling, "a shower first, all right? That's the rule. We take a shower first, and *then* we get serious. Right?"

"Scout's honor," he said.

"You swear?"

"Swear."

They peeled off their clothes, stale with the tired sweat of many hours, the smoke of other detectives' cigarettes, the perfume of a dead girl's apartment, the smog of a hot city, and left them in piles on the living-room carpet. Then he pulled her to him, breaking his promise about the shower, and she did not resist.

Ultimately they did make it to the shower; and when the water had turned cold, they made it to the cool sheets of the bed and heated them with a fire that didn't want to go out. She gripped him with a strength that said she would never let him go, and Ridge touched her body as if it held something immensely fragile and yet indestructible; something temporary and yet eternal.

The sun, at the edges of the curtains, woke them, still wrapped in each other's arms.

He kissed her softly and whispered, "I'll see you at work."

"Are you kicking me out of bed?" she said, her voice raspy with the new morning and not sounding as threatening as she tried to make it; of course the grin on her face didn't help her effort at aloofness either.

He pulled her close, kissing her on the top of her head where the sunlight dappled her pillowcase and warmed her hair. She nuzzled her face against his auburn chest hair, soft as sea foam and fragrant with Man. With one ear pressed against the great drum of his torso, she heard the rich rumble in his voice as he said, "If you don't have time to get home and do your exercises and eat your bran buds or whatever else it is that makes you so bionic, and you come to work looking like the woman who made me look like I'm gonna look when *I* show up for work this morning, then you're gonna blame me for ruining your reputation. And I know how you can hold a grudge."

She kissed him hard on the lips and then whispered, "See you there."

Sitting alone in the sole chair in his living room, Ridge wondered whether the hours before had solved anything, had solved the question that "the idea of God's," as Cully would come to call it, had posed.

As he walked to the shower, turned on the squeaky taps, and stepped into the warm spurt of water that splattered against the back of his neck and gushed down his spine, he knew the questions they would face would still be the same.

But that was all right.

He loved her.

25

The morning papers all carried the story. Deputy Chief Rowe released pictures of all the victims, as well as the contents of the note.

Ridge, Cully, Frazier, and Morris returned to the neighborhood where Suzie Kirkwood's body had been found and interviewed every homeowner who lived opposite the bare stretch of parkland. Nobody had seen anything. The street was a throughway, and cars passed frequently at night. And it had been a weekday night and the people who lived in the neighborhood were successful workaholics who liked to get to bed early.

At noon Deputy Chief Rowe held a press conference and asked that anybody who had seen anything put in a call to the Mulholland Station.

Two hours later the sergeant at the Can's switchboard took a phone call. "Mulholland Homicide Division," he said.

"Who's this?" came a voice, low and muffled; was there a trace of accent?

"Sergeant Pamplin. May I help you?"

A pause. "I saw a car leave the place where you found the body."

"Excuse me, sir, what was your name?"

"I don't want to get involved. But I saw a car driving away fast from the park, where you found her."

"That was when, sir?" the desk sergeant asked, doing a good job. Most legitimate callers would identify themselves, but some might not, and he had to establish whether the caller was honest or some crank after attention. "That was right after dawn?"

"No, no. About midnight, maybe a little before. I was taking a friend home from the airport and this car almost hit me."

"You were walking."

"Almost hit my car, I mean. I swerved into a side street, and when I came back out onto the boulevard, I saw he had stopped. It looked like he was throwing something into the drain grate there at Ventura and Woodley."

"Can you remember anything about this car?"

"It was light. Blue, I think, or maybe gray."

"Did you get a license number?"

"Yeah, I think so." And he gave them a number.

When he heard it, the sergeant said deliberately, "Would you repeat that number, sir?" The caller repeated the same number, and Sergeant Pamplin wrote it down with great care. "Uh, sir, it would be extremely helpful if you could come down to the station personally and file a report with us."

"No way," said the voice on the other end of the line. "I used to work for the city, and I know the license codes. That car I saw was a plainclothes cop's."

"Sir—" But the caller had hung up.

Pamplin checked his computer just to be sure, then took several deep breaths before coding his phone for call forwarding and walking to Rowe's cubicle, where he told the deputy chief exactly what the anonymous caller had reported. Pamplin blessed the LAPD's policy of recording every call made to the main number of any police division; without that recording, he might not have believed his own ears.

An hour later Mike Rowe called together the MULHOM detectives, along with Roger the Coroner and Dr. Blein, and he played them the recording Pamplin had made.

As soon as the cops heard the license number that indicated the car belonged to the department, Frazier barked, "Bullshit!" But Rowe held up a hand for silence and let the tape finish. "What a buncha crap," Frazier said.

But Tooda asked, "Who's that car assigned to?"

Rowe let that question hang. "I think we should hear from our other experts before we discuss that," he said. "Roger?"

Roger gave them a report on his preliminary autopsy. "The buwwets were fired into the body after it was killed," he said. "And not just after it was killed, but fwom an angle that indicates that the killer put two buwwets into her after she had been awwanged at the sight."

"Presented," Blein corrected him, and when Roger frowned at him, Blein repeated it. "Presented. The killer presents his victim to us."

"But he never shot one before," Frazier said.

"He wants to be caught. He's bothered by guilt. And," Blein said, pausing because he considered what he was about to say to be momentous, "that's understandable, if he's a police officer."

"What a load. What a *load*!" Frazier said.

Rowe didn't look at him.

Cully said, "You checked the drain grate?"

"I sent some uniforms from Van Nuys out to it. And the caller was right, there were some bullet casings in it. Nine-millimeter."

"So who is the car assigned to?" Cully asked, for all of them.

"Len Bellflower." But it was Ridge, not Rowe, who answered.

"I've already had him arrested," Rowe said.

* * *

There were no secrets on a story that big. Someone leaked the information to Charlie Gulker, and after Gulker's big scoop all the news shows reported that Commander Leonard Bellflower had been arrested for the murder of four women.

Pending the filing of formal charges, Bellflower was detained in his office, unhandcuffed but attended at all times by not fewer than two armed detectives. They accompanied him even to the toilet.

In less than an hour Rowe had a makeshift interrogation room, complete with soundproof panels and a two-way mirror, set up in a back corner of the Can, beside the locker rooms, and it was there that Leonard Bellflower received his preliminary questioning.

Rowe insisted on having Cully McCullers lead the first interrogation. He even suggested that Ridge's presence in the room was a distraction to her and that Ridge could possibly be used better somewhere else, but he didn't press the point. Rowe sat in the observation booth, behind the one-way mirror, and silently watched Cully go to work.

"Commander Bellflower, I . . . I want you to know how sorry I am to be doing this," was the first thing she said.

"Don't apologize," Bellflower said. "Don't ever apologize for doing your job."

Cully stared at him, wondering if that statement was a form of confession. Bellflower seemed so calm about all this. Cully glanced at the mirror, as if she could draw encouragement from the man sitting behind it; Ridge, looking on with Deputy Chief Rowe, stared at the floor or at Bellflower, but never at her.

Turning back to Bellflower, Cully said slowly, "Commander, you are awfully . . . calm."

"Do your job, Detective," Bellflower said. He was like a man who has seen through the plans for a surprise birthday party and wants his friends to know they haven't fooled him but doesn't want to appear too smug, just in case he's wrong and they haven't planned a party for him after all.

"Do you have any explanation for why the bullet fired from your pistol matches the two taken from the body of our last murder victim?" Cully asked.

"Do I have any explanation? That's a good approach! Let's see, let's see, do I have any explanation. Hmm. I don't suppose the idea of a mistake has occurred to you."

"A mistake, sir? You mean a mistake you made with your life?"

Bellflower laughed from his belly. "McCullers, you're a prize, you know that? Har-har! A mistake I made with my life. Right. Kind of a foul-up. Killing those girls was, you know, a little goof."

He snickered again, but Cully was not laughing. She saw in Bellflower's eyes that he was like a hunk of steak thrown onto a griddle; a layer of anger, like fat in the meat, had just sizzled to the surface. "A mistake, for Christsake! How many times has our lab fouled up ballistics?"

"I don't know," Cully said. "I'd guess the answer is 'several.' "

"Several!" Bellflower repeated, not understanding why that wasn't the end of it.

"But you see, sir, that's why we had the FBI lab check it, too."

Bellflower just looked at her, and he wasn't smiling.

"We did a number of test firings," Cully said. "More than a dozen. And every bullet matched."

"The FBI," Bellflower said, more to himself than to the detectives.

"And remember," Cully went on, "we had two bullets to check them against, not just one. The gist of which is, the FBI experts say this is absolutely conclusive. Such a match is over ten million to one that the bullets in that girl's body were fired from your gun."

"That's not possible," Bellflower said.

"Those are the facts, sir," Cully said, only not as gently as before. She had started to see weakness in her suspect, and that was making her tougher.

"Detective McCullers, are you about to ask me where I was on the night of the murder?" Bellflower was still looking at her as if he hoped it wasn't true.

"You're ahead of me, sir, so why don't you tell me?"

"Don't get smart-ass with me, McCullers!"

"Call me what you want," Cully said, "but you better quit this glib shit and tell me what I need to know. This is no joke, Commander, you've been detained on suspicion of murder, and none of the people who like and respect you find that very funny. But you tell me. You want to train me to be a better cop, you tell me!"

Bellflower only stared at her, blankly, as if the beautiful young woman he had known and liked for so long, and whose father had been a friend to whom he had entrusted his life, had begun to dematerialize before his eyes, and taking shape in her place was something he had never seen before, something dreadful, that struck him dumb.

"Commander," Cully said, "please listen to me. It isn't just the bullets. We also located two shell casings, less than a quarter mile from where the last body was discovered. The markings on those casings match the breech of your pistol, right down to the imprint of the firing pin."

Still Bellflower stared. Cully leaned forward and placed her hands over the dry brown hands of this man who had stood by her, who had stood by her father when almost everyone else in the department was looking the other way. She struggled to keep her voice flat and firm so that she would not be tempted to weep. "You'd better come up with a way to explain all that, sir. 'Cause all we can come up with is one explanation, and none of us likes that one at all."

"Look!" Bellflower said suddenly, smiling as if he

were the only one to get the joke. "This is easy! We've got a semen sample from the guy, it's absolutely no problem. That's biological substance! You take a skin sample from me, you do a genetic test, then you compare the genetic fingerprint with the—"

"The sample's gone," Cully said. "Somebody went into the evidence room and took it. Somebody with access."

Bellflower understood at last. He turned and looked with pleading eyes into the one-way mirror, where he knew Ridge was standing.

26

Because the Can had no suspect holding facilities, it was necessary to take Leonard Bellflower to a cell in the Van Nuys Division station, where only a few weeks ago he had served as captain. Frazier and Morris took him there in an unmarked sedan, Morris at the wheel, Frazier in back with his old friend, whose shame lay bright as the sweat on his face.

Mike Rowe went to his afternoon press briefing and made the formal and anticlimactic announcement that the police had detained a suspect in the recent series of brutal killings, but he would not be able to release further details at this time.

Cully had gone out to see that Bellflower was taken safely away. Frazier and Morris had broken every rule of detention by removing his handcuffs until Bellflower was safely in the car so that the reporters outside would think nothing of seeing the captain ride away with two of his detectives. After he was gone, she went back into the Can and found Ridge pacing slowly up and down beside his desk.

"Tom," she said, and he turned to her. "Well?" she said.

"Well. Well what?"

"Well . . . what do you think?"

"I think we're going to have to do the same thing, whether Len Bellflower is guilty or not. We've got to go

247

out and ask the same questions we'd ask, in the same way we'd ask, if we want to prove either possibility."

Ridge rubbed a knuckle across his nose, looked down the long shadowy length of the Can, and walked away.

Left alone, Cully began to assemble what detectives call the Dark Book. Everybody has a self that he hides from everyone else, like a book that holds the secrets he wants nobody else to know. The blunders, the betrayals large and small, the acts of cowardice and pettiness, the situations and choices that people tended not to be proud of . . .

Like unexpected pregnancies, Cully thought.

Bellflower proved to be a fascinating subject. She learned that his wife had died five years before, when his son was a junior in high school. The son was an athlete, lettering in basketball and football. Cully, who had lost her father at about the same age that Bellflower's son had lost his mother, understood some of the agonies that went with that territory. Bellflower's son, his only son, had lost his mother, and Bellflower must surely have wanted to be balm for his son's grief, while he was an open wound himself. That had been the experience of Cully's mother, anyway. Even though her parents had been divorced for two years before Big Jim's death, a year later Ruth McCullers was still disintegrating, and Cully had prevailed on her to see a psychologist.

And now Cully wondered if Bellflower wouldn't have sought exactly the same kind of help for himself.

The police department keeps a staff of psychologists on call, and the counselors run sessions on both a private and a group basis. Cully put in a computer request through the department's personnel section to find out if Bellflower had taken advantage of the service, and in less than thirty minutes she received a computer reply that Leonard Bellflower had attended nearly a year's worth of individual counseling sessions with a Dr. Gillespie.

If Cully could find that doctor, he might have the key to all the chapters in Leonard Bellflower's Dark Book.

She located Gillespie through the departmental personnel services division, probably the same number Bellflower had dialed when he was looking for help four years ago. She spoke with a receptionist—Gillespie had his own office in Westwood—and made an appointment to see the doctor that afternoon.

An hour before she was to be there, Mike Rowe called her into his office.

"I understand you've contacted Len's therapist," the deputy chief said.

"Yes, sir?" Cully said.

"He called me," Rowe said.

"Bellflower called you, or Gillespie did?"

"Dr. Gillespie did. He was concerned that any detective would want to know about another detective's therapy sessions."

"How did he know I wanted to talk about Bellflower and not myself?" Cully asked.

"He didn't," Rowe said. "Not when you called. But apparently the doctor anticipated questions about Bellflower, after word of his arrest got around. Gillespie called me and said, 'A detective McCullers wants to see me. Is she here to ask questions I can't answer?' And I had to tell him I thought you just might be going for that reason. Of course if you aren't, then I apologize for this intrusion. But if you are, I'd better deny you permission. We don't have a warrant to search Bellflower in that way, and if we do it, we could blow the case."

"I know the sessions are privileged as to specifics, sir," Cully said. "And the doctor would certainly respect the confidentiality of his patient's revelations. But maybe the doctor could just give me an idea. He could answer some general questions, such as—was he ever violent? Morose? Depressed? Questions like if you were a betting man, doctor, do you think he could be capable—"

"Those are exactly the questions we can't ask," Rowe said. "Precisely because we can't lose this case by having violated the suspect's right to privacy. We could get this whole case thrown out if his lawyer comes into court and says we violated these confidences."

"But . . . these doctors have testified in other criminal cases. They could probably tell us if they might have information that would help swing suspicion away from Bellflower."

"I want him proven innocent as much as you do, Detective. We've just got to be smart about this thing."

"Yes, we do," Cully said, with what she knew was just a touch too much emphasis on the "we."

It was only the slightest hint of an accusation, that maybe Rowe had less personal loyalty to Bellflower than did Cully, but Rowe's reaction was sudden and fierce. "Detective!" he said sharply, then lowered his voice. "We're all tense here. And . . . and torn apart by this thing. All we . . ." He stopped again, then forced himself on. "All we need to pursue is the fact that evidence points to Leonard Bellflower."

"I'll agree with that, sir," she said. "It's just that there are holes. Bellflower might know hookers, that's true. Most cops, over time, run into enough of them. Maybe the girls got into the limo because the face they knew was a cop's face. But Bellflower didn't own a limo."

"He could easily have access to one," Rowe said. "He could have rented. That's something we have to find out. It all takes time. We just . . . We know we're dealing with an issue here. A complex psychological issue. And we're going to settle it all in . . . in time."

Cully said, "Sir? Whoever did this, it wasn't just the working out of a psychological problem. What he did was kill some women. Mutilate them . . ."

"I . . . I know," Rowe said.

"Beat them to death, butcher them, slam a nail into their skull!"

"I know. I know."

Cully looked across Rowe's desk, at the deputy chief's pale hands pressed on the polished surface, their reflection blurred with droplets of perspiration. "If Commander Bellflower is guilty, then I'll prove it," she said.

He nodded, and she let herself out, closing the cubicle door softly behind her. She found herself pitying the deputy chief; in that last moment in his office he had seemed even less sure of Bellflower's guilt than she was.

Cully wandered the length of the Can, her gaze on the stained concrete, then realized as she reached her desk that the phone ringing so persistently was her own. She snapped it up, hoping for news, hoping for hope, and said, "McCullers!"

"Cully, it's Gail!"

"Oh. Hi." She heard the disappointment in her voice and tried quickly to cover it. "How are you?"

"Better than you sound."

"Well, I've . . . had a hard day."

"Good. Then maybe you'll join us. I'm having some old friends over tonight, some girls from school. Chris, Margitte, people I haven't seen in years. I was hoping you'd join us, too."

"Sounds great, Gail, but—"

"Before you say no, listen to what we're doing! I've got a fortune-teller coming, don't you think that'd be neat? See, instead of sitting around talking about the past, we'll talk about the future! Say yes, come on!"

"I'd love to, Gail, I really would. But I've got so much to do."

"You've got to eat dinner, don't you? Come on. We'll eat, have our fortunes told, and if you need to run, you can. Come on, Cully, it won't be the same without you, everybody wants to see you."

A glimmer of life, outside the darkness of her job. Cully said yes.

Ridge found Odom DeFuller in the chili-dog place across the street from the station. Odom had four dogs side by side on the plate, and a super-large Cherry Coke.

"Mind if I sit down?"

"Hell no. But you're in the way of the blue flame if I burp across these four all-the-ways."

"I'll take my chances. Odom, about Len Bell-flower . . ."

"Buncha shit," Odom said, through his first mouthful. Four hot dogs, eight bites.

"You're not worried at all."

"Can't be worried. It's some kinda mistake."

"We all think that, Odom, but we're gonna have to prove it to 'em."

Odom was about to stuff the second half of his first hot dog into his mouth; his jaws were stretched wide into a bright red cavern. But when Ridge said this he moved the wad of food away from his mouth and set it slowly back onto his plate. "God. I didn't think . . ."

"It's no joke, Odom. It's for real."

"How can I help?"

"You think he did it?" Ridge said.

"Fuck no, he didn't do it! What kinda fuckin' question is that?"

"It's the one the prosecutor's gonna ask, and right now we don't have any answers except that he looks like he could've."

"No way. I know him too well."

"Every killer knows somebody, Odom. What if it *is* one of us?"

"So what if it is. Ridge, you know how many times a cop wants to go out and get even. You know how easy it is to lose respect for other people, and for yourself, when you're a cop. Bell never did that. I know. I was in group therapy with him. He had hit his wife, okay, he had done it. And now his wife was dead and it was tearing him up inside. The grief and the guilt, all tied up together. I saw him bleed. Blood that looked like sweat, but it was blood. Blood and water, like what came out of Jesus' side. Tears too. I saw him cry, Ridge. Len Bell-flower is no killer."

He said this in a hushed voice, like a person standing alone in a great cathedral.

Ridge sat at home, alone, trying to think. He was always trying to think. Wasn't trying to think a kind of thinking?

There was a knock on the door. From his chair he called, "Yes?"

"It's me," Cully answered.

He stood and opened the door. His eyes searched her face, looking for the reason she had come. She looked warm, a little dazzled, as if she had just looked at a bright light. But she didn't say anything until she was sitting on the couch and he was beside her, waiting for her to tell him why she was there.

"I was just at a party," she said. "Some of Gail's friends. And they had a fortune-teller." She smiled, as if amused by how silly she knew she was sounding to him.

"Yeah," he said. "You told me you were going."

She had remembered that. He wasn't giving her time to get going—but how could he? How could he believe anything she was about to say?

"Yeah," she said. "Well, there were eight of us there, plus the fortune-teller."

"Crystal ball?" Ridge said, thinking this was supposed to be a funny story and he was trying to get into the spirit of it.

"No," Cully said, with that same amused, bewildered half smile. "She made coffee—real strong coffee—and when it was your turn to be read, you'd go into the kitchen with her and sit down at the table, and she poured a little into your cup and would talk with you for a minute while you sipped it down. Then she'd pour what was left into your saucer and read the grounds."

"Yeah?"

"She knew I was pregnant."

"Eight young women there? She had to figure somebody was."

"Oh yeah, of course she did. She asked Linda and Suzie and Sandra if they were pregnant before she got to me, and they all said no, but she asked them, and me she just told. And when they said no, she kept saying, 'Well, somebody here is.' "

"Still—" Ridge started, but Cully waved him off.

"I know, I know. But that's not what shook me. It was what she said. When I told her yes, I was pregnant. It was the coffee grounds. Here, I brought it with me."

Cully opened her purse and pulled out a Fitz and Floyd saucer she had protected with a Ziploc baggie. Carefully, so as not to smudge the dried-on stain of the grounds around the saucer's inside indentation, she slipped off the bag and sat the saucer on the table in front of them, then leaned over it with him like two people looking at a picture of some treasure they meant to buy together. Cully twisted the saucer so that the stain, two thirds of the way around the inner circle, was open at the top like a *U,* and with her fingernail she pointed delicately at the curve on Ridge's left. "This is me," she said. "See the bulge here, right where my tummy is?"

Ridge looked and prodded his cheek with his tongue. "Okay, I'll admit it's a long dark drip with a bulge in the middle."

"But doesn't it—"

"It looks like the bulge is pregnant."

"But see this other, lighter shape on the other side, without the bulge?"

Ridge looked, wondering what she wanted him to say.

"This woman looked at me and said, 'Don't worry. Your baby's going to be fine. It's got an angel watching over it.' "

Ridge stared down at the ghostly shape of the far side of the coffee stain, then took her in his arms and kissed her. From her lips to her neck and back to her lips again. He picked her up and made love to her, urgently and yet with all-encompassing care.

Afterward, as Cully slept within the circle of his arms, Ridge lay in the darkness.

Children. A child. His child.

It didn't seem possible.

He had seldom thought of being a father. Children are part of a home, and a home starts with a man and woman who love each other. Ridge had not dreamed of children because he hadn't met the woman he could imagine coming home to.

Until he had met Scarlet McCullers.

Now as her breath bathed the bare flesh of his shoulder, he could not predict what she would do about this pregnancy; so full was his vision of the present, he felt blind to the future. They had just given themselves to each other with the fervor of new commitment. Some silent way, not in the lovemaking but just before it, they had told each other that what was between them would last. That settled something—okay, our relationship is *not* temporary—but it didn't answer the question of this pregnancy. Cully would ask it again; and what would he tell her?

Being honest with himself, he had to admit that he wasn't ready to be a father. When he thought of children, he thought not of swings and parks and baseball games; swings and baseball games weren't part of his life, and the only time he went to a park now was to look at a corpse somebody had dumped there. But Ridge could imagine children; he thought of putting them to bed at night and breathing upon their cheeks and pressing his lips against their hair and pulling the covers up above their ears.

He thought of praying for a child's life. Not for deliverance from some disease, but for the child's *life*, for fullness and kindness and peace. For the willingness to stand against others and not to hate them for their opposition; for the confidence to step apart from a crowd and the inner strength to bear the loneliness of it. For no loneliness at all, if Ridge had his way, though loneliness had made him what he was.

Thinking of a child in that way almost made the child seem real.

That was a dangerous thought, he knew. And when he thought of abortion, it was not with the idea that it was murder. Thomas Ridge had seen murder. Adults gunned down in the prime of life, teenagers dead on the street because the charade of manhood they played out had permanent consequences; and children, too, slaughtered by parents who should not have been parents. That was murder.

So it wasn't the idea of abortion that haunted him. It was the fortune-teller's remark.

An angel is watching over your baby.

And try as he might, Ridge could not shake the feeling that he was the angel, and that little scrap of life growing inside Cully McCullers was going to be the child he thought he might never have, the one whose warm hair he could sniff, and kiss, and cover for sleep.

Ridge awoke from the sound of a bump against his four-poster bed, and Cully's curse: "Dammit!" He looked at the luminous face of his Timex.

"Are you getting up?" he asked the darkness.

"Yeah," she whispered. "Sorry."

"Where are you going at two in the morning?"

"I've gotta find Clarence."

"Porsche's pimp?"

"I've gotta do *something*. I can't sleep."

"I'll go with you."

"No," she said sharply.

"But—"

"But what, Ridge?" She pressed her fingertips against his lips, and he kissed them. She softened instantly; but still she had to go. "Don't try to protect me, Tom. Don't tell me you think I can't do my job. I can handle a pimp. What I can't handle is . . ."

She didn't know how to say it. Ridge tried for her. "It's impossible to believe that we could be so wrong. That somebody we know, and respect, could be a monster."

He could see her silhouette against the dim gray of the curtains. He wished he could see her face. She kissed him softly on the lips, and left like a ghost.

Cully drove down to the Hideaway Motel. Clarence's Clenet was not in the lot. So she pulled into a side street and grabbed a cup of coffee at a curbside diner while she waited. She ordered decaf. Taking care of the fetus, even though she kept telling herself it would never become a baby.

Ten minutes later she saw the white Clenet: the long rectangular hood with the leather straps, the square trunk that looked like a footlocker. It turned into the motel lot and Clarence lumbered out, stretching his big frame up slowly and walking to the door of the room where she had last seen him. He used his key and went inside. Cully paid for her coffee and crossed the street.

She knocked at the door; not softly, but not banging either.

"Uh-huh?"

"Clarence. Open up."

"Who's there?"

"Detective McCullers. Come on, I want to talk to you."

She was waiting, ready to say, "Hi, remember me?" when she heard the click behind the door. Reflex more than anything else made her jerk to her right, and a shot boomed on the other side of the door, tearing out the peephole. Two more explosions splintered the wood, and Cully snatched her nine-millimeter from the holster on her left hip.

"Clarence, what the fuck are you doing?" she screamed, but couldn't hear herself because the noise had deafened her. She dropped to one knee—if the pimp came through the door, he would be high and she could shoot up through his belly—but then some sensation returned to her eardrums and she heard him slamming through another doorway. She kicked through the lock of the shattered door in front of her, dipped around the jam, and saw the second door, on the far side of the room, standing open. That's why he took this room, she thought, it's got a back way.

She whirled and saw his car. Would he just leave it? Why was he shooting? He couldn't be thinking clearly, he'd just be running. But from what? He knew she was a cop. . . . And suddenly Cully understood why Clarence was shooting.

Would he run into the street? No, the cops could shoot him down there if they wanted to. He'd be heading down the back streets. . . .

Cully hopped into the Clenet. The car had Lincoln running gear with standard Ford electronics and she hot-wired it with a hairpin in ten seconds flat.

She tore the car into the alley Clarence had disappeared into and bore down on the accelerator. As she switched on the headlights they lit him full frame, running down the dark left side of the alley not twenty feet in front of her. He turned as if to fire at her and she swung the car directly toward him and rammed the accelerator. He spun again and ran.

She drove straight at him, twisting the wheel to follow as he dodged through the shadows. He climbed halfway up a wall, slid, clawing frantically, and bounced on her fender. His head dribbled off the pavement and he rolled, trying to get to his feet, but his bloodied face slammed into the barrel of Cully's automatic.

"You dumb shit!" she yelled.

Back at the station Clarence told them he had run because he knew the cops were going to kill him. Why would they do that? they asked. Because you protect your own, Clarence said. Your man, Bellflower, he was plowing my girl Porsche, and he dusted her, too. I'd swear to it.

27

Early, before the sun had begun to burn off the layer of gray clouds that had drifted in overnight from the ocean, Ridge left his apartment. In the calm, unhurried motion of the car through the light dawn traffic, he thought back to the seminary, where he had once studied, and recalled the writings of a theologian whose name he could not remember but whose words had scorched his Baptist heart: *The genius of Christianity is that Jesus of Nazareth found the holy not among the righteous, but among the profane.*

Ridge drove to the city dump.

The day before, he had phoned ahead and had reached a supervisor who had a plot map of the whole site, with the schedule of the trucks and their order of dumping. By figuring out how many trips each truck made on a given day, the supervisor could plot within a few dozen feet the dumping location of a given load of garbage.

Ridge located the supervisor, who showed him the spot. Bulldozers had packed the stuff down, but had not yet pushed topsoil over it.

Ridge had rubber gloves and a shovel and boots and coveralls in the trunk of his car, the implements detectives used sometimes for searching for bodies within wooded areas. He went to work, digging through the garbage. Ridge, who was fastidious in his life and liked to use a paper towel when he turned off the water in the men's room, stood ankle-deep in the decaying garbage and turned over scoop after scoop of stinking matter, intermittently and inevitably finding the junk mail that everyone threw away, and thus tracking through the addresses of the people in whose garbage he stood.

He worked for three hours before he found the street he wanted, then kept wading along and digging, looking for the right block, and then the right building.

After another hour he found what he was looking for.

Ridge sat down across from Bellflower in the interrogation room.

Ridge said, "Len, I want to tell you something. I want to tell you so you'll know I'm not lying, that I'm telling you straight from that cold little steel room we all have behind our hearts, where we keep the truth locked up.

"Len, I was born in the south. When I was real small, maybe four or five years old, I saw the separate rest rooms and water fountains, the ones for white ladies and gentlemen and the ones for colored men and women. I want to tell you what I thought then. My mama and daddy, they were good sweet people, and they never taught me to hate or to look down on anybody for the color of his skin, and if they ever used the word 'nigger,' it was never within earshot of me.

"But I saw those separate rest rooms and water fountains, Len, and what I thought was 'nigger.' Not the word, really, but what the word means. I thought, there must be something mighty wrong, mighty nasty about those people, if they can't even pee where I pee.

"From the way you're looking at me I know how you feel about that kind of situation and that kind of thinking. You also know that I'm telling you the truth. I'm telling you how I felt, in my heart of hearts, when I was a boy.

"As I grew up I saw the changes happen. I saw the marches for racial equality, and I want to tell you what I saw. Not everything that was there, but what I saw. I saw a tragedy. I saw stupid, racist cops—every southerner knew those cops were stupid and racist—turning dogs and clubs loose on black people; but I also saw those black people looting and burning. It seemed to me, watching television in the south in the sixties, that every time Martin Luther King showed up, the next thing we would see was a black mob smashing store windows and carrying shopping carts full of loot away.

"And I know the emphasis of that in my mind was a racist emphasis, I'm aware of that, Len, and I'm admitting that to you now because I know you'll know I'm telling you the whole truth and nothing but the truth.

"So you'll believe me when I tell you this. You're the kind of man who throws light on all those dark corners. I don't mean by what you say. Wait, that's not what I mean, exactly. It does have to do with what you say, but it's got more to do with what you do. It's who you are. And I can tell you that I see you as just a man, not a black man, but a man—but I think you know that can't be completely true, not to a guy who saw the separate rest rooms when he was a child.

"In you I've seen dignity and courage and character and leadership, and all the things that I admire. And I have to say I've been proud of my friendship with you because I've felt that friendship has endorsed the best part of me. Not that I'm to be congratulated for liking a guy like you. What I mean is, it gives me faith in the human race when I see how easily the barriers of the past, that seem so indestructible, can be blown away by the right contact with the right person.

"You, Len, are the right person. And I know you're looking at me now, and you're knowing what I'm getting at. I have to have you look me in the eye and tell me what you know about those girls. What you had to do with them."

Bellflower looked right back across that green table at Ridge and said, "Nothing."

"That's too bad, Len," Ridge said. "I went to the dump. I went through your garbage. And I found the pictures of the first victim that you cut up. It's right there, mixed in with your junk mail."

Bellflower began to cry. He wept for a full two minutes before saying anything, and then he poured out everything. He told Ridge he had slept with hookers, and he did not have to say he was ashamed; his whole proud face had melted into a puddle of despair. He said he had wanted to keep his encounters with them totally random. But after a few months he had found himself growing comfortable. That was the word he used— "comfortable"—in a way that suggested to Ridge that Bellflower had found a kind of temporary peace in the company of certain rented women.

He told Ridge he had tried to keep his job out of it —he wasn't stupid. He knew if hookers and their pimps got to know him too well, they'd be calling for favors he would be unwilling to perform, for he would never compromise his job, he swore. But a surprising number of street girls recognized his face—and Bellflower laughed when he told Ridge that, and said, "I guess they're in so many motel rooms, they watch a lot of television." So to stay anonymous, Bellflower had started borrowing the limousine of a friend; it made it easier to pick a girl up, and he never had to worry about his LAPD sedan being spotted.

Then Bellflower's eyes, yellowed whites rimmed in red, drooped wearily, and he shook his head. "I didn't kill anybody," he said, without looking at Ridge. "But I can't ask you to believe me."

"But Len," Ridge said, "how do you explain the bullets matching your pistol?"

"I don't," Bellflower said. "I can't understand it."

"What about the friend who loaned you the limo,

Len? Maybe he can help us establish an alibi for you on the nights the girls were killed."

"I don't think so," Bellflower said. "The friend was Josh Lannon. But he can't be much help. Some nights I had it, nobody died. But every night a girl got killed, I had borrowed his limo."

Bellflower lowered his head. Ridge watched as the great tears rolled down his ebony face.

Blood and water.

The detectives of MULHOM pushed everything else aside to work on Bellflower's case. Their orders to do so, as if they needed any, came directly from the office of the chief—for the only thing worse than having a police officer commit a crime was having the public think he was allowed to get away with it. The detectives attacked the case with fervor, all of them sharing the same belief: if this bunch of hotshots can't prove Bellflower did it, then maybe he didn't do it.

For most of the day Ridge and Cully ran in different directions. She, John the Baptist, and Banana Santana went to work again on Clarence, now supported by an abrasive young public defender in MULHOM's makeshift interrogation room. After listening for two hours to Clarence spouting his unshakable conviction that the police commander whose picture he had seen in the newspapers was the man he had seen picking up Porsche, even though he had told Cully and Ridge at separate times that he had never gotten a look at whoever was in the limo that took the girl on her final ride—after listening to all this, she and Dewey and Santana were exhausted. They had a cruiser from the Hollywood Division come up to drive Clarence to a cell there, held over on the charges Cully planned to file against him for having shot at her, though she knew that his accusations against Bellflower would cloud any prosecution against the pimp. Maybe that was why Clarence made them; she couldn't think straight anymore.

Because the victims had been exposed to varying ranges of outdoor temperatures before they were discovered, Roger the Coroner could provide times of death only within a broad range of several hours. But still, for a while, Ridge, Tooda, and Cowboy Condell thought they had an alibi angle working, based on whatever the actual times were when the girls were killed. The detectives had been instructed by Deputy Chief Rowe to keep Josh Lannon's name out of the whole affair, since he had been an innocent party; but they figured that if they could find any witnesses, like the man from the tattoo parlor, for instance, who might have seen one of the victims alive *after* Bellflower had returned the limo to Lannon, then the actor might prove to be the first thread in a whole tapestry of alibi that they hoped to weave. Once again they hit the streets of Hollywood with pictures of the victims, and this time they took along Bellflower's picture, asking the hookers along the way if any of them had spent time with him; if MULHOM could find any prostitutes who could swear to have dated Bellflower, the very fact that they were still alive might cast doubt on his being a compulsive killer. But that hope and all the others crashed on Highland Avenue, where a young whore jumped when she saw Bellflower's picture and said she had been with him just a few days before in the hotel across the street. She described him as "spooky" and "scary," and to prove she had been with him she produced Bellflower's LAPD business card.

At eight o'clock Cully and Ridge walked out to the parking lot of the Can together. The night was chilly. The eucalyptus trees rattled overhead in the first steady breeze of autumn. It could have been a beautiful night; but neither of them was able to see beauty in anything right at the moment. He stood by her jeep and seemed to want to talk, and yet he volunteered nothing.

"I'm tired," she said, for both of them. "Let's get some sleep."

He nodded, turned without a word, and they drove off in different directions, she toward Coldwater, he toward Laurel Canyon.

28

Josh Lannon wore a creamy linen suit, pale blue shirt, and a tie the color of daisies. Everyone else was dressed in darker fall colors, but the interview he was granting would not be published until spring, and he wanted to look freshly contemporary when it appeared.

For a time Josh Lannon had stopped giving interviews, but lately he had reversed his policy. His popularity continued to grow in Europe, and that, he thought, should help him at home. When his press agent called him with a request to meet a writer for the largest news syndicate in Europe, Lannon agreed to meet her at the Polo Lounge, the Beverly Hills Hotel's haughty watering hole.

The interviewer was from Rome. She wore remarkable eyeglasses; they looked as if the halves had broken and the nose bridge had been glued at a mismatch, so the left goggle sat a half inch above the right. The whole arrangement was then encrusted with gold flecks and rose to points at the temples. The woman never smiled, she was far too elegant for that; when she shook his hand in greeting, it was with cold stiff fingers.

Lannon asked her not to take notes; he told her he always asked interviewers to depend on themselves to listen and to capture the flavor. He was not worried about being misquoted, he told her; if anybody wanted to write lies about him, who could stop them?

He did, however, carry a tape recorder hidden inside his own coat, in case he ever did want to force a publication to print a retraction.

The woman with the glasses told him in a husky accent that she wanted "to focus on a new penetration" about him, namely "the man behind the man," and she said the phrase as if it had never been spoken before. Then she pursed her heavy lips for a moment and said, "What was the first cinema you ever saw?"

He looked at her, and saw his own face in her glasses.

An urge began to rise inside him, and the urge had a voice. It whispered: *Tell her. Tell her the truth.*

He hesitated. All he could see of her face was that wall of eyeglass lens and those puckered scarlet lips beneath; she sat motionless while she waited for his answer.

Tell her. Tell her.

How could he tell her?

He would remember the day of that first movie as long as he lived; there were nights when its feelings returned to him in such vivid recollection that he was sure even death could not take the memories away. Josh Lannon sometimes feared that when his body was lowered in a coffin, that movie would unspool forever upon the closed lid above his lifeless eyes, and the emotions of the day he first saw it, as a boy of five, would course through his rotting body. Stronger and more toxic than formaldehyde, those feelings would drive out the poisons of decay, and preserve him in eternal pain.

His mother's dance review had traveled to a town somewhere; Josh had blotted out the town's name, or else had never known it, for he had been too young at the time to note the names of the towns or even the states where the carnival traveled. His mother did not have to bother with setting up the tents; the man who owned the carnival did that, and she paid him a flat rate

—only a token, since she and her girls drew men past the turnstiles.

Josh had grown up playing around the swing rides, the ones like chain-and-metal maypoles, with throbbing gasoline motors and creaky greasy joints and scrambled orbiting surges that slung the farm boys against their girlfriends. Around the age of four he began fetching tools and drinks for the men who assembled and operated them, and they sometimes let him take tickets. But in this particular town one of the main support beams of the roundup had snapped when they were setting it up, and the ride would be out of service for days. That put the operators in a foul mood, and they ordered him away from them as if Josh had caused the problem.

He went back to the rusty Winnebago his mother traveled in and found her just coming out its backdoor with Deets, the carnival owner. She shoved a bill into Josh's shirt pocket and told him to go into town and "see a movie or something."

Josh didn't know what a movie was. He didn't know where the town was either. But he asked one of the guys at the milk-bottle booth and the guy jerked the only thumb he still had toward the carnival gate and said, "That way, idiot."

Josh walked into the town, a place with a court-house square and a brass statue of a soldier. On the back side of the courthouse was a theater, and on the marquee red letters said *BAMBI*.

Josh could read. One of the girls who traveled with his mother had taught him, using the comic books she liked to buy for entertainment in the camper as they rode from town to town. She read to Joshy, as she called him, and he began to recognize words like "Whap!," "Bam!," and "Pow!" When he began to look at the cartoons and say those words himself in the right places, she had begun to point out the other words with the tip of her polished fingernail. She had taught him to write his name, and she had showed him hers. Her name was Bambi.

When Josh gave his money to the man at the theater, he thought that whatever a movie was, it was about the Bambi he knew.

He was frightened when he went into the theater. Not from being alone, he was used to that; but the place was dark and cool and unlike any place he had ever been in. But it smelled like popcorn and spilled soft drinks, just like the carnival, and when the music started and the whole wall exploded with color . . .

Josh sat, not moving a muscle, afraid that if he did, the beautiful magic in front of him would stop and disappear. Then he began to laugh, as the other children did, to encourage Bambi from his seat in the theater, and the fawn on the screen heard him, the fawn flourished, Bambi was real. Little Josh's rapture was total— and utterly unnoticed by anyone around him, until the fire sequence, when Bambi and Bambi's mother are running for their lives, and five-year-old Josh Lannon knew the mother was not going to make it. He clutched at the metal armrests of his chair and screamed at the colored wall: "Run, Bambi! Run, Mommy! *Ruuuunnnn!*"

But Bambi's mother did not survive.

And when the kind old stag told Bambi that Mother had died, Josh Lannon began to scream and cry.

He couldn't stop. "No!" he sobbed. "No! *Nooo!*" People around him turned in their seats to look.

"Hey, boy, where's your mama?" a broad country woman demanded from the row in front of him.

Still Josh cried. The woman walked back up the aisle and came back with the manager; she pointed to him.

Josh darted out of the theater and ran all the way to the tent where his mother's dance review performed.

The music was playing; that made him pause. He had been told more than once that he was never to interrupt or even come into the tent once the music was playing. But he had to see his mother, he had to feel her, to be sure she was all right. He slipped around behind the railing and walked to the back, and came through the double hung canvas that kept out the light.

His mother was on stage.

He had seen her undressed before, but never like this. She kept her shoulders back, her spine arched, and her breasts pressed forward, and they looked enormous. All he saw was the nipples, impossibly red; the breasts were like two blimps, taut and projecting. The men in their overalls were transfixed, speechless. She moved slowly, shifting her pelvis, licking her lips, and fondling her breasts.

His crying had stopped. He watched her in fascination. Strutting, rubbing, caressing her own body.

She pranced fluidly off the stage, glancing back just once at the men in the room. Josh must have become invisible, for she did not look at him at all.

He moved toward the stage to follow her; he had climbed on that stage many times, but never when the tent was full of men. Deets, working as master of ceremonies, grabbed his neck, his fingertips biting into Josh's throat like ice tongs. "Get outta here, you little bastard! What the fuck's wrong with you?"

He slung Josh toward the door and Josh stumbled out into the sunlight. He peered back inside and saw two men in overalls already talking quietly with Deets.

Josh ran around the side of the trailer and tried the door, but it was locked. He banged on it and began to cry again. The window curtain pulled back, then the door sprang open. "Josh, what the hell?" his mother said.

"Mama, the deer—" he started, but he didn't know how to get the words out, to tell her about the deer and the fire and the fawn without a mother, and how much he loved her.

"Just a minute!" he heard Deets say behind him,

not to Josh or his mother but to the farmers he had brought up with him. Deets strode up, glared at Josh, and then exchanged a glance with his mother.

"Get back out on the midway," Josh's mother snapped at him. "And don't come back till we close."

"But—"

"Get away!" his mother said, and she smiled at Deets and at the farmers, and began to follow them to Deets's trailer.

"Mama . . ." Josh cried, running after her.

She whirled on him and grabbed him with both hands, one behind the neck and the other under his chin, and began slamming his face against the metal side of the Winnebago. Again and again she hurled him against the trailer, her teeth clenched as her words pounded with the rhythm of the blows: *Get. Away. Get. Away. Get. Away . . .*

Josh woke up in a hospital. When he asked the nurses how he got there, they told him he had been hit by a car—not the answer to the question he was asking, but enough for Josh to know to keep his mouth shut. Two days later Deets picked him up, paying the bill, smiling a lot, and telling the nurses the police had no leads on that hit-and-run driver, but he was thankful to the Good Lord that little Josh was okay.

Deets drove him back to the field, where the trucks were already packed and formed up to convoy. Josh's mother gave Josh a hug and held him in her lap in the Winnebago and fed him ice cream all the way to the next town. Every time she hit him, she fed him ice cream afterward.

Now Josh Lannon, sitting in the Polo Lounge in Beverly Hills, looked across the table at the journalist from Rome and said, "My first movie? I'll never forget it. It was *Spartacus*."

He drove home from the Polo Lounge, changed into spandex shorts and a sweatshirt, and spent two hours in his home gym. He relaxed in the sauna, showered, then dressed in a plain navy sweater and safari pants, the kind with broad pockets that covered up the bulge of his thighs.

He moved to his makeup desk and sat down before an ordered array of powders, paints, and cosmetic magic. He went to work on his face, covering it with an artificial pallor that did more to disguise his suntanned superstar appearance than any other single piece of visual artistry. His lips were the hardest to disguise; he had to use a pipe for that. Cigarettes just amplified the pout he was known for, but sucking on a pipe pursed his lips and changed their look completely. He pulled out one of those carved ivory pipes with a ski-jump stem. He combed his hair the way a man does when he's going bald—parted two inches above his left ear. His hair was still thick, but it was amazing how much change in his appearance that little alteration made.

Before he left his room, he got out a trash bag and the sandbag that he used to hold down his weight rack. He tucked the sandbag into a leather satchel.

He locked his mansion, set the burglar alarms, fetched the limousine from the fleet of cars in his garage, and drove out of Bel Air.

The Santa Ana winds had risen late in the afternoon, blowing a sudden warmth through the valley. In the previous coolness of that October Cully had snapped in the plastic sheets that fitted in the glassless window openings of her jeep. They distorted the storefront rainbows of neon she now passed on her way down Ventura Boulevard and blurred the headlights of the cars she saw in her rearview mirror, but tonight she was too tired to bother with removing them, so she drove toward home with sweaty heat lying between her back and the bucket seat. It seeped into her bones, where the anger and frustration were already simmering.

It was all over as far as Cully was concerned. Len Bellflower had done it.

She had doubted it at first. She had wanted to doubt it. But the pieces fit too tightly together.

Ridge was different. He wouldn't give up. And she believed he was doing it, was arguing with her, because he was angry at her. Was this a competition? Hell yes, it was. And she had won. They had different instincts. Hers were better than the great Tom Ridge. And the great Tom Ridge couldn't handle that fact.

The thought jolted her. She was being hostile and competitive.

How could she be doing this to Ridge, a man she loved? Well, Ridge was domineering—not by being a bully, but through the strength of his mind and the arrogance that strength gave him. And Cully was never going to allow herself to be dominated.

It wasn't easy being a woman. And by God she wasn't going to complain.

She wasn't going to back down either.

And the baby growing inside her didn't make it any easier.

No, not a baby. Not even a fetus. A sperm and an egg that just got their timing off, that's all. She'd deal with that. Sometime. Sometime soon.

She reached her apartment, parked on the street, and clamped in the iron locking bar that joined the steering wheel and brake pedal into one unstealable unit—for even cops could get ripped off. She shuffled down the concrete path, musky with the mulch of the pansy beds the landlord had planted that day, and entered her apartment, locking the door and switching on the lights in one habitual motion. Suzie Kirkwood's black cat—Spanky, Cully had decided to name him—padded in from the kitchen with a soprano bray, then scrambled back to his bowl. Cully dumped in a handful of food and rubbed his arched spine. She paused to watch him eat, then crossed the living room, undressing as she went. She reached her bedroom, tossed her clothes onto the bed, moved into the bathroom, and turned on the water for a long hot soak. But before she could climb in, she thought she heard the doorbell. She twisted off the water and listened; the chimes came again. She slipped on her robe and went to the door, knowing it was Ridge even before she looked out the peephole.

"I think we ought to talk," was the first thing he said.

"Yeah. You're right. Come on in."

He sat down on the couch. Spanky jumped straight into his lap, and Ridge petted the cat absently. Cully sat in the armchair. She still had on the thick white socks she had worn under her boots, and she put her ankles together and tucked her feet up under her. She knew she looked defensive but if she moved from that position she'd look nervous and edgy and even more defensive, so she forced herself to sit very still.

Ridge didn't say anything. She realized he was trying to get words out and she felt warm for him the way she always felt when she let herself look at things from his point of view. She was ready to go hug him when he said, "You're mighty sure, aren't you?"

"About Bellflower?"

"About the . . . pregnancy." He lifted Spanky off his lap and set him on the floor.

"I don't want to talk about that right now. I just . . . I can't talk about it. Right now," she added, though at that moment she couldn't imagine when she would ever feel like talking about it.

Ridge paused. Fatigue marked his face, as she was sure it was lining hers. "All right," he said, "let's talk about Bellflower for a minute. Let's say he didn't do it. I'm sure he didn't, but maybe I'm dead wrong. I can say that. You can't."

"I don't understand. I can't say what, that I might be wrong?"

"Exactly."

"Okay, you're right, I can't say I might be wrong. Okay, then, maybe I'm wrong, but I'm not."

"That's what I mean. You won't let yourself believe you might have taken the wrong trail."

"If you end up at your destination, Tom, then by definition you didn't exactly take the wrong trail. We found the guy. It's clear. He doesn't admit to it, but none of them do. Right up to the gas chamber, they don't admit it, until it's too late and the pellets are hitting the liquid."

"I know he's acting guilty," Ridge said. "He doesn't know how to act. This kind of thing breaks the boundaries of anything Len Bellflower has prepared all his life to be. Think about that for a second. We have to analyze a killer's motivations from the mind of a killer. And Bellflower's reactions seem consistent with that, if you assume he is the killer. What we don't want to admit is that a perfectly innocent man might react exactly the same way as a perfectly guilty man. For entirely different reasons, of course, but his external actions might be exactly the same."

"Ridge. This is too—"

"And while we're at it," Ridge plowed on, "a woman with a pregnancy might have the same reactions to the pregnancy, whether she meant to keep the baby or not."

"We're not talking about pregnancy."

"She'd be afraid. She'd be full of all sorts of dark doubts. Her whole life would be turned upside down. But that doesn't mean anything, it doesn't mean she shouldn't keep the baby."

"And it doesn't mean she should."

A small fear, like a warm liquid, puddled in the center of her chest, then spread slowly, so that the whole middle of her body began to feel watery. Could Ridge have made a leap, in the silence of those moments when his thoughts were his own and his heart whispered secrets known only to God and himself? Had the union of that sperm and egg already become a life to him, a life that he was now trying to save?

The thought of this terrified her—for him. For her, for them. In the eyes of the man she loved, was she about to commit murder?

She would never remember getting out of her chair. She must have; he must have seen her move and met her halfway. But suddenly they were both kneeling in the middle of her living room, hugging each other. She was crying, but she could do it without making noise. She could do it and wipe the tears away with the back of her hand, and all she looked like when they stopped hugging and he looked at her face was that she was about to cry, not that she had.

"Cully . . . I wish I could help you. I feel like this is all on you. I swear . . . I swear to God . . . I won't blame you afterward. Whatever you decide to do."

"Whatever I decide? Why can't we do this together?"

"Goddamn, Cully! First you're telling me it's none of my business, and then you're asking me why I don't take any responsibility!"

She was about to argue with that, but she couldn't find a comeback. He was right. That was exactly what she was doing. Maybe with the pregnancy she wasn't thinking straight.

"I know," she said. "I know." She just hugged him, her hair against his ear, her cheek against his neck, and his warmth felt good against her. We'll come up with something, she thought. It'll be all right. That's what she wanted to say, but she didn't say it. And yet she felt it there on the carpet of her living room, holding him in her arms.

Lannon pointed the limo toward the airport, where twenty-four-hour clubs along its main approaches advertised nude reviews to L.A.'s new arrivals.

Maybe here the girls wouldn't even recognize him.
Maybe they would like him. What were their typical sexual partners like? Who were their usual customers? The
girls would think he was just another poor lonely social
reject who couldn't get sex free, and then when they saw
his body, they would be impressed enough to put something into the grunting and sweating.

He parked out under the harsh lights, not worrying
if anyone saw the car. Limousine services worked the
airport just like cab companies; anyone seeing him
would think he was just another driver taking a break.
He strolled into the bar, a place done in Japanese-
meets-lumberyard. Music poured from a jukebox. An
actual jukebox! The shabbiness of the place both re-
pulsed and delighted him. The walls had been painted a
matte black, then covered with the kind of latticework
they sold at discount stores. Plastic ivy poked from bur-
lap pots and snaked down the far wall, where there was
an aquarium, for some unknown reason. Only one fish
swam in the pale waters. This place didn't worry about
people coming back; it was a trap for the millions of
travelers moving in and out of the city.

At the bar sat four Koreans, all of them in identical
black glasses. The girls danced on a table in the corner,
a single harsh spotlight hooked into the ceiling above
them. The others moved about, topless, serving drinks
or asking customers to buy one for them. Their faces
looked clouded, used and empty, like dry wine glasses
smudged with lipstick. Lannon figured they didn't even
run a good prostitution hustle in this bar. The Orientals
probably just talked with the bartender and asked him
straight out where they could find some companionship,
thinking it was bad manners to ask the girls directly.

Lannon took a seat in the center of the room, and
when the waitress came, he ordered a beer in a bottle.
She never even looked at him.

He watched the first girl, the one on the table when
he entered, dance to a new song by the Rolling Stones.

She was soft around the middle, and the g-string she wore was an inch smaller than her butt, which made up the difference by spilling out over the edges.

Staring at her, Josh Lannon realized why he had come to that seedy bar. He wanted a victim. He wanted someone to destroy. And he wanted someone who had a hint of innocence about her. Innocence in a prostitute. How interesting. And how deceptive—the suggestion that they were experienced professionals when really they were star-struck girls inside.

He thought again of Mike Rowe. Lannon had admired Rowe, at least had envied him, when they first met. Rowe was a real cop. Lannon had played cops three times in movies. He had studied them, even trained with them at their academy, if training means running the obstacle course a few times and shooting on the range. He didn't have time to waste in the classroom. But he did the fun things and played with the toys. Mike Rowe was real, though. And yet, when it got down to it, Mike Rowe wanted to be humiliated by him, by Lannon, a man who was an illusion.

Two more girls had climbed up on the corner table and danced while he pondered this. He had scarcely seen them. But the girl stepping up there now caught his attention. She was different. She was in shape. Not the health-club kind of shape; she looked like she had danced a great deal, and she moved as if she actually liked it, her pelvis snapping in and out right on the beat of the music. But there was something different about her dancing. Most of the others were hookers who thought dancing meant pretending to fuck. This one danced like she thought fucking was just another way of dancing. She was young, too, maybe twenty-three, twenty-four. And best of all her hair was platinum, if that was her real hair. Yeah, the way she tossed her head it had to be. It was like she was a British rock-and-roller. Lannon bet she listened to all that Rolling Stones stuff in her apartment, wherever that was, and danced to it. Her apartment . . . he imagined it: it would be one of those double-row, two-story jobs with a courtyard of tropical plants in the middle and a name like the Bali High. He wished he could go to one of their places sometime, that would be a real experience, he could draw so much from that. But it was too risky.

Lannon realized that death was here, and he was it.

The girl finished her dance and gracefully stepped off the stage. She threaded her way through the tables, and as she passed him he reached out and touched her arm. He did not grab; he knew she would resist that. He kept his fingers on her arm. She glanced down. "Excuse me," he said. "Are you interested in being in a movie?"

So simple and direct. A question she had to answer. She answered by looking at him more closely. At first she didn't recognize him, and yet there was something familiar about him. "I can't show my face here," he said quietly, even with the jukebox playing, so that she had to lean down close enough for him to smell her bath powder. "I'm scouting for a film I'm doing."

It would have been a repulsive line from anybody else; she'd even had men try it on her before. And she was not a prostitute. But there was something unique about his voice, and she recognized . . . Josh Lannon!

"You're exactly right for it," he said. "I wonder if you can act. You actually don't have to act, I mean I don't act, and I don't want actors who act, I want people who are magnetic just being themselves. And you've got it. Real magnetism. And—" He frowned toward the jukebox, as if the effort to talk over its throbbing was too distracting.

"Excuse me," he said, "I didn't ask your name."

"Janet," she said. "Janet Ladle."

"Well Janet, I'd like to . . ." He frowned toward the jukebox again. "I've got to fill this part right away, we're going to be shooting in Paris and I have to catch a plane there right away. It's probably too short notice for you. . . ."

"Are you kidding?" Her voice was light and sweet, like spring sunshine, and full of little-girl thrill. "To be in a movie? With you?"

He had her. "Could we get out of here and talk?"

It would take her two minutes to pull on her clothes. She wasn't supposed to leave, and the bartender, who was also the owner, would tell her that if she walked out, she shouldn't come back. But that was okay, she didn't want to come back.

But while she was pulling on her blue jeans and T-shirt she wondered if this guy was for real. Sure, he looked like Josh Lannon, but what if he was an impersonator, with a perfect line? She congratulated herself on being smart enough to wonder this. She decided that she would take a second hard look. If the guy didn't look righteous, she would turn right around and walk straight back into the bar.

She opened the backdoor, and he was standing at the driver's side of the limo. She walked toward him slowly, taking her time, remembering the warnings the dancers had all discussed, about strippers dying. As she drew closer he pulled the pipe from his lips, slid a hand back through his hair to rake it into its natural position, and gave her a half smile, an expression she had seen numerous times, when that same face was pumped full of light and projected twenty feet high. Josh Lannon! No doubt about it.

Janet got into the car. She didn't care if the bartender fired her, she wasn't ever coming back.

29

Lannon stood in the shower, the water turning to steam almost before it hit his back. He scrubbed himself hard, but not hard enough to hurt. Only the water and the soap could touch him. He lathered and rinsed three times. But he was not tired. He couldn't be tired. There was still more to do.

He dried off and took some Dexedrine. He could sleep tomorrow. When he slept, it would be peacefully.

He picked up the telephone on the wall beside his toilet, next to the television set, and dialed Rowe's number. He knew he would find him at home; Rowe's wife and daughter had taken their annual extended weekend at her family's condo in Colorado, and Rowe had begged off to stay at the helm of the good ship MULHOM as it wallowed in the rough seas of Bell-flower's arrest. The deputy chief was left to rattle around the Hancock Park house alone. He had been telephoning Lannon almost hourly, at first recording an awkward message on the answering machine that Lannon used to screen all his calls—*Josh? It's me. I guess . . . I guess you're not there, give me a call when you get a chance, okay?*—then leaving an even more humiliated silence as he kept checking in after that without wanting to say his name. Lannon knew who made those gaps in his message tape, but he had waited to call back until now, when he was ready.

Rowe answered on the first ring, saying only,

"Rowe," in that official, cool, masculine voice he used to let the men he commanded know that he was a leader.

"Rowe," Lannon said, mocking him in an affected baritone.

"Josh," Rowe said. "I've missed hearing from you."

Lannon laughed. "You must have heard my voice a lot. Haven't they been playing you tapes of the anonymous caller?" Rowe said nothing from the other end of the line; Lannon realized he was the only one laughing and instantly turned serious. "I need to come talk to you," Lannon said. "Tonight."

"About what?"

"It's just . . . I need your strength." Lannon watched himself in the bathroom mirror as he said it.

Lannon took the Range Rover and reached Hancock Park in fifteen minutes. There was a party going on in a house down the block from Rowe's, and Lannon blessed the number of cars crowding the parking space out along the street; he could tuck the Rover among them and no one would remember it. He moved unseen to Rowe's door and tapped instead of ringing. Rowe opened the door immediately, then closed it quickly behind him.

Rowe made no sign of welcome. They stood there looking at each other in the foyer, not touching. "Let's go back into my study," Rowe said, and led him to a corner room.

It was Lannon's first time inside Rowe's house. It was exactly as he had pictured it, done up in conservative colors and traditional fabrics, with Rowe's study upholstered in hunter-green wool, adorned with prints depicting riders running to the hounds. A desk almost identical to the one in Rowe's cubicle at the Can sat in the center of the room; Rowe was a predictable man.

He leaned back on the front edge of his desk, half

sitting, half standing, facing Lannon. Lannon studied his eyes and saw a wariness that alerted him.

"I just wanted to see if you're okay," Lannon said, and then wished he could call for a retake on the line because he heard it sounding wooden and phony.

"I'm not okay," Rowe said. "Why would I be? In the last two days, even as I tried to do the right thing . . . everything . . . everything in my career and my personal life is turning out . . . not like I wanted it."

"It's terrible, Mike," Lannon began, and took a step forward, but stopped as he saw Rowe pull back.

"I've been thinking, Josh. I just can't stop thinking. I know Len Bellflower's guilty, I *know* it. But I still can't stop thinking."

"Thinking what?"

"About the psychological profiles. Dr. Blein, have I told you about him? I can't remember what I've told you and what I haven't. . . . But the things he said . . . about killers like this. He's studied the personality that drives somebody to do something so awful as this, and what's scary is that, to hear Dr. Blein talk, that personality isn't so different from the normal—what we think of as normal—human being walking around anywhere."

"No, it—"

But Mike Rowe needed to talk and wouldn't let himself be interrupted. "There are killers everywhere, Josh, I know that. Maybe anybody could be one, I don't know, but not just anybody could do what we think Bellflower did. Somebody who does something so awful, was he born that way, or made that way by circumstance? Or was he born with the tendency, and something ugly brought it out in him? Right from the beginning, Blein talked about this killer's mother. He said the attack on the breasts was a rage against motherhood, and nurturing, or the lack of it. And I thought about your mother. . . ."

"I had a zero in the mother department," Lannon said easily. "No doubt about that."

"And I thought about your career. The way you've been worshiped . . . and the way things have turned around for you in the last few months."

"Nothing's turned around," Lannon said harshly, but even his frown didn't slow Rowe's rush of words.

"I thought about rage, and ego, and passion—all the things Dr. Blein talked about. And I thought about when these murders started—right about the time your mother came back into your life."

Rowe was staring straight at him. Lannon met his gaze with the look of clear, easy innocence that he had mastered long ago. "I know exactly what you mean," he said. "If you start thinking this way, you can suspect anybody. I mean hey, when my mother first got here, I wanted to beat my face against a wall, the way she used to do it for me. I thought it was better if I went out and found a girl to lick my face instead. And you should see it, Josh, what those girls are like. They do worship me. They'd do anything for me. But they don't know about my mother. They don't know about me. If I try to talk to them about my mother, they get bored. They want me to talk about me—who they think I am. They want to kiss and lick and suck who they think I am. They don't know who I am, and that makes me angry."

Lannon paused, wondering if he had gone too far. "God knows what I'd be like, if I was a man like Bellflower." He squeezed his eyes shut; tears appeared at the intersection of the long lashes. "I just . . . all this is so awful, and I feel so awful that you and I have gotten so caught up in it. I wish I'd given you more comfort."

Rowe stood blinking, confused, watching as Lannon sank to his knees and wept like a sinner before a revivalist. A sadness filled Rowe's eyes as he looked down at the blubbering red face. Lannon struggled up from his knees and held his arms out toward Rowe. "I came here to hold you, Mike. I need to hold you."

"Josh, I—"

They were Rowe's last words. Lannon snatched him by the right wrist and jerked the arm up around his throat, pivoting to Rowe's back and applying the choke hold he had learned in the classes he had taken at the police academy, when he was studying for the role that first made him famous.

Deputy Chief of Police Mike Rowe struggled at first, but his strength had never been equal to Josh Lannon's. With the flow of blood to his brain pinched off, his body sagged, as if all its bones had turned elastic.

30

Doubting Thomas Ridge, purified by the grace of something nameless within him, something that provided no answers for the personal dilemma that he and Scarlet McCullers found themselves in, and yet somehow went beyond all answers, drove home to his bare apartment.

He felt it right to be alone now, to leave Cully to her rest and her solitude. They were both exhausted.

But even before he was inside his door, he knew he did not want sleep. And so he took his place within the armchair that had been a gift to his grandmother before she died and that was now his lone piece of furniture, and snuggled there within its leathery embrace, he set his mind free to float upon the currents of the night.

I saw him cry, Odom DeFuller had said about Bellflower. *Blood and water. Like what came out of Jesus' side.*

What was the biblical significance of that? The orthodox theological interpretation was that blood represented Christ's humanity, and water His divinity. But Ridge had never accepted answers that seemed too easy; was there a deeper meaning behind the gospel writer's report that something extra gushed from Jesus' veins?

Ridge had tried to give up such questions long ago. He tried to give them up now. He pondered the old saying that blood was thicker than water. What did that mean? That relationships of blood ran deeper than relationships sealed only by emotion and promises?

> *I saw him cry.*
> *Jesus' side.*
> *Blood and water.*
> *I saw him cry.*
> *Blood and water.*

Cully McCullers, alone in her own apartment, took her bath and went to bed. But she, too, could not sleep.

Thoughts boiled around in Cully's brain, making sleep impossible. But while Ridge mused over biblical mysteries and cosmic symbolism, Cully pondered pistols and found herself wondering how in the hell, if Bellflower was *not* the killer, bullets from his gun found their way into the body of Suzie Kirkwood.

Not ten minutes after she had turned out the light, Cully sat straight up in bed. Then she threw on her clothes and drove up to the Can.

When she turned in off Mulholland Drive and her headlights leaped across the empty parking lot, the old building looked small and derelict, its flaky, rusted walls frail, as harmless as a dying animal slouching off to search for a shallow place to make its grave. But when she stopped the jeep and switched off the engine and lights, she found herself in the inky shadows of moonlight, and the Can loomed before her. The lunar sheen reflected along its pitted surfaces with the phosphorescence of a nightmare reptile, and the wind raked the brittle eucalyptus leaves around its crooked corners and across its tin roof like claws upon the inside of a coffin lid.

Cully felt a moment of fear. She remembered what Louie had said about seeing the tire tracks of a limousine that had parked at the building's rear, an observation that she and Ridge had discounted as irrelevant to the murders. She was not even sure she believed Louie. But she believed him now.

She took her pistol from her purse, shoved it into the waistband of her jeans, and got out. She forced herself to the dark door, cursing herself for not bringing a flashlight. A padlock guarded the hasp, and though the hasp was old, the lock was not, and it snapped open quickly once she twisted her key into it. She pulled the hasp aside, hung the sprung lock on the door loop, and pushed it open.

Inside, the floor space was jet black, but moonlight slanted in from the door and she was able to find the switch box and illuminate the little fleet of lost spaceships that lit the length of the building. She shoved the door shut and walked squarely down the Can's center, wishing the department had funded an all-night message patrolman for MULHOM instead of bouncing all its off-hour calls through the Van Nuys Division station; and she wondered: If somebody had been at this place all the time, would Bellflower be where he is now?

She reached the locker room first and stopped in front of Bellflower's locker. Nothing she could see there now could be confirmation of the suspicion that brought her here, and yet as she looked at the simple padlock she knew she was right. She moved down the cinderblock corridor, switching on lights as she went, and came to the shooting range. There, on the floor of the far right lane, she found what she was looking for.

She was coming back through the corridor into the locker room and had just switched off the corridor lights when she heard the door from the outside pushed softly shut, the sound loud as a whisper in a churchyard. She pressed her back against the cold wall of the locker room and pulled out her pistol. Breathlessly she listened to the footsteps approaching steadily across the concrete floor, and then she heard the familiar male voice. "Cully?" he called.

"Ridge? Ridge! Oh, Jesus." She tucked the pistol back into her belt before she stepped fully around the corner, not wanting him to see how jumpy she had been.

But she couldn't resist hugging him. "I wasn't sure it was you," she said.

He stared at her as his brain put it all together. He nodded, with a faint smile of satisfaction that he had figured correctly. "I called you," he said. "And when you weren't home, I got nervous. And then I realized that if it had hit me, it would hit you, too."

"You mean the pistol," she said. "The ballistics. How the hell could Bellflower's bullets be in that dead girl if Bellflower wasn't the killer."

He nodded again, and his eyes took on their distant stare. "I started thinking about lies," he said, "wondering where the lies are here. I started asking about that anonymous witness on the telephone. And then I thought, 'How obvious!' "

"We were stupid," Cully said.

"We were stupid!" he agreed, grinning, and with growing excitement, rattled on quickly. "Once I saw that one lie, the others became obvious. Bellflower didn't remove the sperm sample from the evidence room! I mean, if the theory is that Bellflower wants to be caught, and that's why he shot the body, then why would he destroy that evidence?"

"It's the one piece of evidence—"

"That can prove his innocence!" Ridge barked. "Exactly. And that left ballistics." Ridge was having so much fun that Cully stood there meekly, her hands in the pockets of her jeans, and let him lecture, forgetting that she had gotten to the Can first. "How could the bullets have the markings of Bellflower's barrel? Because somebody changed barrels with him. It would be easy. When your pistol is in its holster, all you see is the handle. You could have it for days and never notice a switch had been made. You could even shoot with it, because you only see the points of your sights, not the barrel itself. And a switch would be easy, if you had the master key to all the padlocks in the locker room."

"Rowe," she said.

"Rowe," Ridge repeated quietly. They both paused to let a chill pass; it was hard to say the name of a cop who would frame another cop for murder. Then Ridge went on, "But the stroke with the anonymous caller, about the fleeing cop dropping something in the storm grate, that was brilliant. We found the shell casings, and they matched Bellflower's gun precisely, there was no doubt about it."

"The bullets had the markings of a barrel, that could be switched. But nobody would consider that, since we found the brass casings, because they matched Bellflower's pistol, the pistol he'd had in his possession constantly, the pistol he'd never denied having. How could he, it had been registered to him eighteen months."

Ridge smiled with slow satisfaction. "The casings did match, of course. And they were from Bellflower's gun. But they weren't found at the murder site."

"No," Cully said. "They were picked up at the shooting range, at the spot where Bellflower practiced." From her pocket she pulled the handful of casings she had just found at the right-hand range lane and spread her palm open, displaying them for Ridge.

His eyes locked onto her hand, and it all hit him then: she had been there first; she had thought faster, by a more direct route; she had beaten him to it. Not only that, but he had stood there gloating over his own brilliance.

He did the one thing he could have done, and have her still love him the way she did. He grinned. "Good work," he said. "Damn good work."

"But I don't think it's Rowe," Cully said, all her ego jousting with Ridge now vanishing with the gravity, the sheer ugliness, of what she was saying. "Why would a hooker go out with him, without checking with her pimp first? But his good buddy Josh Lannon . . . He has access to the Can, and Lannon . . . can you imagine a stripper being invited on a private date with him, and

not accepting? He also owns a limo, silver. I checked."
She took a breath. "So now we're left with one question.
Did Lannon do all this alone, killing the girls, framing
Bellflower? Or did Deputy Chief Michael Rowe help
him?"

"Why don't we go ask Deputy Chief Rowe?" Ridge
said.

From Cully's desk they telephoned the Van Nuys
Station and asked for the deputy chief's emergency contact numbers; MULHOM procedure dictated that he
could always be reached. The night sergeant said Rowe
had logged in from his home at nine that evening. The
sergeant said there was no question; he had spoken with
Rowe himself, and the deputy chief had been definite
about his location and availability; with his second-in-
command in a cell facing murder charges, Rowe intended to provide emphatic leadership. It was now a
quarter past midnight.

They telephoned Rowe's home. No one answered.

Detectives Ridge and McCullers drove to Hancock
Park.

Neither of them had ever visited Rowe's home before. The living-room curtains were drawn but faintly
backlit, as from the glow of a single lamp. They parked
in the driveway behind Rowe's car and rang the doorbell. It gonged with an aristocratic solidity, but no answer came. They rang again, and then knocked. Still
nothing. They backed up into the front yard, gazing up
at the second-floor windows and wishing for a light. Still
nothing.

A thin slit of uncurtained light brightened the pane
of one of the living-room windows, and Ridge and Cully
moved to it. He peered in, then pulled back. He
squeezed his eyes shut.

She looked. Through the parted curtains she could

see the spacious, shadowy living room of Michael Rowe.
The deputy chief hung from one of the mahogany raf-
ters, a noose around his neck and a dining-room chair
kicked over at his dangling feet, as if his last step had
been a desperate leap from despair into oblivion.

31

Their first call was to Rose Nose Dugan. He was the Immediate Number Three for MULHOM, behind Rowe and Bellflower. They made the call from their car, not wanting to touch anything in the house until the forensics teams arrived. Then they sat in the car and waited.

When the lab boys rolled in, Cully entered the house with them and floated along at their shoulders as they poked through Rowe's personal papers, looking to see if he had written any expression of disgrace and despair over the collapse of his dreams, brought about by Bellflower's guilt, before he hanged himself—and though they found no such note to explain the suicide, nobody showed a single doubt that it had been exactly that. Ridge remained in the car, as if he could ask and answer every question within the sanctuary of his own mind.

An hour later he appeared inside the house. "We've got a body," he whispered in Cully's ear. "Up on Balboa Boulevard. Dumpster driver found it."

"I'll meet you there," she said. "You take the car, and I'll come over with one of these guys when they're finished here."

"See you there."

He was already gone when she realized he didn't mean they had discovered another corpse, unrelated to the others. Ridge would have left only because something they radioed him had led him to believe that this newly murdered girl was sister to the others, and the death of Mike Rowe had ended nothing.

Two long one-story buildings, mirror images of each other, lay at right angles to the boulevard. A sign above each listed the street number, with letters of the alphabet all the way through J to distinguish the different tenants, specialty repair shops for vacuum cleaners, cellular telephones, car radios. Ridge parked along the street, got out, nodded to the two young uniformed cops as he stepped over the yellow-tape barrier, and walked slowly down the length of the alley toward the three vehicles parked there: a patrol car with its blue lights still revolving, the medical examiner's van, and a garbage truck.

The alley was quiet. There was none of the loud talk and gross humor that men who work the graveyard shift usually use to keep their spirits up when cleaning up murders in the grim hours of the night. That hush was Ridge's first sign that something about this murder had them scared. He felt what he always did when approaching the scene of a murder: a narrowing of the world until all that existed was the victim whose life had spiraled to an abrupt point of death; a killer whose life spiraled away from that moment in an ever-widening spin, so that the farther he got from that lethal instant the more meaningless it became to him; and Ridge himself, who stood at the exact middle of both those spirals, reaching simultaneously forward and back, like Hercules between two teams of horses, to pull those two spirals back together into a single event of furious death.

It made time slow for Ridge. Details stood out. The doors to his left and right, sliding out of the periphery of his vision as he passed; the sound of his heels against the grit of the concrete; the faint red glow of the night sky in L.A., the city light diffusing through the smog; and the revolving blue light of the police cruiser, pulsing down the stucco walls of the alley. By the time he reached the garbage truck, Ridge wore his Doubting Thomas stare.

It was a small group beyond the truck. Rose Nose Dugan, two young uniforms, two Hispanic body baggers from the coroner's office, and a fortyish, puffy truck driver who looked as bloodless as a vampire in the flashes of the revolving blue light. "This is Larry Buell," Dugan said to Ridge. "Mr. Buell discovered the body and was good enough to call us."

Ridge looked at Buell; the man was visibly quivering. "It was the smell," Buell said, needing to talk. "Ain't nothin' like that, man. Nothin' like that!"

Ridge glanced over at the trash container, still two feet off the ground and hanging on the forks of the Dumpster. Then Ridge looked up at the top of the truck. It was clear to him that whatever Buell had found was inside the truck already, and he would have to climb up onto the cab to see it. "You knew, just from the smell?" Ridge asked.

"I smelled it in 'Nam, man! Fresh bodies, dead in the field a few hours? You never forget that smell, man! Jesus, I—" Buell's voice went high; tears suddenly poured from his eyes like his whole head was full of water and his shaking sloshed them out.

"Take it easy, it's okay," Dugan said.

Ridge took Buell by the shoulders and stooped so that their eyes were on the same level. "Larry?" Ridge said. "It's okay. This ain't 'Nam. That's all over. This is just a dead body and you helped us find it. This ain't 'Nam."

Buell's eyes locked on Ridge's and he stopped crying. He cleared his throat. "I came to make this pickup. I was hungry, man, I always eat after this stop. And I always keep the windows open because this Dumpster is usually full of Chinese food they make down here someplace, and it gets rank, so I gotta keep the cab blowed out so I can choke down my Big Mac, ya know? Only I smelled somethin' different tonight, man, *that* smell, ya know? I told myself, Larry, man, it's just that day-old mu shu pork, baby, chill out, ya know? I punched the Dumpster, I pulled it up, and then . . . I bout hadda stop and puke, the smell was so strong. I crawled up there with my flashlight and looked. And . . ."

Buell looked away, out of words. Ridge turned to see that Cully had walked up. They exchanged a glance, and Ridge reached out to one of the uniforms and took his five-battery flashlight. Ridge climbed the truck on the ladder up the side of the container section. He reached the top and stood there for a minute, shining the light onto the garbage, and at last he climbed down again and handed the flashlight to Cully.

She climbed easily, grateful she had worn jeans and cowboy boots instead of a skirt that Dugan could look up. She peered over the edge of the white steel container and shined the light down onto the sea of garbage.

The refuse stretched the full length of the container and appeared to be at least six feet deep, with a mound toward the cab section where Buell had made the last couple of pickups without yet using his compacter. At first Cully could distinguish nothing. Then she trained the beam on the mound and saw the rusty color of blood. It was on a canvas sack, exposed through the ragged edges of a dark green plastic trash bag. The sack itself had ruptured, and from the split spilled platinum-blond hair.

32

At four in the morning, Cully sat in the Can, the only human in the big tin cavern. All the other detectives were either still out at Mike Rowe's house, milling around in the front yard and mumbling about the inevitable demise of MULHOM, or they had driven to the Dumpster on Balboa Boulevard to gaze at the new mess there. Ridge had stayed with the body and Cully had taken her turn at being alone with her thoughts and her dancing stomach.

She heard the door open and Ridge entered. He drifted over and sat down in the wooden chair across from her. "The body was in pieces," he said. "It was in a canvas sack, like a seaman's duffel. And all that was inside a heavy-duty plastic trash bag."

She knew what that meant. The same killer. Bellflower was in custody, of course; he couldn't have done it. But the trademarks of the other killings—the garish presentation of the victim, the cynical notes that had so vividly marked the other killings—were not an aspect of this one. A jury, even a good, thoughtful one, would only shrug its shoulders at this new murder and say it would have to be the object of a new investigation; but as for the girls with the notes, their killer had already been found, and his name was Leonard Bellflower.

Ridge went on: "Whoever put her there didn't mean for her to be found. Blood had seeped through the canvas, but it contained everything else, and the plastic bag sealed that off—or was supposed to. But the Dumpster was behind a little Chinese catering service, and they would dump their scraps in it. The rats . . . they liked the pork marrow and the chicken entrails, and while they were scratching around, one of them tore open the trash bag. When that happened, they smelled the blood, and after that they gnawed through the canvas, and then into the body." Ridge paused again. She knew he was wondering whether to try to protect her from nightmares, and she stared back at him in a way that said he'd better not try. "As nearly as I can tell, they've eaten off her face. But we'll have to wait for the autopsy to be sure."

Cully's hands felt cold. She knew her face was pale.

"You okay?" Ridge said.

"Sure," she said. She took a deep breath, sucking in the cold air. "For somebody who's at absolutely rock bottom, I'm just fine. Mike Rowe dead. Bellflower will be blamed for that, too, know why? Because the department will feel that Rowe was such a thoughtful, feeling officer that Bellflower's crime gave him an overwhelming sense of failure. And don't tell me I'm wrong, Ridge!" she snapped, though he was not about to do any such thing. "I *know* the department likes to write it's own history! The department feels what it *wants* to feel! The department . . ."

Cully's eyes closed tight and she slowly shoved herself back from the desktop and put her head between her knees. Ridge understood; nausea shadows every cop in a homicide investigation, to strike in odd moments, when the levels of distraction and adrenaline cross and the detective's stomach goes critical.

But instead of retching, Cully screamed, like a lioness roaring, the sound bouncing off the concrete floor and up into the jungle blackness above the rows of dim lights in the Can.

"He can't help doing it," Ridge said. "He can't stop."

She said nothing, just kept her head down.

"Cully . . ."

She lifted her body just enough to rest her elbows on her knees, and still staring at the floor, forever stained by the black drippings of the asphalt, she said, "We'll never prove it. Not with what we have."

She was right, Ridge knew that. Their explanation about the switching of the pistol barrels and the planting of false evidence against Bellflower would sound like the raving fiction of cops trying to salvage the reputation of their ravaged division.

"He's going to keep killing. Like you say, he can't stop. Compulsion has become an obsession. And obsession has turned into sport." She paused. "We're going to have to catch him in the act."

He understood, and said sharply, "Now, you listen to me. . . ."

"I'm going to be his next victim, Ridge," she said, sitting upright, her face flushed. "I'm going to put myself in his way and make him come to me. Then he's gonna be mine."

He started to say something. His lips closed, and he looked away.

"The pregnancy?" she said. "I guess we should talk about that now. I need to tell you that . . . I've decided to have the abortion."

Ridge sat in silence for what seemed a very long time. Both wanted no part of this discussion now; but if not now, when? Ridge said, in a raspy voice, "Cully . . . Look, I . . . I don't know how to do, what to say. I want to bear my share of the decision, and the responsibility, if that's what all this is. I just . . . I have to tell you what this feels like to me, what scares me. You say you're not ready. Maybe you're not. Maybe things happen in life that we're not ready for until we do them. The kid who goes off to school for the first time, is he ready? The kid who doesn't know how to swim and stands at the edge of the pool, about to jump in for his first swimming lesson, is he ready?"

"God, come up with some tough examples, would you?"

"I'm sorry, I'm not trying to make this hard."

"Sure. Right."

"I mean . . . Okay, what about the couple that stands at the altar to be married? Say they've never been married before. Even if they've lived together, they don't know what it's like to be married, because marriage is a commitment. And if they've never lived with that commitment, are they ready for it?"

"They're all ready to try," Cully said. "I'm not."

There wasn't much Ridge could say to that one. "Okay," he said after a minute. "Okay. You're not ready. But if you say that now, is it going to make you less likely to be ready in the future?"

Cully started to answer, thought a minute, then said firmly, "No. It's not going to influence what I do in the future . . . except be more careful about ever getting pregnant when I don't want to be."

"Are you sure about that? You're not tying this pregnancy in with marriage, or anything like that?"

"What are you saying, Ridge?"

"I guess I'm saying I don't want you to close the door on the idea of marriage. Because . . . because I can see that happening for us."

She looked at him. She seemed to be holding her breath.

"Really," he said.

"I've got to do this, Tom. I can't stop it. I'm not ready to be a mother. You've got to understand that. I'm not saying I won't ever be ready, but I'm not ready now. It's the opposite of what you think. I'm afraid that if I have this baby, then I won't ever be ready to be a parent. If I don't have this one, I may be ready. And I don't just mean ready to try, I mean able. Able to be a mother. Able to be a good one. I know I'm not able right now."

Ridge nodded slowly.

Then Cully said, "I've just got to ask you to forgive me."

33

The air smelled sweet here. Los Angeles, beneath the skyscrapers and the freeways, was a desert, but here in Bel Air it was a garden. The mists of a million sprinkler heads poking up through mulch, nourishing ten thousand varieties of flowers, made the air cooler and softer, turned Southern California into Eden.

Eden, where Cain killed Abel.

Cully sat alone in her car and watched the gates far down the road.

How would he do it? she wondered, and wondered how many nights she would have to wonder.

An inexpensive, highly polished American sedan turned in at the driveway, and through her binoculars Cully caught a good look at the driver as he passed through the light of the gate lamps. A slender Hispanic with fastidiously barbered hair; Cully guessed he was a house servant.

She waited. She understood why cops smoked and drank coffee and then peed into the empty cups. Stakeouts made your back hurt, your bottom hot and sticky and itchy. She wore a clingy black dress with long sleeves and a tight skirt ending above her knees. It was elegant enough to go anywhere Lannon might lead her, but simple enough to blend in almost anywhere, too, for the code of California is that nothing a man wears is ever considered too casual, while nothing a woman wears is ever thought of as too formal. The dress was shiny as silk and almost as smooth, but it was polyester, which was great for resisting wrinkles but after a while made her feel like a sandwich encased in Saran Wrap.

Two blocks away, at one of the outlets of Lannon's neighborhood into Sunset Boulevard, Ridge was parked and waiting just like her. Knowing he was there made her less lonely. She wondered what he was thinking now.

She cranked her seat back and did some isometric exercises, then saw heat lights ignite the burgundy bracts of the bougainvillea across the street from the Lannon mansion. The silver limo floated out of the driveway and cruised away, in the direction of Hollywood.

Cully had parked with her lights off, on the darkest part of the street, and when the limo turned down the street, she had to struggle not to follow. If she and Ridge were right, Lannon would not be able to deny for long the dark passions that had broken loose inside him; the new girl in the Dumpster was proof of that. But that new corpse—and Mike Rowe's—showed that he was cunning enough to vary his routine and hide his tracks. It was Ridge's sense, from the cruelly arrogant notes left on the first set of victims, and the oddly cultivated relationships between Lannon and cops like Rowe and even Bellflower, that outperforming the real cops, dominating them through his ruthlessness and his intellect, was as much a part of the psychic payoff for Lannon as the thrill of killing was. Lannon would know that somebody from MULHOM might suspect him, even follow him—and he would try to throw them off, maybe by using another unsuspecting friend to drive the limo, or a servant, like the one she saw arriving.

If they were wrong, Cully may have just let another woman die.

She and Ridge had hand radios but had decided not to use them just in case Lannon had a scanner and might be monitoring their bands; she had hers tucked into her console. Now she pressed its talk button twice, to send Ridge the two bursts of static that meant "no." She waited five more minutes, long enough to decide she had been wrong and Lannon really had been behind the dark windows of the limo, when the Land Rover swung out of the driveway and came toward her.

It did not have its lights on, and Cully almost forgot to duck. But she did, and had just tucked herself down behind the dashboard when the Rover's headlights, behind chrome grille protectors designed to blunt the damage of a scrappy rhinoceros, threw their candlepower down the street and lit the headliner in her car. Cully flattened herself all the way to the floorboard, wrapping her body around the gearshift.

She waited until the taillights of the Rover had flared at the end of the street and turned off onto Sunset before she punched her hand-radio talk button once, started the jeep, and went after him. She had checked the map and the approaches into the neighborhood, and had spent the last hours rehearsing all this in her mind. She did not want to leave the neighborhood by the same street that the Land Rover took, or else Lannon might be watching his own rearview mirror to see if anybody was following. So she gambled again; she went the way the limo had, and when she reached Sunset, sure enough the Land Rover rolled past her, having doubled back, and that's when she knew for sure that she was right.

She followed Josh Lannon, driving himself toward the lights and the sex and the false and misleading advertising of Hollywood.

She saw an ugly gray sedan in her rearview mirror, far back, and gave him another single punch in the radio. She heard a single punch in return.

Keeping Lannon in sight was easy. She decided not to worry about staying out of sight herself. Most of the traffic snaking east on Sunset at ten o'clock at night was going all the way to the Strip, and ducking in and out of it would be more noticeable than just staying behind the Rover and moving with the flow. Cully was improvising. She tried to make her mind go white, like Ridge told her. *See everything.*

Beside her on the passenger seat was a black satin clutch bag, and tucked into it was the small .38 she had inherited from her father and a camera no larger than two sticks of licorice stuck together. It was autofocusing, self-winding, nearly silent, and loaded with 1000 a.s.a. film, which produced photographs of good resolution even by candlelight. At home at her kitchen table she had practiced holding the camera so it wouldn't show; the best way was to prop her elbows on the table and rest her chin on the backs of her fingers. It was a natural posture, and the camera tucked below her palms like a harmonica. Her right thumb could press the shutter, and in a dim room nobody should notice the camera at all. It didn't need to be aimed, just pointed in the right direction; its lenses took in a broad field. The camera was a marvel, really, one of the little gadgets Mike Rowe had scrounged up for MULHOM. Now Cully wondered how well the film would work in the flashing red-and-blue lights of the strip joint that Lannon was parking across from.

She got lucky; a car pulled out of a metered parking space in front of the record store next to the strip-tease club, and Cully tucked the jeep into the spot and followed Lannon.

She had been here before. This was the place where the second victim had worked. A sign above the door said AMATEUR NIGHT. Was that what Cully was being, an amateur?

Close those thoughts out, Cully, doubt is nothing but noise.

She stopped at the Plexiglas window in front of the strip joint. The woman behind the window looked her over and said, "You working?"

"Huh?" Cully said.

"You don't free-lance in here, honey," the woman said.

"Oh. No," Cully said. "Just picking up technique. For my boyfriend."

"Six dollars," the woman said, and Cully paid her admission. She moved through the curtain of pink plastic beads that set off the entry, into the same long rectangular room where she had been before, on her search for Porsche. At the bar to her right a tattooed three-hundred-pounder in a T-shirt tended the glasses of half a dozen customers, slouched in the glow of amber neon. Further on, at the rear of the room, was the sound booth. At the opposite end, to her left, was the low stage where the strippers worked. A girl bouncing her breasts there now attested to how little Porsche's fate had scared any of them away; or maybe they figured that with Leonard Bellflower in jail, all the danger was gone.

Cully took a seat near the corner of the stage so that she could glance the length of the room without being obvious. She had anticipated that Lannon, in trying to be just one more dull face among many, might settle in with the anonymous mass of men in the middle of the room, but instead he slowly picked his way back through the tables and took a seat against the rear wall. Cully's angle was good, but the light was bad, and even in this smoky dimness Lannon wore a pair of mirrored glasses. A photograph at this distance would be very poor evidence, so she decided not to even try to use the camera she had brought in her purse.

Ridge moved in and took a table close to the bar, about a third of the way back. Lannon did not seem to notice. And though Cully could not tell what his eyes were doing behind the sunglasses, Lannon's face never angled in her direction.

He watched. And watched. The spotlight bored a white tunnel through the feathery drifts of smoke hanging above the heads of the men crowded at the small round tables throughout the room and glanced yellow off the brass pole on the stage where one dancer and then another rubbed and writhed. The pole reflected like twin golden toothpicks in the lenses of Lannon's glasses, but still he sat, as lifeless as the reclining nude, painted in Day-Glo pink upon a field of flat black, that stretched from the front to the rear of the room along its eastern wall.

Other men in that room sat just as still, unmoved by the dancers or the pounding music, lost in the spell of their own fantasies; but to Cully, Lannon's inaction was torture. What was he waiting for? What if he did nothing tonight, and the pictures and the surveillance and the efforts to catch him in the act were all a waste of time? Now that Rowe was dead, was Lannon's drive burning out, to flare again later? How long could Ridge and Cully keep this up? *What was he waiting for?*

The right girl. Some girl that would move him.

She was going to catch him in the act, and there was one way to do that.

She stood, tucking the camera with her thumb against the back of her purse, and moved over toward Ridge, brushing by his table and dropping the camera into his lap as she went past.

She walked up to the bartender. Spirals of black hair tangled around his thick neck and on his arms beneath the tight T-shirt, as if his torso had been mowed and sprayed white. He grinned at her and said, "Hi, baby, how can I do ya?"

"This amateur night?" she said.

He looked her over. "You want to dance?"

"Let's say it makes me horny," she said.

"You can't be a pro," he said. Girls who looked like her could do porno movies; but he had seen it before, the professional woman whose life unravels and who wants to get up on the stage and expose herself.

"I'm a lawyer," Cully said. "Announce me."

"Go back to your seat," the bartender said. "This is a pro set. After this girl is finished, we'll get you on."

"Let me leave my purse with you," she said. "I tend to get forgetful when I start having a good time, and I wouldn't want to lose it."

She hated to separate herself from the pistol, but places where commodities like sex and drugs were sold tended to be wary of unsolicited offers from strangers. They were always on the lookout for cops wearing hidden microphones; leaving her purse was an act of wide-eyed sincerity. The bartender visibly relaxed as he accepted the black bag and slid it under the bar for safekeeping; Cully hoped that if Lannon was watching, she had just disarmed him, even as she had disarmed herself.

As the bartender motioned the emcee over, Cully went back to her chair. Five minutes later the girl on stage was down to nothing and had strutted off, to a smattering of applause.

"Dudes and dudettes!" the emcee called. "We've got one of those unusual pleasures. A rank amateur! An absolute beginner! A lady who'd like to try the stage for the first time. She's . . . I think she said she's a lady lawyer, and she didn't even tell me her name. But from the looks of her, I'm willing to see the rest of her, how about you?"

Catcalls and whoops. Josh Lannon, in the back of the room, watched impassively behind his sunglasses. The spotlight searched the audience, and Cully stood.

Cully smiled. She looked nervous, and she was. The spotlight swung past her, swung back, then stuck to her like a blaze of bright glue. It followed her as she climbed the stairs up onto the stage and squinted into the light.

The music started, a low steady thump. She ignored the music, it wasn't there. It was like she was undressing at the end of the day, and a hundred men were in her bedroom watching. She began with the three cuff buttons at each wrist, undoing them casually one by one so that her hands would be free to slide out of the tight sleeves. But once the cuffs were loose, she seemed to lose all interest in the sleeves, raking her fingertips through her hair and fluffing it back off her shoulders; the last time she had been there, she had seen enough to know that delay, in stripteasing, was everything.

She turned her back to the spotlight, and slowly, very slowly, her left arm bent and the fingers stretched up the center of her spine; she arched her back slightly so the tips of her thumb and forefinger could pinch the flap of the black zipper. As slow as syrup, she pulled it down, and the taut black fabric spread apart to reveal the smooth living field of her back.

The men in the room before her held their breath. If this was an act, it was a great one. Strippers were one thing, but a girl watching from the audience and getting up to do it herself—man, what a fantasy! Any moment they feared she might stop and say that was enough. But she kept going.

She turned again and faced them, her eyes on something in the smoky air above the men's heads, her fingers undoing the belted clasp at her waist. The dress hung now like a loose toga; she shifted her shoulders once, and it fell into a black puddle at her feet. Cully couldn't tell if Josh Lannon was watching. She knew Ridge was.

The music changed, seguing into "Like a Virgin." The sound man had found just the right tacky tune. Cully remembered him from her last visit to the club, when she had pretended to be looking for a missing stripper. He had helped her then, had bought her line about being a family friend of the lost dancer. What was *he* thinking now?

The owner, Carpazian, made a big "okay" gesture to the sound man, who stepped out of the booth to speak to him. They stood right next to Josh Lannon. "Perfect, just perfect!" Carpazian said. "We gotta add a act like this!"

The sound man sniffed and rubbed his index finger under his nose. "Better be careful with this one," he said. And Josh Lannon, sitting beside them, turned his head.

"Why?" Carpazian said, loudly over the music.

"She ain't no lawyer. She's a cop," the sound man said.

And Josh Lannon, entranced by Cully's striptease, turned his eyes back to the stage. He had noticed her when she had first stood from her seat at the table and moved to the bar, but he had not been sure; this hot little thing with the wild blond hair and the clingy clothes and the bouncing body was so different from the disciplined, controlled young woman that Rowe had secretly pointed out to him at the Can that day.

Lannon watched steadily. For a few moments he seemed far away. And then he smiled.

Cully was down to her silk camisole and stockings; stepping out of the collapsed dress without snagging her high heels and tripping was tricky, but she had managed it. Now she was hesitating, and the guys in the room were shouting, "Don't stop! Don't stop! More! Do it to it, baby!" They began to clap to the beat of the music, to pound on the tabletops, to drive her on.

She sat down on the edge of the stage chair and peeled off her stockings. She was down to her camisole, with bikini underwear beneath. She stretched her fingers up on the pole, like she had seen the other strippers do, and she began to move to the music. Covered as she was, it was far more tantalizing than the bare-all strippers had been. Her breasts rolled beneath the silk. Her legs were smooth and taut.

Josh Lannon's mind raced. He looked at the bartender, with whom Cully had left her purse. He glanced into the sound booth, where a telephone blinked on the wall. He turned to the sound man and said, "Gentlemen, may I use your phone?" Neither he nor Carpazian heard, so Lannon stepped up and lifted the receiver.

"Hey, bub, that's a private line!" Carpazian said.

Lannon tossed twenty dollars onto the top of an amplifier. "Local call, okay?" he said.

Carpazian looked at the bill, tucked it into his pocket, and said, "Sure."

Ridge, glancing back from his table, saw Lannon making a call, and wondered whom he was trying to reach. Was it personal? Was it business? Did it matter?

Lannon dialed one of the other numbers on the punch buttons of the phone, and the bartender answered, "Yeah?"

"Hi," Lannon said. "Please don't look around, I'm calling from your sound booth, and I'd like to offer you two thousand dollars cash for a slight favor."

After a slight pause the bartender said, "What's the favor?"

"There's a girl dancing on your stage right now. You have her purse under the bar. If you'll look into it, check her driver's license, and write down her home address, I'll give you two thousand dollars, plus an additional thousand if we decide to use her in the magazine."

"Two thousand?" the bartender said. "What magazine?"

"Penthouse," Lannon said. "The woman dancing is a cop; you'll find her badge inside her purse, probably. We've been after her to pose for us, and she's holding out, but obviously she's interested. Just the home address, that's all I want. You'll have to hurry."

The bartender rummaged a minute and said, "Hey, you're right, man. She's even got a little pistol in here."

"Just the home address is all I need," Lannon said easily.

Cully danced; she suddenly found it easy, and the yells of the men watching sounded far away. She thought of Ridge and then closed her mind to him. She locked her thoughts onto Josh Lannon and tried to pull his eyes with her body.

The sound man stepped back into the booth and cued another record, this one louder and more driving, but she had shown all she was going to. She stopped and bowed, pressing her hand against her chest to keep the top of her camisole closed. "Don't stop!" they yelled. "Don't stop!"

She lifted her clothes and carried them backstage to dress. She could let them see her take them off, but she couldn't stand the idea of them watching her put them back on.

The dancers from the club, waiting their turn to go on, stood chewing one side of their mouths and watching her as she dressed.

She walked out the side door and stepped down to the bartender. "How was I?"

"Come back anytime," he said.

She looked at Ridge's seat. He was gone. She glanced back to where Lannon had been sitting. He was gone, too. Then Ridge came back in from the entry. "He left," Ridge said.

"When?" she said.

"During your . . . performance. He didn't even wait to see it end." Ridge knew he was being cruel. He felt like being cruel.

Cully took a long breath. "Okay. All right." She didn't want to look him in the eye.

Ridge led her to the door and they watched Lannon pull out of the lot, then hurried to their car and followed him. He went straight home.

They sat in Cully's car under the canopy of the bougainvillea, and said nothing.

"Were you ashamed of me?" she asked at last.

He was silent.

"Because I wasn't," she volunteered. "I wasn't then and I'm not now. I want to stop him. I'm going to stop him. I'll do anything to stop him."

"Then you don't need to be ashamed," Ridge said softly.

*   *   *

They sat for another half hour in silence, wondering if they could be wrong about Josh Lannon. About Bellflower. About each other.

They walked back to the corner where Ridge had left his car. "I ought to see you home," Ridge said.

"Why? I'm fine."

If that was how she wanted it, then that was okay with him.

Thirty minutes later Josh Lannon left home again.

She found a parking spot near her apartment and she left the car there on the street. She walked along the path, past the petunias and the trellis covered with the lavender trumpet vine, then up the stairs to her door. She was endlessly tired. She wanted to flop straight into bed and sleep forever.

She locked the door behind her, threw the security bolt, and moved into the bedroom. She took her clothes off in the middle of the room and carried them all straight to the hamper; the dress she wadded up to take to the cleaners the next day. She turned the shower on.

Outside, the Land Rover pulled to a stop along the curb, just behind Cully's car.

Ridge sat in his apartment with the lights off. Smoke from the strip club clung to his clothes and felt like a stain within his nostrils. He stared out at the glare from the streetlight falling across the sliding glass door out onto the balcony and showing every smudge and pit on the glass. Lit like that and seen from this angle, the glass looked like waxed paper.

Ridge thought about the glass. He *reflected* on it, and thought about the way thought itself can distort things. He thought about perspective. Seen from outside, the glass would be like a dark mirror. From inside it was like a wall. In different lights it was different things.

And that led him back to Cully. Thinking, not feeling. Thinking, away from the feeling. Thinking, it all seemed simple. The cells inside her were human. Left alone, they would become a person. But it was best not to think too much about that. They were not a person right now.

Logic was simple. This wasn't a child yet.

Thought without feeling.

Feeling. Dangerous to thought. But Ridge had one problem. The only true way for a detective to think was to consider feelings as he thought. Ridge had lived for most of his life by escaping feeling by thought; but something about his feelings was breaking in on him.

It was the possibility that slapped him in the chest. Something he had come to think was impossible was lying out before him in the phantom mists, like the pattern on the glass, waiting for the right light, the right glance of perspective, to become visible. And he knew it without seeing it. He had loved before—his parents, his brother, his grandmother—but that love was distant, just a memory, an echo; but this was his first time with a woman. At least it felt that way.

And if they could love, couldn't they have children together?

And if they, if she, no, if *they* decided not to have this child, would that mean they would never have a child?

Don't worry; there is an angel watching over this child.

This child was real to Ridge. He loved this child already.

There stirred in him a grief so great that he felt pressed down into the chair. It lay on his chest; he could barely breathe.

Ridge tilted his head back and looked at the pattern on the ceiling. The little inverted stipples of spray-on plaster that glowed white on one side from the street lamp and cast sharp shadows behind them like mountains on the moon.

Things you never see unless you look at them the right way.

He thought of Lannon making his phone call. Who was he calling?

A pimp? Calling for a date? He wouldn't do that; if he killed the girl, the pimp would connect them.

It was a call with a purpose, though. He talked. Then he went to the bartender, paid, and left.

Ridge sat bolt upright. He looked sharply to his left, then just as suddenly swiveled to his right, as if somebody might appear there to tell him the thought was crazy.

He jumped from the chair and ran from his apartment.

Josh Lannon heard the water running. She was in the shower. Nobody could hear anything in a shower. He was amazed at how simple everything was.

He covered a pane in the door glass with tape and broke the glass with his elbow. It made so little sound the neighbors couldn't hear, much less the stripper in the shower. He reached inside carefully and twisted the knob. The lock button popped out, but the door still wouldn't open. He thought at first he had made a mistake; the thought was like panic. But then he reached above the knob and felt the latch for the dead bolt. It turned easily, and he was inside.

He shut the door quietly and crossed into the bedroom. He approached slowly, savoring. He took off the cap, the glasses; he stopped at the living-room hutch and finger-combed his hair. He turned and froze, surprised by the black cat who had materialized behind him. Lannon jerked his arms suddenly, making a face, and the cat scampered into the bedroom. Lannon followed silently. He was almost into the bedroom when he heard the shower turn off, and his feet paused on the carpet.

He heard her push back the wet curtain and step out, the bath mat muffling her step. He thought of the towel hanging between her wet breasts as she dried the patch between her legs. It made him excited.

He waited until he heard her move again; he didn't want her jumping back into the bathroom and locking the door before she got a good look at him; once she did, she wouldn't resist, he was certain of it. He heard her move into the middle of the room, and he stepped inside.

Her back was to him. She had her head cocked to one side and was scrubbing the towel against her hair. It fell in heavy wet strands across the slender muscles of her neck and shoulders. He drank in this view of her body, this vision that she had so tauntingly denied him earlier when she was on the stage. Now he enjoyed his own private showing. He watched her in a moment that seemed long and luxurious to him. He had all the time in the world. The dresser was just at his right elbow, and he saw the black purse resting there on a white Irish linen doily. He slipped the purse open with his thumb and slid the pistol out.

She must have heard the sound of the purse clicking open. She turned to look, then froze.

He smiled.

She darted.

The movement surprised him in its suddenness, and it spooked the cat into running beneath the bed, but as far as Lannon was concerned, it was futile. She had instinctively jumped toward the door, but he was blocking it already, so when he shifted his shoulders fully into the doorway, she had to stop and back off.

Clutching the towel to her chest, she stared at him, her gaze darting down once to the pistol in his hand.

He smiled again. "Hi," he said. "I'm Josh Lannon."

"Get out," she said.

"You want me, don't you?"

She said nothing. Her dark green eyes were on him and he was surprised at the anger in them.

"I can have you any way I want," he said. "I can shoot you. I can cut you. I can beat you to death. I can do anything."

"Okay," she said, "let's see how good you are." She hurled the towel at his face and moved toward him, but he saw it coming; her kick grazed his testicles and landed harmlessly on the bulging rock of his thigh muscles. But she followed it up with a raking of her fingernails that caught him in the eyes and gouged three trenches down his face. His face! That enraged him; he fought her, crushing her in his arms and throwing her onto the bed.

She screamed and kicked. He snatched a pillow and rammed it onto her face, then fought to wrap her within the bedspread. He had a hell of a time keeping her down. She threw her slender body fiercely from side to side, and just when he had her hips pinned beneath the weight of his left side and locked up inside his armpit, she broke her head and shoulders free and he had to let go of her hips and use both hands on the pillow to crush it against her face. Finally, by mashing his own head against the top side of the pillow and keeping his body spread out onto hers, he pinned her down and drew up one side of the spread. Then he punched her four or five times in the ribs to take the fight out of her. He felt her body flail and then go still beneath him.

It was sloppy, but he had her. He knelt over her, gasping and feeling the blood trickle down his face. Warm. Bloody. It felt good. It felt real.

He could kill her any way he wanted. He could shoot her through the pillow. He could stab her. But he wanted her to see him.

Smothered inside the blanket, Cully lay in a dark muddle, her brain working so fast that time moved like a slow dream and every sensation was enormous and every thought shouted in her brain. *Am I out? Did he knock me out?* She blinked against the blackness and felt the nap of the blanket like sandpaper against her eyes. Lannon's body lay on top of her with the crushing weight of an avalanche, and a voice inside Cully screamed, Not my baby! Don't hurt my baby!

Then another voice, muffled to Cully, yet clear, said, "Lannon. You fuckin' bastard."

Ridge.

Cully felt Lannon's body, already stiff as rope, snap into a hard mass; the barrel of his gun pressed against the back of her skull; in the vivid sensations sparking through her body, her nostrils twitched with its oily smell.

Above her she felt the damp heat of Lannon's body and felt his voice vibrating in his lungs as he said, "I can blow her brains out right here, right now. You shoot me, my gun will still go off. I'm not afraid to die, I'm dead already. So put your—"

And all the while he was saying this she was thinking, thinking like Ridge, standing there in his place, crying out inside for him to *do* something, anything that would give him a chance to—

Cully screamed, snapping her knees toward her chest, bucking and wrenching.

Poom!poom!poom!poom! Four shots, she *saw* the muzzle flash, even through the blanket, and Lannon's body lay only half on her now, a thick leg, and an arm, twitching. Ridge yelled from his belly as he shoved Lannon off her and shot again, *poom!* This time Cully was sure she heard the bullet burst through Lannon's skull, but by the time the body clumped against the floor, the vivid images in her mind were all gone, and she became aware that she was weeping and realized that she was hearing a relentless, panting scream, and that it was hers.

Then Ridge dug her out of the blankets and buried his face against hers.

From beneath the crooked curtain of bedclothes Suzie Kirkwood's cat stared with wild unblinking eyes at the shattered face of Josh Lannon.

34

It was raining that day. Los Angeles in the rain is a different town. The storms move in off the Pacific and the rain falls in wads, swamping windshield wipers. Torrents run through the gutters and the drains; the once-dry ditch of the L.A. River becomes a torrent. Even the disc jockeys become depressed and tell their listeners over the radio that this can't last long and if they keep their spirits up with some good music, they can survive.

Ridge drove Cully through the rain that day, and when he heard the disc jockey say exactly that, he switched off the radio. Then the silence in the car was too loud, and they had to listen to the suck of the tires on the freeway groves and the beating of the wipers.

They reached the doctor's office. Ridge rode up with her in the elevator, walked with her down to the waiting room, all done in peach wall fabric and gray furniture, with Degas prints on the wall. He squeezed her hand as a nurse led her away. They told him she'd be ready to go in thirty minutes. Ridge sat down on a soft couch. Three women were in the room with him, their bellies bulging round and tight beneath the copies of *Parents* magazine they were thumbing through.

Ridge went back down and sat in the car.

He thought of the way Cully had screamed.

No matter what anybody tells you, no matter what you see on the silver screen, terror is terror and it is not nice to look at. When she lay wrapped in the blanket, not knowing Ridge was coming for her, she was sure she was about to die horribly. She was screaming. The blood splashing over her scared her to death.

All Ridge could do was hold her and rock her.

Like a baby.

Tears welled into his eyes. He wiped them away and forced himself to think. To remember.

He had sat there on her bed and rocked her and explained to her how it had finally struck him what Lannon was doing at the telephone, that he had put it together when he thought about Lannon paying the bartender before he left.

She stopped crying, finally. Just stopped.

He wanted to tell her he loved her. He knew it didn't matter. She knew it, and it didn't matter.

He looked up and tried to see the sky through the flow of water sheeting down the windshield. He thought of children. He didn't want to, and he did.

It seemed to Ridge that somewhere in the unseen world beyond this one, babies drifted, traveling a dark universe. Not just babies, but his baby, Cully's baby.

And that baby was being denied entry into this world of sun and rain and love and terror by the instruments the doctor was applying to the door inside Cully, the door into the universe.

Thomas Ridge prayed. Thank you, God, for Cully. Take care of this baby, wherever it waits. And don't hold this one against us. For next time.

And Ridge understood that he loved Cully McCullers and that there had to be a next time.

He went back up to the office and stood at the window. The nurse at the desk glanced up at him and gave him a bright smile that scorched him like acid. After a few minutes the door into the procedural area opened and a young woman stuck her head out and said, "Mr. Ridge? I'm Dr. Finnerman."

"Yes," Ridge said.

She pushed the door open wider, and he went through. "Last room there on your right," Dr. Finnerman told him.

Ridge found Cully getting dressed, beside a table with the steel stirrups. Crisp paper covered the table's surface, and it rattled as Cully sat back against it and carefully drew on her boots. Ridge bent down and tried to help her, but it was a one-person job; as he had all day, he felt useless.

He stood to his full height, took a deep breath, and said, "That didn't take long."

"No," she said. "I couldn't do it."

"Couldn't . . . do what?"

"I couldn't have the abortion." She said it quietly, without pride or joy, as if a part of her felt she'd had a failure of will. "When I got here, I asked Dr. Finnerman to tell me if the baby was still alive, after all that we had been through. And she looked at me like she knew right then that if we found out it was okay, my decision was made. She did an ultrasound, and there it was, fingers and toes, a heart beating outside its body. And I couldn't let it go."

Tears rolled down her face, and Ridge grabbed her to him. "I'm not ready to be a mother, Tom. But I feel like this baby fought to be alive, and I just couldn't let it go."

"I love you," he said. "I want to marry you."

She pulled her head back and looked up at him. For a long moment she said nothing. Then her eyes filled with tears, and she nodded her head.

They set their course to bring a baby into a world where friends betray, where lovers kill, and where angels watch over the hearts of the unborn.

ABOUT THE AUTHOR

A native of Jackson, Tennessee, RANDALL WALLACE graduated from Duke University. Currently, he writes and produces scripts for television and feature films. He is the author of three previous novels, *Blood of the Lamb, The Russian Rose* and *So Late Into the Night*. He lives in Los Angeles with his wife and two sons.

— LIZARDSKIN —

The newest police thriller from
New York Times bestselling author

Carsten Stroud

Sergeant Beau McAllister of the Montana State Highway Patrol has a formidable service record, an engaging wit, and a quick trigger-finger. When violence touches Beau's life on a slow Friday afternoon, it arrives in a rattler-fast strike. When the smoke clears, a Dakota boy is dead, Beau McAllister has been forced to shoot, and his problems with the law have just begun. And what appeared to be a bizarre incident fueled by hot tempers is actually the first crack in a conspiracy of astonishing corruption.

Once again, with laser precision, Carsten Stroud has penetrated the thin blue line. *Lizardskin* touches a raw nerve and lays open the painful, private, perilous world inside the policeman's soul.